PRAISE FOR PATRICIDE

"In D. Foy's *Patricide*, the prose is so sharp and evocative that I feel as if I'm watching camcordered home movies that I both treasure and fear. It is as if Denis Johnson wrote *Jesus' Son* with an anvil. There is blood and violence and there is heartbreak and heat and there is life and death on these pages. This book is a conjuring even as it is a killing."
—*Linsday Hunter*

"Those of us who've been following D. Foy's writing for a while will be gratified to find, in *Patricide*, another marvel of emotional intelligence, another heady cocktail of high linguistic invention and vernacular speech. Foy's writing contains such energy, such sheer firepower, it's tempting to cast him as a word merchant in the Stanley Elkin vein, a superlative technician working in the dark American shadow of Melville, etc. Only—such a description would omit Foy's greatest virtue, namely, his wisdom. It's one thing to describe the bleaker corners of experience with such full-throated vitality, and yet quite another to do so with as much empathy and equipoise. I already knew Foy was a genius. Now I'm beginning to think he's a saint."
—*Matthew Specktor*

"*Patricide* is a torrent: bruising, beautiful, impossible to shake. D. Foy writes with an intelligence and a ferocity that is exquisitely his own."
—*Laura van den Berg*

"Biting as Beckett and honey-hued as a Tom Waits ramshackle ballad, *Patricide* is a spiraling and spiteful spire of memory's two great gods, nostalgia and blame. With it, Foy has delivered a true work of art—addictive, hypnotic, relentless."
—*Scott Cheshire*

"*Patricide* is a novel of abuse, addiction, and conflicted love in which D. Foy bends language around the patriarchal until it screams. It's a knockout of a book. Read it now."
—*Terese Svoboda*

"The fraught relationship between fathers and sons has been poured over by the likes of Rick Moody, Ivan Turgenev, Steven King, Pat Conroy, Philip Roth, and Cormac McCarthy. What D. Foy does in *Patricide* is blast fully into the ranks of the masters. A frightening, touching, challenging, and emotionally charged masterpiece."
—*Christian Kiefer*

"I'm a fan of Foy, not just for the crazy tales he cooks up, but for his formidable use of language. He writes sentences that are both beautiful and volatile at the same time. *Patricide*, like a lovely concussion, will leave you dizzy and desperate for the next page."
—*Joshua Mohr*

"The literary superstorm that is *Patricide* reads as though it had been brewing for decades before D. Foy, in a torrent of inspiration, was forced to blow. As Karl Ove Knausgaard explodes life's quotidian moments with cool, clockwork precision, Foy expands phenomena ecstatic and traumatic to degrees that not only evoke lived experience but transport the reader to their very essence. When finally the novel achieves its full cyclonic shape, you're caught in its horrid eye, confronted with the kind of diamond-cut awareness typically offered only to the broken, the abused, the fully-surrendered. The screaming inner child—help me, save me, love me—is torn to bits, giving rise to a quietude that demands nothing less than acceptance of things as they are. Foy's been there, and lives there still, and this book offers up his battered jewel."

—*Sean Madigan Hoen*

"Warning: This book, *Patricide,* is not messing around. This book is going to take you with it. Do not fight this book, it will win. This book will bite, but you will like it. This book will hurt, but in the best of ways. Do not be afraid of this book. Be thankful D. Foy has made it for us."

—*Elizabeth Crane*

"Hurricane Father rips through the pages of *Patricide.* We stand there stunned, surveying the wreckage, only to realize that this is just the eye: another wall of storm is coming—Hurricane Mother, Hurricane Addiction, Hurricane Marriage. D. Foy animates and maps these weather systems of life, but he's less a meteorologist in a studio than a storm chaser with his head out the window of a van, screaming brilliance dead into the wind."

—*Will Chancellor*

"*Patricide* is a brooding, painful, and beautifully written book about being raised into damage by a damaged man. D. Foy has given us a how-to guide for the excision of the father and—just barely—the survival of it."
　　—*Brian Evenson*

"If *Patricide* is a book in which love and survival are at constant odds, D. Foy is the only one who can broker a truce. Baleful and beautiful, Foy's words braid a destructive tapestry that gets at the heart of what it means to grow up in a world that won't have you. It's also a story of resilience and resistance on a razor's edge. Once you start reading, you won't be able to stop, no matter how much it hurts."
　　—*Samuel Sattin*

"D. Foy's sentences are a storm, and his second novel thunders its own beautiful, brutal weather. *Patricide* is a gale-force to be reckoned with."
　　—*Anne Valente*

"I want to be seared by what I read. Marked. Branded. Every book I open, I want to be changed by what I find inside. Too often that doesn't happen. With *Patricide* it did, glory be. If you're looking for a novel that makes you feel good, don't pick this one up. But if you want to be marked—if you want an education about life and all its brutality and tenderness—this is the book for you."
　　—*Ron Currie*

PATRICIDE

ALSO BY D. FOY

Made to Break

D. FOY

PATRICIDE

STALKING HORSE PRESS

First paperback edition published by Stalking Horse Press, October 2016

The author would like to thank the following publications in which various forms of this book's pieces first appeared: *Guernica, The Literary Review, Midnight Breakfast, NAILED, Post Road,* and *Revolver.*

www.stalkinghorsepress.com

Design by James Reich
Icarus derived from "The Four Disgracers" by Hendrick Goltzius, 1588

Stalking Horse Press
Santa Fe, New Mexico

Stalking Horse Press requests that authors designate a nonprofit, charitable, or humanitarian organization to receive a portion of revenue from the sales of each title. D. Foy has chosen Mid-Atlantic Bully Buddies.

www.midatlanticbullybuddies.org

CONTENTS

Sleep - 15

The Father -19

The Boy - 27

The Witness - 53

The Coward - 111

The Seeker - 139

The Exile - 199

The Drunk - 259

The Man - 307

The Fable - 373

The Letter - 387

Wakefulness - 391

For Jeanine

PATRICIDE

It does not matter who my father was.
It matters who I remember he was.
— *Anne Sexton*

SLEEP

The condition of alienation, of being asleep, of being unconscious, of being out of one's mind, is the condition of the normal man. Society highly values its normal man. It educates children to lose themselves and to become absurd, and thus to be normal. Normal men have killed perhaps 100,000,000 of their fellow normal men in the last fifty years.

— *R.D. Laing*

I was ten years old, and I was stoned.

And soon enough, by thirteen, I'd be drunk, and soon enough again—garbage head that I became, blazed on whatever—too drunk and stoned and high, too far down and far too wild for thoughts of any sort, much less for thoughts about myself.

You were hell on wheels! my father said when I told him what he'd made me. *I didn't have anything to do with that!*

Which was the point, of course, and my father's spin. Had I had the means to study my life, I'd never have needed to escape my life flying away with Mary Jane. My conditions made those means impossible. Lacking the means to study my life, dreaming the dream of Mary Jane, *every single day*, was the only choice I thought I had.

But I do wonder if he was right, my father, that I was born a junky, born a drunk, somehow my best enemy, who, absent my father as mentor in the ways of the user and drunk, would've gone out to *find* a mentor in the ways of the user and drunk.

Whatever he had, whenever he had it, I wanted every bit. I wanted his booze, I wanted his weed, I wanted his cigarettes and cigars. That I wanted these, though, because my father had forever already given them, or that my father gave them because I'd forever begged—these, I think, are the questions whose answers will remain eternally up for grabs.

The memory of my father with his amber glass reaches from the depths.

I can hear the boy I was asking what he's drinking, can I have whatever it is.

I can see my father's glass and hear my father's words. *Go easy, hot shot, this stuff'll burn.*

And I can feel it, too, the promise of the stuff fulfilled, that fire in my nose and through my face and ears, and that fire in my belly, and what it would become, the wonder I'd grow to cherish more than love, and then abjectly crave.

I can see my father take the glass before I pinched another sip, which even then I wanted worse than bad, I can hear my father's promise I'd someday have my own. *Time goes fast, hot shot, time goes fast.*

Memories of my father's cigars, little puffs of his cigars, memories of his cigarettes and dope: they're all there, murky and swirling as the rooms of smoke they made, which I loved also, whose smells I loved and was so madly delighted to help to make, my father's cigar in my greedy lips, my greedy puffs and sighs—*thooooooooo . . .*

They are there: the smoke from my mouth, my lips, the smoke from my father's mouth, the smoke from my father's lips.

THE FATHER

He was our father, and he fucked us.

— *Rod Steiger*

SUICIDAL, APT TO CRUMPLE ON A DIME IN FITS, I WAS FLOWN out to my father's in his dustbowl town, where nothing was expected, said my father, the place would be all mine, take a job when you're ready, said my father, or anything you like. I'm looking for my own work, said my father, but we'll fix you up, and if you need it, said my father, we'll go find it, that's what really counts. You've only got to get here, said my father, that's it. We'll be together then, and together we'll be good.

I STARED INTO SPACE AT MY FATHER'S HOUSE OF GLOOM FOR the days it took to find a piece of my old self, then turned into a freak, running miles at a pop and busting calisthenics. And then I was reading again, then I was rolling through the country to marvel at life in the fields of rye. I wrote foolish letters to my girl in California. I wrote awful poems and a story with no end.

Between my sadness and my guilt, taking from my father in his own bad luck—mortgage in arrears, sharks at his door—I couldn't eat more than a taco a day and a bite or two of beans. One morning I spied a tub of cream in the fridge, and my mouth began to water. But just as I'd got the tub on the counter and cream on the spoon, ready to smear my taco up, my father, as usual, appeared.

"Put it back," he said.

"What?"

"We're saving that for a special occasion."

The double take, that's what I gave my father. He was serious, his face a stupid stone.

"You mean for the gala we're having Friday night?" My father kept his stare. "It's a dollop of sour cream, *Dad.*"

"I don't care what it is," my father said with The Voice he used so well at times like these. "When you're in my house, you'll live by my rules."

"You have got to be kidding."

"Next time, make sure you ask."

Decades vanished, then, and I was a kid of seven. "But why?" I said.

"Because I said so, that's why."

After that, I'd have been stunned to see him roast a wiener, but a few days later my father announced our dinner that night with Suzie, the woman he'd somehow lately taken.

Compared to my mother, if just by looks, Suzie was a turd on a satin sheet. She had a mannish face and brittle hair, acid-washed jeans with blouses from Walmart and Sears. Add to these her arrogance, her coarse guffaws and filthy mouth— "You're getting so skinny," she said to me once, "you're going to fall through your asshole and choke yourself!"—and you were face to face with the best of the worst, as in the best-lack-all-conviction worst.

My father was getting naked with this cretin.

My father was sticking his penis in this cretin as she grunted her imperatives.

And the more I saw my father curtsy like a dolt in two left shoes, and the more I caught my father jumping at her orders and laughing at her jokes, the harder it became to look him in the eye.

We were greeted by a waitress in suspenders plagued with buttons. There were bogus flamingos and bogus plants and tuck-and-roll banquettes. Roy Orbison-cum-Muzak sealed the mood, and stale air. Then, as the waitress told her "specials," my father said, under his breath, "Nothing fancy, got it?" I looked at him, like before. "Chicken or pasta," he said.

Suzie gobbled up her surf and turf, then sucked her teeth and told a joke with pitchforks and dead babies while my father used his card to pay the bill. On it, where the tip should've been, was a zero.

THANK GOD FOR CALIFORNIA GIRL.

Three weeks later, in mid-June, she flew out for a visit. We got nice in the honkytonks on Route 66 and, for all the chumps to see, screwed at dusk in my father's yard. And then she was gone, to our city by the bay, and I was left to stumble from my dream.

Two weeks on again, when I could take no more of my quarantine or my father, she bought my ticket home, where I let a flat with a couple psychotic Irishmen. One got me hired by a builder, then attacked me with a hammer when the boss put me in charge. The other was a creep who murdered cats and stabbed his friends with darts when they were drunk.

MY FATHER WAS THE MAN WHO NEVER LET YOU SLEEP WHEN he couldn't sleep, the man who came to you before the sun had risen to drive to the mountain to see it rise, then, stoned as ever, head down to the donut shop where none but old men and reprobates gripped their cups and spun their yarns through clouds from hissing batter. My father hauled you down your paper route then drove you to the creek for pollywogs and snakes. My father saw your glories and defeats on baseball fields and soccer fields, and listened to the stories of your exploits in the hills, your blacktop brawls, your reasons for loss, your little white lies and confessions of guilt, your knock-knock jokes, ridiculous, the piss-pot woes of your teenaged heart, all the while withholding his own, hidden in his beard, his buzz, the days he didn't show, his omnipresent haze of fear—of the truth of his life, the grief he'd not tracked for what could only have been a cavalcade of losses and defeats from the childhood he'd survived himself: here expelled from the contest for his drawing of a stag his teachers judged a fraud—there bereft of the father he'd never had save in lore, dearly beloved anyway, as you knew forthwith when my father spoke his father's name—here yet again, a man, trapped in the marriage my mother's father had forced my father into when my mother told the monster she was pregnant at sixteen—and there again yet, blasted, with three sons at twenty-seven, his dreams on the wind and little in the bag but the hump along his path of failure and defeat.

And that was my father, now, trapped in his house, more a tomb than a home, the tyranny of his ruin bearing down.

Before I'd got out to my father's, he was so much more than that. My father was my confidante, my cohort, my comrade in crime, my father was my mentor, my dealer, my captain, my king. And then, by the time I'd left—how can I say?—he was gone, my father, a wretch. I didn't merely dislike my father, then. I *hated* him. But more than all the rest, even as I hated the man, I loved the father, still.

Denial's the grace that shelters us till shelter is ourselves.

The truth of my father had always lain before me. And though I knew it had, I didn't know I knew, nor could I have said it.

I didn't want to know. It was just too much to know.

I avoided and denied the reality of my father as surely as my father had denied and avoided the reality of his own.

And nothing I did could obliterate my mother.

You couldn't deny the illness of a woman who beat her son often, molested him in measures, tortured him a thousand ways. You couldn't deny the illness of a woman whose kleptomania risked her family over and again, whose generally awful ways wrought disgrace in the least affair, from family gatherings and vacations to common times at bars and pools, or on a field trip to see how men made salt.

The logic of a child's urge to flee such a woman, always, of the terror of a child made to live with such a woman, of the hunger of such a child for a spoonful of comfort and trust—none of these, either, can be denied. A child in these conditions, a child with just a sliver of will to survive, would cling fast to the human best ready to meet these needs.

For all my father's weakness, my father was my haven, beyond which I saw just waste.

My mother tore my hair and clawed and slapped my face and neck.

My mother touched me with her hands and fucked me with her eyes, and with her words she fucked my mind, and when at last she'd finished, if merely for a time, she thrashed me with her spoons.

By contrast, punishment at my father's hands was mild. My father whipped me with a belt sometimes, for reasons he explained: "You know why I'm whipping you, Son?"

Had these times made the whole of my harm by my father, they might have been excused. But these times did not make the whole of my harm by my father, or even just a few. When my father pressed together his first and second fingers, like a wooden dowel, he had a dowel with which to jab a chest. Equal pain, of course, through different means—accepted then for standard castigation—was brought down, too: curling, then squeezing, your son's pinky, or with a finger thumping your son's head, or dragging your son by his ear into banishment, the room of his exile, the corner he'd be made to stand.

And no matter the sentence, it was doled out always with The Voice of Paternal Law, The Voice of The Father, giant. My father may have deigned at times to spare these trials, but never The Voice of The Father, which alone sufficed to warn that past the limits of good faith, pain did lurk.

Still, when all was said and done, I felt a little safe knowing the worst that could happen by my father was a whipping with a belt. Some pokes to the chest? A twist of the ear or thump to the head? What were these to a beating with my mother's spoons?

But wicked as they were, the creatures I'd seen in my father's zoo of horror were not by far the worst. Behind the curtain behind the desk, rougher beasts were slouching yet.

THE BOY

Nobody can think and hit
someone at the same time.
— Susan Sontag

OUR MOTHER AND FATHER HAD GONE INTO THE MALL AND, like always, left us in the van.

"I've got a game," I said.

"What game?" my brothers said.

"You'll see," I said, like my father.

"What do we do?"

"Hold up your arm, like this," I told X, and showed him mine.

"Like this?" he said.

I took X's arm above and below. "Now relax your shoulder and make a fist."

"But what do *I* do?" little Z said.

"*You'll* see. Just watch X's arm."

"This is it?" X said. "This is all I'm supposed to do?"

"Keep your shoulder relaxed," I said, swinging X's arm.

"Like this?"

"Act like you don't even know you have an arm. But not your fist. You have to keep it tight."

"But what do I do?" little Z said. "I want something to do!"

"Just look straight ahead," I told him.

I'd been swinging X's arm with increasing force. The instant Z looked off, I shoved X's arm hard into his little face.

X's mouth fell open. His eyes turned into UFOs.

This was a boy who thought he was a sorcerer. Or at least when he was mad he thought he was a sorcerer, at which point the rest did, too.

"I'm a dark and powerful sorcerer," my brother would cry. "Tonight when you're sleeping I'm going to turn you into an ant, and when you wake up, I'll tear off your legs and burn a hole through your guts with the sun!"

One day he'd threaten to spike my pizza with oleander leaves—"They're *extremely* poisonous," he'd say with narrowed eyes, "*extremely* deadly."

Another he'd promise to cut me to pieces if I entered his room without him in it, which he would know, because he was a dark and powerful sorcerer.

He chased me round the house with a butcher knife once, screaming, "I'll kill you! I'll kill you! I'll kill you!"

Another time, claiming I'd eaten the last of his candy, he flung a pair of scissors my way: they stuck into a book inches from my face.

And now X had clocked his brother on the jaw without a darn of effort. I'd never seen X so full of glee.

Z, meanwhile, the more fragile for his two lost teeth, had shrunk back, stranded between pain and the showing of it.

Any second now he'd explode in tears, the way he always did when we wronged him even slightly. He was the baby, charming as a baby, and when he cried, the world stopped to listen. Knowing this, that wrath would descend like flies on the brother that hurt him, Z had learned to blubber on cue. And escape was fantasy, then, and struggle vain: no matter what, *you were going to get it.*

Without our mother and father, Z's howling face was for X and me the best fun we could find. Z blubbered and howled, and we roared ourselves dead with laughter. And the more we laughed, the harder he cried. And the harder he cried, the louder and more we laughed.

We were boys, all right, innocent and cruel—two sparrows on a moth.

Our pleasure drew from little Z's pain, doubtless, but beyond that pain's short-lived face, we didn't care a penny. We never wanted Z's suffering to vex him past the moment. He could've been anyone—Fred Flintstone crushed by Barney, Curly squeezed by furious Moe, some kid face-planted in the hall at school. And anyway, it wasn't Z's pain that got us, really, but his impotent confusion. All we wanted was to mess with him. Three days later, the grief he'd got was a cloud long gone. As for X and me, what we'd done yesterday, much less two minutes back, ate at us about like a distant war.

And then it was over, our moment of slow-mo swapped out for fast-mo, our clarity for chaos and fear.

"Look!" X shouted. "There's Mom and Dad!"

Just as he'd said, my mother and father had stepped from the mall. Z knew what was what. His time had come, he had the hand, the old table had been turned. And X knew it, too, and just to rub it in, when Z started howling, X leered at me and said, "You're going to get it now!"

I wouldn't be thrashed by my mother today, not here in the parking lot, but I was sure as hell going to catch it from my father.

I could feel my ear in his fingers, my pinky in his fingers, his fingers on my chest.

I could see my father's Angry Face.

I could hear my father's Father Voice.

And I could see my exile for the weekend from friends and TV, too—*ABC's Wide World of Sports* and later doorbell ditch, *Good Times*, *All in the Family*, or *Happy Days* that night, and, in the morning, cartoons, *Bugs Bunny* and *Porky Pig, Popeye, The Flintstones, Land of the Lost.* I wasn't going to see any Stooges, either, for the next few days, or any Bowery Boys, or Laurel and Hardy, or W.C. Fields.

Misery, for sure, right down the line, was the gremlin on my back.

And then, sudden as a belch, it appeared, my *idea.*

"Listen," I told Z, glancing toward my mother and father. "If I let you punch *me* in the face as hard as you want, will you promise not to tell?"

As fast as my brother had conjured his fit, the fit disappeared. His face still shone with tears, and his nose still ran with snot, but his blubbering had quit like a gadget unplugged. "As *hard* as I want?" he said.

"Yeah, with your fist, okay, just not on the nose. Go ahead," I said, and gave him my chin. "Right here."

"With my *real* fist? Where you made him hit me?"

"But you have to promise you won't tell Mom and Dad."

I turned to X. "And *you'd* better not, either."

A car backed out and stopped my mother and father. I had a minute to go, if that.

"You'll never get the chance to do this again," I told Z. "Don't you want to slug me?"

"I guess so," he said.

After what had happened, and with all the times I'd tortured him, this must have smelled like more of the same.

"You won't do anything else?" he said.

"Promise."

"Do it!" X said.

Had their places changed, X would've socked me three

times over, cackling all the while. Then he'd have sworn the instant I made to get him I'd be turned into the frog he'd carve up with his razor.

Z popped me on the jaw when I spun to glare at X. My head snapped back, my ears blew out, the world went foggy gray. My brother's face, the jerk, was a wheel of passion— bewilderment to pain, doubt to fear, satisfaction to delight. X, meantime, was snickering like a villain from a comic strip.

"What are you laughing at?"

"He really did it! He socked you *right* on the jaw!"

"Hee hee hee!" went little Z. "Hee hee hee!"

"Now we're even," I said. "Right?"

"Yeah!"

And then our mother and father were on us.

"Hey, guys," my father said. "Look what I've got!"

From a large brown bag, he took three smaller bags and passed them round. Each was full of my father's favorite treat—double-dipped chocolate peanuts.

YOU DON'T NEED YOUR FATHER'S WHIPPINGS, YOU DON'T NEED your father's pokes or thumps. Your father's disappointment is enough to kill another piece of you, the way your father's disappointment always kills another piece of you, some little part of you hidden beneath the other parts you never knew that you still had. Your father might whip or poke or thump you, or your father might not whip or poke or thump you, but he will never not talk down at you with the voice he uses to let you know you've failed him yet again. And then your father will leave you, and the sun will be blown away, and you'll be left to stumble through your waste of fear till your father comes to take you back. And though your father always takes you back, you can never say for sure he will. Each abandonment is the last abandonment, each abandonment another betrayal, another little death. And your mother's betrayal, with each of the lies in her endless show of lies, will never fail to be followed by your father's own, told in nearly perfect faith. And this lie of your father's is the lie he'll tell again and again by acting in every way possible as though he believes the lies your mother tells are truth, when for years he's known that all your mother tells are lies. Once your father leaves the house each morning, he's a void till night, he might as well be gone for good. Your mother calls your father with tales of your villainy, but those tales when you hear them from your father bear no semblance to the world you were in. And what's more, there's nothing you can do. Your father's gone, your father is a void till night, you don't even know the first three digits of the number to your father's phone. The one time you can speak to your father is those few moments alone on weekend mornings, when your father gets stoned and takes you off for his drive through the hills. You tell your father your mother's lying the way you always tell your father your mother's lying, the way you've always told your father your mother's lying, but you only hear what you've always only ever heard, the "I'm-sorry-it-turned-out-that-ways" and "there's-nothing-I-can-do-about-the-pasts" and "I'll-have-a talk-with-hers" and "if-you-didn't-do-anything-wrong-you-wouldn't-have-any-troubles." Over and over, you beg your father to leave your mother, over and over, you beg your father to take you from your mother, "Please, Dad," you say, "please, don't let her hurt me again." You tell your father you see his pain, you tell your father you know how much he hates his life, but always you hear the same old stories, the same old lies, the "I'm-working-on-its" and "your-mother-and-I-are-trying-new-ways" and "it's-your-mother-who-wants-to-argues" and "if-it-was-up-to-me-your-mother-and-I-would-never-fights" and "you-don't-understand-hot-shot-someday-maybe-you-will-but-your-mother-is-hard-to-satisfys." And then you're bribed with candy or donuts, or a movie or trip to the lake. And then the bribe disappears and the show begins from the beginning. None of it matters, why should you care, who cares what you say or do when not a single stitch will matter? You know what will happen, you know absolutely what will happen. Your perceptions will be twisted, your feelings denied, your words wiped clean by a pop on the head with a wooden spoon, a slap on the face, a bark to shut your hole. And, really, why should your mother and father do other? You don't trust yourself any more than your mother and father trust you, any more than you trust the rest. It's been so long since you trusted yourself that you can't remember when your distrust began. Neither can you recall when you began to feel like you were just an absence with skin and hair. Neither can you say the moment you saw that, regardless of where or when, you weren't "you" or even a semblance of "you" but just a notion of "you" from a vaguely conjured story—a crappy-ass impostor, a crappy-ass fucked-up lie. You know you began to hate liars, but like the rest you can't remember when that began, either. You know only that you hate liars, you hate cheaters, you hate swindlers and fakes and frauds. You know only that wherever you go you can spot them, like stains on a pretty dress. And the more these swindlers and frauds tell you to tell the truth from one side of their mouth, even as they lie from the other, the greater your confusion and deeper your fear. You can't remember the last time you met someone who wasn't a fake or fraud. You can't remember the last time you felt what people call "trust." But even as you hate these people, all people, really, you hate yourself most of all, because you are one of these people yourself, though you can't remember when that began, but that it began. And in the same way that you can't remember how it was that you began to see that everyone's a liar because lying is the single way to make it through this flaming world, all you know is that one day you saw that if you want to live, if you want to survive on this douche bag of a planet, you must continue to lie, you must never stop lying for even a flash. But because you can never admit these things, because you must deny you're a liar almost always by lying about the lies you tell about your lying, and because you must avoid any situation that might set the truth beside the phony you've become, your lies themselves, your first wave of lies, must be very subtle, very crafty images of the truth, stories you yourself can believe if only you tell more lies, super lies, lies within bottomless lies.

IN THE AUTUMN AFTER THE SUMMER MY FAMILY HAD MOVED to the town of Y in the country to the east of the bay, when I was ten and my brother eight, we had a fight that drove him to a rage. Probably I'd smashed a castle he'd made with dirt and stones, or broken a stick he'd carved, or freed a creature he'd planned to kill.

Whatever I'd done, he didn't like it. And I knew exactly how much he didn't like it because there on the hill outside our little cabin X became the devil that had tried to stab me the year before and, a few months prior, believing I'd eaten his candy, impale my face with scissors.

I noticed this change with real concern, but stayed put to see that he could hack it. Luckily, I thought, the hoes were in the shed, the knives in the kitchen, the scissors in the roll-top desk. But then a shriek poured from him, and he scurried through the grass toward the patch of dirt whose brush my father had us boys clear so he could plant his weed. Round the patch, we'd stacked piles of rubbish and stones to haul off in a cart. My brother, I saw, was after the stones—the kook was aiming to come at me with stones.

I scooped up a few of my own, then hid behind a tree. I could see X through the grass, working himself into the frenzy I knew would soon break, casting the spell that would stop me long enough for him to stone me down like a sinner from the Bible.

"You're dead!" he cried.

His stone was too big for any sort of grace, yet fueled by his wrath it arced my way and whacked against the tree. When another hit the dirt a few feet off, I thought how crazy my brother was, his stones were packed with menace, those goddamned stones could truly actually *hurt* me. And then it struck me that beaning X with my little stone might make him see the pain his big one would invite. But no sooner had I popped him on the chest than X let out a bloody howl and threw himself my way.

My path as I ran fringed a knoll that kept X out of sight. For a minute I thought he'd scuttled off to yell at the sky, but there he stood, now, hugging a rock the size of my head. I looked up in terror at this fiend that was my brother, backlit by sun pierced with boughs of oak.

"I hate you so bad!" he said.

All I knew once the treetops had spun was the dirt in my mouth and acorn in my face. The doubtful had become the possible, the possible the feasible, the feasible painful fact: my brother had just smashed me with a *boulder*. Had he let time take my courage, too, I might've stayed down, but then the nut began to hammer me with fistfuls of pebbles and dirt. In half a minute, I'd scrambled up the hill, flung him to the weeds, and pinned him beneath me to pound at his chest.

"Ahhhhh! Hrahhhhh! Ooahhhhh!"

My brother's face was shiny with tears and snot. His hair was full of twigs, and a pill bug squirmed in the gunk on his cheek. But just when my fun had about topped out, a clap of thunder split my head.

"You little monster!"

It was my mother. She'd boxed my ear and was now in full attack.

"Please, Mom —" *thwap!* "— he smashed me with a —" *smack! smack! thwap!* "— a boulder —" *claw! smack! claw!* "— I didn't do it all —" *smack! smack! smack!* "— please don't, Mom, please . . ."

The single power my mother obeyed was collapse, and my mother had just started. I'd be lost if I did nothing, I knew, so I dug my fingers into the hand with my hair and pitched myself away.

"He threw this," I cried, pointing at the boulder. "He tried to kill me."

"You get back here," my mother said.

"It's not fair."

"You get back here, right now!"

It didn't matter where I ran, but only that I ran.

I thought of the fort by Randy Bartlett's—Randy Bartlett, who with his goons next year would beat me to shit, because I was a slicker from the city, because after Bruce Ledbetter had called me out when I said he could fuck himself for saying I was a slicker I'd kicked his ass across the park—where I could read hot rod zines and comic books for the wink of time I'd have until my forced return.

"Just you wait till your father gets here," my mother said when I walked in.

X and Z were at the table with their cookies.

"You're going to *get it*," X said.

"He threw a boulder at me," I said, and showed my rising bruise.

"Get in your room."

"It was both of us," I said. "He did it, too."

"Get in there!"

"It's not fair," I said.

"You're really going to get it!" X said. And then, "Mom, may I please have more milk?"

I went to the room I shared with X and climbed to the top of our bunk and stared out the window at the patch we'd cleared and didn't hear my father's car till dusk.

My brothers had left the house again to do whatever, my mother had left to do whatever, I was alone in the house waiting for my father to arrive and with his Fatherly Power mete out his Fatherly Justice.

What use would it be to show my father my bruise? What use would it be to beg my father's mercy? None of it mattered, nothing I did would matter. Darkness would fall. Gophers would dig, and deer graze. Then light would rise, and dew gather, and goldfinch sing, *and I was going to get it.*

From the porch I watched my father drive, grim behind the wheel. I saw no one, there was no one but my father. He stepped from the car and slammed the door and turned my way, a storm in his face, like nothing I'd seen in my father's face, which, black as it was, couldn't be called a face.

My life fell away, then, I might've been nothing, I felt I was less than nothing. Up the drive my father strode, up the stairs my father strode, no means or ends or life at all, that was what I had, nothing was what I was and had, and then my father made the porch, but still I was nothing, and less than that, I had nothing in me but nothing, and without a word he struck my jaw with his full might, his giant fist, a blow, just one, that slammed me to the floor.

And then the swirling haze . . . And then his Face, all black, my father's, my father's giant Voice . . .

IT HAD BEEN REAL, YOU WERE THERE, THE BOY ON THE FLOOR, yours was the jaw that met the fist. You'd seen his face, your father's, you'd watched it swim above you through your haze. It was no less real, this moment, than when you whacked that girl with your little hoe, fell ten yards to a bed of rocks, scored the goal that won the match, got beat to shit by six big men, found your mother with your father's friend, caught that fish, roared with glee when your father lit his fart. No, it, the moment, your father's betrayal, was no less real than all of these, no less real, not a whit, than when you took your brother's stone against your chest. It was real. It was realer than real, and yet you were buried in an avalanche at the bottom of a mountain of lies, versions of a story nothing like your own, your story canned as fabrications, exaggerations, hallucinations, lies. Your brothers don't remember. Nor does your mother, nor, most significantly, totally unbelievably, does your father. To this day, your father denies having touched you at all. Over a decade back, in answer to the letter you'd written the year after you left him to his dusty tomb, your father went so far as to commit his lie to paper. *The biggest shock of all & the most painful to me,* he wrote, *was to hear you tell me I abused you, that I hit you & beat you as a child.* Could it truly be your father remembers what your father says, a history of benevolent paternity, free from punishment, violence, abuse, free, for that matter, from any harm at all? What if what your father says had happened is what in the end really happened? If so, how could that be, and what does it make of you? Did none of what you remember happen? Do things not happen that are said didn't happen? If no one speaks of this or that, had this or that ever been to speak of? Did any of what you remember happen? Did it happen the way you remember? Did your father not punch your face? Or did you only imagine, or think you imagined, your father punched your face? What all else must you've thought you imagined in this thing through which you believe you're passing, this "life"? Has the whole of your life been a trudge through a maze in a dark mirage? Or solely official portions? If portions alone, which? And of that which, what part were you? And of that "you," if "you" are *you,* which part is the real and which the false? And what part of the face of you that you are not did the man that is your father never punch? Without the part of the face of you that you are not, much less without "you" your

41

"self," how can you know your face was or wasn't punched? Is this some story you raised, the memory of a story you raised, the version of a version of yet another faintly dreamed, one step forward, three steps back, ad infinitum? And just what are these lives of ours, anyway? What makes our lives real? What makes our lives unreal? What makes our lives lives at all? But as for this blow you believe you think you know you suffered at the hands of the man that is your father: *It was Real.* Or . . . or was it really? Is it possible, as your father would have it, as your father's always had it, that what you say has happened hasn't really happened but merely been *conjured up*, that what you say has happened is all perchance a product of your fancy, or less than your fancy, that it's perchance a sad hallucination of a bad mistake, or a mis-take, or maybe just an old missed ache, a slip, you know, a lapse, perchance, a shtick beyond your father's natural physic, temporary madness, act one, scene one, wrought by a crick in your father's ethical neck, picric in his soul's alembic, all refinement tainted, all humanity lost, ah, for just one instant, a lunatic fashioned, molded, made for that—flash!—jiffy-lark-zing smack on the yick—quick, quick, quick!—as the flick of a cobra's tongue, as the sick on the lamb, as Yorick's wit, as a Gaelic jab, as a battle ax, Nordic, as a john's dirty dick in a whore's dirty quim, as pop at a flick, as a '69 Buick, as a bootlicking cleric, as a yardstick brandished in an old nun's hand, as a gun in a gunslinger's hand, as the smack and tang of fine tomato aspic, as a mystic's kenshō or Bolshevik tiff, as light, as sun, as quietus running, quietus quick—*O my father!*—is it? Or was your father possessed perhaps by devils—*O my father!*—his body worked from depths within? Or was your father strung instead to threads unseen and controlled by fingers in the sky—*O my father!*—dancing in the sky, these fingers, these hands, was it do you think perchance solely this or these, that old committal, hideous, vulgar, foul, inexcusable yet excused—*O my father!*—a needful crime in the name of stuttered truth—*O my father!*—was it yes? was it no? was it hey diddy ho, dear father, yes or no, or no or yes or no, dear father, hey diddy ho, hey diddy—*O my father!*—was it? Or does none of it matter, this act of his—*O my father!*—this or any other, your understanding of this act or that, any more than your understanding of any thing else: planets round stars, the journey of whales, an afflicted child, love? It doesn't matter. It couldn't have mattered. This or that happened, or this or that did not happen, who was to say, that was then, and this now, or yet this or that was *was*. Or was it? It was, as they say, what it was. And this is what it was: a *shattering*.

HOWARD KISSLING SAID HOW COOL IT WAS LAST WEEK I'D kicked the ass of David Cook, he hated him so bad he'd wanted to kick his ass himself but wasn't sure he could, he still might've tried anyway, that's just how much he hated David Cook, but so what now anyways, Howard Kissling said, now it didn't matter, he said, hells yes, because I had done it for him.

Probably I'd have kept my big trap shut had Howard Kissling not thought me cool. But Howard Kissling had thought me cool, which I had never, so I had to make him think I thought I was cool, and the best way to make him think I thought I was cool, I thought, was to say I'd kick Jeff Longman's butt—the bully of all school bullies, a giant of a kid, with size ten boots and grown men's shirts and his father's massive ring. The words just leapt from my big fat mouth, and once they had, I couldn't do much but make like I believed them.

What I hadn't judged when I told Howard Kissling I'd kick Jeff Longman's butt was just how big the mouth of Howard Kissling was.

The Stone Age was where we still lived—hi-fi stereos, eight-track tapes, slot cars, walkie-talkies—but that didn't keep Howard Kissling from telling the world I'd said I'd kick Jeff Longman's butt. I hadn't made it to school Monday morning before Ken Hummel and Phil Bradley and Tommy Madison and the rest were yelling how Jeff Longman wanted to "see" me.

But Jeff Longman didn't want merely to see me across the playground and shake his mighty fist. Jeff Longman didn't want to tell me in person, either, that though he was disappointed to hear about my ludicrous boast, he understood how things get away in the moment and that, considering we two had never had a rift, and in light of his currently beneficent mood, he'd let me slide this time with a warning. Jeff Longman didn't look at anyone. Jeff Longman didn't speak to anyone, any more than he warned them. What Jeff Longman did was pulverize kids, eviscerate kids, what Jeff Longman did was hang-and-draw-and-quarter kids. But I'd opened my big fat mouth and bragged I could kick his butt, an ultra-major blungle that lumped me in with the pack of boobs everyone knew he'd made mincemeat of.

Ways roundabout and secret became my deal. I hid in class at recess, claiming to read or draw or study my teacher's snake. At the house, I peeked through the curtains to see Jeff Longman wasn't blighting the place like a kid from a field of corn. In the dark, Jeff Longman's twin, a ghost, hovered by my bed. Minutes were a pain, hours a plague, days a manifest horror.

A week passed, and then a weekend of dread for Monday. And then Monday came and went, and no Jeff Longman. All I saw was mouths.

Jeff Longman says he's going to beat the crap out of you! Jeff Longman says he's going to kill you! Jeff Longman says he's going to make you eat shit! Jeff Longman says he's going to make you wish you were never born! Jeff Longman says he's going to make your face look like a baboon's ass! Jeff Longman says he's going to tear off your head and spit down your neck! Jeff Longman says he's going to knock your teeth down your throat! Jeff Longman says he's going to rip your arms right off! Jeff Longman says he's going to mutilate you! Jeff Longman says, Jeff Longman says, Jeff Longman Jeff Longman Jeff Longman . . .

And then it happened: "Hey, *you, Rice*!"

If ever a voice had had a life, it was the voice of big Jeff Longman. His voice by now had hair on its back and scales on its feet and a crown of wings from butchered hawks.

Somehow the giant had waited for me to slip across the field at school, through the hole in the fence, and, from there, two backyards and a cul-de-sac, knowing I'd come out on that very street and make my way down this one and that one and this one again till I'd turned onto my present way, what I'd thought to've been a million days from nothing, but which, obviously, was just another cursed trap.

I turned round as commanded, convinced of my doom, to Jeff Longman striding my way like Andre the Giant himself. And if his catching me there of all rotten places wasn't the worst, a mob of kids had followed.

Jeff Longman strode toward me like Andre the Giant and said not a word while I stood there like a dope.

I thought for sure he'd lay me low with a hook to the temple or cut to the jaw. I thought for sure he'd crush me in the kidney and then the ribs, and I'd keel over while he mashed me into paste. Instead, Jeff Longman stopped two feet off and snatched me by the neck. And that was it. Jeff Longman didn't so much as shake me. Jeff Longman stood there, that was it, and squeezed my neck with both his giant hands. From Jeff Longman I hadn't deserved of a single blow. The guy wouldn't soil a knuckle on me, I was so pathetic. He'd throttle me to my craven death, that was it, then leave me on the walk for some old lady to hobble to clucking from her porch.

I could see his face as I had in my dreams, yellow hair and bloodshot eyes, which had fixed not on mine but on the hands with which he was choking my life away. For a good minute, at least, I hung motionless in the vise of those giant hands.

I'd never done such a thing—stood idly by while some jerk had his way with me. I'd always fought back, always, in fact, I'd won. But this kid had terrorized me with his person—with the myth of his person and his massive size—and then, with his simple brutal ploy, he'd rendered me inert.

I could feel the throb of my blood, the *pound pound pound* at the sides of my head. Darkness had slunk into my vision, dizziness had shot me through, and nausea, when at last it appeared: the mind to win. From the moment he had snatched me, I'd remained wholly quiet, an effigy of myself. And yet, as sometimes happens in need, you see the blessing that had been your bane. My paralysis had saved me, lulling Jeff Longman into something close to worriless ease. Jeff Longman, it seemed, had thought I'd stand to the end like a twerp. And likely I'd have done just that had my body not taken over. To struggle against this giant, my body had known, would've been to give him a gift. He'd have choked me, and I'd have thrashed till I passed out, and he'd have kicked my teeth down my throat and my dick up my ass and walked off laughing as he wiped his hands. I didn't resist him, then, but lurched straight at him, this giant, the last he'd expected, my body somehow knew.

And *that* was it.

The second Jeff Longman dropped his arms, I cracked his giant nose.

The world vanished, then, and all my thoughts and all my terror, in place of the world had risen the tide of power with which I'd merged, which actually I'd become.

I felt the nose crunch beneath my fist, I saw the eyes roll at the blood from the nose, I watched the hands fly to the bloody nose.

I could've howled with laughter at this monster in ruin, I could've punched his balls, I could've buried him in a pile of guts and bones. I hit him again, as hard as I could, this time on the jaw.

He fell back, Jeff Longman, cross-eyed now with trying to see his nose. So again I smashed his nose, and then his jaw and both his eyes, and knew as I did that he was scared, as shocked to find himself as screwed as I'd been screwed the minute before, limp on his knees, his face no longer the face of death but some kid who'd crapped his bed. I windmilled that face as hard as I could, till the kid tried to throw himself against my legs.

I'd wanted to break Jeff Longman's face. More, I'd wanted to terrify him like he'd terrified me, to shame him like he'd shamed me, to disgrace him so awfully badly he could never

47

show his face again, so awfully terribly badly he'd change his name and move to Venezuela.

But whatever I did, after the bottomless days I'd spent in stone in his state of terror, I was going to take my pound of flesh from him, and gobble it up like a king his dish of caviar.

I turned with him as he fell my way and looped my arm round his neck, then over and over I smashed his head. I smashed his head and smashed his head, and even after his body had given, I hadn't had enough.

"Say 'Uncle!'" I said, and struck him again. "Say it!" I said. "Say 'Uncle!'"

I'd never in one of my scraps thought to say something so retarded. It was just a thing I'd heard old-timey kids yell on *Dennis the Menace* or *Andy Griffith*, some goofy thing you made a guy say when you wanted him to beg. And if the guy didn't say it, well then, you smashed him till he did.

"Say it!" I said as I hammered his skull. "Say 'Uncle!' you dick! Say it!"

"Kill him, Rice!" said the kids that had followed Jeff Longman to watch him mash me into paste.

"Mess him up!" they said. "Kill him!"

"Get him, Rice!"

"Say 'Uncle!' Longman!"

"Make him say it, Rice!"

"Mess him up! Get him, Rice! Kill him!"

I'd almost lost faith in this monster's ruin, and my hand was hurt from mashing his skull. But then, his face at my hip, I heard Jeff Longman yelp.

"What was that?" I said, and smashed him again. "What was that you said?"

"*Uncle!*" Jeff Longman said.

"*Uncle! Uncle! Uncle!*" the kids all said.

"He *said* it. Longman said, 'Uncle'!"

"You did it, Rice, you kicked his butt!"

All I'd had to do was let him go, and he'd have hit the deck. But I wasn't ready to let him go, not a teensy bit.

"And who kicked your butt?" I said.

"You did," he said.

Jeff Longman would never look at me again. Jeff Longman would never step on the same field again if I was on or near it. Jeff Longman would never forget me, and I'd always remember him.

"And you're never going to mess with me or any of my friends again, right?"

"Right!"

I threw Jeff Longman down and watched the kids close in with horror and glee.

"Right on, Rice!" they said.

"That was rad!"

"Cool, dude!"

"You totally kicked his butt!"

My shirt was soaked with blood. The hip and leg of my pants were soaked with blood. My sneaker was thick with blood, and clumps of dirt and grass.

A half hour later, I guessed, my mother would likely beat me to hell, though not if I'd been hurt, maybe, though that'd be tough to prove, given my chance to prove it. My face had not a scratch. My mother would know it was another kid's blood on my good clothes. I'd have been out raising the same old Cain I'd always been out raising.

My hand was swollen, my knuckles torn. My shoulder burned, and my neck hurt so I couldn't turn my head.

And then, for no reason I could see, none of it mattered, not my broken fist, or screaming kids, or screwed-up clothes, or hell. Jeff Longman, crying, lay in the grass. *But so what?* I thought. *So the freaking what?* A man across the way had been chasing his dog. Now he stood watching, the dog at his feet. What difference really did it make? *So what,* I thought, and took off running.

YEARS LATER, AFTER THE NUTHOUSE AND YOUR START ON the road to health, you'll hear a man tell the story of how he'd buried his mother, who'd died of drink and drugs. He'd forgotten the events of his childhood, he'll say, but with his mother's death the memories had returned. The man will begin to weep, then, the tears, which he won't hide, streaming down his face. On a Sunday morning, the man will say, when he was twelve, his father took him to the barber to force on him another cut that made him look a fool. He hated his father for that, the man will say, and for more than he could count. His father was despicable, he'll say, he hated his father with his whole being. "I hate you so much," the man will say he'd told his father as they drove home, "I wish you'd die." It wasn't noon when they got back, but his mother was drunk and bore into his father. This went on, the man will say, while his mother drank and drank. From his bedroom the man heard his mother and father cut themselves down till he could take no more and rushed out to beg them to quit. But it was too late for that, the man will say. In that very moment, his mother slammed a knife into his father's heart, and his father, the man will say, died then and there. The man had wished his father dead just hours before, and now his father was dead. Questioned, the man's mother had no notion of what she'd done, nor would she ever believe she had. "The bottle," the man will say as he weeps, "is powerful. It's stronger than prison," he'll say, "stronger than death, and stronger for sure than love." His mother had shown him that, he'll say. His own disease, he'll say, which he'd got after years of drinking in the face of what he'd seen it do, despite what his mother had endured, and those at her hands—how she'd kept at the drink no matter what, not because she wanted to, but because she couldn't stop—all of this had shown him that. And now his mother, too, was dead, he'll say, died of her disease. And now he'd had to bury her, and doing so recall again what drink and drugs had done to him and his, and what it might do yet without his eye against it. And it will be then, in that moment, so many years after you'd dangled by your neck in the hands of the giant boy, that you'll recall not only that, but all of the times you've stepped so close to death. In a baffling rush, they'll pour through you—the illnesses and accidents and ODs and wrecks, the beatings and floods and falls and brawls, the depression, relentless, the endless call of suicide— that tightrope over fire and ice—the trip through mountains, deserts, islands, seas, secret towns and cities of black, through madmen and addicts and hookers and thieves, and gangsters and conmen and who knows how many killers, time and again placing your fate in the true unknown. Since boyhood, you'll think, your life's been a row of brushes with death. How is it you've managed to live? By what measure have you been let to stay here on this globe? For so long now, you'll think, your life's not been your own, but that of a doll dragged through a play writ by some old clown. One time after the next, you'll think, you've sunk to the depths and given your last, then been yanked to the surface, groping for the hand that saved you but finding merely emptiness. And the times you've been restored some sense, you'll think, it's to squint into faces of confusion and dread. And the more you think, you'll think, the more you realize it's not so much the engine that drives these vanished years that scares you, the reasons behind the things they hold, as why they return at all to appear in the distance of your memory, the way on desert plains a thunderhead will be where there'd been just spacious blue. The greater the sense you try to make of those years, you'll think, the deeper you find yourself in the whirlpool of memory, knowing very well that the harder you try to remember, the more incomprehensible things become, that the more pictures you try to gather, the more certain you are your past isn't as you thought but a baffling meld of lunacy and grace. And then you'll return and know it doesn't matter, the reasons for this or that, because if you understand, things are such as they are, and if you don't understand, things are such as they are. *This, and only this*, you'll think, *is all that matters—right now—life and death, death and life, the one the other and the other the same, all of it* now, *the single thing in this wide world you know is true, though you can never express it truly.*

THE WITNESS

The ordinary response to atrocities is to banish
them from consciousness. Certain violations of
the social compact are too terrible to utter aloud:
this is the meaning of the word *unspeakable*.

— *Judith Herman*

HE'D HEARD ABOUT CHAPARRAL AND SEEN IT FROM A distance, but never walked through it till now. *Coyote bush, sage, monkey flower, oak,* he had read on the placard. *Ceanothus, manzanita, chamise.* Of course he'd read *poison oak,* too. And of course, too, his father with his can of beer had singled out the shrub and warned him from it. But he had ignored his father's warning or more likely just forgot it.

One moment found him after lizards, the next a walking stick bug or snake. Another he scanned the ground for spiders, or looked to the sky in search of hawks, or chased a covey of quail. He slid down a canyon, the stream at its bottom full of minnows and gnats, and found a bed of newts, their bellies in the current orange as rust. He scrambled back through the roots and stones, as dry by the time he reached the top as he'd been wet at the bottom, covered with dirt like soot.

In the morning his teacher told him not to scratch at the rashes over his body and face, but the burning had kept him from anything else. At lunch, the pain more than he could stand, the nurse sent him home. Now, alone on the street, he felt like a spirit trudging through fire, blind but for snatches of this and that—a plastic flamingo on a yellow lawn—a sparrow in a hedge—a geezer on a porch—a boat in an oily drive. A fever had gripped him, nausea gripped him, he was boiling, itching, burning, and in his head throbbed a storm of wasps. He kicked his lunchbox toward a flowerbed and threw himself down to claw his neck. Home could've been the dandelion by his face or the streak of cirrus miles above. Then a gap appeared, and he went on.

He knew straightaway his house had changed. Until four-thirty or five, when the neighbors returned, the street stayed pretty much empty. But today someone had parked their car right in front of the house. Whoever it was had even made sure the door lined up with the path through the grass between the walk and street.

He looked back, then whirled, expecting a man or shadow to rush at him, but by the time he'd stopped no man or shadow or even a dog had come. All that moved were eyes, his own, through stillness. The palm tree in the yard. The paper in the drive. The rocks laid down after two old men had ripped away the lawn. The barbeque by the cart by the gate to the house of the widow next door, who smelled of mothballs and puke. The car before the house he lived in. The car before the house, metallic green, with its necklace of macramé and beads dangling from the mirror. The green metallic car which wasn't any old car, because his father had told him just what kind, every time his father had seen such a car, his father had said its name, with details about its year and make: *Corvette*. The car before the house was a green Corvette, metallic, with big mag wheels and a macramé necklace on the rearview mirror, a necklace, he knew with assurance, exactly like those his mother had been making since Easter.

A voice said to move, and without any effort his body began to drift.

Less than an inch above the ground, it felt, he glided toward the green Corvette.

And then he was peering through the Corvette's window at the necklace of beads and hemp, each bead the size of a large pea, but not green like peas but cobalt blue with a circle of white lined in red and a tiny dot of gold, the same as the hemp and beads which at this very instant lay in a box in his mother's room.

He looked away, into the console, knowing what he'd see there, afraid as he looked of what he knew he'd see.

And naturally it was there: a black-and-white picture of his mother.

He thought it was his mother, it *was* his mother, and yet it wasn't any mother he had known.

The woman who looked like his mother, the woman who looked like a shade of his mother, gazed from the picture straight into his eyes, like a dark siren working to steal his mind.

But the woman was not trying to steal his mind. The woman was trying to steal the mind of whoever had taken the picture, of the man who'd taken the picture, since after all, no one but a man could've taken the picture, which he knew as surely as he'd known he'd see the picture the man had taken of the woman who looked like a shade of his mother when he looked away from the necklace he knew his mother had made.

He gazed into the woman's eyes as dark as the entrance to a cave, struggling to perceive the meaning there, struggling to escape that meaning, to escape its awful pull. At any moment a cavern might open beneath his feet, and he'd be helpless but to plunge away.

Then he understood that the woman wasn't trying to steal his mind or the mind even of the man who'd taken her picture, but that her own mind had been stolen, that she herself was lost, though willingly, that she had given herself to the man whose eyes she gazed into, that the eyes into which she gazed hadn't just stolen her mind but mastered it, that she was ecstatically enslaved.

The day had evolved, it must've been two, the heat was at its peak.

Up and down the street nothing had moved, nothing had changed, nor was anything moving. Nor could he hear the hum of traffic, nor so much as a chirping finch.

He looked back to the house, expecting perhaps to find his mother at the door, a spoon in hand, but the house was still.

A shaft of light had pierced the Corvette's window and revealed the woman's every mark. Framed by a curtain of raven hair, her face was that of someone transfixed—the chin dropped, lips parted, black eyes ringed with white.

If the man who'd struck her to this degree wasn't a warlock, he was a doctor with a needle of dope, the sort of doctor he'd seen in old-time flicks, who snatched bodies from graves and kept eyes and brains in jars of chalky juice.

He thought what this man might look like, whether his hair had gone silver or stayed always black, worn long as the alchemist whose picture he'd seen in an ancient book, beneath a skullcap stitched with spells and chants, or cropped at the neck and parted with smelly grease. He wondered if the man wore robes, also stitched with spells and chants, or maybe just an old white smock and putrid suit, reeking of sweat, tobacco, and blood. He wondered about the man's face, too, whether it had a mustache, patchy and thin or heavy as fur, tainted with bits from yesterday's stew, or perhaps instead a pointy beard under brows so thickly long they looked like antennae from some race of sinister beings.

But also he wondered if none of these were true. The man might not have anything like silver hair or the mustache of a walrus rank with crumbs or a bloody smock or the eyebrows of a fiend. The man might not be a doctor, even, or even, for that matter, a man.

A wagon left a drive and set his way. The girl had freckled skin and tawny hair swept up with pins. She had an ample mouth and wide green eyes and rings on the fingers of the hand on the wheel. The guy beside her wore glasses with gold wire frames and lenses of green. His hair glowed, too, and so did his skin. When the wagon passed, the guy donned a cap and spit out some gum that bounced off the grass and stuck to the walk. A cloud of exhaust trailed the wagon, bitter, what he'd always thought the smell of burning hair.

A cat screamed, another in reply. He smelled cooking food, he couldn't say what, lamb chops maybe, and maybe boiled spuds, somewhere some mom was making up a batch of spuds.

A few houses down, Pedro Jones's mother, whose pubic hair he'd watched her son pluck as she lay naked on the couch in a stupor, stepped out for the paper. He could see her as though just feet away. An enormous breast drooped from her robe when she bent down, crazy with freckles round a nipple the size of a plate. A dove had lit on the wire before her house, but flapped off as she rose. And then the screen slammed shut, and the porch was bare.

A snake of flames had encased his throat. Ants were chomping his skin.

He had to get inside but was afraid.

The gate stood across an ocean of lawn.

Waves of heat drifted from its surface, and golden skippers flitted and bounced.

He looked back into the green Corvette, at the picture of the woman who looked like a shade of his mother, he looked again at the gate.

Hours passed, and hours more.

By the time he'd made it to the gate, he had just the strength to spring its latch.

His dog was at the door to the kitchen, like always, wriggling with her sad dog's eyes and cut-off tail. Typically this would've thrilled him, his little dog had never not thrilled him, she'd thrill him again, he knew, he'd roll on the floor with his trusty old dog while she licked his face, yet the fire was howling, he was swimming through a lake of fire. The dog cried at his neglect, really she'd scarcely whimpered, but he hadn't heard her for the horror running through him, that he would be discovered. Why he should fear this he couldn't say, but there it was, a void in his belly, as if someone had scooped out his guts.

His whole being strained against the urge, yet limb-by-limb he crawled to the door across the room, craning his head for the slightest creak or groan.

The house's silence was greater than the silence of the street. It was as if just beneath its surface roared a punishing howl.

He knew what would happen, or thought he knew what would happen, or rather he knew what would happen was the last thing in the world he could ever want to happen, but he kept on just the same.

Past the door ran the hall to the room he slept in and the rooms of his brothers and mother and father. Across the hall an arch gave onto the living room, as empty and still as the rest.

Could he have explained it, he'd have said the house had been lifted right out of entropy. Ten thousand years ago this house had sounded and smelled and felt like this. It would sound and smell and feel like this in ten thousand years again. Nothing moved, nothing changed, silence and stillness were all.

His dog appeared beside him, the smell of her filled his head, the smell that was hers alone, of the faith and earth that was dog. For an instant he felt that old sense of safety run through him. Curled up beside his dog he'd never come to harm, care bound the world and watched its sway, he was safe in the heart of a lullaby.

Then a door opened, at the end of the hall, he was sure he heard the squeak of the door at the end of the hall, he knew the sound of the door to the room of his mother and father. And then a voice sounded, manly and strange, speaking to his dog. "Come on, girl," said the man, and his dog stepped forward. "Hurry up, now," said the man, "come on." His dog disappeared round the corner, the door closed. "Up!" his mother said. "Up!" "Not while I'm here," said the man. And then with the same voice his father used when speaking to the dog, "Just because we let you in doesn't mean you're getting up here, too. Lie down."

Ancestral portraits lined the hall, most of whose figures he hadn't met and many of which, because they were dead, he never would. Some were prints of daguerreotypes. Certainly the people there were dead. Gilded in silver, embalmed with years, they were specters now, with cheerless faces and clothes from dramas of yore. They could've been a thousand years old for all he cared. They were dead.

The man in the room with his mother moaned. His mother moaned with him, and then again. Then the man gave out a vicious grunt, and then a series of grunts syncopate with his mother's shrieks and moans and the sound of a rapping stick.

The dead on the wall stared out with their dead eyes. Most of the living stared out with dead eyes, too.

He sat there, still on his hands and knees, trapped in the hall of the dead while some strange man did some strange thing with a woman he thought was his mother in the room that didn't belong to the man, in a house that wasn't the man's but his mother and father's. It was the man whose green Corvette was parked before the house he lived in, the Corvette with his mother's necklace and the picture of a woman who looked like a shade of his mother.

The man was nearly hollering, now, his mother was shrieking, it sounded worse than slaughter. He wondered if the man might be killing his mother or maybe just maiming her for good. A part of him feared the idea. Any time, now, the man would rush from the room, bloody and wild, and drive away in his sporty car, leaving him to his mother killed on the floor by her bed, her throat slashed or belly full of holes, or perhaps she'd just be beaten and throttled. He would find her, he'd try to wake her, and when she failed to respond, he'd dial 911. But another part of him felt that all of that would be fine. His mother would be gone. They would take her away, she'd be gone forever, and he'd be fine, he'd be more than fine, he'd be fine with everything.

But right now nothing was fine. At any moment the strange evil doctor man would step from the room of his mother and father and find him there on his hands and knees. The man would gag and tie and stuff him in a bag, then throw him in the trunk of the green Corvette and drive to a castle on the mountain to cut him to pieces for his jars of chalky juice.

The man and his mother had gone silent.

The house lay still again, the world itself was stillness.

The best he could think to do was return to the past, before the man had opened the door of his mother and father's room and beckoned to his dog, or before that even, before he'd walked into the house. If he could go back, the man would never have been there, and what he knew would happen could never happen. But he couldn't go back, but merely edge along a limb at a time until he'd reached the island between the kitchen and den and lean against the island to wait.

He'd been clawing at himself in a fever, his anguish as pure as grief or bliss. At last a voice pierced the silence, someone calling through murky water, and a door opened, and his little dog's nails clicked across the floor.

Footsteps followed, his mother's barefoot shuffle and the man's shod tread, coming his way. Then, as if the moment had been planned, his mother appeared, the man's big hands on the back of her hips. Then the man's foot appeared, and the man's knee and thigh, and then the whole of the man, the unbuttoned shirt, the thick dark hair, cropped at the brow, the bluish jaw and mustache black as boots. The man was strong and tall and roughly handsome, like a hero, more or less, perfect in stature and form. Or, still better, the man looked like another man, whom he'd seen in ads in magazines, smoking Camel cigarettes, The Camel Man.

There they stood, not his mother but the woman from the picture in the green Corvette who looked like a shade of his mother, and The Camel Man from ads in magazines, framed in the door like a living picture, oblivious to him as he sat on the floor gazing up.

When the man spun his mother round and drew her near, she laced her arms about his neck and rose to her toes to kiss him.

Never once had his mother and father kissed this way.

Never once had he seen anything like it, not on TV or anywhere.

As his mother's face approached the man's, the man's mouth opened and his tongue flopped out. Then their mouths joined, and their jaws grew violent. A thread of saliva bridged their mouths when at last they drew apart, then broke beneath their darting tongues.

His mother wore a short silk gown, the man had pulled it up, he could see the flesh of his mother's buttocks rolling beneath the man's big hands, the skin there lighter for her bathing suit, a pale olive hue just beneath the surface that shimmered as it moved.

And then their faces parted, and they opened their eyes.

His mother's heels touched the floor.

The man let go his mother.

His mother's gown recovered.

Neither his mother nor the man had looked his way. It wouldn't take much, he knew, to draw their gaze, the least little movement or twitch.

"Thanks for having me," said the man with his low voice.

His mother's arms were still around the man. She freed them now and ran a finger along the man's ear while a hand rested on his shoulder.

"I missed you," she said. "I'll miss you when you leave."

"Let me know when it's good to come again," said the man.

A strand of hair had come to rest between his mother's lips. The man preened it loose. He smiled and kissed her nose.

"Tomorrow," his mother said.

"Your hubby thinks I'm having lunch with Todd Stove."

His mother pouted. "I know," she said.

"You are a stone fox," the man said, and opened the door. "But you know that, too."

His mother turned to him as the door shut, then froze, struggling to veil her shock. She had neglected to secure her gown and was exposed.

He saw her naked daily, every morning she and his father pranced naked about the house, but seeing her now, anxious like this, made everything about her new.

Her breasts looked different.

Her belly looked different.

The tuft of hair at her pelvis looked different, also.

Everything about her looked entirely other, she was frozen in terrible newness for one second more, the woman beyond his mother.

And then she vanished, the woman who looked like a shade of his mother, and his mother appeared, with the eyes he knew so well, gone from startled transfixion to venomous beads, his mother with the mouth he knew so well, turned from luscious summons to hideous purple knot. Then her body was also gone, taken by her gown with a practiced wave.

"When did you get here?" she said.

His dog had scurried over and pushed her face beneath his arm. "I'm sick," he said, extending his hand. "I have poison oak."

His mother took the hand and yanked. "Get up," she said. "Right now."

"I have poison oak."

He tried to stand, but the floor was somehow wet, and he slipped.

"What did you see? Tell me what you saw, right this instant."

"The nurse sent me home," he said, and began to cry. "I swear."

"If I hear one peep about this to your father, so help me." His mother nodded to the puddle widening about him. "Look at you. I thought you were a young man, but now I see that isn't true."

"Please, Mom, I didn't see anything. I have poison oak."

"What did your father say to do? Did you put on that lotion he gave you? Why are you here? When did you get here, and what have you been…"

He thought of the snake he'd caught the day before, a gopher snake three feet long, how as he held the snake behind its head the way his father had taught him the snake had writhed about his arm, squeezing with all its might.

Far in the distance, close to where he thought space must begin, a single cloud stretched across the miles. The men of the Apollo had landed on the moon two or three years before. He remembered his father calling him to see the man on TV as he stepped from the rocket in his white suit, impermeable to everything, outer space, gravity, the coldest ice. When the man wore the suit, he could feel no harm. He could soar to the moon, then step from his rocket to wander its plains.

To get to the moon, the man and his crew must've torn through a cloud like the one above him now. On the other side of that cloud, that's where Earth ends and space begins. If you looked down from your rocket, you'd see it, the whole Earth, just like on TV. It would look like a marble of blue that looked like a great blue sea you'd never dive into again, not for the rest of your life. But by then it wouldn't matter. In a day or two, you'd be on the moon.

MEMORY'S A TOWN WITH A FARAWAY LOOK—IT COULDN'T exist but on a card. Memory's a dance you want to say has been with the girl you never got. Memory's the smell of your love in a vial, which you'll take from a drawer of letters and gloves and scarves years off, whose days in the smelling will as soon be the smell of Regret. Where do they come from, your memories? Where have the images that make your memories been hiding across the years?

THAT SATURDAY, ON HIS WAY HOME FROM THE QUIK STOP where he'd blown his allowance on sweets, near the edge of the field, he saw a pack of cigarettes. Had the brand been Benson and Hedges, or Vantage, or Pall Mall—anything short of Marlboro or Camel, which to his mind even then were the only cigarettes worth their smoke—he might've kept on. But they were Marlboros, and not Marlboro Lights, in the white and gold pack, but Marlboro Reds, in the soft pack, totally superior. It wasn't that he could not *not* look at this package in the weeds. He could not *not* stop looking at this package in the weeds.

Already the cigarettes had him, already he was theirs.

Blue skies ruled, sunshine ruled, summertime would come with its water balloons and swimming pools, milkshakes and barbeques, mornings late in bed his father gone to work, cartoons daily, mischief with pals come afternoon, baseball practice and baseball games, the A's on the tube, the Paradero's hideout, camping in Y, and—best of all!—firecrackers and firewheels, roman candles, M-80s, bottle rockets and Piccolo Petes . . .

On the street now and then a car hummed by, the drivers

thoughtless of his schemes—some stupid kid staring at a field as he gummed his lollipop and farted.

Three or four robins bounced through the sprinklers on a lawn, and cabbage moths roamed the field at whose far side, near the eucalyptus by the freeway, stood a fort, actually just a big bush in whose hollow boys pretended they were gunners in their nest or hunters in their hutch, and older boys banged their girls or jerked off to the honeys and bunnies on the pages of *Playboys* and *Hustlers* left behind for fledgling crooks like him.

The willow before the Elks Lodge up the way had begun to bloom. Late last summer Mike Paradero had bared his ass from a fork in its branches to shit on him and Paul Paradero and Pedro Jones, that weird redhead kid who just a few weeks back had led them to his yard to peer through the window as he, Pedro Jones, sneaked up to his fat mother snoring naked on the couch and plucked one of the hairs on her belly and thighs.

A block past the Elks Lodge, a lab at his heel, an old dude dumped a catcher of grass into his truck. The sun was shining. The sky was blue. Some doves swept by, then circled round to settle in the willow at the lodge. The sun was really shining. The sky was really blue.

The pack was still half full, he could tell, or thereabout. He picked it up, and, by golly, there they were, eight of them, just as he'd thought, almost half a pack of real-life actual cigarettes.

Obviously he couldn't walk into the house with them: *Hey, look what I found!* His father would take them. *Thanks, hot shot*, his father would say, and light one up.

But he had found them. They were his, and he was going to smoke one or maybe three or four if that's what he decided. And plus by himself, as in totally alone. And no one could stop him, no one, for that matter, would even know. He looked around again and saw the same—lazy cars, robins, the willow with its doves, an old man down the street, that was it, and sun and sky and breeze.

He wedged the pack between his belly and belt, then set off for his room at the house to stash them in his dresser, beneath the PJs he never wore.

Then he flopped on the couch by the tube to watch a dragster explode, the commentators yelling as men tried to save the driver from his pit of flaming steel. For hours he went between the couch and the tube, shuffling through the channels—a baseball game, the Astros and some other team; the PM matinee, *One Million Years, B.C.*, with Raquel Welch; a boxing match announced by Howard Cosell; a ballet—*yuck*; a talk show—Lawrence Welk interviewed by Merv Griffin or Mike Douglas or Dick Cavett—*yuck*, and *yuck*, and *yuck*, and *yuck*; Bob Hope in seafaring costume spazzing on a set like a tropical island; Bob Barker yelling, *Come on down!*—*yuck*; shots of a plain full of antelope, egrets, cheetahs, and giraffes . . .

His mother had been doing laundry, he realized, she'd go through his stuff at any time. He moved the cigarettes to a shoe in his closet, and then again, before bed, slipped them under his mattress.

Later that week he stole a box of matches from the tray his father worked his weed on.

Some days after that, once he'd fed the dog, and cleared the dishes, and vacuumed the rug, and edged the lawn, and swept, he told his mother he was off to the school for ball, but headed to the field.

He wove through the grass, stopping now and then to

check a log or stone for lizards and snakes, even if lizards and snakes were the last things he cared about now. It was just a bunch of fakery, same as every one else's, this act of looking for lizards and snakes. He wanted to know he was alone. If someone entered the field, he'd wait them out looking for lizards and snakes. And if he found some jerk in the fort when he reached it, simple, he'd come back later and do the same. But apart from the moths and flies and hoppers and bees, he saw no one and heard nothing but a couple of singing larks. From fifty yards out, the shrub that was the fort looked empty. He craned for a sign—a cackle or snore—but heard nothing again but the whisper of grass and purr of bugs, the whistling of blackbirds, too, and the freeway humming and, really far away, the shouting of a man.

Traffic along the path for the last few yards had made the place human, though that didn't change the fort, which looked still like the shrub it was, five feet high and fifteen or so around. Only after you reached the other side could you see its purpose. Beer cans, soda cans, paint cans—milk cartons, candy wrappers, tarps—newspapers, planks, empty packs of cigarettes—magazines, lone shoes, and twine was what you found. Bums had been living in the fort, Mike Paradero once told him, but really they couldn't stay for long because the cops went out to roust them, and sometimes guys from high school messed them up, as well. He'd actually gone into the fort a couple times at most, the last maybe six months back.

In his memory the place had glowed with exotic smut. Now it was grody with the stench of shit. He shuffled through the beer cans and butts and pages filled with naked chicks to the milk crate across the way and found that someone really had taken a dump, probably just an hour before. And whoever it was that had taken the dump had used the crate to launch it: teeming with flies, a load of shit, four logs high, gnarly in its glory, there it lay, whoa. He might've had to smell the shit, but no way was he going to see it. Most of the paper had been ruined by wet, from last week's rains or morning dew. They stuck to the dirt like leaves, and when he tried to scrape up this one or that, the earwigs and pill bugs there went nuts. Finally, he managed to gather enough junk to cover the shit—a branch, and two empty Tab cans, and a wad of slimy paper, and a plastic bag gummy with moldy jam. Then he moved the crate to the other side and went out and gathered up an armful of grass for the crate.

He took a cigarette from the pack and smoothed it tip to butt. He tapped it on his hand, the way he'd seen his father do, then brought it to his lips and struck a match. Then he lit it, and then he puffed, and then he squinted at the smoke. Then he drew super hard and sucked in all the smoke.

For the longest time he'd wanted this most of all. He'd wanted to cradle the smoke as smoking men did, deep in his lungs, like a promise or a vow, he'd wanted to vent the smoke as smoking men did, slowly as he talked, his words embraced by smoke, and watch the smoke as it drifted off in arty wisps. He'd wanted this smoke inside him oh-so-badly for oh-so-long, and yet now that he had it, his body refused to help. His eyes watered, his ears burned, the world began to buzz. And then with a heaving retch, the smoke poured burning from him . . .

But so freaking what, his will was strong, too strong for this lame-o piece of paper and weed. Mastering the cigarette was like mastering the rest, the bike, the bat, the fist. He'd smoke this cigarette down to the butt if it was the last thing he goddamned did. Then he'd smash the butt beneath his heel, like the roughneck at the lumberyard smashed it beneath his heel, like Clint in the sand and Bogey the fog, like his father in the lot a butt beneath his heel.

His head was spinning, now, and his stomach, too, the air had grown thick and hot. When again the seizure struck, he struggled with all he had, and in a bit the danger passed. But still his mind buzzed, inside his head the machine hummed on, *bzzzzzz, bzzzzzzzz, bzzzzz.*

He looked at the cigarette. The smoke twined up in gentle loops, the smell so good, a smell he'd always loved. Again he placed the cigarette to his lips and squinted at the smoke, again he drew, though easier now, again he took the smoke inside and felt the burn, and the burn of his cheeks and brow and ears, the branches and leaves areel before him, the lady on her page, reeling and reeling, the beer can by his foot. He held the smoke long enough now, though not too long, he didn't gag, he didn't lurch, and then—*thooooooooooooooooooooo*—he let it go, gentle, easy, all the smoke, all *his* smoke, vanishing now in the branches and leaves. And now again the buzz set in, better than before, and now again the nausea, worse than before, and then it faded, the nausea passed, and . . . he was something else, somewhere else . . . *high.* . .

He took another drag, he felt the rush, felt the burn, felt the crazy buzz . . .

A wave rolled up then slipped away, and then a wave on it . . .

And then the cigarette itself had passed, the cigarette was gone, he dropped the butt and smashed the butt, he heard the hiss he heard his father hear as his father smashed a butt, he saw the smoke, dying at his heel . . .

Yet it was something more than fear he felt counting the rest of the pack. They had to go, he knew, these seven cigarettes, though how he didn't know. But no sooner had he been bound than like a whip the answer cut his doubt away—*smoke them!*

Not once did he set this choice to another—burying the cigarettes, say, or tearing up the cigarettes, say, and scattering them across the field, or throwing them in a dumpster, say, or even just leaving them with the rest of the junk in that icky little fort, maybe under the crap whoever it was had taken. The thought—the *command*, more like it—to smoke the cigarettes had rung out, and he lit another, a head without a body, a body without a head . . .

Time passed, now quantum, now huge, he was there, the boy in the dirt, the nothingness of the sky . . .

Stars wheeled, crypts decayed, flowers bloomed and blooms waned . . .

Bees by the billion, stewards of the earth, swarmed the fields, life on the breeze, ruin in sun, famine, mishap, joy, war, the secret, the truth, never before, never then, but through and all, through and all, he knew it all, and he knew none, how could he know more, better, how, or why, when he was but a cipher, a boy in a bush—how could he?

Hours passed . . .

He had no clue.

BELIEFS ARE POWERFUL. THEY'RE THE MOST POWERFUL things in the human mind, and when they're spawned from misunderstandings of the way things are, everything you do will fly in your face like piss in the wind. Say, for instance, you grow up believing the thing that will make you a man is a dying mouse or piece of rotten fruit. Your core will be infested with doubt, you'll be a houseful of the lowest of spooks: the syndrome kid in a silo—the moron daughter fed to hogs—the nincompoop whacked by a maid—the flipper child drowned in oil. And the fear will come. Your life will be a trance of fear run amok, and of hunger run amok, a trance of hunger for love, of fear of love, of fear of losing the love you long to hope you have, of hunger for the things you hope might win you love, of fear of losing the things you hope might win you love, of hunger for the thing you hope might cure you of your illness, purify you, save you from your fear of your hunger for the thing you hope might save you, and the disappointment and sadness of your failure to attain it. And you will know weakness, you'll know neglect, you'll know powerlessness, frustration, confusion, yes, and you will know discontent. And so you'll know hatred, too, and rage, you'll know hunger for destruction, and fear of destruction, you'll know selfishness and harm and greed. Like some crippled phoenix, your sadness will slither from the bed of your failure, doomed to creep through a maze of scum till at last it sees—though, as always, with that certain false sense of hope—that its sole chance for respite lies where others fear to go, into the chaos of rage. No longer a crippled phoenix, now, no longer even a bird, your sadness will rise with wings of fire, a dragon laying waste to the pure and shamed alike, the shamed especially, the conspirators of your harm, and those especially in whom it smells so much as a whiff of your rotten self, which is punishment for your weakness and despair, for having allowed yourself to have been so irreparably crushed, time, after time, after time . . . And then the day will come when you see there's nothing you've not poisoned, nothing you've not harmed. You'll have destroyed the whole of your path, there's nothing you'll not have wanted to smash, you'll long to crush the world itself because the world, you'll believe, is your tyrant. And hatred will consume you, and turn your heart to waste. Fed by your regret, your sadness and grief and shame, and now too by your rage, your hatred will attain the strength of armies. And, like armies, your hatred will devour everything before it till nothing remains but to turn on itself, a frantic dragon bloody with the blood of its own heart—you in your hatred of yourself for hating, you in your hatred of hating and of the harm wrought of your hating, and of your selfishness and greed. But most of all you'll hate yourself for your helplessness before your hatred, before your selfishness and greed, before the senselessness of your harm. And you will know without knowing you know that you are not a dragon, but a puppet in the mask of a dragon flouncing through its trance of fear, controlled not by some god, but by your own hand, *by the hand of your mind*, of the beliefs by which your mind is owned, which are lies, whose impenetrable walls, however much you may assault them, with whatever force of weaponry or will, toss you back again and again into your impostorhood, ridiculing you, scorning you in your irrelevance, you, the world's butt, you, creation's lackey, broken child devoured by the Wolves of Doubt, vacant man owned by the Clowns of Fear, laughable, pathetic, terrible in your pain—ha! ha! ha!—a Monster of Mendacity—ha!—a Menace of Melancholy—ha!—a Mongrel of Mortification—

ha!—the mewling Mayor of All—Misery, Misfortune, Malice, All—ha! ha! ha! ha! ha!

"Hello, little man," she said.

He'd never liked showers, even before the ritual had begun. What boy liked showers? What boy didn't like dirt, and, more, *his* dirt? But he didn't merely like his dirt—he adored it. His dirt was the stuff of ventures in the wild, of black frontiers, of secret maps, of kingdoms lost and found, of monsters and myths, of victory and defeat, of deepest, sweetest, scariest dreams. Dirt was the stuff of dragon slayers and mountain men, of captured soldiers, and of convicts and spies. Dirt was the stuff of football players and firemen, of Indian warriors and racecar drivers, of cowpokes and workers of steel, and of villains, and of ghouls. Dirt was the stuff of tunnels, caves, castles, forts, the stuff of wigwams and tents, of fields of play and fields of war, of horses and hogs, of stags and bulls and roaring bear, of death and dying and bleeding wide-eyed life. Colonel Hogan was dirty. Fred Biletnikoff was dirty. Lennie and George were dirty, and Leatherstockings, too. James Bond was dirty, sometimes, and sometimes Mario Andretti was dirty, also. Steve McQueen was dirty. So were Yul Brynner, Charles Bronson, James Coburn, Paul Newman, and Robert Redford. Aragorn, he was a king, and he was always dirty, just like Bilbo Baggins, and Frodo Baggins, and scheming treacherous Gollum, and Gandalf, a wizard, no less, and Gimli the Dwarf, and even Legolas the Elf, even he got dirty, green-eyed, shining Legolas. Sitting Bull was dirty, Chief Joseph was dirty, and Geronimo, definitely he was dirty. All of the people he admired, all of the people he really loved, were dirty, including his father, who was pretty dirty at times, at least on the weekends, when they pulled weeds or mowed the lawn or laid beneath the car, wrenching this and that. When he was dirty, he wasn't himself, but beyond, where no one could touch him, where no one could tell him who he was or what to do or how. When he was dirty, he was everyone who'd ever lived to know the dirt, to fall in the dirt, to roll in the dirt and fight in the dirt, to rise from the dirt to brush it off with a shining grin and word of joyous cheer. He couldn't have said it then, nor for a long time after, but his feeling for dirt was like a saint's for God. Dirt was earth, dirt was safe, dirt was the final home. When you were in the dirt, you were on the ground, in the grass, or the mountains, or forest, or fields—where you ran and played and drifted and dreamed, free from home, that other home, which was a lie, free from the impostor you became when you stepped through its door, a shape shifter of sorts, skittering from one guise to the next like some barefoot kid across a lake of melting ice, there in your realm of resentment and loss, your anger, your nerves, your fear, that realm of confusion, where you could place more faith in the forecast of a witch doctor throwing bones from his bag than in anything you could conjure, never knowing as you did whether you'd be hailed—smart as a surgeon, suave as a star—or reviled—filthy as a bum, evil as a fiend—a useless hated urchin condemned to having your hair torn out, your face clawed, your body wracked with fists and spoons—your head, your arms, your shoulders, your legs, your back, your scrawny-ass little butt—whether for a tussle with your brothers that had gone too far or having badly answered a question or command you'd misunderstood or hadn't heard or complained about even, knowing it was wrong. None of these things obtained when you were in the dirt, not a single lousy one. Dirt never lied. Dirt didn't have to lie. Dirt had no stake in anything, not even in itself. It had no place to be, it had to be nothing, nothing but itself, ever present, ever stable, true as the sun and moon, the ever-rolling years. Dirt you could trust. You could trust dirt so well you even always knew when it was near. Dirt smelled, and better than anything he knew—better than pizza, better than cake, better than tacos or lasagna or ice cream or tea, and better even than dogs—or maybe almost better, since if a dog didn't smell of dirt, it wasn't really a dog—and better than jasmine at night, than blue-belly lizards, than salmon eggs or cheese balls, rivers and lakes, gasoline, even—better, really, than anything ever in the whole wide world. Home itself wasn't dirt, but that didn't mean you couldn't bring your dirt back to it.

Only when the ritual that was his evening shower approached did the spell get broken. The call to shower was the moment he was stripped once more of everything he knew—his clothes, his dreams, his fantasies, his trust, his faith in the way of things, his faith, finally, in the world itself. His father would order him to remove his clothes when his mother called, and then to enter the bathroom, his mother still in it, naked herself.

Not always, but often enough—exactly when he never knew—his mother would lay her hand on his shoulder, before he could slip into the tub. Then, turning him to her, she'd kneel down, and, with the same words, always the same words, like those of some seductively mad woman from the silver screen— Joan Crawford, Karen Black—take his penis in her fingers.

"Hello, little man," she said. "What do we have today?"

She herself had just stepped from the bath, yet the fingers with which she clasped him were cool. Now, with two fingers from her other hand, she was lifting it to examine his testicles, pressing them to one side and the other, squeezing them lightly, too, as if she were studying a mouse, a newborn mouse, sick, so sick that at any moment it might die.

Her head was wrapped in a towel, her olive complexion still bright with the hue from her time in the steam. He could see the small beads of sweat on her face. He could see the pores where she'd plucked her brows.

On the wall beside the sink hung a print in frameless glass—eight different-colored hearts floating in splotches of grey over which had been scrawled, "Red, Orange, Yellow, Green . . ."—the same print he'd seen in the bathroom at his mother's rich brother's house up in the hills of Y, the house of the man who'd tried to drown him the summer before.

A rag lay in the sink, a towel on the floor, between the cabinet and toilet, whose lid was open, a big no-no. One of his father's hairs lay on the rim, thick and black against the porcelain white. Inches away, three or four drops of urine, orangey-yellow in the center and pale at the edges, had been overlooked, also. A spot of rust dotted the knob on the cabinet. The walls were oozing with steam. The room stunk of soap. It stunk of cleanser and bleach.

Somehow she'd turned on the shower, heat was building, shrouding him and the rest, but inside he felt cold, like he'd been running for hours through a winter's noon.

Next to the toilet hung another picture in pen-and-ink, of some gaunt old knight on a nag, windmills spread across the distant plain. The murky glass before it blotted out the lopsided sun and most of the man on the pony beside him. The knight was a vanquished shell-man alone on an empty plain. He didn't think this then. His thoughts held no matter. The broken man on the broken horse had conjured in him the remnant of a scarcely remembered age, a monochromatic void of sadness, that was all.

He didn't need to see his mother anymore. He could feel her—that never changed—and smell her, too—Dove soap and Vaseline lotion, and her shampoo, Johnson's. There was nothing to do but wait. At times, if the spot where his mother had caught him was tight, hedged in on one side by cabinets and the other by the toilet or wall, one of her nipples would brush against his arm or waist, or sometimes press against him whole, the way they were now, and a shudder would trip through him. He looked at his mother again. He knew her body almost better than his own, so often had he had the opportunity to study it during the eternities that were these judgments.

His mother's face was beautiful. He'd always felt that. He'd always loved his mother's face, save when it shriveled to the beady-eyed mask of her rage. His mother was known for her face, her olive complexion, supple and smooth, her dark brown eyes and hair, her forehead, broad, the sweeping line of hair, the Nordic nose, strong yet soft, the lips, full, the soft but ample chin. In her loveliest moments, his mother resembled Katherine Ross or Ali McGraw—an inexplicable woman, her inexplicable face, with calling eyes and flowing hair, like a woman from the shadows, a woman who though you met her in the light of day appeared always to be pulsing from the shadows.

Men wanted his mother, he'd always known this, too, he couldn't remember not knowing this, the way they clamored about her, the way she urged it on. Perhaps for them, perhaps for his father, also, his mother's body held equal enticements, though even then he wondered and doubted, knowing her body wasn't like those of the other rarer women, who with their long legs and feathery arms, supple waists and tiny round buttocks, floated through the world. Wherever they were, he knew these women as he knew those in whose midst they floated, the lesser ones, the difference between these women and his mother, wherever they were, in the market, the mall, the station, the pool, especially at the pool, in their bikinis, fresh and tan, emitting their bottomless light.

It wasn't that his mother's body was malformed or even ugly, not at all, but that his mother simply lacked a certain grace, that the grace of the other women had eluded her by some twist, barely, the same faulty turn that would've deprived Marilyn Monroe's darker lesser sister.

His mother was shapely enough in the waist, but her buttocks, large at the top, around the hips, and tight at the bottom, where they tapered to her thighs, were somehow always a trace too full. And her legs were on the thick side, right to the ankles, their backs dimly pocked, the inner thighs laced with veins. But it was her valgus knees that barred any hope for grace. Because of them, his mother waddled some, so that watching her move about with those short hurried steps, you felt she was permanently clenched against the pull of gravity itself. As for her breasts, they were large, or rather they weren't small, the breasts of a sleepy matron. And that she was a woman who never worked was clear from her arms, soft from shoulder to wrist, with flesh that rippled at the backs when she raised them to apply deodorant or take some item from a shelf. But his mother's hands, her fingers—the same fingers with which she was holding him now—these were different. Her hands were so lovely, her fingers so long and tapered, with strong clear nails, that sometimes as he watched her making sandwiches or drawing the zipper on his coat, he was filled with the sense that if they held him for an hour, he could melt into them and soar through her veins, straight to the heart of forever. He'd be in heaven, then, he'd never go back again.

But instead his mother used her hands to slap him, to roughly comb the knots from his hair, to scratch him, to beat him, to squeeze him daintily while pushing back his skin for some magically surfaced blemish. She held him at times, she did, lying on the couch of a Saturday night after a plate of pie, a sitcom on the tube as she ran her fingers through his hair, and yet the moment rarely lasted more than minutes. Soon enough his mother would dig into his scalp—scanning like a monkey through the roots for some crumb of leaf or sand—or prod at his forehead or ears in search of the blackheads that were somehow always there.

His yearning for that endless moment in his mother's hands was just a dream, he knew. He'd stopped hoping for it long before. It was especially apparent now. He knew what would happen. It was common as the chiming clock, and dinner, and school. His mother would squint into him till at last, troubled to see nothing to treat or fix, she'd frown as she flicked him away, like a bit of rotten fruit.

She guided him to the tub. "It's very handsome, honey," she said. "Get in there now, and scrub it good."

YOU ARE STRICKEN WITH WONDER. BUT THIS WONDER ISN'T a wonderful wonder, this wonder is no wonder of serenity and grace. It's a wonder of madness, a wonder of terror and doubt. It's a wonder that civility, concern, humility, kindness—that compassion itself—haven't utterly collapsed. And sometimes when you look at man's inhumanity to man, growing as you watch, you can't help but to ask how the day hasn't come that we erupt in a turmoil of slaughter, like the men in *Jacob's Ladder*, when gassed in a test in the jungles of Nam the squad goes wild, as the Vikings went wild, cutting each down to the least helpless man. Our very births hurl us from primordial bliss into a matrix of delusion, of Brughelian malice and Goyaesque brutality, of turn after turn of the desire, fear, hatred, and rage that lead us to the black of domination and defeat—the makings, on the whole, for the pornography that's been your life: your father in the shadows at the end of the day, after the fight with your mother, who that afternoon, before your father came home, broke spoons across the body that was yours, who'll corner you by the bath in an hour—your mother—raped by her father, raped by her brothers—who fucked your father and all your father's friends, who took you, her boy, her eldest, to bed to fondle as you "slept" through your "naps," and who, years later, having divorced your father—the man that stood by as she did her crimes—would marry another—a psychopath in prison, life sans parole, for killing his woman with her gun—while in the distance of Dustbowl Central—the same as ever, for years and years—your father withered in his house of gloom, broken, befuddled, stoned.

HE'D BEEN STANDING ON THE BLACKTOP WITH THE BALL in his arm, telling David Cook he was nuts, his shot had not passed the line, his shot had landed at the farthest point of David Cook's corner, impossible for David Cook to reach, a perfect shot, that's right, if he did say so himself.

But David Cook went on and on that he was wrong, a claim, as any dope could see, that was the fattest joke he'd ever heard. Even Kathy Lucas was on his side. She pointed to the mark the ball had left in David Cook's square and told David Cook he was out, but the kid crossed his arms and shook his head and called Kathy Lucas a tard.

And it was then he understood with total clarity that nearly always, more than anything else, others only got in the way and mucked things up. They stepped into the middle of things and distorted the truth till the truth was no longer the truth. They denied the existence of the truth or refused to look to see the truth. They lied, knowingly and otherwise. They got in the way.

Kathy Lucas stamped her foot and called David Cook a butthead, a butthead, moreover, with a birthmark on his face, and David Cook's eyes filled with tears, everyone could tell David Cook would start to cry, what a puss, and called Kathy Lucas a twat. Her face turned red, her eyes, too, like she'd jammed a clip in a socket and been zapped a thousand volts. That was it, Kathy Lucas cried, David Cook was a liar and a butthead with a birthmark that was going to get it from Mrs. Kalashian, the recess monitor with the mole near her eye and breath like a rickety dog, who Kathy Lucas knew for a fact hated David Cook because Mrs. Kalashian had told her, Kathy Lucas, that she hated every kid who was a butthead with a birthmark on his stupid face. Then, with her skinny legs and scabby knees and the panties he saw when her dress flopped down on the monkey bars, Kathy Lucas ran across the yard, David Cook chasing and shouting *dirty stinky twat!*

Mrs. Kalashian appeared with Kathy Lucas and David Cook to demand what the heck the problem was. He told Mrs. Kalashian Kathy Lucas had been right, David Cook was out but wouldn't quit. David Cook was a liar wrecking everyone's time and wasting recess, too, there were ten minutes left, the ball had landed in the corner, right there, on the spot Kathy Lucas had said. Then David Cook said he was a liar. Then Kathy Lucas called David Cook a big fat butthead with a birthmark on his face whose father was a has-been, but instead of calling her a twat, the way David Cook had called her a twat before, David Cook began to cry.

Mrs. Kalashian snatched Kathy Lucas's arm so hard she almost fell. Mrs. Kalashian said if she heard one more bleepity-bleep out of her, Kathy Lucas would find herself on the hot seat in the office of the principal. Then Mrs. Kalashian told him to start the game over. She didn't want to hear anymore about it, Mrs. Kalashian said, she had no way to sort the mess out than to let David Cook play again. Kathy Lucas was near crying, now, writhing about, trying to get loose from Mrs. Kalashian, all of which, he could see, made David Cook happy, the jerk wore a grin, now, huge, the jerk was gloating was what, that was the name for what David Cook was doing, his father had said, acting like a rotten winner, like a big shot better than the rest, and better especially than the guy who'd got the short end of the stick.

And this was how it had always been, he saw, as he stood hugging the ball to his chest while David Cook tried to take it—David Cook, whose face, it was true, had a big red birthmark on it, like a glob of blood from the wrong tube had squeezed out of David Cook's mom before David Cook was born and stained the side of David Cook's face—always some David Cook was there to get in the way and muck things up, to step into things and warp the truth till the truth was something else, to deny the existence of the truth or refuse even to look to see the truth, to lie, to get in the way and bungle and flail and muck the whole thing up. And this was how it would always be, he knew, this was how it would be.

Yes, and the same was true at home. It didn't matter that he knew the truth there, either. People knew the truth, everyone everywhere knew the truth, but they mucked it up or distorted or ignored or denied it, and, in the end, one way or other, turned it to something no one wanted, a broken broom or chewed on Styrofoam cup.

His father said not to think so much. His father said he had some imagination. His father said he conjured things. His father said he, his father, would have a talk with his mother. His father said he, his father, knew what he meant but there was nothing he, his father, could do. His father said they'd just have to wait and see. His father said he, his father, didn't have time. His father said he, his father, was sorry he felt that way. His father said to keep his head down. His father said life wasn't fair, but sometimes we had to do the best with what we'd been given, as if what we'd been given, however crappy, was a gift we had no choice but to hold. His father said he, his father, loved him.

But soon the day arrived when he stopped telling his father what he knew because he knew very well what his father would say. He never went to his mother anymore. He'd stopped going to his mother so long ago he couldn't remember when. But no matter whom he went to, and no matter how sure he was he knew what he knew, somehow, far in the core of his knowing, a spot of doubt had appeared, which for all his efforts he couldn't kill. He scourged it with his mind, he smashed and clawed and tore it with his mind, but instead of weakening or shrinking, the spot of doubt leapt from one piece to the next, like a germ in the heart of a city. Before long he no longer had a voice in his head, his own voice, but three and five, then seven and nine or more, none of them his, most of them yelling at once, so much so often they kept him from anything else.

He'd seen a documentary about chimpanzees. He missed the start, when one chimp had somehow wronged another. The camera only showed how the bigger angry chimp began to harass the first chimp, viciously slapping and biting it. After a time, as if irked with its results, the angry chimp got other chimps to help. Of course the angry chimp said nothing. That was what amazed him, how the angry chimp did nothing more than madly parade before the others, converting them to its purpose by example. One minute the angry chimp would stamp and flail as if in a game of charades, another it would rush in to smash the beleaguered chimp. "Come on over, guys, and give me a hand!" it might as well have said. "This is going to be a splash!" No wonder, then, that two or three others had soon joined it. And once they'd begun, the beleaguered chimp was trapped. It tried to run, but its tormenters cut it off. It tried to submit, lying down before them, but none of them would be soothed. The camera filmed the assault dispassionately, now zooming in on this chimp or that as it bit or punched the beleaguered chimp, now zooming out to present the disaster whole. A sinister inevitability had infected the scene. A dozen or so chimps had closed in on the beleaguered chimp, and then more yet, a mob, now, actually, sliding moment by hellish moment into the madness that broke without warning, and they fell on the chimp tooth and nail. A few minutes back the chimp had been quietly goofing around, flirting or trying to glean a scrap of fruit. Now it was getting slaughtered. It took but a moment to finish the work, which wasn't yet the end, because without pause the killers began to eat the chimp's privates, and not in the frenzy of before, but calm as a baby its banana, the brain, as well, got at with a stone, and the rest after it. He never forgot the chimp's face as it emerged from the fray like a horrible mask, its mouth so wide he could see the back of its throat. Then a claw took it by its neck, and the chimp was gone.

One day soon, he figured, if he didn't look out, he, too, would be torn to bits and gobbled down, if not by his mother and father then by the David Cooks and Mrs. Kalashians of the world. The notion kept him bound for weeks. And if for moments or days he managed to find some respite, the voices hauled him back. His doubt had made a permanent place, he realized. Maybe the voices were right. Maybe he didn't know much of anything. It might even be, as his father said, he didn't know diddly-squat.

He tried to think exactly when he'd thought to set off once and for all. It must have come from a film, one he'd seen long enough ago it had been always in his mind: a hobo with his bundle and stick, the sum of the hobo's world. The hobo sat on the bed of a train, a line of cars before and after, the knotty stick, torn straight from a tree or found on some trail, angled across the hobo's shoulder as he, the hobo, rested his arm on a knee, weary with his travels but content just the same, the bundle on his stick made from a bandana. The image hovered in his mind as gray as the bandana, everything weathered, everything gray. The hobo wore two odd boots, and for the patches on his pants, cinched tight with rope, a hole had worn through the knee. On his head was a newsboy, at his ear a stogie, and in his mouth a spear of wheat. Fields stretched into the distance, untold miles off. Life may not have been rich on the train, forever rolling on, but it never grew dark or cold, and hunger, that bony hag, never reared its head. There on the train, golden light was the worst you'd know. The sun shone everlastingly.

The day before leaving, he stole a bandana from his mother and a branch from the tree he robbed each year of cherries, then shaved its leaves with the knife he'd got from his mother's mother's father. The day he left, with his matches and twine and candy and crackers and cheese, he packed the knife in the bandana he'd tied to his stick, then waited for his mother to busy herself with chores. Pretty often on Fridays his father came home early, but that wouldn't be for an hour at least. He'd already donned the best of his clothes, the jeans from Mervyn's for the new school year, his thickest flannel, his whitest socks. He'd need them in the days to come. He would not look back.

His mother was on her knees at the kitchen sink. A bottle appeared beside her, then another, then a sponge, then towels. Presently she'd flap off to the bath attached to his mother and father's room, and he could split. He crept to the end of the hall with its pictures of the dead and stood at the door to his mother and father's room—the same door the strange man had passed out of a few weeks back, whom he hadn't seen before or since, about whom, owing to his mother's threat, he'd said nothing to anyone—waiting to hear his mother start her work.

He looked at his room. What would he do on a train with a toy from *Lost in Space* or, for that matter, with a Rock 'em Sock 'em Robot, or Ants in the Pants, or a Space Tilt Labyrinth, or Legos, or, easy enough to haul, a Slinky? He was a hobo, now, or would be soon, his own man, alone on the endless road.

He hadn't made his bed. He hardly ever did, or rather he tried not to, despite the hell he always caught. He'd been beat with the spoon for leaving his bed, and for talking back when his mother told him what for and he said what for what. But he hadn't made the bed that morning, and he wasn't going to make it now. He'd never make that bed again.

What would be best, he thought, was to set the bed on fire. He could go to the shelf above the bench where his father kept the fluid he filled his Zippo with, next to the box with his father's weed and his father's things for weed, and return to the bed and spray it with fluid up the yang. He could throw a match on the works, one of the same wooden matches he'd packed in his bundle, and, then, to make sure the bed would burn to the end, he could douse the bunch with another shot of fluid. He'd seen someone do this in a movie, too, set a bed on fire. He could set a bed on fire as well as anyone, his own bed especially.

But then if he set the bed on fire, his mother wouldn't find the bed unmade. It would be better for his mother to find the bed and know he'd left it for her. A messed up bed would make his mother way more pissed than a bed on fire. If his mother hadn't already seen the unmade bed, she'd be sure to see it soon, when she finished in the bathroom.

And that would be it. Right away she'd holler out in the voice he'd come to hate so well—*Pa—aaaaattt!* His name would sully the house, grating as the fuzz that woke him at night when the tube went dark, his father passed out, the roach in the clip at his side. But this time he wouldn't obey his mother. Never again would he obey his mother. He'd be far away, on a train beneath the great blue sky, once and for all alone. And anytime anyone did try to tell him what to do, he'd smile and walk away. Ha, he'd say, just like that, and move to another car, because the train he'd ride had cars enough for him to change often as he pleased.

He'd be his own man, then.

He would be alone.

And his mother would still be in her house, hollering about his unmade bed. And when his mother had finished about his unmade bed she'd holler about the money she needed to buy her sofa, or the busted vacuum, or the patch of mint she wanted torn from the yard, sick with toads as it was, or the duckling his brother had killed two days back that moldered in the box on the side of the house, or the drapes in want of cleaning, wrecked with wine, and for absolutely positively sure she'd holler about his father's spinelessness and his father's limp dick, that was what his mother had said his father was, a little limp fucking dick, they'd been fighting over money, or mostly his mother had been screaming about money while his father stood by with his jaw clenched up, his mother shrieking on about her poverty and misery and headaches and back and doubtless, too, about the little limp dick his father didn't know what to do with, what kind of a man was his father that he didn't know how to use his limp little dick, his puny little joke of a dick, and his father had stared at his mother with his grinding jaw, his eyes glassy and wet like the eyes of the pony the woman with pigtails had brought to school for show and tell, and then his father had walked across the room toward the garage the way he did the times his mother and father fought and his father had had enough, when he'd go to his bench to get his pipe and light it up for a toke, but this time, instead of storming through the door, his father slammed his fist into the wall so hard it blew a hole right through it.

No way, Jose, one thing was sure, no way was he going to be there when his mother started screeching, not one more time, not, that is, ever again. He'd be his own man, then, split for good on a huge old train. A pair of socks lay in the corner, a pair of underwear, too, actually all of the clothes he'd stripped last night and flung onto the floor. Big fat donkey dicks, it could all stay there. He wouldn't touch a thread.

Then he saw it, the book, *Tortilla Flat*, and knew he couldn't leave without it. If his bundle couldn't hold the book, he'd wedge the book in his pants, it didn't matter how he carried the book so long as he carried the book.

The book made him think of what he'd do. He would get on a train to Monterrey. When he was nearly there, just north of town, he'd jump from the train and hitch a ride to Tortilla Flat and join the *paisanos* and live the way *paisanos* live, like Danny and the Pirate and Pilon and Jesus Maria, loafing on the porch in the sun, drunk with wine, hooting at the folly of the ones who'd lost the way to live. That was what he would do. That was how he'd do it.

His bundle and stick were where he'd hid them, in the corner by the garbage by the gate. He laid the stick on his shoulder and opened the gate and peered onto the street. Mr. Vernon, the widower he and the Paraderos had spent the summer doorbell ditching, stood hunched by the hook on his house for winding up his hose. Mr. Vernon had one glass eye, and the eye that was good had yellowy whites round a cloud like dirty milk. Mr. Vernon also wore a gadget behind each ear, the color and shape of kidneys, what Pedro Jones had said were hearing aids. Without the aids, he figured, Mr. Vernon couldn't hear a bomb explode in his toilet, much less someone crying fire. Alice Cooper could be jamming with a whole huge band in Mr. Vernon's kitchen, but Mr. Vernon would be snoozing like a dog. It didn't matter how many times they'd doorbell ditched Mr. Vernon, the old man acted like he never knew who'd rung the bell when he knew exactly who'd rung the bell. More than once Mr. Vernon had seen them running from the house, but to prove his kindness, what else could it be, every year on Halloween Mr. Vernon gave out the bossest candy, not the crappy little pieces of cinnamon or butterscotch or root-beer flavored crud but whole huge bars, Reese's Peanut Butter Cups and Milky Ways and Snickers, totally the best.

The other way down the street, while it wasn't really hot anymore, Mary Anne Mumford, a year older, in fourth grade, was romping in the sprinkler with two girls he'd never seen. Mary Anne Mumford didn't strike him as pretty, yet when he thought again she wasn't ugly either, not to mention she was always super nice. Once when he wrecked his bike in front of her house—looking down to change his gears, he'd slammed a car and smashed his head and cut his face—Mary Anne Mumford rushed from her house to promise he'd be fine.

The coast was clear, now, he saw, just some cars from time to time. An hour later the world wouldn't have a clue. Tough titty, too-bad-so-sad, they could call the FBI and suck old slimy eggs. He set off toward the field at whose far side, near the fence between the freeway and it, stood the bush someone had made into the fort where he'd smoked all those cigarettes he'd found at the edge of the field. He could use another pack of cigarettes. He hoped he'd find another pack, maybe in the field again, or maybe in the fort, and definitely on the train. Till then he'd have to bum them from his hobo pals. That would be cool.

Mr. Vernon called out to him. "Taking a trip are you, Mr. Rice?"

"No, Mr. Vernon, I'm not."

"No?"

"Nope. I'm moving."

"Well, I sure do envy you," Mr. Vernon said, his hose in one hand, trickling its last drops, and a sprinkler in the other. "That has got to be the easiest move I've ever seen, and I've seen a few."

"Maybe I'll catch you around sometime," he said.

"Don't forget to cross your T's and dot your I's!" Mr. Vernon said.

He would have to get a map. He'd have to ask the way to the station, too. Meantime, he'd bivouac in the fort at the back of the field where he'd smoked up all the cigarettes. He'd have crackers and cheese for dinner and a Snickers for desert, and come dawn he'd nab some peanuts at the Quik Stop, plus, if they had one, a map. In his pocket burned seven dollars and forty-three cents, the last of his earnings from mowing lawns. That would carry him, till he reached the train, at least.

After that he wouldn't need much. One hobo might share a sandwich, from a gentle heart at the diner. Another might have some whisky. He could drink whisky now, if he wanted, he could drink coffee and beer and wine. Another hobo would give him an apple core, or maybe the whole apple. People on the road shared everything.

But if they didn't share everything, he'd be all right just the same. Pretty soon he'd hit Tortilla Flat. The *paisanos* would share with him for sure. He'd flop in the sun with the wine he'd swapped for two old shoes or maybe the gin for a holster on the road.

No one would tell him anything. In Tortilla Flat, or even on the train, if that was where he stayed, he'd never have to tell a soul he knew the truth because everywhere anywhere every soul he saw would also know the truth. If everyone knows the truth and no one lies, the truth becomes as common as the rest. It was the way things were. It was easy.

He turned onto the street Ken Hummel lived on, his best friend till last month, when he'd kicked Ken Hummel's butt. His brother X had found an egg in the bush by a house on the way back from school. It wasn't an Easter egg someone had forgot, but an egg some goons had stashed in a bush a month or two before Halloween last year, so it'd be rotten by Halloween. If you got hit with a rotten egg on Halloween, you could count on stinking like you'd got blasted by a skunk.

Last Halloween, both Pedro Jones and Brian Dee got popped with rotten eggs. Brian Dee's mother threw out his pants and shirt, Brian Dee said. The goons that drilled Pedro Jones, he said, were dressed in costumes like the rest. Neither could tell between the goons and the rest any more than the goons were bigger. That had been their scheme, said Brian Dee. The goons dressed up to get close enough to pop you, but instead of candy in their bags their bags were full of rotten eggs. And when the goons ran out of eggs, they loaded up from their stashes in the bushes.

X looked like a kid who'd just won money. He and Ken Hummel asked what had got his brother's panties so mussed, and X held out the rotten egg. Ken Hummel must not have known what he'd do just then, when he, Ken Hummel, saw the egg, because he, Ken Hummel, gawked at the egg as stupidly as he and X and asked X where he'd got it. Not till X had pointed at some house with bushes did the idea to do what Ken Hummel did enter Ken Hummel's mind.

He knew that was when it had entered Ken Hummel's mind because he knew Ken Hummel had been there when Pedro Jones told about the goons with the eggs on Halloween. And anyway, he'd seen Ken Hummel's face change into a rat's. Ken Hummel was Ken Hummel, and then he was a rat. Ken Hummel's eyes went cold, and his face grew long with snaggleteeth. And then—like that!—with his dirty rat's claw Ken Hummel flipped X's hand into X's chest.

That was how it went. And when the egg popped like an egg and like an egg splattered over X's clothes, X's face turned as sure as Ken Hummel's face had, from a piece of happy gold to a saint betrayed. First X stared at the hand that had held the egg, covered with slime and bits of broken shell, then X stared at the other hand, empty but clean.

A grody gnarly stench—worse, he imagined, than the grody gnarly stench of a body in a ditch—spread so fast anyone with smell might have died. A witch took his face and frogs his throat, his stomach coiled up like a poisoned snake, he was a step from hell and dying.

By now Ken Hummel was cackling, pointing at X like X had turned into a dancing fetus or barfing clown. But X was not a barfing clown. X was not a dancing fetus, either, or a diarrhea ballerina or stupid weeping bear. X was a wound, alive but breathless, in which all of mankind's pain had been distilled. The rage he felt at X's pain appeared to him that pain's cut-off twin. He felt X's pain to be so thick and pure that when X couldn't hold the rage that should've come from it, like some bodysnatching spirit, the rage leapt straight to him.

It wasn't blood that shot from beneath his fist when he smashed Ken Hummel's nose, but muck, white and thick. Any other time this would've shocked him. But he was in his fury, now, thought taboo, helpless but to storm Ken Hummel's face with blows, with blow after blow that drove him up the walk of the house where X had found the egg. When Ken Hummel reached the stairs to the door, he, Ken Hummel, fell back with his arms at his face. Actual blood was flowing from Ken Hummel's face, now, from his nose and his mouth, Ken Hummel was crying, begging him to stop, but he wouldn't stop, he couldn't hear the words that might convince him to stop. It made no difference, either, when the old lady stepped from the house demanding with her reedy voice he let Ken Hummel be, he went on through his fury beating Ken Hummel till it dawned on him the lady was between them.

And then, as it had started, it stopped.

He simply turned away.

"You were going to kill him," X had said to him as they walked down the street, "weren't you, Pat?"

He looked at his brother and smiled. "You stink!"

"I'm going to turn him into a possum," X said, "then cut

his throat and skin him. I'll hang his fur on a rack and send it to his family for Christmas."

Three blocks past Ken Hummel's house, he turned onto the street where the Elks Lodge was, and the field with the fort. He saw people looking from their cars and wondered that they'd never seen a hobo. He was, after all, an honest-to-goodness hobo, now. He had no home, no place to go, he had no place to be. He had his own stick with his own bandana, like a proper hobo should, in which he'd packed his necessaries, his crackers and knife and cheese.

He didn't need more, he didn't need less, he was on his own for the rest of his days. Everyone else could eat fat choda.

At the field, he had no such luck as the day he found the pack of Marlboro Reds. He couldn't even find the nubbins of a Marlboro Red. He walked past the field to the Quik Stop with the ashcan people stubbed their cigarettes in. What he found there would be the actual best. Real hobos didn't smoke new cigarettes, but what the rest had tossed away. Twelve or fifteen butts were in the can, most half-smoked, if that. Someone had snuffed out a cigarette they'd taken just a puff from, even. Beneath the tray of sand he found an empty box of Camel Lights to hold the butts, fourteen in all, none of the filters gunked up with lipstick or slobber. One butt had no filter to speak of, one of those Pall Malls he'd seen Mike Paradero's father's bachelor buddy smoking in the garage that day the bachelor buddy had told the story about the chick he wanted to do that was kind of foxy.

He slid his bandana from the end of his stick and stowed the pack of cigarettes. Then he stuck his finger in the payphones and dispensers. He pulled the lid on each of the dispensers and slammed them shut, then with his thumb pushed the refund buttons hard. The phone had a dime, and *The San Y Mercury News* coughed up two whole quarters, that was cool, which he slid into the hip pocket of his jeans, and set off for the field.

The days had cooled, but seen no rain. The eucalyptus was more red than green, and what in the spring had been a quilt of head-high grass thick with poppies and vetch was now a maze of straw. A trail marked the way to the fort. He would spend the night on a bed of straw covered with paper and rags.

Fifty feet out, he scanned the field to see if he'd been followed by some kid or high school boys or maybe some guy with his dog. Or maybe some stinky dude that wasn't a hobo but a bum that had seen him head that way, maybe the jerk that had laid that crap with its gnarly horde of flies he'd had to cover with branches and cans.

He could hear the whistles of the meadowlark, the *conk-a-reeeeees* and *o-ka-leeeeees* of the blackbirds that popped from the straw now and then to check for hawks and crows. They hadn't been there in the spring, but somehow a charm of goldfinch had invaded the field, as well. He listened again, straining to hear a coughing bum or laughing kid, but heard just the birds and bugs and constant hum of traffic.

The bush that was the fort looked the same as ever. So did the way around it. He pushed through the straw until it gave way to the glut of waste that had repulsed him before, shriveled after months of drought: magazines, lone shoes, twine; cigarette boxes, newspapers, planks; milk cartons, candy wrappers, tarps; empty cans of beer, and soda, and paint.

He sniffed for a hint of shit as he entered the fort, but smelled warm straw instead. He smelled old paper, too, then, and something sweet, a Tootsie Pop or Popsicle, maybe, or maybe forgotten licorice. The milk crate was still there, and trash. But what he hadn't found before, and which he couldn't believe he'd found today, was a *Playboy*, brand-spanking-new.

Its cover featured a dusky woman who looked like an angel dropped into a whiteout. She stood before a sheet of white, bent over to adjust the strap of a platform with six-inch heels for sure. More than these, she wore a long sleeve shirt patterned like the scales of a fish. She'd stretched one long leg a little before the next, whose skin in shadow was darker. The effect, catastrophic as clever, was to draw his gaze to the bliss where her buttocks stuck out from her shirt. If her legs hadn't been so nice, and her hair a little longer, when he squinted, she might have been his mother.

He brushed the leaves from the crate and set the magazine on it. His bundle and stick he leaned against the branches at the edge of the hollow, then cleared a space to fashion the bed.

He wondered how so much junk could've got there: a knotty branch, three empty cans of Bud, a black doll—naked, with its legs torn off and half its hair cropped to the scalp—a Dr Pepper can, crushed, a wire coat hanger, a pair of aviator glasses with the lenses smashed, two miniature Coke bottles, two more porns with most of their pages stripped—a *Hustler* and a *Oui*—the front section of the *Y Tribune*, an old *Sports Illustrated*, a copy of *MAD*, a catalog from JC Penny, the banana seat for a bicycle a lot like the one he'd left behind, and not a single crummy rag. The magazines, paper, and catalog he put away until he'd gathered some straw. The rest he chucked into the mix of crud outside.

Again he took stock—just three boys across the way, older,

the best he could tell, grab-assing as they went. He walked through the straw until he found a section free of thistle and vetch and began to rip it out.

Once he had a pile, he hauled it to the fort, then stacked three layers, the first one way, the second crosswise to that, the third to that again. Then he tore the last pages from the *Hustler* and *Oui*, mostly sections of articles and ads, which sucked.

More than a few of the pictures—smaller than the others—included a naked lady with a naked man, like the one with some weirdo dude in a cowboy hat and boots and calf-skin gauntlets, swirling a lasso over the head of a lady on all fours, a bell round her neck and a mask like a smiling cow, with black-tipped horns and everything.

He laid the pages down the length of straw and covered them in turn with sections from the paper. A whole bunch of sailors had been killed off the coast of Vietnam, he saw, and some bigshot scientist had also croaked, the one who'd got famous finding bones in Africa.

He sat on the bed with his knife, eating crackers and cheese. He was thirsty as a camel, but so what? He once heard a man say a man on his own had to suffer. He guessed the man had meant something like crackers and cheese sticking to the roof of your mouth with no hope of water for miles.

Dusk was here and gone by the time he'd finished. And it wasn't night that had fallen, but darkness unremitting. He was caught in blackness, and everything he heard sounded dead and new. The birds were no longer singing. The bugs had started to scream.

He rooted through his bundle without knowing what he wanted till he knew what he wanted wasn't there: a flashlight.

He felt a stone beside the bed and picked it up, then fumbled again for the matches he'd packed, and struck one against the stone. In the flame's pale glare his lodgings looked grimier than he'd thought. That might've been okay, but then a shadow flashed by, of a wild dog.

He stared toward the hole in the bush, listening with his whole being for the sound of panting or claws on the prowl, but the match burnt his fingers, and he dropped it, and the world went blacker than before. A pack of wild dogs must have crept down from the foothills at the edge of town. If he looked outside, a dog would be there, he thought, waiting to bite his face. And then, holy crap, his knife had disappeared. He groped among the paper and straw, feeling his brain would melt if he didn't find the knife, but, yes, there it was, beneath his leg, exactly where he'd left it.

He sat in the dark, clutching the knife of his mother's mother's father. Over the drone of the freeway a horn blared somewhere close, maybe from the lot nearby. And now every cricket in the field was chirping, thousands of them, together with the croaking of an army of frogs. A wind pushed through the trees, and far away a siren wailed. He hadn't heard anything like the sound of paws in the dirt, but that didn't mean the dogs hadn't settled to wait him out. A dog might try to eat him—so what, he had a knife, sharp as hell. He would stab the crap out of that dog, he decided, or get munched trying.

From the hole in the bush, he stuck his head into the night. An owl swept across the sky, silent as the sky. Against the stars the swaying trees made him think of voodoo women in fire. The pack of wild dogs was nowhere. There wasn't even one wild dog. There wasn't so much as a gopher. The shadow of a swaying tree—that was what had scared him, the stupid shadow of a stupid tree.

He stood and looked across the field, toward the street, then stooped to set his eyes against the top of the line of straw, to spy the shape of anything against it. All he could see, like a lake of bronze, was the shimmering field of straw.

Back at his bed, he lit another match and held it over the woman on the cover of the magazine. Then the flame expired, and the darkness swallowed her and the world with her.

He sat in the dark thinking how to find the train. He hadn't gathered straw enough, he realized, the ground was lumpy as hell, gnarly, actually, a goddamned gnarly rock or lump was blazing at his back, and a dent in the ground beneath his head made a crook in his neck that now began to throb. Danny and the Pirate and old Joe Portuguese had to've had it better than this, even if they slept on floors with nothing beneath them or maybe just a blanket. And the more he ached, the colder he got. The rains hadn't come, but sure enough autumn had.

The cigarettes he'd found that afternoon reeked like the breath of a hundred dying geezers. He picked one out and struck a match on his stone and puffed as he touched the flame to the cigarette's broken tip. The smoke burnt like fire and raised a fit. After a time, he put the cigarette to his lips again and squinted at the smoke, then brought the smoke inside and held it, thinking how he'd cradled his brother the day of his brother's birth. He'd forgotten his brain would change. He was high like before, now, and now, too, he was sick. Dizziness took him, he might even barf, but the dizziness passed and, like before, he was high, that crappy head without a crappy body.

The crickets and frogs and trees and straw and sirens and

horns and wind had risen like a wakened sea. But instead of blotting out the rest, how strange, every scratch and squeak boomed inside his head.

He couldn't see anything but heard it all—the worms in the earth, the ants in the earth, every last breath of the moths in the grass, and the blood of the crickets in their veins. Somewhere in town a little boy screamed, somewhere an old woman cried. Men bellowed in the bars, and their women brought them beer. And a girl squealed, and a commentator barked, and some idiot boys smashed their idiot trucks. A jet passed overhead, a big old jumbo, the sound of its engine awful. And then he heard it, some kid saying a joke.

"'But I can't give you cyanide to kill your husband,' the pharmacist told the lady. 'We'll both be in jail the rest of our lives.' That's when the lady showed him the picture of her husband banging his wife. 'Well, why didn't you tell me you had a prescription?' he said!"

The laughter of the kids with the joker faded to the clanking of glass. The sounds reached him with such clarity he thought the kids couldn't have been more than ten feet off.

He scurried round the bush to peer above the line of straw.

Four figures, just as he'd thought, were making their way straight toward him, two guys and two girls, he guessed.

He dashed back in to tie his bundle to his stick, then hurried to the rear of the bush.

The kids, all pretty big, were likely in high school, grownups, more than less. They'd give him a beating or worse for finding him on their turf. Or maybe they'd pants him instead. They'd strip him of his underwear and smack his butt, then yell at him to scat. They'd laugh like hell as he ran off crying through the grass. Or maybe they wouldn't do any of that, maybe just ask his business in their bush, and, when he said, drag him to the Quik Stop to make him call his father. A few minutes later, his father would appear, scowling, and thank the kids. Once in the car, his father would ask him what he, his father, thought he, his father, should do with him, whether he deserved a whipping or restriction or both. But who cared about his father—whatever the kids might do, he didn't want, and whatever he did, he had to do now.

"This is it?" one girl said.

"It's just a big bush," the other girl said.

"Who wants to get in a big bush?" the first girl said.

"We do!" the boys said, and broke out laughing.

"Eeeeewww!"

"Don't knock it till you try it," one of the boys said.

"You'll see," the second boy said as they reached the other side of the bush.

"Come on."

"Did you guys set this up?" a girl said.

"Set what up?" a boy said.

"I don't know," the girl said. "It looks like a bed."

"What?" the boy said.

"Killer!" the other boy said, and they all laughed.

The lights round the Quik Stop glowed like lights in space.

Cars came and went, each with a pulsing halo. He imagined robots at the wheels, or aliens, or maybe nothing at all, just a computer like the one that took the spaceship in that movie.

He thought this scene would be what an astronaut saw when he neared the outpost of a planet light years off, dark and cold and silent but for the engines of machines run by robots and computers.

Throughout the day, planning his escape, he'd had the sense that nothing could touch him. If no one needed him, so what, he didn't need them, either. And not only did it make no difference whether he was needed, but if he was, even if just to use and hurt, it would make no difference what was said or done, because he had traveled beyond them, now, beyond gestures and words and pain. He'd made himself his own man, he'd made himself a hobo.

But somehow his faith had left him.

He was alone.

On the side of the Quik Stop, beneath the teeming bugs, he whittled a stick from the field and thought about the chimpanzee its fellows had killed and eaten. Cars came and went, men, all in all, buying their Friday beer. Most of the stick lay in a pile before he noticed the guy above him with a six-pack in each hand. The guy's bellbottom jeans covered all but the tips of his shoes, and his hair was as long as his mother's.

"What's up, dude?" The guy wore a light blue shirt with the words, SOCK IT TO ME! When he didn't answer, the guy said, "Someone leave you hanging, or what?" He looked at the guy, right into his face, but said nothing. "Dude, what are you doing here all by yourself? It's like almost midnight."

He remembered what he'd said to Mr. Vernon, what felt like millennia back. "I'm moving," he said.

"Tell you what. My sled's right here. Why don't you let me and my buds bump you home?"

He looked toward the field, and then at the guy. The guy's hair had grown so long it covered one whole side of his face, which, from the half he could see, was the face of a hero. The guy looked like a rock star, like Peter Frampton or Robert Plant, if they were Argentine or Mexican.

"I told you. I'm moving."

"But you got to be crashing some place tonight, right?"

"Maybe."

"So then let's hit it, man."

The guy nodded over his shoulder at two other guys smoking cigarettes as they leaned against a red Camaro. Like the guy, they wore hair down their backs and bellbottom jeans.

"Those are my buds. Just let us cruise you to your pad, and we'll catch you on the rebound. Cool?"

"What's your name?"

"Roberto. What's yours?"

He wanted to ask Roberto if he could just go with him, where Roberto and his buds were going, but somehow knew Roberto would say no.

He didn't want to go back to his mother and father, even if had to, at least until he could make a better plan. He'd sneak in the house and get into his messed up bed and go to sleep and make another plan tomorrow.

Roberto set his beer on the ground and tucked his shirt.

Four kids were walking through the field, laughing as they came. One of the girls spun round, she was a total fox, and kissed the kid behind her.

He wondered whether he'd been wrong about everyone getting in the way and mucking things up. Roberto seemed pretty cool. He didn't know it, not the way he knew to figure fractions or peel a spud, but somehow just the same he did. He could trust Roberto, and if Roberto loused up, then he would know he hadn't been wrong, people really did lie, they got in the way and mucked things up.

The kids walked by as couples, each hand in hand. One girl, the foxy one that had kissed the kid, her hair was full of leaves.

He shut his knife and rose and kicked the pile of chips.

"That's a pretty tough car," he said. "Is it yours?"

"No doubt."

"Does it burn rubber?"

Roberto smiled. "Dude, for *miles.*"

IT'S AS IF ALL YOUR LIFE YOU'VE BEEN SORTING THROUGH a box of pictures, randomly choosing this or that, only to see your ignorance of their meaning in the scope. And yet in this oblivion, you're reminded, spookily, not just that the person in the image representing this or that moment is "you," but that until now, you—the "you" who peers with wonder into the image, eldritch as a face in a lake—*have forgotten both the moment and the experience of which it was a part.* Nearly always in this process, the quality of the memory fails to hold sway. Sometimes, like a picture, it's badly focused, its composition skewed and perspective stale. Others, its clarity and precision are spotless. Others yet, however apt, are tedious as crumbs of bread. In every case, regardless, you "see" the image in your mind, the recognition dresses up, assumes its form and status, you acknowledge this and this and that and this, but feel no more than for a homely child. Ample as it is, or stingy as it is, the memory does its work, it asserts itself. It's far too much—the mere knowledge of what lurks about the image the memory's made of, everything connected to the image, vague or clear, like fuzzy options round a coming time or planets round a star—or way too little—an absence of connection to other moments or events, an image in a void. But finally, too, in each case, with whatever fault or force, the recognition's one with whose appearance you're assaulted by doubt—embarrassment, nostalgia, sorrow, shame, longing, penitence, fear—any one of which, alone, should you fail to struggle, will drag you to the depths.

THE COWARD

I cannot think of any need in childhood as
strong as the need for a father's protection.
— *Sigmund Freud*

IN Y, WHERE MY TRIP THROUGH THE DARK BEGAN, MY FATHER kept on the mantel a brown ceramic jar eight inches wide and ten inches high or so.

Together with its contents, this jar would once have been considered our *lares and penates*, the deities worshipped by ancient Romans in exchange for protection of body and home. A sandwich baggie of weed—usually Columbian or Acapulco Gold, but sometimes, the special times, a lid of Maui Waui or Humboldt Sensimilla—was this jar's principal deity, though also it held: a baggie for roaches and one for seeds, plus rolling papers (Zigzags or Jobs), and a rolling machine, and pipe cleaners, and roach clips, and matches, and lighters, and screens. And always beside this jar sat my father's "rolling tray," of redwood or cedar, I don't know, ten by fourteen or sixteen inches, imprinted with a fading name, a cigar maker likely, and bound at the edges with trim a half-inch high.

The weed my father left on the tray I never touched, not because it was somehow taboo to touch, but because I didn't know my father would miss it if I did.

Looking back, now, I see this restraint was mystic.

Even at ten years old, the sixth sense most every doper has from birth—that knowing-without-knowing what to do and when in matters shifty and base—served me well, kept me safe (to the extent it's safe to get so high you forget your name), told me when to take my father's weed, and how much, and from where, and where to smoke it, and when.

The liquor store that sold the papers my father liked stood at the foot of the canyon three miles off. Riding my bike to town and back, which I did seldom, and strictly on weekends, entailed a half-day's effort at least. But it wouldn't have mattered had the place been right next-door. I couldn't walk in and demand the guy at the counter sell me some papers because I'd stolen my father's weed and was going to get torched with my pal from school. Nor could I steal the papers, nor could I buy them: they were kept in a rack with the rubbers and smokes and porns. So while I stole my father's weed, I stole five or six papers and a book of matches, and placed them in the baggie my father kept his own stuff in, which I nabbed from a drawer in the kitchen.

My father never got stoned alone, or not often, if he didn't have to.

Almost always he smoked with my mother, and when my mother was gone, my father smoked in the presence of my brothers and me. And as much as my father liked to laugh, and as my mother did, too, they seldom laughed together with no one to hear it but their three sons.

It was mostly when friends stopped by on weekends, or my mother's brother and his wife came on holidays, and my father got everyone stoned, that they were taken by chatter and razz and laughter, and, for a few hours, at least, I could forget the limbo of madness that were the days before the fun, when my mother succumbed to devils, and my father succumbed to her, and my brothers and I to them.

The disgrace we suffered was the routine disgrace of millions.

That the moments from which these shames were born had so much more at stake down the party stretch, however, infused them with hyper-absurdity and dread. The things that needed doing before our guests arrived would never not be done. For my mother, the chance our family appeared to others as anything less than she'd imagined—as utterly ordinary, as utterly *petite bourgeoisie*—was impossible. No task could be done too soon, and surely none too well.

This, I guess, was why the fate of the world in these endless hours seemed always to balance on the attainment of some hopeless ideal, expressed in the fuss with which the laundry was washed and folded and stored, and the smallest trinket dusted, and the floors swept, and furniture placed, and carpets cleaned, and bathrooms scrubbed. Nor could chance say why the yard on these days had got so foul its overhaul was crucial, any more than the weather could say why at least one errand demanded running, and typically several.

Later, as the time drew near, we boys were made to scrub and trim our nails, and brush our teeth, and comb our hair, and don our Sunday best, which at some point my mother had managed to press with the same hostility she unleashed on everything else. After she'd inspected our bodies for the boogers and sleep and dirt and wax and crust and snot and jam she found despite our greatest efforts, my father confirmed we'd tucked our shirts rightly (their buttons were to be in line with the button on our pants, and the loose cloth at the waist folded at each flank equidistant from the spine), gird our belts (whose buckles were to be centered at the button on our pants), arranged our collars, tightened our socks, laced our shoes, and cleared ourselves of lint.

Of course it was never these embarrassments alone that sent me to the realm of tick-tock horror, but the gloom that whipped them on.

Unless we'd misbehaved grossly, my father wouldn't hit us. His Fatherly Face and Voice, together with The Poke to the Chest or Thump to the Head, sufficed to keep us straight.

But what worked for my father rarely pleased my mother. A slap on the face, a jerk of the hair or jab to the neck—these stood fair game always, in addition to the verbal grief, any of which could be doled out any time—including a beating with wooden spoons—for as little as a scowl before a command, and certainly for talking back.

In short, high anxiety was the norm in our house, and our lives were lives of dread.

And when holidays and weekends came round, things got worse. These brought guests, and with them hell, and whenever hell once more revolved around, my dread would turn to terror.

WE TEND TO THINK THE ATROCITY THAT WAS THE TWENTIETH century is some paradigm epoch of man's inhumanity to man, but the truth is, the history of man from day one is a catalog of horror.

Good men and women have come and gone, but few of their names have been added to the list. The ones who were really good, the best ones, had no names to add. When they came, few, if anyone, knew it, and when they left, nothing remained to mark their passing but perhaps a new way of seeing.

Aside from these, man has largely proven himself a cannibal since before he took his knuckles from the dirt.

He devours his fellows without the least hint that with every mouthful he destroys himself the more. The best I can fathom is a parody of the ouroboros—some cursed man gnawing his guts as he draws them from the hole he stabbed.

The day X confessed his wonder he'd escaped a serial killer's doom, I knew how profound our horror had really been, however different his was from mine.

His profile, he said, and the profiles of more than ninety percent of serial killers, are the same.

To start, X is a white male. And while he's also frighteningly intelligent, he did poorly in school, and for most of his life has labored in kitchens. His family was volatile, his father absent and mother domineering, her own history, not incidentally, and that of her family, filled with alcoholism, addiction, mental illness, and abuse. X hated our parents to varying degrees and suffered cruelty at their hands and others'. He's never tried to kill himself, but, like me, he's been suicidal, thoughts of which he's drowned and revived in his own abuse of drink and drugs. X, moreover, had been obsessed with fire, and, what's worse, with torturing and killing animals. But scariest of all, he said, was the way he spent so much of his youth plotting to kill the people who'd hurt him, from the way he'd trap them, he said, to the things they'd say and do as he fucked them up, to how he'd get rid of them once he'd had his fill of fucking them up.

Today I know it's precisely from the sort of snafu scenes I endured as a boy—one here, another there, mounting in the head till at last they've merged into a demon—that most of the world's atrocities are born.

From what else could the compulsion for the power and destruction of our tyrants derive if not the homes in which when children they were as systematically plagued as the masses they delight to crush?

Mao suffered an unendurable childhood beneath a father so miserly and vicious that to escape one of the many beatings he administered, Mao threatened to jump into a winter pond. When Mao's father demanded Mao beg forgiveness and kowtow before him on "both knees," Mao parleyed a deal that his father not hurt him if he performed a "one-knee kowtow."

And Hitler, who suffered famously under what Alice Miller describes as the "machinery of annihilation that in turn-of-the-century Germany was called 'child-rearing'": as a boy, he once told his secretary, Hitler had so numbed himself against his father's beatings that he'd been able actually to count his blows, right up to thirty-two, he said. This, Miller says, was just one of the many strategies by which the Führer became so powerful "a master of violence and of contempt for human beings."

And Stalin, too, the only one of three siblings to have survived his beginnings: that poor fiend was the last of a drunken shoemaker who beat the kid till he was five, then left him to the priest with whom he spent a childhood from which, because of bad blood and small pox, he emerged a virtual dwarf, notorious for his pitted face and wasted arm.

And if we weren't looking at Hitler, Stalin, or Mao, we could as readily turn to any number of monsters, from Attila the Hun, Alexander the Great, Genghis Khan, Tamerlane, Caligula, and Napoleon to Saddam Hussein, François Duvalier, Idi Amin, Pol Pot, Suharto, and George W. Bush. The list goes boldly on, and not a brutal man on it, I think it safe to say, grew a hair on his balls without having first been made a brutalized boy.

I HAVEN'T WITNESSED SLAUGHTER, MUTILATION, OR TORTURE or the like, but what I have amounts to a tale told by that old idjit, full of sound and fury, signifying not just nothing, but all—everything and nothing with sugar on top.

Most of us can scarcely hear such tales.

To witness or, God forbid, actually experience them, is out of the question.

Certainly I'm no exception. The horrors around me I escaped through the lessons of my father.

I locked myself up. I drank the booze and took the dope I could short of dying. I sought out women broken as myself, women in their own despair who were blind to mine, women who, if I were lucky for a while, might even believe me somehow able to save them. And when I wasn't lost in these quasi-fatal distractions, I scratched out this or that parable of broken love, elegies for the death of life and love as we knew them at the century's end:

A girl I know wades through parties with her tongue stuck out that folks will give her pills. Later she assaults riders on the subway, and later yet, alone in her flat, cuts her arms and legs. Once, she said, when the cutting wouldn't work, she broke her jaw with a hammer . . .

A friend of a friend went to sleep one night while his wife continued to crack out in their den, five days' worth of huffing having failed to get it. In the morning, my friend's friend found his wife's head against the blaring tube. He tried to wake her, my friend's friend said, but his wife was dead. Whether she'd been watching the episode of Good Morning, America *when she died or had died before it aired, he couldn't say . . .*

Another friend was once so desperate to get at his bottle that when he couldn't pull the cork, he broke its neck on the street. He cut his face as he gulped his wine, then stumbled into a club where, later, he came to with his face in a urinal, the whole of him rank with piss and shit. None of that did much to daunt him. He lurched back to the floor to shake his stuff. The last thing he remembered, he said, was crawling through a field in a storm, coughing up blood, blind past the mud in his eyes . . .

The brother of a friend's friend met a psychic who convinced him that his brother—my friend's friend—had killed him in a former life, in a duel, no less. Frustrated as he was, my friend's friend said, he had no choice than to bear his brother's rage. Nothing he did would change his brother's mind. "How the hell can you prove a thing like that?" my friend's friend had said in the park, tossing pebbles at a shrub. "My brother says I'm lucky. The only reason he doesn't stab me when I'm sleeping, he says, is the fear I'll return in another life to kill him again, with poison or an ax or whatever, and then we'd both be doomed to ride that wheel of revenge." Later, the brother of my friend's friend got AIDS. Later still, when his liver went bad, my friend's friend ordered his sedation. And then the brother of my friend's friend died. "Who cares if I killed him in another life," my friend's friend said. "I killed him in this one . . ."

Still another friend had just returned from a visit with her parents. "One morning," said my friend, "my mother found a bird in her driveway—dead. Her neighbor was minding his own business when she hit him with the bird, shrieking that he shouldn't take her for an ass. 'I know you killed that bird and put it there,' my mother said," my friend told me. "'You're just jealous all the birds hate your feeders and eat at ours instead . . .'"

And then that moment at the Marina Abramović retrospective, at the Y Museum, when I stood watching the man and woman *before the film Abramović and her whilom partner Ulay had made of themselves screaming into each other's faces, as loud as they could, till exhaustion: "Aaaaaaaa! Aaaaaaaa! Aaaaaaaa!" The woman turned to the man and said, "This reminds me of my brother's first marriage. They married each other twice."*

ONCE THE HOME LAY READY—MOTHER DARKLY RADIANT in the dress I'm sure she'd stolen for the fête, father supremely stoned and groomed, we boys granted muster—the family posed, as ever, for the camera.

The photos, naturally, had to include all five, so my father was made to erect a tripod and prep his timer for autoshoot. Meantime, my mother would arrange us to her fancy, generally albeit. While like mannequins we'd have been placed on marks, the tilts of our heads wouldn't have been set, nor the details of our faces—the twinkles in our smiles and eyes, how many teeth we showed. But after a day or more beneath the yoke of my father's latent rage and my mother's growing madness, the last thing I wanted was to beam for a gizmo.

Picture-time in the '70s was old-school picture-time—no batteries, no digital storage, no analog storage, even—just mechanical ingenuity, with a manual camera with actual rolls of emulsion film that had actually to be developed. You took a picture, especially if you were a hobbyist, and you didn't know what it would look like till you slipped it from the pack outside the store that had developed it. For my mother, this meant snapping a lot of pictures. But ten of them could flash rotten while the one rolled out supreme. This was all she wanted—the waller, the one for the album, that shipped out come the holidays, proof we were The Family of her dreams.

"Don't do that," she'd say to X after he'd got chubby, "it makes you look like you're overweight." Or, to little Z, when he began to fidget, she'd say, "If you blink, sweetie, you'll ruin it for everyone." Or, to me, my face like fire, "You look like a victim. Is that what you want the world to see, poor little me?" Or, to my father, "You're much more handsome, honey, when we can see the other side of your face," or, "Just once I wish you'd trim your beard. It's so uncouth."

Nothing mattered but that my mother got her waller before the guests arrived. Only the waller mattered.

As for the guests, they'd arrive the way they always did, and the laughter that peeled from the mouths of my mother and father went on till the guests had driven home. And the more weed they smoked and booze they glugged, the greater and louder their laughter.

The dread that had made laughter so hard for my brothers and me had vanished.

For the span of an evening my family had hatched from an egg in the Land of Telefilm, a cross between The Partridge Family, The Brady Bunch, and The Munsters.

In one moment we were commonplace and sad.

In the next we were a millennial blend of funky-strange, sexy-gorgeous perfection thirty years before its time.

The house sparkled.

The couple shone.

The booze flowed.

The music pulsed.

The dope burned.

The food amazed.

The talk rocked.

The kids acclaimed.

We were wondrously pure, goofily playful, playfully ghoulish, appealingly polite.

Our guests came dry, but departed wet with ardor and steam.

And then it was over, and I wouldn't hear the laughter till the next guests came, and life, that double-crossing brute, trudged pathetically on.

MY FATHER CAME FROM WORK EACH DAY AND CRACKED A beer or poured some wine, then gave a doobie to my mother, she more than happy to join him. And that was all I needed to know the lay. This is how the big folks live, I saw, this is how the world goes round. You come home from work and light a bowl. You eat dinner, then sit in your chair with your stuff and your book till you pass out and a son fetches you to bed. Weekends you rise in the quiet of dawn. You brew up your java and coco for your boy and drive off through the breaking glow, to a road on a hill with a view, a peacock sky in the works to the east, or fields of tomato or corn, a peacock sky in the works there, too, or some river through trees with magpies and crows, your doobie at hand, which, come first chance, you most happily indulge. Then your eyes slip into that yellowy pink, and then again that hooded way your family knows so well, sleepy and kind but somehow sadly distant. And then your face softens to that partial smile, and your voice becomes a sybarite's with his meerschaum traced in gold. You speak to your son in your sweet tones, you promise him that all is well, hoping to make him think his life's been a vision, terrible, he's wakened from, at last. Your son's awake now, you say, he's back now, you say, in the arms of the great old world, looking at his father's face, which, to your ignorance, frightens and soothes him both, which imparts in him the worry he'll someday call distrust. Your son shares his vision, he tells you how scared he was to be in it, whose devils he hopes will fade by the light of your face, its cool, as you well know, the lie you cling so fearfully to, because in the dark at night that's all you have, this lie, it's your life, really, the whole of it, that your son before you tells with such awful truth. Listening to him, sensing the clarity with which he sees so much, his life and yours, the mask that hides your sadness falls away, and you give in, again, for a time. You don't know it, but your sadness is why your son feels he can sometimes believe the stories you tell, your grounds for going on. It, your sadness, is why your son feels some sense of bond with you, that you two share a thing no one else can grasp. And though it's true, however incompletely, that what you share is a sadness so violent and profound it will crush him and all he has as surely as it's crushed you, you do not, nor will you ever, share the viewpoint toward it. You in the blindness of your stupor have never had a point to share. Later in the morning, before your endless tasks and chores, you head to the garage at the top of the drive to take from its spot on the shelf one of your old cans, in which, beneath a rag, you keep your stuff, and, after rolling a doobie or packing a bowl, you have another toke, one or two or sometimes three, rarely more, just enough, as you say, to hold your buzz. Fortified anew, then, you mend a carburetor, trim a hedge, you wire a lamp, patch a tire, or frame a print, you run your countless errands, always about but somehow always absent—the head, as your son himself will learn too soon, without a body, that body without a head—returning through the day to the weed in your can to hold your precious buzz. And then it's dusk. Your chores ended for the time, you repair to the house to change the beer of your day for the booze of your night, Chivas Regal, neat, the happy hour nip and the one post-dinner, always mixed with another toke, always another toke, and maybe now and then a fat cigar.

AS A BOY, YOU DON'T HAVE WORDS ENOUGH TO NAME THE things you know.

I couldn't speak the name for what drove my father to do as he did any more than I could speak the name that followed. And even if I had been able to speak that name, I knew it was yet unspeakable. I didn't know the name, then, but I knew the thing.

My father roused me from sleep those dawns that we could drive into the hills alone, where, after having smoked enough to excuse his pledge to the hell that was his marriage, he worked to sway me, too, and to prove his love for me, and his knowledge of my pain and its source, and his real compassion.

But the more I poured out my woes, and the more I begged him to save me, the further he retreated.

As if I were a prisoner with whom my father shared a cell, consoling our mutual fate, as if I had no more choice than, like him, to bear his awful burden, he said he felt bad for me, he said he was sorry I felt the way I did.

I love you, Son, my father would say as he walked off, hands above his head.

If my father bore no blame for a crime he couldn't stop or stave, his paralysis before it couldn't be seen as caused by fear.

He could float away in his cloud of weed, up above the world, and there in blameless repose watch events unfold below. And anything that failed to meet such reasons he dealt with by established rule—amnesia manufactured.

My father standing by while I was beaten and debased, I saw, was to help your friend find his wallet after you have ripped it off.

For all the years since, as helpless to speak these truths as to escape them, I'd somehow had to find a way to walk inside their shadow. It was a task at which, until quite recently, I failed.

AS THE MEMORY GOES, WE'RE IN A HARDWARE STORE OR lumberyard or maybe out in the parking lot of the hardware store or lumberyard, or maybe rather at the county dump, near the foot of a mountain of waste, millions of tons of waste ceaselessly crushed beneath machines in which hunker like droids enormous men with piggy eyes, the rumbling earth and swooping gulls and rats by the score scurrying through the mountains of waste.

But no matter where, my father is the same.

In the hardware store, he studies a rack of goods while I stand by with forced concern, bored as I've always been by such. I don't see the man with whom my father's having sudden words. I don't hear the words, either, but know only that my father's spoken sharply, as I rarely hear my father speak outside the home, or when he isn't in his car. Then his hand's on my shoulder, and we're rushing off, and then we're in the lot.

In the lumberyard, too, my father moves from aisle to aisle until, as in the store, I hear him and some man in red exchange, after which my father's hand's on my shoulder as we scurry away, out into the lot.

At the dump, there are rows of trucks and cars hitched to trailers against the mountains of waste into which men heave all manner of this-and-that: burned out fridges, logs and leaves, rotten washers, rotten dryers, bales of rope and mounds of grass, fucked-up sheetrock, fucked-up pipes, fucked-up ladders, and fucked-up bricks, couches wrecked by children and cats, lawn chairs, board games, benches, and stands, defunct strollers and defunct carts, obsolete prints in busted frames, betrayed loafers and ravaged boots, water faucets, hose bibs, insulation, glass, flaccid footballs, basketballs, soccerballs, and nets, shit-stained beds, piles of clothes, antique phonographs, ancient tubes, telephones, scissors, books, and wigs, reams of paper and spools of twine, cabinets from kitchens and claw-foot tubs, rickety crates and easels and desks, smashed-up wardrobes, jars by the case, and ear horns and bull horns, and doll houses, doll clothes, and dolls by the score, and humidors, and go carts, and bongo drums, and scales, and rotten meat, rotten fruit, rotten bread, and rotten grain, and booze bottles, wine bottles, beer bottles, cans, and empty cans of sauce and tubs of wormy fruit, and old rubber water bags, and moth-blown blankets and pissed-on quilts, and milk cartons, and burlap, and voided cans of turpentine and thinner and house paint and glue . . .

In the memory at the dump, the reek of the dump pollutes your mouth, your skin, your lungs, and through your lungs your blood, and through your blood all your vessels and all your veins, and through your vessels and veins the backs of your eyeballs and all of your teeth. The reek of the dump is a reek like no other, moribund, vital, noisome, sweet, the smell of everything everyone's used to its last, the smell of sorrow, the smell of thanks, the smell of endings and of no thanks, and of death on a dirty pillow.

My father's mouthed off to some man my father didn't think could hear, a man, my father must've believed, who'd fail to oppose the urge to contest my father's words, if truly the man had heard them, though clearly my father was mistaken, because now in the parking lot by the hardware store or lumber yard, or by the dump truck against those mountains of waste, the man's appeared, from harmless nothing to furious something, to snatch my father by his shirt and press his face against my father's face and speak to my father his lethal words.

This man has giant arms thick with hair, on one a girl by a palm tree and waves. His shirt is stained with sweat at the pits and round his gut, his jeans are soiled with grease, and a patch of steel in his boot gleams from the toe where the leather's worn through. The man's lined face, baked with sun, is glowing crimson, now, and a vein is pulsing near his eye.

My father had hurried away, anxious to ditch the hardware store or lumberyard, or to get round the truck at these mountains of waste, but by then it was too late.

Before my father can escape, the man's taken him by his throat and pressed his face into my father's, which hovers in slack-jawed terror. My father's vanished, he's a bag of goo, dangling from a giant fist.

My father's arms droop as the angry man talks, my father

says nothing, his mouth hangs open, his face is white, his big eyes flutter and blink. The man's fist at his side is swollen clichéd white, and the veins in his arm are swollen, lacing through the hula girl, ready in a flash to strike.

My father's been reduced to his least, a rabbit caught by a troll.

THE MAN WAS STOCKY AND THICK AND PLAINLY VERSED in carnage. In his day, he'd held the collars of other men, and slammed his fist into the heads of men and would hold the collars and slam the heads of many others yet. The man was an angry man, doing what angry men do. His answer to my father's words, whatever they were, couldn't have been but excessive to those words, since the man was nothing if not excessive.

And since clearly my father wasn't ready to brawl—my father, as I was to learn, beyond the blow as a boy he threw against his younger brother, and the blows with which later he struck his sons, had never thrown a blow against another man or even a boy in boyhood—the one response my father could've looked on with a scratch of pride, knowing he'd handled himself with grace, was to've confessed his blunder and offered his regret. *Yes siree, buddy*, my father could've told the angry man, it's true, he, my father, had spoken out of turn, he, my father, had no ax to grind, nothing worth coming to blows about, *So once again, I beg your pardon*—and from there gone about his way, his son no wiser for the lapse.

But my father didn't do this or anything like it.

My father mouthed off to a man he ought to've stayed well clear of, and in the moment of truth, when the man bore down, my father fell to panic, he froze in his terror like a rodent in the hand of a giant.

Almost daily I was faced with proof my father wasn't through and through the stuff I longed for him to be all through—the stuff, that is, of *The Father*.

The father's never anything but The Father.

Either the father is The Father, or he's just some other guy.

Because The Father is invincible, indefatigable, impermeable to bribery, sleaze, and vice, beyond corruption of any sort, purity incarnate, authority supreme.

The moment of The Father's tainting is the moment of The Father's death—he crashes into the slime of being with all its hateful masses.

Of course if The Father's been tainted, it's because he was never The Father but at most a fraud whom time alone could out: had the father been actually The Father, he could never have been tainted.

This, at least, was the fantasy I harbored in some yet-hopeful place, despite that from the outset I'd seen my father for who and what he was and understood that what my father said he was had never lined up with who he showed himself to be.

It had benefited me, I see now, to live my life inside this dream—hence, despite what I knew, my insistence that my father had been my haven. So long as I remained in that familiar place, I'd never have to change, nor confront myself, nor, in what would be more painful yet, confront him, this man who was my father.

AT HOME MY FATHER TOOK AN AIR OF POWER WITH HIS sons, the aura of The Father.

My father was the master, and we his servants.

My father's rule was never to be quizzed, and all was rule, from sweeping dirt from corners, to washing blots from cars, to mowing lawns three ways to foil errant blades.

Attitudes and methods were taught with wisdom and goodwill, and guidance of our fledgling starts the same.

Left at length to our duties alone, we struggled like heroes only to see our fingers in the garden had missed that stem of clover, our broom had passed this grain of sand, our brushes, run too quickly along a tire's rim, had missed that spot of grease.

Fresh demonstrations were offered with incentives, implying—since this knowledge was ancient, abstruse, occult, my father's most common expression to this effect being, *Watch now, hot shot, I'm going to show you an old Indian trick*—that among the world's billions we alone had been let to a secret order.

Results were scrutinized, oversights analyzed, mistakes dissected, weaknesses measured, techniques adjusted till perfection had been had.

Future deviations were noted and admonished.

To preempt slips, third, fourth, and, heaven forbid, fifth offenses were suitably reproved.

And because we'd been taught with perfect knowledge, our lapses could have followed from stubbornness alone.

Minor slips were met with scorn, and always disappointment.

Graver errors received the same, plus the infliction of some choice torment—ear-tweaking, for instance, or chest-poking, or head-thumping, or finger-wrenching, and the like.

Graver errors yet received the same plus a sentence of endurance, such as standing in a corner.

And, finally, chronic lapses, such as abandonment or

lateness, acquired the whole package, plus the universally common poverty of amusements and/or movement—such as: restriction to a room, the house, or the house-and-yard, depending—such as: the confiscation of bicycles, skateboards, and/or TVs, depending—such as: etc., etc., etc. . . .

In the home, my father spoke of self-defense and self-esteem, of waiting till a boy struck you before striking him, of never starting a fight but ending one always, of letting the world see you were honest and fair but not to be played. In short, my father taught silence while holding a massive stick.

And my father spoke of taking no prisoners in matches and games, and of looking both ways before you touched the street, and of the dangers of failing to watch your back.

My father spoke of honesty and obedience and loyalty and rigor and bravery and honor and power and force and strength.

My father spoke of The Real, my father spoke of Truth, my father spoke of Fact.

Yet all of these, together with his willingness to terrorize his boys through a shifting mix of disappointment, anger, and threatened or actual pain, stood in blank opposition to his acts out in the world—to his aversion to the slightest conflict, and to his reluctance to suggest as much to others.

Out in the world, my father was a yes-man, and as helpless.

It was only from a distance, on foot or behind the wheel of his moving car, that my father ventured to insult a man, or to complain, and when he did, it smacked largely of the mean.

My father cursed beneath his breath as he turned from the person by whom he felt slighted, as he did that day at the hardware store or lumberyard or dump.

But more often my father waited till he'd crept away before

speaking loud enough for his pest to hear but low enough, always, to question.

On the highway, when someone cut my father off or refused to let him merge or turn, he flipped them the finger as they passed, then, snickering or grumbling, swung in behind them with his high beams on, to blind them from their rear view mirror.

In the city, he did the same, but there he could roll down his window to flip people off and shout *fuck you!*—ready, always, to cut and run.

ALREADY MY MOTHER AND SHAME WERE TANTAMOUNT, THE way Lee Harvey Oswald and assassination are tantamount, the way AIDS and death are tantamount, the way 9/11 and terrorists and war mongering and greed are tantamount.

Every time we left the house, I was bushwhacked by horrendous shame. The mere thought, truly, of attending her—at the grocery store, a movie, the swimming pool or mall, of standing by as she engineered this dolt or that, heedless of status or rank, fearing meantime that her victims would know I was her ghastly little son—filled me with the meanest sort of dread.

My mother had distilled haggling to its essence.

Already her ceaseless, frequently successful efforts to wangle discounts and refunds were bad. These weren't street fairs or flea markets she haunted, but department stores, boutiques, and liquor stores, and such. There, then as now, as the smallest children know, you pay the declared price or take your business on. But my mother had grown impervious to such etiquette. The mutterings and glares of bystanders had not the least effect. Nothing stunted my mother, nothing thwarted my mother, no amount of intimidation could dissuade, much less fluster, my mother.

She had fixed her aim well before and resolved to bleed to get it.

The minute she saw something might not go her way, she began to complain about her disappointment with a product or service, which, naturally, she was bound to report to this or that bureau, not to mention her wide circle of "influential" friends, accusing the employee at hand, even, man or woman, of various moral deficits and damage, threatening him or her and their employer, too, with a range of punitive and legal actions, and so on and so forth.

And when my mother brought these manners home to attack my father, the amnesia that had in the past redeemed my humiliation vanished.

Shame was no longer something my mother fashioned in a moment, then left behind to mark her way.

My mother had crossed the line.

She'd transformed, turned into shame itself, avatar of disgrace.

I was stripped of defenses, then, in the house and out.

I needed something to hold onto, just one thing, if even to a lie.

Now and then it crept into me that my father's ways were as wrong as my mother's, but I did exactly what my father did when a thing upset him, exactly what my father had been teaching from the start.

I tried hard not to look, and when I did, I tried not to look too hard.

What I saw, when I saw, I denied, and took every measure to avoid the chance I see it again.

Still, often as I looked away, I saw what I saw and knew what I tried not to know.

And the older I got, the clearer the truth of my father became, and the clearer that truth, the scarier, more insufferable my life.

But because I couldn't accept, much less admit, what I knew my father to be, my knowledge festered, a formless dread that bloomed with epidemic sway.

Too many times I'd seen what happened to my father.

Too many times I saw what my father did, and saw what my father didn't.

I'd never wanted to see my father, not like that, but I did.

AND THEN OBLIVION CALLED OUT WITH HER PROMISE, AND I obeyed.

I didn't know why I couldn't resist that call but simply that I couldn't resist, and so I just obeyed. And I obeyed by stealing and smoking my father's weed. And once I'd tasted the gift of that obeisance—the ability to escape my pain at will—I couldn't conceive its loss.

Stealing my father's weed with silence and stealth and style, and never a hint of my father's doubt, I thought then, was the best way possible to wound my father and regain some little power.

But not until decades after those ways had begun would

my father know these things—that I'd been getting stoned from the time I was ten on weed I stole from him—when, in response to his denial that Z had grounds to disown him, I'd tell my father that in truth Z's stance stood not merely in my father's avoidance and denial and the addictions thereof, but from having turned his three sons into addicts and drunks, and from having trained them in the ways of avoidance and denial, and of failure, which training didn't start late in life, as my father to this day claims—"after you and your brothers had left the house" or were "old enough to know"—but from the day each of us was born.

I began to steal and smoke my father's weed when I was ten, I'd tell him, surely from despair and rage, but just as surely from my obsession for revenge.

Because before my mother's abuse, my father stood by in silence.

Because I had no way to stand the nightmare of my life but through the trance of Mary Jane.

Because I had no way to ease my rage but through the trance of Mary Jane, to which I'd never have had recourse had my father not placed the tray on my lap when I was seven—which to this day also my father denies, which memory, as he's always claimed, I "conjured up from he doesn't know where"—yes, my father's tray on my lap with its papers and weed, the buds he had me break with my little hands—*just so, just so,* he taught, *just so, just so*—and then, when finished, when the weed lay in a mound on the tray on my lap, to use the cover of the papers to scoop up that weed and pour onto the tray, which, again, as my father taught—him, the master, him, the lord—I propped on my lap at his ordered slant till the weed was clean, the seeds tumbled to the bottom of the tray, massed along its rim.

And yet decades later my father would deny the least of this account, just as my father's denied all my memories my whole life. And as my father wouldn't know I'd begun to steal and smoke his weed when I was ten, neither would he know anything else about my secret life till I chose to tell him decades on, when none of it, really, any longer mattered.

None of which is to say that meantime I hadn't struck out at him. Because meantime I did take him at his own game, with silence and stealth and style, and made of him—*O my father!*—a greater fool than he had made himself.

Meantime I lied to my father as he lied to me.

Meantime I betrayed my father as he betrayed me.

And I could do these things, with silence and stealth and style, I told my father decades after I'd begun, like a coward, I said, because he had taught me well, because he had taught me well.

THE SEEKER

I sensed that in truth I had neither memory nor the power of thought, nor even any existence, that all my life had been a constant process of obliteration, a turning away from myself and the world.

—*W.G. Sebald*

HE CONSIDERED DOING IT ALONE, TELLING NO ONE, EVER.
Whatever happened doing it, he alone would know, what he saw doing it, he alone would know, what he heard, what he thought, once he'd heard and thought it, he alone would know.

Without silence secrets had no meaning, without which they had no power.

He knew this, in his bones he knew it, not in his mind but his body. The knowledge was as much a part of him as his blood and guts. He knew he knew it, the same way he knew he knew the instant he spoke his knowledge, if just to a hole in a tree, that it would no longer be his alone but the world's if no one else's, the tree's if not the world's, if not evident to the world then at least exposed, sort of like an image-in-an-image, like the image of the man with the boner in the image of the camel on the pack of cigarettes Mike Paradero's sister had shown them, whom, the man with the boner, Mike Paradero's sister had said, most people didn't know they were seeing even when they looked right at it, the image of the man with the boner, right there in the leg of the camel—the same way, he understood, that anyone who saw the tree would see his secret, too. And whether they knew they'd seen his secret, they would still have seen his secret.

In the end that wasn't so important, either, their knowing or not knowing. He would know they'd seen the tree and seeing the tree seen his secret, or rather not his secret anymore, but, now, merely knowledge.

And that was everything.

Once someone had so much as seen his secret, his secret would no longer be secret but just plain old knowledge.

What good was knowing something everyone else also knew? That, he thought, was totally bogus.

He didn't remember who'd mentioned it—maybe Burney McCarthy had, or maybe he had himself—but only that one day after school over at Burney McCarthy's house he and Burney McCarthy had talked it over.

His mother and father did it all the time, he told Burney McCarthy. His father was always taking a toke. Every single day his father got loaded, totally.

Burney McCarthy's uncle did it, too, Burney McCarthy said. Every time Burney McCarthy's uncle visited, he, Burney McCarthy's uncle, had a lid or a doobie or at least a roach that he, Burney McCarthy's uncle, went out on the side of the house to smoke.

We should get our own weed, he had said to Burney McCarthy, and Burney McCarthy said, *Yeah, we totally should, that would be rad, we could totally get stoned, too.*

But since neither he nor Burney McCarthy knew how to get any weed of their own, they talked about the mag wheels they both wanted for their BMXes. He'd got a Mongoose last year with its crappy-ass rims, he told Burney McCarthy, which totally bit, already the rims were warped, they couldn't hack dooky dong. Burney McCarthy said that wasn't squat, Burney McCarthy had an old Huffy that couldn't hack even one piece of dooky, it was a Huffy, right, and not only had the rims warped but the frame had cracked and the gooseneck, too, and how much did that totally majorly bite?

But still from then on practically his single thought was how to get some weed of his own.

He knew he couldn't ask his father for some weed of his own. He had already asked his father one day when his father was toking on a doobie if he could take a toke, the way his father had let him puff on his cigarettes and cigars and drink his drinks. But his father said, *No, this is different, someday you can, hot shot, there'll be plenty of time for that, but not today.*

A couple of months had passed since he and Burney McCarthy had talked about getting stoned.

Now it was winter, the coldest he'd known, so cold actually it had snowed, which for this part of the country, his mother and father said, was unheard of. It had never snowed in this part of the country, not that they knew of, his mother and father said. It had snowed but a couple of inches, yet it was snow just the same as any snow anywhere else. Plus it had been cold enough the day and night it had snowed for the snow to stick, crucial, his father had explained, because just because it snowed didn't mean it was cold enough to keep the snow from melting once it hit the ground, it was a lot colder a few thousand feet up than down here on the ground, his father said.

He had talked to his father before it snowed, the same as ever. He had never not talked to his father. But talking about the snow with his father was the first time he had even halfway wanted to talk to his father since the day his father had punched him in the face and knocked him out after his brother had crushed his chest with a boulder and his mother had beat him for making his brother crush him in the chest with a boulder, and then his mother lied to his father about what had happened so his father was mad enough to want to punch him in the face with a full-on fist, which, though his father had whipped him with a belt before, and though his father had poked his chest and yanked his ears and crunched his pinky in his fingers, he, his father, had never done, punched him in the face with a full-on fist.

His father had hurt him plenty with all of the stuff his father did to him when he got in trouble, which, most of the time, like that time, meant when his mother told his father what a monster he was, what a devil, he *antagonizes* his brothers, he *tortures* his brothers, then he talks back and lies and refuses to listen to her or do as she says, it was awful, his mother would say, just awful, she couldn't stand it anymore, this son of yours, his mother would say, he's horrible, *horrible*, the last thing she needed, if it weren't for him, she'd say, she wouldn't be stuck here in this terrible hell, she could've been happy, if anything made her miserable, she'd say, it was him, she'd say, the little monster, she'd say, he'd ruined everything, everything, *every*thing, she'd say, she could barely stand the sight of him, and when was he, his father, going to do something with this son of his to make him stop, but because his father had never even slapped his face, not once, the way his mother, for instance, always slapped his face or hit him on the head with her wooden spoons, he'd never feared getting slapped by his father, much less getting punched in the face so hard by his father that he'd be knocked out cold, or actually almost knocked out cold, since it had got like a dark blue fog and his head had just crazily spun instead of like when he fell far into sleep, where he knew nothing of the world.

He had hated his mother before, but he'd never hated his father.

But now, for that, for his father knocking him out and

for his mother making his father knock him out, he hated his mother and his father, too.

Who he hated more he struggled to say—his mother for everything she did to him almost every day, plus how she lied to his father and turned his father against him until his father punished him in addition to whatever punishment he'd already got from his mother, more than enough, whatever form his punishment took, for anything he'd ever done or could do or even think of doing—or his father for never listening to his side, for always doing what his mother told his father to do, for letting his mother do everything she did to him, and now, too, especially for punching him in the face so hard his father knocked him out cold and afterward never said a thing about sorry, not once, *I'm sorry, Son, for hurting you, that was wrong of me, I should never have done that, Son, forgive me, Son, I'm sorry, please forgive me.*

But worse than hating his father, he hated hating his father.

Hating his mother felt like breathing air almost, he had hated her that long.

Yet when he hated his mother *and* his father, he suffered much, much more than when he only hated his mother.

When he hated his mother *and* his father, he was left with nothing, he was totally alone, an aloneness that wasn't solitude or even seclusion but just an endless aimless stumbling across the plains of loneliness.

And that, actually, he realized one day as he combed the hillside for arrowheads left behind by the people that lived once in these parts, the Chochenyos, he'd read in a book, made him hate his father even more.

His father had made him hate his father so much that he

hated the hating in addition to hating himself for that hating, which triple hate hurt three times as much as just hating his father alone, and eventually made him hate his father still more, if that were possible, for his father having made him hate his father so much that together with hating his mother, hating his father, hating hating his father, hating himself for hating his father, and hating hating himself for hating his father, all so badly he had no one to turn to, not even himself, which quadruple hurt, again, wounded him way, way more than what in comparison was the simple pain of hating his father and hating hating his father plus hating himself for hating his father and hating hating himself for hating his father even more for having made him hate his father and his mother and himself so much that he had nowhere to go, no refuge at all, no safety, he was totally alone, he had nothing, not even himself, which meant he could do nothing, much less tell his mother or father he hated them, because if he did tell his mother and father he hated them his mother and father would punish him the way his mother and father always punished him, nor could he so much as think about finding some way to hurt his mother and father as remotely as badly as his mother and father had hurt him.

Today, mostly instead of thinking about all of that, he thought about how to get some weed of his own.

By now, really, the thought of feeling better occupied the whole of his waking life, and most of his dreams.

He dreamed of being a hobo still, but for all kinds of reasons when he tried to split for good he'd been stymied and failed.

He knew he'd feel better by getting stoned, because when he asked his father why he, his father, got stoned so much, his father told him that it made him, his father, feel *fantastic*. That was the word his father had used, *fantastic*.

Despite his having heard tons of people say the word *fantastic*, his mother included—*Fan-taaaaas-tic*, she'd say about a hundred times a day in hope or approval of this or that—something about the word always hovered just beyond his grasp, like the face behind a voice on the radio.

He felt he understood the word's meaning, yes, it suggested everything super and great and trippy and huge and fine, but somehow the word itself emanated a power greater that the sum of what it suggested.

Then, the moment his father explained to him that getting stoned made him, his father, feel *fantastic*, his puzzlement had vanished.

Seeing that a place or a thing or some special person could be *fantastic* meant one thing. Knowing that feeling *fantastic* meant feeling super and great and trippy and huge and fine, *all at once*, meant another thing.

He wanted to feel *fantastic*, too.

Feeling *fantastic* had become his most treasured wish.

He wanted to feel *fantastic* far more than he wanted, say, to become a soccer pro or rock star, and definitely more than he wanted the mag wheels for his bike, or a new fishing pole, or even a camping trip to Y.

These things might bring him joy, and maybe even lasting joy, but none of them, singly or together, could take him to the kingdom of *fantastic*. One thing alone could do this, and that was getting stoned.

Why else would his father want to get stoned as often as his father got stoned?

His father's life was a life of sadness and dread. Who could blame his father for wanting to get stoned all day?

Getting stoned filled you with the sense that the whole world, that life itself anywhere you went, was super and great and trippy and huge and fine, that the whole world—every living thing down to the tiniest atomistic being—was beautiful.

This much was clear. This much he totally understood. What he totally did not understand was why his father should always feel *fantastic* while he himself had always to feel only crappy and hateful.

The more he considered this difference, the clearer his understanding that that difference amounted to yet another rock of hate to throw on his pile of rocks of hate.

And then one day on the stupid yellow bus down the canyon on the way to school, when Bruce Ledbetter was hassling him, calling him a city slicker, a pussy-breathed city slicker bozo with his ass jammed full of city-slicker zits, over and over like that, and he could hardly think of anything but how much he hated Bruce Ledbetter almost as much as he hated his mother and father, how stupid Bruce Ledbetter was, nothing but a cretin, nothing but a skin-bag gooey with malice and stupidity and fear, and, more, how badly he wanted to kick Bruce Ledbetter's butt the same way he'd kicked Jeff Longman's butt before he'd moved out to this crappy bunghole of a town, hammer and crush Bruce Ledbetter's face into a blob of knocked-out teeth and blood—and he could do it, too, and he would, if Bruce Ledbetter kept at him, it would be just a matter of time—when all of that was moshing round inside him, that was when the thought had come—how he could get some weed of his own.

One minute he was gritting his teeth, thinking about Bruce Ledbetter's bottomless cretinous stupidity.

The next minute there it was: the *answer*.

He didn't need a way to find his own weed.

That would be majorly dumb.

He already had his own weed.

His father had weed, a lot of weed, and his father having a lot of weed was as good as he himself having a lot of weed.

All he had to do was take his father's weed.

That was all. It was easy.

All he had to do was take his father's weed.

His father left his weed where his father always left his weed, up on the mantel in the plastic bag inside the clay jar with the rest of the works for the weed.

After he thought about whether he would smoke the weed he took from his father and never tell anyone, the same way he had smoked the cigarettes alone and never told anyone, or whether he would smoke the weed with someone else, and if so why not with Burney McCarthy, since Burney McCarthy and he had already talked about getting stoned, and Burney McCarthy had made it clear that he, Burney McCarthy, wanted to get stoned as much as he himself wanted to get stoned, he told Burney McCarthy that he knew how to get some weed and did Burney McCarthy still want to get majorly stoned.

Burney McCarthy was jacked.

Burney McCarthy's old toads never came home until six at least and sometimes even seven, Burney McCarthy said, so they could totally get stoned at Burney McCarthy's place, anytime, totally.

He told Burney McCarthy cool, he would kipe the weed pronto and book it on his bike straight to Burney McCarthy's.

The door of the stupid yellow bus only faced the side of the canyon his house sat on when the bus drove down the canyon. No one could leave the bus if they had to cross the road, so every day he had to wait until the bus had driven to the top of the canyon and halfway back again before the driver let him off.

Bruce Ledbetter, the idiot cretin, he was the bully of the school who thought he was buff but was really just a turkey, together with Brad Hanson and some other idiot turkeys, hassled him the whole way home, the same as they'd hassled him that morning the whole way to school, the same as they'd hassled him every day since he'd moved to that cruddy, crap-ass, spit-wad on the map they called a town.

Bruce Ledbetter had no idea what he could do or, worse, for Bruce Ledbetter, at least, no idea what he really *would* do in a month or so, when, helpless to keep his peace any longer, he'd turn to Bruce Ledbetter and tell him to *shut the fuck up, you fucking stupid idiot asshole*, and Bruce Ledbetter, proving him totally right in his judgment that he, Bruce Ledbetter, wasn't just a turkey but a dickwad cretin, would blink like a jerk in the sun while the rest of the kids on the bus, as if in united disbelief, sucked up a lungful of air that sounded like *Cthuhhhh!* "What did you say?" the idiot Bruce Ledbetter would say idiotically. "You heard exactly what I said, you stupid fucking redneck dweebus," he would say to Bruce Ledbetter. "That's it," Bruce Ledbetter would say with his idiotic scowl, "I'm calling you out, city slicker. You'd better be up at the clubhouse for your ass kicking in one hour, or tomorrow I'll start kicking your ass everyday you get on this bus." By the time he and Bruce

Ledbetter would stop fighting that day, after an hour and a half in the mud and rain, despite Bruce Ledbetter's cheating, pushing him over Brad Hanson after Brad Hanson had sneaked up and kneeled behind him, despite the other jerks who'd try to hold him down while Bruce Ledbetter punched him, but who released him after he slugged them, the jerks, a couple of times, also, he'd give Bruce Ledbetter a black eye and bloody nose and hammer the crap out of Bruce Ledbetter's ear so many times that, once it swelled up all bloody and purple, sort of like a slice of pomegranate, Bruce Ledbetter would finally tell him that he, Bruce Ledbetter, wanted to quit, and that he had won. The giant Jeff Longman had never spoken to or even looked at him again after he had kicked his, Jeff Longman's, butt, and neither would Bruce Ledbetter after he had kicked his, Bruce Ledbetter's, butt, as well.

His mother when he got home was laid up with a migraine. She was absolutely nauseated, she told him from beneath the ice pack on her brow, the same as she always told him every time a migraine put her down.

He didn't know what a migraine was, he only knew he didn't want a migraine.

But probably he'd get a migraine, too, sooner or later, just like everything else he got, all of the sicknesses his mother got, plus a bunch more, colds and flus, and bronchitis, and walking pneumonia, and measles and mumps and chickenpox, and poison oak so bad he'd been hospitalized, plus not to mention the countless injuries, the stitches on his face and arms and hands from cuts and dog bites and crashes and falls, that splinter in his leg the size of a needle, the broken finger, his pinky, whose nail had fallen off even, the second he smashed it against the wall he ran into the first time he rode a motorcycle, it was Randy Bartlett's motorcycle, and torn ankles and knees from football and soccer, and busted ribs from the pony that stood on him for an hour as he lay on the railroad ballast after he'd fallen off the pony that day trotting bareback down the tracks behind the post office, and allergies with their vomiting, and needles and shots and horrible vicious tests for allergies, like when the doctors scooped the skin from his back with their tiny knives, and concussions from crashing on his bicycle and skateboard and the fevers and delirium from the concussions from crashing on his bicycle and skateboard.

No way did he want a migraine on top of all of that—that would be totally uncopasetic.

He fetched the glass of water his mother had commanded, then took a plastic baggie from the kitchen drawer and from the mantel in the living room his father's stoneware jar.

The weed, he knew, had been waiting in the jar all this time, waiting for just this moment, for him to come and take it.

He unrolled his father's baggie of weed and guesstimated how much it would take to roll two fat doobies, then put the guesstimated weed in his baggie. Then he leveled the weed in the bottom of his father's baggie, rolled the baggie up nice and tight, like a couple of fat cigars, licked the top of the baggie the way his father showed him when his father rolled the baggie up, to create a seal, his father had explained, the same as when he licked the glue at the top of the rolling paper rolling his father's joints, sealed the baggie, and placed the baggie back in the jar.

Next, he counted out seven papers—between the Zigzags and Jobs he chose the Zigzags, he liked the man in the picture with the long hair and beard and doobie trailing smoke from the man's mouth—then stacked and folded the papers, then placed them in his baggie and rolled the baggie up the way he'd rolled his father's baggie up.

Then, finally, after taking one of the five or six books of matches in the clay jar, he tucked it and the baggie of weed in his jacket pocket and hollered to his mother he was off to ride his bike.

Right up till he'd set the glass of water on the nightstand beside his mother, his heart had raced with the thought of stealing his father's weed. Yet once he'd gone inside, a wash of calm swept through him: in lieu of the haze that typically ruled the periphery of his vision whenever his excitement reached a certain pitch, his vision had assumed some supernatural clarity.

Not as if *he* were looking through a microscope, but as if his brain had been put *into* a microscope, aspects of his surroundings to which he'd never been privy—the far edges of his vision, where no matter how dull the moment life existed in perpetual ambiguity, where this or that thing in the world was always only this or that or perhaps neither this nor that nor anything else—the whole of this world was part of his waking thinking life, now, as real and sure in every detail as an amoeba dancing through a drop of water blown up a thousand times. Every last thing in his field of vision, for at least 180 degrees, he perceived with crystalline exactitude. What was more, he did so without astonishment, with astonishing detachment, really, as if such power had always been his.

Without a squeak of effort, he realized, he could see the cobwebs chunky with soot in the corner of the ceiling and wall, plus the painting on the wall beneath the cobwebs, with its vertical bands of color—ocher, chocolate, tan, mocha, cream, black, and green—and especially the red-hot circle three-quarters up from the bottom of the band of black. Also without looking, he could see each of the scores of colors in the warp and woof of the old Persian rug, the crazy delicacy of flowers and vines running round the medallion at its top and through the borders before him, the thinner then the thicker at the dirty fringe, and the arabesques and glyphs in the spandrel, where the corner of the rug met the hearth and the claw that was the foot of the settee beneath the painting. He could see the hatchet on the hearth, the eleven split logs of oak and the kindling and splinters from the kindling his father had chopped a few days back, and the andiron over the ash, and the poker and broom against the jam, and the soot on the jam, and piled on the settee the afghan his aunt had crocheted for him the Christmas before last, and Greta, his mother's calico cat, curled on the afghan, and beside the afghan J.J. Walker and Freddie Prinze back-to-back, holding bananas like pistols for a goofy duel on the cover of *Bananas* magazine.

And as he saw these things, everything, with perfect clarity and perfect calm, he realized, as well, that not just his vision, but all of his senses had been mysteriously honed, the way they'd been mysteriously honed that night he'd run away with his hobo bundle and smoked the cigarettes alone in the black of the fort in the field, and heard the men at their women, the blood in the veins of the crickets and worms, and caught the scent of finches drowsing.

The jays that marauded the cat food on the porch everyday had set up a discord of squabbling against which his mother was moaning for peace.

He had heard that for sure. He had always been able to

hear that for sure, day after day, the squabbling of the birds on the porch.

But what he could also hear, which he hadn't been able to hear before, was the clatter of silverware and dishes across the glen, in old lady Scott's, and the snoring of the Dobie on the porch of the couple the next house over. He could even hear the scratching of the mice in the couple's walls.

His head, he realized, flowed abundant with stuff, a vast profusion of minutiae that always till now had manifested at the periphery of his consciousness as the sum of immateriality that, could he explain it, comprised what he'd thought of as the bounds of reality but which today he was somehow able to parcel into their constituent federations, rank on rank of sights, sounds, and smells in the caper of dependent co-arising and -collapsing he knew wasn't merely reality's bounds but its infinite totality.

The smell of his father's weed, and the resin in his pipes, and the dirt in the rug, and the milk-pissy scent of the cat on the settee—these swam through his head with the rest, pungent as socks or tar.

He could smell his mother's breath in the other room, he realized, sour with pain, he could smell the grass and leaves rotting on the wintry hills, the trees in the cold, the water of the creek along the road that ran through the canyon, and the things of the creek, as well, the crayfish and striders and minnows and moss, and the horses, too, he could smell them up the way in their paddocks of dung, and the leather of their tack in the barn and the hay in their stalls, and the chickens pecking gravel in the yard before their coop.

The world spun on its axis, the laws were in place, he knew for an instant the void of hurry and rush.

The weed was in his pocket now.

Already he felt better.

The readiness was all.

Okay, okay—that was what he was, now, *okay.*

And then he was on his bike. And on it, the wind in his ears as he booked it down to Burney McCarthy's, he kept touching his pocket to remind himself the weed was there.

He knew he'd put the weed in his pocket but kept tripping on it anyway.

He'd worked up a sweat already, despite the cold, and his ride was all downhill. His jacket was a good jacket, with a collar of fur, or in any case a collar made of fur that was fake, and neither of its pockets had a hole.

He had checked both pockets three times already to see if there was even a tiny hole in either, but now, again, he couldn't remember and stopped on the road to check.

The weed was definitely in his pocket.

He wanted to take the weed out and look at it, but then someone might see him.

Anyone who saw him would know what he had. If he saw a kid on the road holding up a sandwich baggie full of stuff that looked like oregano or dirt, he would know what the kid had for sure.

The kid would have a baggie of weed, and, as far as he knew, no kid was supposed to have a baggie of weed, and especially not a kid who was ten years old.

But he wasn't any old kid.

That was why he had a baggie of weed.

He'd been to Burney McCarthy's house just once before, the first time they'd talked about people they knew who smoked weed and plus then getting their own weed to smoke. The house was a way down the canyon, which meant if he rode down the canyon one way he'd have to ride back up the other.

It would've been better had he had to ride up the canyon to get to Burney McCarthy's so he could ride down the canyon to get back to the crappy house he lived in, because, first, except for school and the doctor's and the crappy house, nearly anytime you had to leave anywhere, it sucked, and second, if you had to ride uphill after you left instead of downhill after you left, it sucked a whole lot more.

Probably he'd have gone to Burney McCarthy's house more often had Burney McCarthy lived up the canyon.

But really probably it wouldn't have mattered where Burney McCarthy lived, up the canyon or down the canyon or even right next door.

The truth was, he'd been to Burney McCarthy's house just the once, because in Burney McCarthy's house he felt almost as sad as he felt in the house of his mother and father.

Burney McCarthy was waiting for him at the top of the drive.

Burney McCarthy hadn't even put on a sweatshirt, just a tee shirt and pants and socks.

"Did you get it?" Burney McCarthy said.

"Uh huh," he said.

Burney McCarthy snapped his fingers. "Rad!"

The beam of sun through the curtains seemed to've cut the room in half. Motes of dust whirled through the beam in a kind of slow-motion chaos. That was what his brain must look like. If they sawed through his skull and took the top half off like the lid off a jar, his brain would look like the motes of dust reeling through the beam of sun.

But the dust, he remembered now with revulsion, was not just dust.

He might not believe it, his father had told him as they dusted the bookshelves and coffee table and bric-a-brac and stuff, but dust consisted mostly of dead human skin, plus the carcasses and fecal matter of *dust mites,* his father had said, *Dermatophagoids,* his father had said.

And guess what? his father had said. *The mites ate almost exclusively dead human skin.*

Scarcely a week had passed since his father had told him about the dust mites before the thought had slipped into a sort of abstract obscurity. Just the same, he had thought the dust mites pretty gnarly when his father had said what his father said, pretty damn grody, to the point he'd gone about the house looking for dust mites in his sheets, and in the clothes in his closets and drawers, and in the furniture, too.

No doubt about it, this part of Burney McCarthy's house was creepy.

Burney McCarthy's whole house was creepy, actually, dismal and gloomy and full of invisible bugs, dead and alive, invisible bugs, moreover, which basically ate human beings, revolting invisible bugs called *dust mites.*

An awful smell had flooded his being, a smell so awful it had to've flooded Burney McCarthy's house right down to the splinters, from the fabric of the crappy carpets and couches and drapes, to the paper in the news on the table and floor, to the ruins on the tray beneath the old-timey rocker, a TV dinner of Salisbury steak with carrots and gravy or some such crud, and even to the twine of the dream catcher pendant from the dead potted plant, and the board of the banjo in the empty vitrine, and the shells of the walnuts in the pot on the shelf, and the vinyl of the record by the door, Three Dog Night, and, behind the rocker, the rubber and metal and plastic of the training bike no one had used since Burney McCarthy's birthday in 1964.

He had smelled other people's houses before, a lot of full-on shit storms, as he'd heard a guy from high school say. Some smelled like a jug of cat piss and disinfectant and model glue and chicken gone bad. Others smelled like hair spray and roses and chocolate. One house, Angela Barker's, smelled like dirty grease, that was all, and another smelled like mothballs and medicine and cookies with almonds and sugar.

Burney McCarthy's house smelled like all that together, plus maybe a quart or so of pus and spooge. A geezer that smoked four packs a day could've been hiding with a fart machine in Burney McCarthy's basement, a filthy old geez with the gang of dead pigeons and skunks whose ghosts sneaked through the house each night, drooling on all they passed.

He set the baggie of weed on the table. The table had a glass top tacky with rings of soda and wine, plus an ashtray spilling with disgustingly lipsticky butts. Pills of tin foil lay scattered about the table, and pencils with broken tips, and paper covered with doodles of pussies and dicks, armies fighting battles, and crashing planes.

"Your mom smokes a lot," he said.

"Yeah, and she nigger lips everything. That's what Thomas says."

"Who's that?"

"He's my lame-o stepdad. He never lets my mom smoke his cigarettes, he says, because she always nigger lips them."

Burney McCarthy picked up the baggie of weed from the table. "You kiped all this from your old toad?"

"That's a hundred percent Acapulco Gold, dude."

Burney McCarthy held the baggie of weed out before him. "How are we going to smoke it?"

He took the baggie of weed from Burney McCarthy and then a magazine from the couch, a *TV Guide* with Angie Dickinson on the cover, and set it on his lap. He poured the weed, mostly still in clumps, onto the magazine and began to break it apart. The seeds popped out here and there while the weed he continued to crumble. Then he opened his book of matches, scooped the crumbled weed onto it, and poured it back onto the magazine, which rested now at the angle he'd created by lifting his heels from the floor to raise his knees. While the crumbled weed stuck to the top of the magazine, most of the seeds bounced down to puddle in his lap. He did this a few times, then picked a couple of stems from the little mound of weed. Then he was ready to roll the doobie. Burney McCarthy sat there watching.

He licked the glue on one of the papers then stuck that paper to the bottom of another, what his father had called an old Indian trick for making a single mondo paper. With the matchbook cover again he scooped up the crumbled weed and poured it onto the paper between his fingertips, then dropped the matches and spread the weed evenly across the paper with the fingers of that hand. He held each end of the rolling papers between his first two fingers and used his thumbs to press the portion holding the weed into the empty section of paper above it.

Now all he had to do was lick the glue and feather it over

the doobie to make the seal. That was the hard part. If you put on too much or too little spit, the seal would fail, and the doobie would break. He'd done that a lot rolling doobies for his father. His father had told him it was training. Everyone that does anything well had to practice, his father had said, and a lot of practice meant training. But he licked the seal with the perfect glob of spit and lay the seal down like a pro and handed the doobie to Burney McCarthy.

"Whoa, dude," Burney McCarthy said. "That is bitching."

Burney McCarthy put on his jacket and shoes. They walked through the kitchen to the garage and through the garage onto a concrete walk between the house and the wall on the canyon side.

"You ever smoke cigarettes?"

"Uh huh," Burney McCarthy said. "With my brother and his friends when I visited him and my dad out in Y."

"It's the same with this. Except don't blow the smoke out right away. You have to hold it in, like this," he said, and took a breath and held it. "But see, you can still talk," he squeaked. "Just hold it in as long as you can."

"Cool," Burney McCarthy said.

"You go first," he said, and tore off a match. "Just puff for a second till it gets going."

Burney McCarthy put the doobie to his lips and held it there with a finger and thumb, while he struck the match for Burney McCarthy and put the flame to the tip of the doobie. When Burney McCarthy was sure the doobie was lit, Burney McCarthy sucked in a massive toke. But almost instantly Burney McCarthy burst out coughing. Burney McCarthy's nose ran, Burney McCarthy's eyes watered, and a thread of spit dribbled from Burney McCarthy's mouth. He held the doobie for Burney McCarthy so Burney McCarthy could wipe his face.

"You took too much," he said, recalling his lesson smoking cigarettes in the fort in the field. "You only need to take a little. Then hold your breath. Check it out," he said, and toked on the doobie.

He could feel the smoke pressing in, it was killer, he'd taken a killer toke. Then, just as his lungs got full, it hit him, too, the way it had hit him when he smoked his first cigarette, the urge to cough, though now he refused to give. Not till the last, when he couldn't hold his breath another instant, did he release the smoke.

The exhalation was like any other exhalation after he'd held his breath forever, like when he swam a length and a half of the pool under water. But instead of the river of smoke he'd expected to see pouring from his mouth the way it had poured from his mouth when he smoked the cigarettes, there was just a curl of ribbon.

Scarcely had this worry appeared before a giant pressure set on him. He was being smashed beneath a monolith, and at any second he'd pop, a giant balloon full of guts and shit. Still, weirdly, the more the pressure mounted, and the closer it got to critical mass, the more he found he could stand.

He felt Burney McCarthy taking the doobie from him, pretty trippy, because he wasn't in his own body any longer, but someone else's. Burney McCarthy's fingertips were touching someone else's fingertips. They were his fingertips that Burney McCarthy was touching, and yet they weren't his fingertips. They were no more his fingertips than they were the fingertips of the king in the picture he'd seen, the King of Siam.

And now Burney McCarthy was speaking to him, but he couldn't make out Burney McCarthy's words. Nor did he care what Burney McCarthy said, nor did he care that he couldn't hear what Burney McCarthy said.

He couldn't say he liked these sensations, not at first, he only knew he'd never felt a single one of these sensations, not even when he'd smoked the cigarettes.

Forces were coming to take him away. Forces were coming to free him. His body by turns grew heavy as iron and light as fun. The crystalline perfection he'd experienced standing before the mantel in his house not an hour before might as well have been the shadow of someone else's dream. He'd been cast into a tunnel the size of a roll of toilet paper, whose edges were a hectic mist. His eyes couldn't focus on anything smaller than a grape, and anything outside was swallowed by the mist.

Burney McCarthy's face had become an avatar of repose, he'd have said had he the means to say it. He thought of his father's face when his father got stoned, the droop of his father's eyes and his father's budding smile, the simultaneous nearness and distance they conveyed. The same ribbon of smoke that had leaked from his lips leaked from the lips of Burney McCarthy.

Burney McCarthy's fingertips were touching his fingertips. He could feel his fingertips absorbing the entity of the doobie, and then the weight of his hand behind the fingers, and the arm behind the hand. His hand had risen to his mouth, the doobie in it, the person he was taking in more smoke.

The smoke, now, manifested as an age-old friend bearing gifts of power.

And then just as quickly the smoke had become a ghoul entering his body to steal his soul.

He felt at once terrified and thrilled.

And both were true, and both were false.

He had the smoke inside again, but this time, just as the fingertips with which he felt Burney McCarthy's fingertips were his fingertips and not his fingertips, the lungs that held the smoke were his lungs and not his lungs. Whose lungs they might've been he couldn't begin to say.

No more than a twinkling had elapsed before this thought abandoned him.

He cared whose lungs they might've been less than he cared whose hand had grown the weed whose smoke the lungs now held.

The urge to cough tore through him once more, which again he resisted. And then again he watched the ribbon of smoke dribble from his lips, and felt the unknown being throw its weight down on him, and the limit of terror tighten its circle, and the angel of profusion blow it away.

He knew it was Burney McCarthy who stood before him offering the doobie, but he knew just as surely he was staring into the eyes of an ancient fraud. A stranger had materialized before him in the perfect semblance of Burney McCarthy.

But knowing very well the identity of this person while struggling to maintain his composure before what could've been nothing but an alien filled him with doubt.

He felt outright beleaguered and downright alone.

He knew he knew, he knew he knew nothing at all.

Neither he nor Burney McCarthy had spoken. Ages must've passed, yet seeing they two had gone through barely a quarter of the doobie, it couldn't've been more than minutes.

Not just the world lay far beyond him but he himself. Nothing happened inside, but only out there.

He witnessed the passing of each moment despite his helplessness to know it was he who'd witnessed it.

Everything he thought or saw hurled him through a gauntlet of fresh dispute, by turns furious and ridiculous.

Burney McCarthy's blinking eyes sent him into a cataclysm of wonder, as though he'd been zapped into the eyes of the entity that saw Burney McCarthy's eyes, as though for the first time in his life he'd seen the eyes of another truly blink, as though this were the first time he'd really seen eyes blinking—the lowering lids, the fluttering lashes, the moisture when the lashes and lids rose again . . .

And now Burney McCarthy's lips were moving, while in the brown leaves of the hillside behind Burney McCarthy, beneath a skeletal bush, a towhee scratched in search of bugs and seeds, and he knew how lovely and terrible this was, that a boy could move his lips while life and death played out its woe on a screen behind him, the boy as safe from the woe as numb to the rest.

Yes, Burney McCarthy's lips had moved, Burney McCarthy was speaking, the entity into whose ears he'd been dropped heard the words, *This is gnarly, man. I feel like I'm swimming through a block of ice* . . . And then, *Are you buzzed? Because I am stoned to the max* . . . And then Burney McCarthy was gone, Burney McCarthy had vanished, and the can at the end of the walk, and the sky above, and the towhee with the bug on the leaf-strewn hill—

—*You're being held in a woman's arms, perhaps your mother's arms or the arms of your father's mother. A woman in a cap adorned with faded flowers is swimming in the pool a few steps off. The water licks the pool's tiled edges, the hands of the woman in the pool slap against the surface of the pool, you hear the tinkling of ice-filled glasses, the clatter of forks and knives. From nearby shrubbery birdsong lilts, a woman beside you erupts with laughter, somewhere close a smoker hacks. The woman in the pool has skin so white, you see, her skin is the color of paste. You can see the pale blue shimmering beneath the surface of the skin of the woman in the pool, you can see the veins in her ankles and behind her knees, she isn't young, or even middle-aged, but old. The sky is clear. The grass ripples, a tree's branches purr, and in the distance you hear a scream. A bumble bee emerges from the hedge by the fence and sets toward the woman in the pool, zooming low to the surface of the pool, bouncing close, dangerously close, three or more times, six or more times, again and again till at last it sticks, the bee is stuck to the pool. For the briefest moment silence descends, you hear nothing but the sound of your breath and the water in the pool. And then the bee begins to struggle. But the bee isn't struggling to escape the pool, but to attack the woman in it. A wind sweeps through your head, a terrible howl, you're sick with terror as you clamor and squirm, the woman that holds you can't see anything, nor the woman in the pool, she just plops and slaps, blind to the bee that's inches off from killing her. And now the bee is ready to strike, now it's ready to kill, now your dread is past all hope, you're thrashing now, you're terrified now for the woman in the pool and for yourself, there's nothing you can do, it doesn't matter what you do, no one knows the danger, no one your fear—*

—And then the doobie was rising toward his mouth again, this memory, he knew, cut short with the same boggling speed with which it had appeared, as if a film had snapped on its reel, leaving him with himself once more, with the person who was him, with nothing but the sense behind it all of bottomless grey, regardless of his efforts to will another frame from the reel, regardless of how far he tried to delve.

There was nothing but his life again: Burney McCarthy staring at the ground, a spider on the wall, dead, a banana slug by the garbage can, the heavy clouds, the roar of a jet, somewhere beyond the clouds.

He gazed into Burney McCarthy's face, and knew he'd known Burney McCarthy forever. Burney McCarthy had eyes bluer than any eyes he'd ever seen, bluer than X's eyes, bluer than the eyes of the man who played Butch Cassidy, and that was super blue. He had always thought Burney McCarthy had blond hair, like anybody's blond, take your hundred picks. But he had been wrong. Burney McCarthy's hair was a hologram of goodness—orange as egg yolk, yellow as straw, gold as rings, red as a red felt pen. The way Burney McCarthy's hair hung down over his, Burney McCarthy's, eyes, Burney McCarthy could've been the son of an elf king, Elrond or Celeborn, or even Fëanor far in the West.

He'd definitely been wrong about his friend. Burney McCarthy had secret powers even Burney McCarthy knew nothing of. The adults Burney McCarthy lived with, Burney McCarthy's nasty stepdad and cigarette-huffing mom, were a couple of fakes, total jell heads that had found Burney McCarthy under a bench, then dragged home to heat their TV dinners and do their chores and yell at when they got bored. They had no idea what sort of ultra-human being whose company they'd been graced to share.

One day Burney McCarthy would step from his room, and Burney McCarthy wouldn't be wearing the same pants as last week with a shirt from his older brother who lived in Y and

167

his toes poking out of smelly socks. Burney McCarthy would be wielding a sword and gird with a coat of mithril forged by the sons of Telchar of Nogrod, his flaxen mane down the cloak woven for him eons past by the ladies of Galadriel.

At the moment Burney McCarthy's fake stepdad and mom understood the depth of their delusion, when the anguish of their blindness plunged like ice through their hearts, Burney McCarthy would begin to fade, atom by tiny atom, returning as had been foretold—little did they know, puny mortals—to assume his, Burney McCarthy's, place among his people in their time of need.

Burney McCarthy's fake stepdad and mom would cry out for mercy as they knelt to wrap their arms about their charge, but it would be too late, in their arms they'd hold but a memory, false, and Burney McCarthy would be gone, the last of Burney McCarthy's smile burning in their eyes like an ancient flame.

No one knew Burney McCarthy, no one had praised Burney McCarthy's gifts, none had divined Burney McCarthy's golden fate.

And thinking this, he knew at once how amazing the world was, how far past beauty the world truly was if only you opened your eyes.

And he knew at once what his father must've known, as well, why his father couldn't live without his precious weed.

He, too, felt *fantastic* now.

He'd seen behind the veil, and what he saw was so much more than good.

Something burned—the tips of his finger and thumb. He looked at them, shocked to see the doobie gone, more or less. Between his fingertips he held a roach. That was all.

"Check it out!" he said, pointing at the banana slug.

Who knew, it could be the banana slug was no slug at all, but, like the frog in the tale restored to his princely self by the kiss of a loving princess, an errant knight or warrior king cursed by a witch from the marsh. Or, who knew, it could've been just a plain old banana slug, and that would've been fine, too, because now that he looked at it, banana slugs were pretty cool.

"It looks like Thomas's dick!" Burney McCarthy said, and broke out laughing. "Ha! ha! ha! ha! ha! ha!" he roared. "Ha! ha! ha! ha! ha! ha!"

They were busting their stupid guts. The canyon boomed with laughter, and with more than laughter, with the madness that was their laughter and the thing that had filled them up with such bottomless insane laughter, the idea that Burney McCarthy's lame-o stepdad, the sort of man who hated when his wife smoked his cigarettes because she nigger lipped them every time, had a banana slug for a dick.

That was pretty funny, even if you didn't know who Thomas was or looked like. He'd never seen Thomas, but the moment Burney McCarthy said the banana slug looked like Thomas's dick, a picture of Thomas, naked no less, appeared in his head, a runty little man with a little runty stache and a bald patch on his egg-shaped head, and long thin hair pulled back in a tail, and dirty fingers, and a shrunken chest, and a banana slug for a dick.

Yar! Ha! ha! ha! ha! ha! ha! Yar! Ha! ha! ha! Yar! Yar! Yar!

And then out of nowhere, madly laughing all the while, Burney McCarthy picked up a brick and smashed the banana slug flat.

"Psych!" Burney McCarthy said.

When Burney McCarthy lifted the brick to see the

destruction there, nothing remained of the slug but a motionless jam, nothing like what moments before, he now understood, had been a majestic algae-tinted yellow. What lay smashed across the soggy paper . . . He couldn't say what lay there, he couldn't say at all, he saw just a shimmering blob that once had been the king of its universe because in its universe nothing existed but it and certainly no notion beyond it of king or universe or even existence, which purity of being had accounted precisely for the majesty that had been its bananaslugness and nothing but its bananaslugness. Nothing remained of the banana slug now, or of its bananaslugness, but two antennae the color of muddy snot.

"Bet he had no idea that was coming!" Burney McCarthy said.

Everything swirled, everything spun, nothing made any sense.

The colors of all things, as many as there were, had been, were now become one, merged into a single hideous color whose name he couldn't say because until this moment he'd never been set before it—not blue, not gray, not green, not brown, nor any mixture of these, nor of any colors he'd known, just a single repulsive color whose defining trait he described as simply change.

And then like fog in fast motion the horror of that unspeakable color vanished, and he was on his knees before what had once been a banana slug but was now he didn't know what, made that way by the stranger beside him, whose name he didn't know.

He had known anxiety. He had known fear. And certainly he'd known dread. But what he knew now surpassed them all.

Doom was near, doom was coming, and not merely for himself, he realized, but for all things, for the world itself, and maybe for the universe, too, whatever it was and held.

In a moment the world would explode. The world would explode without warning, and so fast not a creature would feel the least sensation, not the least glint of pain or intimation or fear of pain. He wouldn't feel pain, either, yet he'd feel fear, the fear he felt now, this terrible insufferable dread.

But that would be all.

He, too, would've exploded like everything else had exploded. It would be as if he'd gone to sleep. He'd know nothing of the world, or of the things of the world.

The things of the world themselves would know nothing of the things of the world, for all would be black, that was all.

"Oh, dude," Burney McCarthy said to the mess before him, "you are *so* faced. Did you see that?" Burney McCarthy said to him. "*Doooooosh!* Doesn't look like Thomas's dick anymore, does it?"

Once again the creature that had possessed Burney McCarthy while they were toking on the doobie had taken Burney McCarthy. Burney McCarthy, or the entity that looked like Burney McCarthy, whichever, was the ugliest thing he'd ever known, uglier than the leper on the tube, trembling earless in bed, uglier than the Elephant Man, whose poor frame he couldn't see bearing another mangled cell, uglier than the girl born faceless, with boils for eyes and a mouth for a nose and an ear the shape of broccoli, and way, *way* uglier than the mess of glop on the soggy paper before them, what had once been a majestic banana slug.

He thought of the UFO he'd seen with Vincent Greco

while camping on the ridge last summer. As the spaceship glided across the valley, straight toward him and Vincent Greco, to suck them up with a beam so the aliens in it could make their grisly tests, the world had been engulfed by silence.

The woods till then had been rich with the lowing of two or three cows above a sea of crickets and frogs, and the wind in the trees, and the animals moving through it. He and Vincent Greco had been a part of that universe, also, two tiny but real lives in a fathomless universe of lives, the whole of them in the scheme of things communing as one.

Then—just like *that*—the world's voice was gagged, and there was only silence, and the menace beneath it.

He and Vincent Greco sat straight up, the ship glided on, straight toward them, he could've sworn, a ship like none from here, a teardrop, enormous and metallic, hulking and sleek, down whose back ran a predatory fin.

He watched the ship ease toward them, knowing as he watched that a crew of alien cosmonauts, in all their otherworldly hideousness, manned the ship's controls. He had seen pictures of aliens that the artists who drew them claimed were real, based on descriptions from people the aliens had released, most of them versions of a great bald skull that tapered to a chin above which, nearly always, in place of a mouth, peeked a faint slit or hole. The beings in these pictures rarely had a nose, either, or anyway much of one. What he remembered most about them was their eyes, almond-shaped cavities of black from whose centers, as from the centers of the eyes of a panther, glimmered two horrific lines of gold.

But however true these pictures may have been, they had nothing to do with the picture in his mind. The aliens in his

172

mind were something very near to the mess of glop that was a banana slug before Burney McCarthy had smashed it.

Each alien was its own continuity of protean glop with a supermotility and superwill on a scale no earthling could gather.

Each could slither, leap, and hover, plus, depending on its predicament and needs, sometimes even fly.

Plus, depending on its predicament and needs, each could assume forms unknown to man.

And if these weren't enough, like two drops of water melding to one, each alien could merge with any other, or even with all of them at once, to create a gargantuan superalien whose intelligence and power transcended the wildest concept of synergy or coaction.

Of course, too, these aliens were never anything but hideous. And the more aliens that merged as one, the more hideous that one alien grew, until, at last, having completed their merge, the entity they formed achieved a hideousness so almighty that any earthling who looked on it would disintegrate at once.

And it was just this hideousness that he saw when he looked at Burney McCarthy. Burney McCarthy was so hideously ugly, he thought, that even the aliens in the UFO he'd seen on the ridge that night with Vincent Greco couldn't stand to look at Burney McCarthy. Burney McCarthy was so hideously ugly that for a moment he wondered why he hadn't already died to look at the hideousness Burney McCarthy was. In the face of such hideousness, how could he speak? And if in the face of such hideousness he could speak, what could he say to what that hideousness had said that would make a bit of sense?

The best he could think of was to roll another doobie, to

smoke another doobie, to get even more stoned than he already was, so he would feel even more *fantastic*.

"Let's go roll that other doobie up," he said.

"Dude, you're not totally stoned?" Burney McCarthy said.

"That massive patch of snow on the other side of the road?"

"Yeah."

"Let's roll that other doobie up and go over there and toke it up and have a snowball fight."

"Whoa."

"Right?"

He wanted nothing less than to go back inside Burney McCarthy's creepy house with its noxious smell and colonies of millions of revolting dust mites. He wanted to smoke that other doobie. If they headed over to the patch of snow and had a snowball fight, fine. But if they didn't head over to the patch of snow and have a snowball fight, fine, too.

Smoking that other doobie was the sole thing that mattered, because the sooner he smoked that other doobie, the sooner he'd feel even more *fantastic* than he felt or had felt until Burney McCarthy had smashed the banana slug and turned into the ugliest thing he'd ever seen, uglier even than a leper or the Elephant Man or the baby girl without a face or the hideous blobby aliens that manned the ship from outerspace that in the middle of the night last summer he and Vincent Greco had run from fast as fire.

But that was the thing. To smoke the other doobie, he had to go back inside Burney McCarthy's creepy, smelly, dust-mite riddled house.

The beam of light that had cut the living room in half had become a rectangle of light split between the couch and a piece of carpet stained the color of shit. Other than this, he made himself ignore the things he hadn't ignored when he arrived.

His brain had gone to the kingdom of *fantastic*, and in the kingdom of *fantastic*, he was the controller. If he didn't want to see a thing in the kingdom of *fantastic*, he didn't have to see a thing.

A voice in his head had told him this.

The voice spoke the truth.

The weed lay where he'd left it, on the *TV Guide* with Angie Dickinson's face. He saw it the moment he entered Burney McCarthy's living room and went straight for it. He put the magazine on his lap, joined two rolling papers, and rolled up the doobie, a big old fat bomber of a doobie he had used every last speck of the weed in, it was twice as fat as the other doobie, totally majorly killer. Then he ran the back of his arm over the magazine. Then he tossed it on the couch and stuffed the baggie in his pocket.

Burney McCarthy had sat beside him meantime, but instead of watching him roll up the doobie in silence as Burney McCarthy had before, Burney McCarthy stared at some spot across the room and air-guitared the riff from the song he'd heard Kyle Bowdritch's big brother playing in his basement that day a few weeks back, "Iron Man," by that super heavy metal band, Black Sabbath, that had that madman guy who worshipped Satan, Kyle Bowdritch's big brother had told them.

Burney McCarthy had slipped into a trance. He'd finished rolling the doobie and Burney McCarthy hadn't noticed. Burney McCarthy just stared at some invisible spot and repeated the buzz-riff from "Iron Man," over and over and over.

"Dvvf, dvvf, dvvf, dvvf, dvvf—nrr-nrr nrr-nrr nrr-nrr nrr-

nrr nrr-nrr nerr nerr nerrrr! Derr, dirr, derr, derr—dirr, derr derr derr da dirr dirr derr . . ."

It was almost as if Burney McCarthy had gone blind. Burney McCarthy still had eyes, but both, unable to see, were useless.

"Dvvf, dvvf, dvvf, dvvf, dvvf—nrr-nrr nrr-nrr nrr-nrr nrr-nrr nrr-nrr—"

"Dude," he said.

"—nerr nerr nerrrr! Dvvf, dvvf, dvvf, dvvf, dvvf—"

"Dude, check it out," he said, and stuck the doobie in Burney McCarthy's face.

"*Dude,*" Burney McCarthy said. Burney McCarthy's eyes looked liked his father's eyes, now, just smaller and redder and glossier. "That is a full-on gnarlzathon."

"Right?"

"Totally."

They headed toward the front door this time, back through the creepy hall they'd walked when he arrived. They made down the driveway, across the road, and up the side of the canyon, picking their way through bushes and trees, slipping on leaves, clawing at roots and stones till they stood in the shade beside the patch of snow spread along a slice of open hill.

A chunk of leaf had wedged beneath his nail.

The longer he stared at the leaf the stranger it grew.

Ten inches from his face, the chunk of leaf seethed with motion, scarcely perceptible, but motion like the rest. Then he realized the motion had nothing to do with the chunk of leaf but something on it, in the grime stuck to the chunk of leaf, the tiniest living thing he'd seen with his bare eyes, a pod of things, actually, he didn't know what else to call them, smaller than the pores of his skin, squirming in confusion.

He hadn't thought of the story for a long time, but now with a rush it returned of a piece, *Horton Hears a Who!* Somewhere in a closet or box or maybe on one of his father's shelves, he still had the book by Dr. Suess. It made him warm, the thought of the book waiting for him whenever he wanted to read it again. He knew it was just a story, but in the story Horton the elephant had heard voices calling to him from a speck of dust, the voices, as it turned out, of the Whos that lived on the speck of dust in an actual city called Whoville.

Maybe the pod of seething things on the chunk of leaf wedged beneath his nail was an entire city of microscopic beings, the littlest thinking beings in the galaxy, whole families and schools and factories and stores running and driving and flying about the same day he and the others of the world were running and driving and flying about.

But more probably that wasn't the case. More probably the seething things on the chunk of leaf were a pod of protoplasmic amoebae torn from the dark of the mud beneath their leaf, writhing about in what for them must have been the glare of an atomic sun.

Either way, he would never know. Not now, in any case, not today.

Yet whatever this pod of squirming things was, thinking beings or mindless beings, he didn't want to hurt them.

For a moment, he felt that so little as his gaze itself could hurt them, much less the weak gray light.

Tenderness rushed through him, he wanted to comfort the beings on the chunk of leaf, whoever they were, whatever, he wanted to hold them always, like a newborn puppy. Instead, he pointed his finger toward the road and with the folded edge of another leaf filliped the chunk from under his nail and watched it flutter toward a shrub.

Burney McCarthy had taken out his Swiss Army knife to stab a dead mouse rotting in the mud at the edge of the patch of snow.

Now Burney McCarthy slid the tip of the blade beneath the flattened blob of fur and flipped it over. All four of the mouse's feet lay mashed into the little cake, each of its claws like a grimace in the face of doom.

From Burney McCarthy's house across the road, amidst the trees and earth and leaves, the snow had looked terrifically white. Up close, now, in the shade, the snow looked more like a blanket of pale lead speckled with leaves and dirt.

A stone verge ran the length above the patch, which spread out laterally for maybe twenty feet. The snow lay thickest in the stone's immediate shadow and tapered down the hill another eight feet or so, where the shadow gave way and a copse of shrubbery began.

He put the doobie in his pocket, then took a few steps back and charged into the snow, which, to his surprise, stood a good foot deep where he landed.

He scooped up a handful of snow.

The sudden cold in his hands, like a bolt of power, ran straight to his brain, and for a hanging instant his field of perception brightened.

He shaped the snow into a ball, then macked it into Burney McCarthy's face.

He might as well have slammed Burney McCarthy with a bucketful of water. The glossy beads that were Burney McCarthy's eyes popped out of Burney McCarthy's head the way he remembered the eyes of the rubber Goo Goo Doll popping out from the hand of the older boy who'd scared him back when he was too young to know the doll was just a doll.

Burney McCarthy sat with his knife in the dirt beside the snow, sputtering and blinking while he himself laughed and laughed.

"You ready to get tubular, Burney?" he said, and took the doobie from his pocket.

That was the first time he'd said these words. His father had brought him to the job one Saturday morning, and that afternoon his father and a man his father worked with went out to the parking lot to get stoned. "You ready to get tubular?" the man his father worked with said as the man pulled a sneak-a-toke from his pocket. "Because I warn you," the man said. "This stuff is strictly purple."

"What?" Burney McCarthy said.

"I don't think you're trippy enough yet, dude."

Burney McCarthy impaled the dead mouse, then held it up for an instant before flinging it down the hill.

"Is that harsh or what!"

"Here," he said, offering the doobie to Burney McCarthy.

Burney McCarthy dropped the knife and took the doobie and held it the same as before, with a finger and thumb, while he struck the match and lighted the doobie.

He watched Burney McCarthy toking on the doobie and realized that, all along, somewhere far in his mind, he'd been aware of an emptiness inside him, like a hole in the ground craving a mountain of dirt.

Burney McCarthy had held the smoke until Burney McCarthy had nothing left to free. Burney McCarthy's exhalation sounded like the last breath of the man he'd seen die on a show on TV, *Kung Fu*, a vicious bounty hunter, after Kwai Chang Caine had torn the bounty hunter to bits with his Shaolin martial arts. Right away Burney McCarthy's eyes lapsed back to the eyes of his father, blissful but remote.

And then a mist fell over the world, and he found himself shuffling through slab after slab of Arthurian plenty, stuffs he'd only imagined from books—greasy ducks and olives in oils from the East, oranges and grapes, frog legs braised in butter and wine, and quail and venison and snipe . . . Cheeses by the giant wheel, ewers of ale and mead, loaves of fresh-baked bread —all these hovered before him . . . And buttery potatoes and buttery yams, and geese soaked in wine, and pork chops and steak, and berry pies and cream cakes and custards and tarts, and sugar-fraught wafers, and candied apples and candied pears, and cider and cream and icy waters fresh from their spring . . .

He had a dull pressure in his arm. He blinked. The pressure increased. He blinked again and saw the patch of snow, remembered the patch of snow, and the skeletal trees, and the road winding through the canyon. But the pressure wouldn't stop. And then he remembered Burney McCarthy, the doobie, getting stoned. Burney McCarthy was poking his arm. Burney McCarthy was talking.

"Hey, man," Burney McCarthy said. "Hey, dude, hey, come on, man, are you going to toke on that or what?"

He looked into Burney McCarthy's face and smiled. He sensed his arm rising, sensed his hand moving to his face, his fingers to his mouth, the doobie to his lips. He was already high from the last doobie, all along he'd been totally majorly stoned, majorly *fantastic*, but now he was *really* majorly *fantastic*, probably more stoned and more *fantastic* than his father had ever been—way, way more.

Never again did he want to leave this place, where nothing mattered because everything mattered, where nothing was *fantastic* any more or less than anything else was *fantastic*. Love didn't matter anymore, nor did sadness. Nor did boredom, nor hatred, nor hatred of hatred, nor rage. All that mattered purred in his head, round and round in the kingdom of *fantastic*.

Burney McCarthy's fingers pressed into his fingers, Burney McCarthy's face turned toward his hand. Burney McCarthy was trying to take the doobie from him, he realized, as he squeezed the doobie between his own fingers and brought it to his lips.

"Hold on a second," he said. "Hold on."

"It's my turn, now, man," Burney McCarthy said.

He toked on the doobie again, long and hard, much longer and harder than any toke before.

"Ah, man, that's what bogarts do, man," Burney McCarthy said.

"What?" he said.

"My uncle told his girlfriend she was a bogart because she kept toking on his doobie," Burney McCarthy said. "She was bogeying the doobie, he said. You know, like you are now."

In his mind he snorted and said, *Bite me, Burney*. He may also have said *Bite me, Burney* with his actual mouth, but didn't know for sure.

His lungs rebelled.

They wouldn't obey him, they wouldn't hold the smoke.

Then a velveteen roar mounted in his head, a hundred thousand sirens singing in the belly of a dreaming cave. And with every particle of smoke that slipped from his lungs, the song grew more delicious, more and more enchanting, the unlimited happiness of ten thousand sirens, the roar of the sirens of happiness swooning in the belly of a dreaming cave.

Burney McCarthy's face wavered before him, but now it began to recede until—*vooooosh!*—it dropped away. His neck turned rubbery. His head lolled one way and the other, and when his body collapsed, his arm swiped out at Burney McCarthy's face. A swath of heavy cotton brushed his fingers, the treetops spun across his eyes. Then the roar of the sirens vanished, and his vision folded straight to black.

He sat on his butt in the patch of snow with an arm in Burney McCarthy's hand. Burney McCarthy stood beside him holding his arm, laughing the way an actor laughs. Burney McCarthy laughed so hard, with such goofy care and razzle-dazzle glee, that he himself began to laugh, as well. He laughed at himself, at Burney McCarthy, at the totally awesome kingdom of *fantastic.*

"Give me that," he said.

"You are so stoned," Burney McCarthy said, still laughing.

They'd smoked just half the doobie, but already he and Burney McCarthy had roared into outer space, or, rather, into a world *like* outer space, where the rules of the world, the rules of the old world, no longer held. He knew he'd roared into a world like outer space because only in a world like outer space could he have wrested free of the gravity that had always made him see the way he'd seen.

Now, all of that had changed. Everything around him—the trees, the skeletal shrubs, the few last leaves on the trees, the blanket of leaves on the earth and the earth beneath the blanket of leaves, Burney McCarthy's house across the road, even Burney McCarthy, like an actor gone mad—it had all assumed a faint translucency through which he could see into the heart of things, into the truth itself.

Objects weren't objects, nor things things.

Objects and things were a vast complicated lie, a daisy chain of illusory sense.

The whole of his life he'd been listening to the huckster that forged this chain of lies.

But now he saw the huckster.

The huckster was an invalid, desperate to uphold the retarded vision with which it had chained the world.

Burney McCarthy had said reality was "gnarly," and Burney McCarthy had been right. Reality was a shadowy block of ice, a thinking feeling block of ice that spoke one word in a thousand tongues.

Did the branches sway in the breeze, the branches asked, or did your mind?

Why, the dirt said, was dirt "dirt," and why, asked the leaves, were leaves "leaves"?

On what are you standing if your feet have never touched the ground? asked not his feet but the ground.

And how could you have got "here" when there was no "there" from which to have left nor "here" to be got to once you'd gone?

Question after question flowed through him, none in the normal sense. They were questions asked by questions asked with a word that was a thousand words and none. Nor were the answers to these questions answers in any normal sense, either, because the answers were merely questions in disguise.

The patch of snow... The snow... Snowballs...

He scooped up a handful of snow and put out the doobie.

Then he took the baggie from his pocket and placed the doobie in the baggie and the baggie in his pocket.

"You know what we should do?"

Burney McCarthy was shaking his head and playing air guitar and fuzzing on and on.

"—Nrr-nrr nrr-nrr nrr-nrr nrr-nrr nrr-nrr—huh?"

"Dude, we should make up like a huge pile of snowballs and plaster some cars when they drive by."

"Heck yeah!"

"Right?"

"Ah, man, that'll be so boss. We can totally plaster them."

"Yeah, huh. But what if they stop?"

"They can't catch us. We'll just book it up the hill. They can go bite themselves."

"Totally, right?"

"Dude."

His hands had gone numb by the time he realized he and Burney McCarthy couldn't use up all the snow making snowballs. That might take days. And besides, probably the snow would melt by then. But he and Burney McCarthy had made a lot of snowballs, anyhow, maybe twenty-five or thirty, enough to plaster as many cars as would drive up and down the canyon before it got too dark to see, by which time, he remembered dismally, he'd have to go back to his mother and father's house.

Burney McCarthy stepped from the snow patch and stacked the snowballs in a pile as he tossed them to Burney McCarthy. He had three snowballs to go when they heard a car in the distance, driving up the canyon, by the sound of it.

Burney McCarthy's face shone with the biggest dopiest

grin he could imagine, bigger and dopier than any dopey grin his brothers had ever grinned. And then he saw it, a cream-colored Gremlin tootling up the road, so slow he and Burney McCarthy would have to hang themselves for missing it. He had thrown enough footballs and baseballs and rocks and kicked enough soccer balls and shot enough slingshots to know you had to lead a moving target to hit it.

The little car by now had slowed down even more, if he could believe it. The car couldn't have been going more than ten miles an hour. Some total doofus must've sat behind the wheel, some old blue hair or guy with no legs or maybe some lame-o that just got his license.

"Now!" he shouted.

Burney McCarthy threw his snowball at the same time he threw his own. He watched the snowballs hurtle toward the car like each was tied to a line strung between them and the car. Both snowballs would strike the car dead on, he could tell, right on its windshield, probably. And then, sure enough—*palappp! palappp!*—his snowball blew apart across the hood a foot before the windshield while Burney McCarthy's snowball exploded smack in the middle of the windshield.

"Whoa!" Burney McCarthy said when the car's tires screeched and gave out a puff of smoke.

He expected the car to take off once the driver had recovered from their fright and seen the car had only been hit with a couple of snowballs. But then a reedy woman, with hair like Peter Pan's and rainbow suspenders full of buttons and pins, scrambled from the car to glare up the hill. Over a song on the radio, a song he didn't know, made for pussies, it sounded like, whatever, a baby had begun to scream.

"You could have *killed* us," the woman shouted. "Do you know that?"

He couldn't say for sure whether the woman had seen them, though he sensed she hadn't. So long as he and Burney McCarthy remained quiet, the woman would just be yelling into bushes and trees.

"That was terrible," the woman shouted. "Just awful! You should be ashamed of yourself, whoever you are. You could have *killed* us!"

From the moment the woman opened her door, the radio had blared and the baby had screamed and cried. He couldn't see the baby. The baby must've been strapped into the passenger seat. Now the woman leaned into the car and cut the song. The baby's strangled cries, and the woman's effort to soothe the baby, echoed through the canyon louder than ever. The woman pleaded with the baby, telling the baby it was all okay, but the baby wouldn't be soothed.

Then, the moment the woman turned back to the road to holler, Burney McCarthy stuck his tongue out and blew as hard as he could. The sound of a giant fart rang out: "*Pthbthbthbthbthbthbthbthbthb!!!*"

In her preposterous outfit, her face contorted with dismay, the woman looked like a scrawny clown.

"How *dare* you!" she shouted. "That is *not* funny! That is not funny at *all*! You come down here *right* now!"

"You come down here *right* now!" Burney McCarthy said from his shrub.

He couldn't control himself. The laughter that rushed out of him didn't come from him but the entity into whose body he'd once more been set.

"Ha! ha! ha! ha! ha! ha! ha! ha! ha! ha! ha! ha! ha! ha!" he roared. "Ha! ha! ha! ha! ha! ha! ha! ha! ha! ha! ha! ha! ha! ha!"

"Ha! ha! ha! ha! ha! ha! ha! ha! ha! ha! ha!" Burney McCarthy roared. "Ha! ha! ha! ha! ha! ha! ha! ha! ha! ha! ha! ha! ha! ha!"

He'd never laughed like this before, he'd never in his life experienced anything so funny. This moment was so funny, he felt he might die with laughing. He'd seen a skit on *Monty Python's Flying Circus*. The English army had made a joke so funny that anyone who heard it died with laughing. To win the war, the English troops told the joke to the German troops, every one of whom keeled over dead with laughter. He might not actually die with laughing, and yet he couldn't think of what might stop his laughter. He could barely stay on his feet. On and on the laughter went—"Ha! ha! ha! ha! ha! ha! ha! ha! ha! ha! ha! ha! ha! ha! ha! ha! ha! ha! ha! ha! ha! ha! ha! ha! ha! ha! ha!"

Through his tears he could see the woman pacing the length of her car as she hollered.

"That is *not* funny!" she said. "That is *not* funny! That is *not* funny! That is *not* funny!"

Somehow he'd known what Burney McCarthy would do. Given the chance to crush the woman finally and completely, Burney McCarthy couldn't resist.

"That is *not* funny!" Burney McCarthy said in a near-perfect imitation of the woman. "That is not funny at *all*!"

The woman seemed to implode, then, like a building bombed within. She'd been destroyed, just as Burney McCarthy had intended, and she knew it. The knowledge had struck her mid-sentence, cutting the word *funny* in two, so that even the words before it were transformed, turned at once into a vicious summary of and desperate plea for her life itself. "*This*," she unwittingly had said, "is not *fun*."

The canyon echoed with the cries of the woman's invisible baby and his and Burney McCarthy's laughter. The woman threw herself into the car and rolled down the window and stepped on the gas.

"I hope you pathetic little boys are proud of yourselves!" she cried. "I honestly do!"

"I honestly do! I honestly do!" Burney McCarthy said, and fell back into his laughter. "Ha! ha! ha! ha! ha! ha!"

He watched Burney McCarthy convulsed with his terrible glee, unable, someway, to grasp how such glee could take a person so.

Something had changed in him. The woman had been right. He couldn't say why or how, but none of this was fun. Evidently Burney McCarthy didn't see it that way. Burney McCarthy had got on his knees to mock the woman one last time before crumpling up with laughter.

"Ha! ha! ha! ha! ha! ha! ha! ha! ha!" Burney McCarthy roared. "Ha! ha! ha! ha! ha! ha! ha! ha! ha!"

Burney McCarthy wouldn't stop laughing. Burney McCarthy had laughed so long and hard it occurred to him that by now Burney McCarthy might've lost the power to stop, that by now Burney McCarthy might, as he'd heard it said, be stuck that way forever, like some mortal in a myth condemned to his single joy.

And now he was gripped with terror. He hadn't noticed it, but already dusk had fallen and passed toward night. At some point between the woman's arrival and departure, the world had turned and the light dimmed, and what a moment before had been funny and rare was grown inexplicably sad. Plus he still had to ride up the canyon on his bike. And plus for sure he'd be late, if he wasn't already. He was going to get it. He was going to get it for sure. To what extent he'd get it, no doubt, depended on his mother.

Plus now too he realized that Burney McCarthy's peals of laughter had turned to shrieks of terror and pain, that Burney McCarthy was being torn to shreds by the ghost of some monster like the monster from *20,000 Leagues Under the Sea*. With his whole strength, he hurled a snowball down on the ghost of the monster attacking Burney McCarthy, then another snowball, and another, scooping up one and the next.

"Dude, dude, dude!" Burney McCarthy shouted, and grabbed his arms.

He blinked. He blinked again. Burney McCarthy's face floated before him, less than a foot away, mottled with bits of twigs and snow.

"Are you totally gonzo, or what!"

"You wouldn't stop laughing," he said.

He looked about. Usually when he got still he could hear at least a sparrow in the woods, scratching in the dirt, or maybe the skree of a jay, or, in the evening, like now, some lonesome crow squawking through the dark.

He strained to hear even the rustle of leaves or wind through a bush, but stillness had settled everywhere. The world had gone utterly quiet, utterly still. Together with the gloom, nearly opaque, in which he could discern nothing so much as a fly or worm, the world felt menacing and mournful both, the mood of the Edgar Allan Poe story he'd read last month, "The Fall of the House of Usher."

"Listen," he said.

"What?" Burney McCarthy said. "I don't hear anything."

"That's what I mean."

Burney McCarthy cocked his head like a listening dog. "Whoa, huh," Burney McCarthy said. "Is that sort of creepy, or what?"

"And now I'm late," he said. "Now I'm going to get it."

"Bummer, right."

"Dude, you don't even know."

His mother had a migraine. Almost every time his mother had a migraine, or even just a headache, it hardly mattered what he did. Whatever he did would be wrong enough to get it. And freak it now, too, if he didn't have to ride his bike up the canyon in the dark.

"Maybe we should toke on the rest of that doobie," Burney McCarthy said.

Burney McCarthy's face glistened with melted snow and bits of leaves and dirt. Burney McCarthy's hair hung in his eyes, their whites gone yellowy-pink. Burney McCarthy, in fact, all of Burney McCarthy, was filthy with mud and leaves.

Last summer over in Y he'd heard some college dude complain how the pigs had harshed his mellow bad. Now he knew what the dude must've meant. The dude must've meant this. This whole situation was a bummer. He'd been handed the key to the kingdom of *fantastic*, then seen it snatched away. That was what the dude had meant. His mellow had been totally harshed.

And now he had to go home, back to the crappy house with his crappy mother and father. He'd do just about anything not to have to go back to that crappy house. He considered asking Burney McCarthy if he could sleep over at his house but remembered how creepy and smelly Burney McCarthy's house was, and how sad. At least the house he lived in didn't smell like Burney McCarthy's house, like a fat old man who smoked four packs a day and lived in the basement with a fart machine and gang of drooling ghosts.

"Here," he said, and handed Burney McCarthy the baggie with the doobie.

"You don't want any more?"

"I have to book it, dude, or I'm really going to get it."

"Well, I'll save this then. We can toke on it tomorrow."

He started down the hill, slipping as he went along the roots and stones. He recalled with bitterness that he'd pushed his bike up Burney McCarthy's driveway. He had to walk all the way up Burney McCarthy's long-ass driveway to get his bike then peddle his bike all the way up the long-ass canyon, which with his luck would be pitch-black way before he made it to the crappy house, where, now that he thought about it, what with his filthy clothes and being late and all, he was definitely going to get it.

"Dude, that was rad," Burney McCarthy said to him as he was about to leave.

"Right?" he said.

"High five, man!"

He high-fived Burney McCarthy and pushed off down the drive. "Later," he said.

The road up the canyon was bad. In the stretches without houses and the lights from houses, he couldn't see past his tire. Beneath the canopy of trees above the road, he couldn't tell whether a moon had risen, either, much less any stars, though if a moon had risen he couldn't see it. The road itself, the shoulder on one side and creek on the other—the whole of the canyon, actually—had ceased to exist. He moved within a bubble of sight three feet at most, and all around the bubble stretched a limbo of black.

And then a car overtook him, some giant boat of a thing, a Caddy or Buick from the dark, he didn't know, blaring its horn as it roared by inches away. He felt the car's backdraft, then watched with terror as it melted into night.

Loud as the car had been, he hadn't heard it coming. The car could just as well have materialized from the night itself.

Had he swerved in that instant but a foot to his left, had he drifted even inches, he'd have been splattered on the road like some dippy raccoon. He wouldn't have been merely killed had the car struck him. He'd have exploded—*boom!*—splattered to hell like a moron coon.

That old feeling of dread surged through him now. He wondered sometimes at the speed with which this sense of doom worked, how much power it had to steal through his last, most worthless fiber and cripple him at will.

The car's taillights had dissolved in the dark, but not the sound of its engine, nor the smell of exhaust, what he'd always thought must be the smell of burning hair.

If doom stunk, it must stink of burning hair. And if that were so, then doom with its stench of burning hair was near, doom was imminent, yes, he could've sworn it, and the world had no idea, the world knew nothing of what he knew, nor would it or any creature on it know what he knew, since once doom arrived, once the world had blown up like some moron coon whacked by a car on a country road, neither the world nor anything on it could know anything, much less what he knew.

All would be black.

That was all.

His legs were burning. He didn't like to think of walking his bike through the dark, but if he wanted relief he'd have to walk his bike. But the greater his delay, the worse his pain when he got home. Already he was late. The question wasn't whether he was going to get it but how much. It didn't matter. His legs were burning. He'd have to walk.

Then he felt the road slacken and knew he'd entered a dip. If he pedaled hard for that extra bump when the road picked up, he could coast a little before he had to walk. But just as he put down his head, the bike dissolved beneath him, and he was flying.

He'd been right. Doom had been near.

He'd hit a stone with his front tire and got thrown into the night. He was, as he always heard his father say about this or that poor sap, fucked.

The darkness was total, he was blind.

Then the palm of his hand felt like it had been whacked with a bat. Then the palm of his hand felt like it had been sheared with a grater. Then the same bat whacked him on the shoulder, the same grater ran across his chin, and then the bat once again, accompanied now by the sound of clattering, whacked him on the hip.

When he opened his eyes, he was looking at stars through trees, and, yes, at the moon now, too, at the depths of his vision, just above the ridge through a hole in the trees.

He thought, how funny, it was like cartoons, the stars were reeling away. For a moment, it seemed he'd been knocked out, but he hadn't. He'd been almost-knocked-out, the way he had last month when his father punched him in the face with a full-on fist.

He lay gazing at the massing stars. That was the heavens he saw up there, he thought, that was infinity. He could look out into the black night sky shimmering with its countless stars and know for certain he'd never see its end.

His face burned, his chin. His mouth was full of dirty salt. He ran two fingers over his chin and held them to the moonlight, then sat up and spit into his hand.

No way was this the kingdom of *fantastic*. He didn't know the name of this kingdom, if kingdom you could call it. You could call it anything you liked, just not the kingdom of *fantastic*. Crap was better. This was the kingdom of crap. Or, no, not even a kingdom, but a village, or less than a village, even, just a *place*, more like it, the crappy place of crap.

The stink of burning hair lingered in his head. He wondered whether he smelled the real stink of burning hair, of the giant car's crappy exhaust, or whether he merely imagined or remembered the stink of burning hair. It didn't matter. He could smell it. Together with the stink in his nose, the blood in his mouth and doubt in his mind made up the crappy place of crap.

His bike in the road looked like a pile of rotten sticks some jerk had painted silver. If another crappy car came along, especially a giant boat of a crappy car, it would run right over his bike and never know, the bike would crumble like rotten sticks. He knew he couldn't just leave the bike. And yet he didn't want to get the bike, either. He didn't want to do anything, much less get up. And if he did get up, and if he did get his bike, he didn't want to ride it home. Besides, that wasn't home. That was a lie. That was another broken link in that huckster's chain of rickety crappy lies.

He spat in his hand to see his blood. He'd cut his lip good, and his chin, too, his mouth was still all dirty salt. From his ear to his chin, he knew, his face was road-rashed good. Wherever he touched his jaw, it burned like a road rash burned. Tomorrow his face would look like a dog's pussy in heat. His face would look like a big dirty butt crack. Everyone would call him a dirty butt crack, a city slicker with an ass packed full of city-slicker zits and a face like a pussy in heat.

He thought of Ken Maeng. Except for that guy Roberto who'd driven him home that night after he tried to run away with his hobo stick, who was Mexican or Argentine, he guessed, Ken Maeng, the Korean kid in his class whose real name was Byeoung-keun Maeng, was the only kid he'd ever known who wasn't white.

Everyone at school said Ken Maeng was a freak. One kid, not Randy Bartlett or Bruce Ledbetter or Brad Hansen or any of the other idiot jerks, they were too stupid, had said Ken Maeng was freaky as a spider from Mars, which, stupid as he felt thinking it, was why he figured when he saw Ken Maeng that sometimes he thought actually of spiders, and not just any old spiders, but big-ass gnarly spiders like banana spiders and tarantulas.

Ken Maeng's hair was pretty long, longer than his, but not longer than Burney McCarthy's, yet instead of pushing it behind his ears, or just letting it hang down like he and Burney McCarthy let their long hair hang, Ken Maeng kept his hair plastered to the side with about twenty cans of Aqua Net.

Ken Maeng's hair had grown so brittle from the Aqua Net that when Randy Bartlett took hold of Ken Maeng's hair that day last winter it was super cold and dry, Ken Maeng's hair had snapped in two. Randy Bartlett massively tripped out—everybody tripped out massively—then ran off waving a chunk of Ken Maeng's hair, cackling and hollering about how he, Randy Bartlett, had faced the chink.

After lunch, he found Ken Maeng at the terrarium full of mosquitoes the students kept for science, wearing Mr. Spring's tam o'shanter. Ken Maeng must've heard him enter the room. He'd knocked a wastebasket over plus a couple of umbrellas, but Ken Maeng didn't look up. He said hello to Ken Maeng, but still Ken Maeng didn't look. Nor did Ken Maeng answer. Ken Maeng didn't say anything. Ken Maeng was crying.

When he tried to think when Ken Maeng spoke after that, even to Mr. Spring, he couldn't a single time. After Randy Bartlett had broken off a chunk of Ken Maeng's hair, and everyone had massively tripped out, Ken Maeng never spoke again.

He thought of never speaking to his mother and father again the way Ken Maeng had never spoken again, but knew it would be useless.

If he said nothing to his mother's questions, his mother would slap him for saying nothing. His mother would slap him for saying something, and his mother would slap him for saying nothing. And then his father would arrive, and the trouble would start again. Not to mention now, too, he could never say for sure when his father might knock him out by punching him in the face with a full-on fist.

He wished with all his heart he could be like Ken Maeng, strong enough never to speak again.

He heard another car. He couldn't see the lights through the trees yet but thought it best to move his bike. The last thing he wanted was to get hit in the dark on a lonely road by a stupid giant car. He saw the lights through the trees and heard the pitter-patter of the engine and for an instant felt his throat tighten at the thought the car might be his father's. Then the car rattled round the bend, a crappy little Bug, honking away till, like the crappy car before, it vanished into night.

"Jerk!" he shouted, and gave the car the finger. "Fucker," he said. "Asshole fucking bastard," he said.

How lame was he anyhow? He couldn't stay silent for even a minute. No one could hear him. His words meant nothing, yet still he'd had to speak his words. And then he thought, no, it wasn't absurd, he *had* had to speak his words. Nobody else was going to speak his words. Nobody else could speak his words because nobody else knew the words to speak. That sort of silence was bad silence. Sometimes silence spoke, other times silence said nothing. Silence without knowing spoke without meaning. But knowing silence spoke with meaning that silenced meaninglessness. But sometimes speaking silenced meaninglessness, also.

A wind swept through the trees. The moon had risen. He could see it now glimmering through the trees, nearly full but not. Beneath him, just off the road, the creek murmured round its stones. All along, the creek had been running by the road down the canyon, but till now he hadn't heard it. There it ran, the creek full of crayfish and minnows and moss. He could see the creek, now, too. The moon's light was shining through the trees.

He wondered which of the moons was real, the moon in the sky or the moon on the water of the creek. And then it seemed maybe both were fake, and both real. And one was a flower in the sky, and one a flower on the creek. As for the moons in his eyes, they were flowers, too, flowers in his eyes, and everything he knew, and everything he heard, was silence.

THE EXILE

Hell is truth seen too late.
—*Thomas Hobbes*

For months before Christmas, when I was seventeen, I talked of nothing but the ax I had to have to see me on the stage I'd dreamt of roaming, banging my head and smashing shit up like any rocker worth the name—Jim(i/my)s Morrison, Hendrix, Page, Keiths Richards and Moon, Ozzy Osbourne, Ace Frehley, Bon Scott, old Pete Townsend, and youthful Angus Young . . .

I'd played soccer as a boy, till I was a junior at high school, when, stoned and drunk as I'd become, I quit my five teams—the varsity lineup, the city of Y's under-18 all-star squad, Y College, the Mexican squad on which I alone spoke no Spanish, plus another local pick up gang—and, at 6'1"/145, joined the rugby team, a down-and-dirty crew of fucked-up boys gorked to the gills every time we took the field.

Thin as string, I might take this hit or that, the way I did in the first play of my first game, when some kid broke my nose, but none of it stopped me from clinging to every kid I smashed for as long as I could to cover him with as much of my blood as I could. The idea to bleed on the guys I tackled I got from my father's brother. The one time my father struck someone other than his sons had been long before, when as a boy my father punched his kid brother on the nose. In revenge, my father's brother pinned my father to the dirt, then watched my father squirm with horror as he shook his blood into my father's face.

Violence was good, I loved violence, but not enough to kill my dream to rock. The Beatles were my favorite of my father's LPs, and *Sergeant Pepper's Lonely Hearts Club Band* my favorite of The Beatles, though I loved as well *Rubber Soul, Revolver, The White Album,* and *Abbey Road,* plus Mike Oldfield's soundtrack for *The Exorcist—Tubular Bells—*and Pink Floyd's *Wish You Were Here* and *Dark Side of the Moon,* and every piece of wax by Zeppelin and The Stones.

That my father had just one of these was miraculous. My mother hated rock and roll so much, my mother hated *music* so much, to have heard her rant about its evils you might've believed she thought the stuff to be, say, *the roar of some iron maiden, broadcast,* say, *through a bullhorn on the back of a serpent from hell.* My mother hated rock and roll, that was all, my mother hated music, that was all, I was forbidden music with her in the house—that was all.

If I didn't want to suffer a tirade at best or a beating at worst, the times I listened to rock and roll were on the floor before my father's turntable, hidden in headphones, I now realized, my father had got to hide himself. Often I did this for days at a stretch, lost in soundscapes, lost in books, the one refuge I could find past the mysteries of intoxication and violence.

But for all of that, still, my dream to rock wasn't much different than my dream to play pro soccer, or later, for a time, to range some national forest in a funny hat. My dream was just the dream that, without help, was all it would ever be.

My father may have come to a ball game here and there, but he rarely cheered for more. As for my mother, she was ill from the start. In those days, the best I could gather from the fits that drove her to attack me, from her words themselves, was that she'd never have married my father were it not for me, she'd never have been left to the dreary visions of the lower-middle class were it not for me, where breaks were rare as hen's teeth and comets.

Then I met Tommy Dallen, my ax-shredding pal for the next twenty years, and my dream returned. Come golden days or ruin, I vowed, I was going to get an ax. Nor would I take any but a real ax, I vowed, the ax I plugged in and tore shit up with, the ax I bagged chicks with, the ax I joined a motherfucking band with. I didn't need an amp, I told my mother and father, the ax to start was fine, by the time I was good enough to rock with an amp, I told my mother and father, they'd not have heard a peep from me because I'd have earned the coin to score the amp myself and rock in another town.

But the answer from my mother and father never changed: you can have a violin, my mother and father said, you can have an oboe, they said, you can have, they said, in short, any instrument any little puss can play, but you can never have an electric guitar, you can never have an ax.

A FEW YEARS EARLIER, DURING MY FAMILY'S SOJOURN IN that hamlet of cretins and goons to the east of Y by the bay, I'd joined the percussion section of my grammar school's orchestra without say-so from my mother and father and received for practice at home a pair of sticks and little rubber pad. I should've known I wouldn't be let to practice at home any more than I'd been let to listen—my mother couldn't stand *that horrible rat-a-tat-tat*. And it wasn't only that I couldn't practice in the common rooms, or even behind the closed door of the room I shared with my kid brother. I couldn't practice on the deck outside, or in the arbor below, or certainly within earshot of my mother. Still, I had to practice, still, I *wanted* to practice, and so I kept on with my little drummer's sticks, rat-a-tat-tatting on my little rubber pad, heedless of the scolding I took for talking back every time my mother screeched, heedless, too, of the beatings I took when the scolding failed. Then one day my mother said if I wanted so badly to play, I could go right ahead and play. All I had to do was march into the woods with my little rubber pad and my little drummer's sticks and find a good little rock or stump. You march up into the woods and find yourself a rock or stump, my mother said, and you can play till you bleed.

Little did I know when we moved to Y that the woods were filled with poison oak. Hardly would I have survived one attack of poison oak than I'd be slapped down by another. Roughly half those days in Y I spent with poison oak, my body itself a wound. I could scarcely open my eyes or mouth, I couldn't take any but Jell-O through straws and juice through straws, I couldn't rise from my bed without the nastiest of pain, since any time I left the sheets, the pus from the wounds that had turned to scabs were ripped away, like hair with tape. My mother brought water and Jell-O and juice, then placed the straws between my lips. My father bore me moaning to the toilet, where to shit my watery shit was to be cut in two, and wiping my ass made no matter, my ass was a sieve of pus. Potions, unguents, salves proved useless, as well, and the best that doctors could give were Cortisone shots and pledges of a lull in a day or two.

It would be years before I saw that these were the days I first began to brood in thoughts of suicide. I'd always believed

I was born with thoughts of suicide, like I was born with a penis: the possibility of suicide seemed never to have not been in my mind.

Lying in my bed, I remember, I wondered how I might get my hands on the rifle with which in his youth my father said he shot rabbits but now kept in his closet and forbade my brothers and I to so much as glimpse.

I wondered how I might load my father's rifle, then drag myself to the woods to stick its barrel in my mouth and work the trigger with my toe.

I thought to claw my way through the dark to the road to be smashed by a truck, I thought to blow myself up with a home-made bomb, I thought to dive down Half Dome or lie on the tracks at the edge of town, that some moonless night the train would kill me and the animals eat what was left.

I thought to drown myself in a filthy lake.

I thought to roast in flames like a martyred saint.

I thought to slice my wrists and gash my throat and split my guts like the man on TV, a Rorschach of blood in my bed.

That would be best, I thought, to slash myself up in bed, where my mother and father would find what was left and know I'd done it for them.

It goes without saying I soon quit rat-a-tat-tatting with my little drummer's sticks on my little rubber pad. And of course I quit the orchestra.

Largely because of my allergy to poison oak, my mother and father moved us from the hamlet of Y with its cretins and goons to the city of Y by the bay, with its different, more diverse cretins and goons.

No one suspected me an addict yet, getting fucked up

daily on my father's weed. And now through my drug-dealing, booze-guzzling cohorts at school, together with their older brothers and friends, I quickly added to the weed any booze I could find and, soon thereafter, blow, as well, together with a steady mix of pills. And just as I'd found my first drug buddy in Burney McCarthy when I was ten, I found my next in a misfit like myself, good Art Ingram, whose mother had sent him up from the hole in the ass that's the San Y Valley to live with Flip and Drea, his dope-smoking, blow-snorting uncle and aunt.

I was thirteen when I met Art Ingram, thirteen when I met Flip and Drea, and thirteen still when Flip and Drea turned me on to blow. Flip and Drea, I now realize, had to've been dealers, they had so much blow, virtual mountains of blow, what I now realize were ounces and ounces of blow.

Thirteen, and already I was baked on both sides, already I'd slunk on down to the flatlands of Y by the bay—down to the barrio, as it was known, to a caddywhompus shack bounded by the multitudes of caddywhompus shacks in which subsisted multitudes more of booze- and dope-pounding drones, scores of them straight-up gangbangers—where on a thrift-store couch next to Art Ingram and his drug-pushing, drug-gobbling uncle and aunt, I commenced to snuffleupagus mounds of blow at a pop, goggle-eyed by the tube watching *The Streets of San Francisco, The Rockford Files, The Odd Couple, Cannon, Hawaii Five-0*, while from the hi-fi a steady flow of Van Halen and Cheap Trick attended the roar in my head.

And when I wasn't plopped down on Flip and Drea's couch snuffleupagussing mound after mound of blow, I vented my rage in schoolyard brawls, and sawed through the forest on my BMX, and shot down hills on my skateboard, and swung by rope over canyons of rock.

And then my dream came true in flesh and blood and shiny guitars. Tommy Dallen looked like a man, or at least like a grown up, knuckle-headed kid that he still was—by fifteen, the guy stood six-feet-three, with hair so thick he could've been a walking, dancing bear-skin rug. And Tommy Dallen had not one but two bad-ass guitars, a Fender Telecaster, sparkly gold, and a Gibson ES 339, together with the wall-of-sound Marshall through which he made those fuckers wail.

It took just one demonstration of Tommy Dallen's manifestly rock-starish powers for me to resume my pleas for an ax. *Get me a guitar for Christmas,* I begged my mother and father, *I'll find a deal, Tommy knows all about them, he'll help me pick a good one, I'll get an amp later, you don't have to buy me any clothes when school starts, you don't have to get me anything else for the next forty years, please, please, please just get me that guitar . . .*

When a month or so before Christmas I announced to my mother and father I'd found a deal in a pawn shop in downtown Y—a '68 Fender Mustang with that sweet nitrocellulose finish of daphne blue, for just a hundred-and-twenty bucks—my mother and father said in no uncertain terms my wish was out of the question, my wish was off the charts, the price of my wish was past their means, don't ask again, not ever, the answer was now and would never not be absolutely, emphatically NO.

But my mother and father's refusals didn't mean shit. I was a dog, though if I'd not been a dog, but a cat, and as numb, it didn't matter. Until I heard YES from my mother and father, I'd refuse to hear a word at all. *I'll pay you back,* I hounded, *I'll do chores,* I howled, *I'll sell my ass on the street. I'll do anything and anything,* I hounded and howled, *so long as you please please please please please please please get me that guitar . . .*

I'D HAD TOO MUCH FAITH IN MY POWER TO CRUSH THE WILL of my mother and father, which, actually, was how I'd seen our relationship then, as a struggle between two sets of wills.

I survived all catastrophes, smashed all foes. My mother and father could beat me down, the world could beat me down, the world could slash me to the utmost core, but sooner or later I'd rise another time to go another round, as I always had, as I always would, till I smashed my oppressor or through sheer attrition forced my oppressor to yield.

With my will alone, I believed, I could force my mother and father into flustered shame, and in that shame to yield. As long as my mother and father got me that guitar, I didn't care what they said or did. I'd have won.

But I'd been wrong.

Clearly, I'd been wrong.

Christmas Day I found no package by the tree shaped anything like a guitar or even like a box for a guitar. And when my two brothers and I tore the wrappings off our identically shaped presents, we found we had each received identical gifts—*cameras,* Minolta XD5 35mm cameras, *brand spanking new* Minolta XD5 35mm cameras.

As I opened my gift, my mother and father gazed down with their phony expressions of holiday care and then, as I saw what they'd done, as the realization of their betrayal commenced its final assault and my face collapsed with bewilderment and pain, my mother and father's faces transformed from phony care to phony indignity, the only gambit, I saw, as well, they could entertain, being the only gambit that might succeed.

I, their phony faces said, was the ingrate to beat all ingrates.

I, their phony faces said, was the traitor, I, the maker of schisms and grief.

My one response, their phonily indignant faces said, should've been—and was a crime to be other—gratitude and glee.

I had devoted the last of my atoms to willing the appearance in my hands of that blue guitar. I had longed for that guitar, I'd prayed for that guitar, I'd laid in bed at night whispering to myself, *Please please please just get me that guitar, and I'll be your slave forever.*

The boy in *Willy Wonka and the Chocolate Factory*, little Charlie Bucket?—that kid had nothing on me. Charlie Bucket was obsessed with a one-time tour through a factory. Charlie Bucket sang songs about his dream to find a golden pass to a factory, Charlie Bucket wept with fear he'd fail to find a pass to a factory, and then Charlie Bucket lost his little boy's bird when the chocolate bar his poor family had pooled their money to buy didn't contain his pass to the factory.

My treasured guitar, on the other hand, was the means to a whole new way of life, of musicianhood, and freedom, and maybe even stardom, the life I longed to live all day, every day, until the day I died.

But when by the Christmas tree that morning I opened their package and saw what my mother and father had tried to foist on me—a thing I had no interest in and hadn't once expressed the slightest interest in—the tiny ember in my heart, what remained of the fire of hope that had once been my dream, vanished in a wisp, and I was sucked into the void.

I'd been lambasted, I'd been scourged, I'd been beaten,

molested, ridiculed, shamed, neglected, manipulated, and ignored by my mother and father, and now they'd revealed their intentions and confirmed their design, to kill my dream and chain me to their will forever, at all costs.

Yet until that moment, despite the hell I'd endured, my will had also endured, I'd somehow managed to keep my ember burning, with my will I'd guarded my ember like hunters of yore the fire in their horns, with my will I'd tended and nurtured that ember for my life, because, in a very real way, this was true, that little ember *was* my life, my dream of beautiful violence and violent beauty in a life of rock and roll.

Inasmuch as I'd wanted to believe myself other than the rest of the world's children, however, I wasn't one cell different.

The rest of the world's children believe they need others to believe in them to amount to anything more than a parasite in life. And as I'd also been told, so also did I believe.

I needed to know my mother and father believed in me.

Charlie Bucket's family believed in him, ludicrous as his dream was, hopeless as it was.

It didn't matter that Charlie Bucket's dream was but a dream about a dream, a dream in which Charlie Bucket could dream of entering yet another dream, the fantasy world of Willy Wonka, itself a factory of dreams.

Little Charlie Bucket could've wanted a goldfish, a model, a cheap plastic clown, and Charlie Bucket's family would've found a way to get it—at the very least Charlie Bucket's family would've found a way to *try* to get it.

The dream itself, what Charlie Bucket's family gave Charlie Bucket, held no value. The *feeling* behind the dream, the *effort* behind the *feeling*—*that* was what mattered, that was what the dream meant, their love for Charlie Bucket, their unconditional *belief* in Charlie Bucket. What Charlie Bucket's family wanted made not a whit of difference, unless of course Charlie Bucket wanted it, too.

Until I met Tommy Dallen, I hadn't encountered such a family as Charlie Bucket's. When I saw such families existed, in my own little stamp of the world, no less, as Tommy Dallen's family proved—a family that supported the least of Tommy Dallen's wishes, that went to all lengths to support and encourage Tommy Dallen's dream to rock—the paucity of my own family stood so much the starker.

Tommy Dallen's family was Charlie Bucket's family, but with coin.

Tommy Dallen's family had both the means and the heart to help Tommy Dallen sing.

Seeing the love Tommy Dallen's family gave him, seeing the genuine support Tommy Dallen's family gave him, psychologically, emotionally, financially—Tommy Dallen's family actually regularly *requested* that he sing and play for them—I saw as well not just the things my own family had never given me, but all of the things they never would give, all of the things, if I wanted them, I'd have to get for myself, somehow, foremost among them *love*.

As I sat by the tree that morning, scowling at the camera in my lap while self-pity shot me through and through, I was crushed by deprivation, crushed by hardship, crushed by countless mundane failures and defeats.

Yes, I'd been given things, and I knew it.

I'd been given a bicycle and a skateboard, too—a skateboard, even, that my father had gone so far as to make himself from anodized aluminum with tools at his job.

And every year I'd been given a uniform for soccer, and gifts on Christmases and birthdays.

Nor had I ever gone hungry or cold. Had I wanted to be fat, I could've been fat in a thick wool sweater and jacket and snow hat on my head.

Yet, as I'd always vaguely sensed and now clearly knew, I never received anything from my mother and father that didn't reflect some aspect of what they themselves wanted or wanted me to be, and never had my mother and father failed to let me know I should know my fortune for it all.

I received not a stick without the implicit, and often outright, contention that that stick never came from any but the goodwill of my mother and father, that, in fact, the ability to tie my shoes, every bite of food I chewed, all of my power and all of my virtues, had derived from a favor granted by them in their infinite wisdom and infinite grace.

I was told I had a "better" life than most kids, and if not better than the kids in America then than everywhere else. Pictures in *National Geographic*, of Burmese peasants gumming betel with their ruined teeth, and painted Aborigines dancing through clouds of dust, made my blessings plain, as every flag-waving American would agree. Certainly, I was told by my mother and father, along with this and that random flag-waving American, I didn't have trouble like that.

I didn't wake up each day to a pile of dung by my crib of straw, I didn't wake up to fire and blood and demijohns empty of bad water. Nor was I wearing a loincloth of grass before a hut of wattle and daub, picking at grubs as I scanned the shadows for beasts. And for sure I wasn't chained to a conveyer belt, sucking up carcinogens while sifting stones from coal, nor was I bent beneath a devil sun reaping plantains or coffee or mangoes for someone else, in an orchard owned by someone else, whose plantains or coffee or mangoes I myself could never with my labor buy, nor was I suffering any other such deprivation or abuse.

But I had more than cheap paranoia to fuel the certainty that my mother and father weren't striving once and for all merely to destroy my dream but once and for all to destroy *me myself.*

My dream got in the way of the dream of my mother and father.

My dream took them from themselves.

My mother and father, therefore, I was certain, had to crush *me*, at which point neither I nor any dream of mine could plague them ever again.

And the best way to crush me, my mother and father had to have believed—this being their genius—was to crush my dream.

EARLIER THAT YEAR, IN THE SPRING, MY MOTHER AND FATHER told my brothers and me that we'd been robbed.

Though I couldn't see the least evidence of this—no jimmied locks, rifled drawers, shattered glass, gutted beds— none of the damage you see in crime shows and movies on TV—my mother and father told my brothers and me that all of my mother's jewelry had been stolen, plus a number of my father's tools, together with other divers and sundry items, excluding, for some mysterious reason, items such as our stereo system and TV.

Then, a month or so later, or perhaps two or three, as if by actual magic, a grand piano appeared in our house, followed by a duo of suede Italian sofas and a coffee table in two modular sections of polished travertine. A new set of rings appeared on my mother and father's fingers, as well, diamonds in both, set in platinum or white gold or whatever, and then again, to top it off, my mother commenced to prance about in a new fur coat. Other divers and sundry items materialized, too, among them a new bedroom set in my mother and father's room.

Certainly my mother and father had acquired this set by my senior year in high school, since at that time, when they took a trip to Mexico without us boys (the first such trip they'd ever taken—till then, my family had never had a formal vacation, featuring air travel and hotels, but instead only trips in used cars (my mother and father had never owned a brand new car) to campsites in the mountains or the homes of relatives in southern Y and, once, Y in the dusty South), I slept in my mother and father's bed with my girlfriend, Tia Tiller, the sweetest, naughtiest little Mormon an angry horndog like myself could've ever hoped to meet.

As if any of these odd happenings weren't enough to convince me my request for an electric guitar had been warranted, one of my father's relatives, I never learned who, had bequeathed to my father a sum of money too small to do anything major with but large enough to add an entertainment room to our house by fixing up the basement.

Until the days when diamond rings and grand pianos and fancy suede couches began to appear in our house, appearances by which I'd been quietly baffled, money was never something my family possessed much of, nor was there much left after these appearances. If my having ceased to receive an allowance when I was eight or nine hadn't made our situation plain, my mother and father's fights about our seeming penury destroyed that confusion without question.

For the longest time I had no idea where money came from, and even after I'd learned, years would pass before I began to fathom the workings of the most basic economics. Outside my mother and father's fights, neither my mother nor my father discussed money with my brothers or me.

Until the days when diamond rings and grand pianos and fancy suede couches appeared in our house, I had assumed my father simply earned money.

Doubtless my father did earn money, only not the way I'd assumed he earned it, by performing labor similar to my delivering papers. As I collected money at the end of each month from the people I delivered papers to each day, so my father drove off to do some job or other, like adding numbers on a calculator or making expenditure reports with the same ploddingly stoned insistence that characterized the way he raked the yard or prepped a window sill to paint, for which labor, whatever it was, I assumed, my father received money at the end of every month.

More or less, I assumed, adults and children did the same sort of work, but since adults were adults they received more money for their labor than the kids. Once you were an adult, I assumed, all you had to do was work, and at the end of every month you received the money with which you bought your house and car and food and clothes.

By the time the diamond rings and grand pianos and marble tables and fancy suede couches had appeared in our house, my brothers and I had been so well programmed to silence regarding all matters fiscal that I never gave the matter any thought.

Probably I'd assumed (with the same mindlessness I assumed the source of my father's earnings) the appearance of this stuff to have come from the earnings my mother received at her new job with some winery in the foothills to the south, which job I'd also assumed accounted for the appearance of thirty or so cases of wine at the back of our basement, stolen, as I learned years later, by my mother, just as my mother stole everything else.

I knew little of the world then.

Among the countless things whose workings were beyond me, it never occurred to me to connect, on one hand, the appearance in our house of grand pianos and diamond rings and fancy Italian sofas and, on the other hand, the robbery my parents claimed our home had suffered.

Had my father not connected these two events for me years later, I doubt I'd have connected them myself. At the time, I knew merely that something had changed. I knew merely that while the sun of a sudden heyday had risen for my mother and father, the same old fog of drab normality had refused to fade for my brothers and me.

Dimly I sensed that sofas and pianos and rings appearing from the mists didn't gibe with my brothers and I wearing the same old clothes, riding the same old bikes, mowing the same old lawns, throwing the same old papers, and receiving the same old zero allowances, but that was all.

Besides, understanding better wouldn't have changed the situation. Experience had proven so. If doing this or that for us boys redounded in some way to the wellbeing or pleasure of my mother and father, my mother and father might do this or that. Conversely, any inclination to ignore us boys was held against the same criterion.

And while I could never meaningfully articulate any of what I sensed back then—my mother and father's ongoing skullduggery, that is, which I'd been trained to believe was nothing more than the product of a fertile but no less febrile imagination—my father's admission years later that not so much as a lint ball had ever been taken from my mother and father's house by anyone but my mother and father confirmed my sense and justified my doubt.

It was true, after all.

My mother and father were liars.

Our house had not been robbed.

Our house had never been robbed.

Which wasn't to say thieves hadn't slipped through our door. Thieves had very much slipped through our door. Long ago thieves had slipped through our door, but once they'd got in they never left, but like a worm in a body stayed there quietly, steadily thieving.

My mother and father had concocted a scam to swindle their insurance company, and then my mother and father had proceeded actually to swindle their insurance company by submitting a fraudulent claim according to which thousands of dollars' worth of chattel had been stolen from our house. Believing my mother and father's lie, the insurance company reimbursed my mother and father for the thousands of dollars' worth of chattel purportedly stolen from our house. Then, the moment my mother and father received the insurance company's money for the thousands of dollars' worth of chattel that had never been stolen from our house, my mother and father rushed out to spend the bulk of that money on expensive new chattel for themselves and but a pittance of that money— enough to buy three brand new Minolta XD5 35mm cameras— on stuff for their three sons.

THE COMMISSION OF ATROCITIES IS POSSIBLE ONLY AFTER we've silenced the truth by which we discern harmony from harm.

The way we rationalize the commission of atrocities against the whole of existence, and especially against ourselves, differs not one iota from the way the old vivisectionist did when he severed the vocal cords of the animal he was torturing to prevent the animal from screaming.

The matter is simple.

It's the logic on which the history of the writing of history is built.

History as we know it is what the historian says it is.

To *pretend* our atrocities never happened, to *pretend* our atrocities never made so much of history, we need simply ensure no one ever sees or hears them.

But even if an atrocity is seen or heard, if that atrocity isn't spoken, and if that atrocity isn't written, still that atrocity didn't happen, still that atrocity *could not* have happened.

What can have existed or happened that hasn't been spoken or written?

The clash of titans and roar of progress have never made history. Beneath it all, like a chasm beneath thin ice, lays a void.

It is this—*the void*—that makes as much the historian's history as the history the historian speaks and writes.

It is this void, in truth, that makes true history.

True history is never the history we find in the historian's books.

True history is silence.

My whole life, and especially my life as a boy in the shadow of my mother and father, has been an inexorable drive toward quietus.

My mother and father have been the historians.

I have been the history, I have been what my mother and father have said I am or am not.

And the truth has at all costs been avoided.

IN THE MOMENT I GLIMPSED THE CAMERA'S NAME AND MAKE on the box inside the wrapping, I saw, as if for the first time, the utter contempt with which my mother and father must have always seen me.

Rarely will a parent admit such contempt. Typically, in fact, the parent almost always shudders with feigned outrage at the mere suggestion of such.

But what the parent says can never efface what the parent has done and does.

The parent's words align with the parent's actions, or the parent's words do not align with the parent's actions.

I no longer wonder how in one instant I could be praised for the mind of a genius or looks of a star and in the next condemned for an idiot beast, clawed with nails and beaten with spoons, fondled in the bathroom and under the sheets, jerked by the ear, poked in the chest, punched in the face, ridiculed, jeered at, ignored.

I no longer wonder that—to this day—neither my mother nor my father admit to a single instance of their crimes.

Nor do I wonder how, to the contrary, my mother and father still see fit to accuse me of imagining these transgressions, that *I* have conjured up these stories of mine, that *I*, not them, am the liar.

And though I wonder at many, many matters today, none of these matters are any longer among them. Today I see my mother and father not just as they were, but as they have remained.

When I was seventeen, however, there on the floor by the tree with my unwanted camera, these truths, flagrant as they'd become—that my mother and father had never nurtured me, never supported my dreams, never cheered me on with unconditional love, that my mother and father had never once understood me, all of which I was seeing as if for the first time—these and other truths, too, brutal and shocking as they were, back then, when I was seventeen, held nothing for me but anguish.

My difficulty had never lain in my inability to wrest clarity from the dilemma into which my mother and father's position set me. It lay simply and precisely in the task by which I found myself now confounded, in the task, that is, of *accepting* that position.

I hadn't conceded to my knowledge of my mother and father's position for the one reason that *I did not like to concede.*

Once we know the truth of a thing, we can never *not* know the truth of a thing.

I know the sun will rise each day.

I know without the sun's rising the process we know as *day* has no meaning.

And I know I must breathe air, I know I must eat food and drink water, and shit shit and piss piss, just as I know also that I know these things, just as I know also that these are things I can never *not* know.

The knowing, then, was one thing, the conceding very much another.

Concession would have demanded action, and, among those I could've taken, just one would've been acceptable. No matter how young, I would have had to leave.

But leaving, as I'd learned, I couldn't do, not for a time, despite all of my effort and all of my will. As despicable as my mother and father were, I needed my mother and father.

Seeing this need, now, I see as well its damage.

In the same way I'd refused to admit I knew my mother and father's position toward me, I'd refused with equal stubbornness to admit my reliance on them. And I'd refused to concede to my dependence because the moment I conceded, I knew, I'd loathe myself past hope.

Already I loathed myself. Already I held myself in the lowest way. No one was as cruel to me as I was to myself, not even my mother and father. My mother and father could've vaporized when I was seven, but I would already have received from them everything I needed to lash myself ragged for all my days.

My mother and father no longer required a bell to make me slather.

The bell was in my mind, the bell *was* my mind.

My mother and father had put the bell there, and then my mother and father had rung that bell until any difference between it and my mind had vanished.

My mother and father had taught me well to crave reward and fear punishment.

My mother and father had taught me well to believe the laws according to which reward and punishment are meted out, and with such fervor that the instant I went so far as to contemplate an act to one side or other of those laws, I rewarded or punished myself accordingly.

I had assumed the task of administering my own control. I was now at once my own master and my own slave. The hand I held was the hand that held me down.

I realized as I stared at my mother and father's camera that the ties had been broken, the games ended, I was on my own.

I had always been on my own, I knew, but now the break was formal, now there was no going back, now there was nothing to go back to. And for the rest of my life, no matter the people I was "with," I would still be on my own.

The difference lay in my readiness to make good with this truth, even if my readiness was as petty as the rest.

I knew what I knew.

Ready or not, I had no choice.

I no longer had a place to turn.

I was cornered at last.

I had lost.

I was on my own.

IT WAS THEN THE WORLD BEGAN TO SHUDDER.

I couldn't speak any more than think, I'd been rendered stupid and inert.

A long time passed before I saw I hadn't breathed. I may as well have been drowning, I was drowning in my rage. And then somehow my rage thinned for the second I needed to see that if only I took a breath, all would be well, the world would be well, my mind would be restored, reason would return, the universe would show me what to do.

I took a breath.

I took another breath, then, and another and another, until I understood: I was on my own now, and now that was so, *I had no obligation to anyone,* much less to my mother and father, *I could do as I pleased anytime I liked,* yes—*I could simply leave the room.*

And then like a boss yet another insight cut me, a devastating truth: without exception, every single thing I'd understood before had been a lie. *I hadn't been defeated but sanctioned.*

With a gambit intended to crush me, my mother and father had given me instead what, beyond their love, I had craved more than anything else. However indirectly, for all intents and purposes, *my mother and father had handed me the means to buy my treasured electric guitar.*

The brand new Minolta XD5 35mm camera my mother and father had just given me was good as money itself, if not more valuable than the guitar, then at least valuable enough to warrant an even trade.

This camera was mine!

I could do what I wanted with this camera!

I could shoot this camera into space, I could smash this camera in a vise, I could lose this camera in a cave, I could hawk it for drugs, I could grant it to the kids of Thalidomide, anything, anything, if that was what I wanted.

But naturally I wouldn't hawk my new camera for drugs or shoot it into space or grant it to the kids of Thalidomide. I was going to take my new camera to the pawnshop with Tommy Dallen and trade it for my cherished guitar.

Meanwhile, I needed simply to walk away from my mother and father and brothers with my new camera and go to my room in silence. My mother and father had wanted to silence me with their gambit, and they had. But the silence they had bargained for wasn't the silence I'd give them, because the silence I'd give them had *everything to do with me* and *nothing to do with them.*

My mother and father would be the object of *my* silence, now. *I* would be silent because *I* would choose not to speak, no matter what my mother and father said or did. I would be silent because I could be silent, and, more, because I wanted to be silent, because being silent was *my* desire.

With my brand new Minolta XD5 35mm camera, I smiled at my mother and father and walked away.

My mother and father's smiles had disappeared.

My mother and father's smiles had vanished in defeat, I knew, and in agony and despair.

The sound of my mother's choked gasp and my father's demand to explain, which I ignored, confirmed this. I didn't look back, but walked to my room and locked the door.

A moment later my father barked my name and pounded down the hall to wrestle with my doorknob as he ordered me to open up, but I stayed on the side of my bed, smiling at my new camera, which I'd shortly trade for my guitar.

"Just who the hell do you think you are?" my father hollered, and set to pounding on the door. "Patrick? Do you hear me, *Son*? You open this door right goddamned now!" After a time, my father began his threats. "If you don't open this door this instant," my father said, "there'll be hell to pay. I'm telling you, *Son*, I won't be responsible for what happens if you don't open up."

Several times in my fear of my father I almost caved. My power had good reason, but my fear had maybe more. Years ago, in the doorway of the kitchen of our little cabin in the town of Y, my father had knocked me into oblivion by punching me in the face with his giant fist. I'd waited for the day my father would punch me in the face again, but that day didn't come till I'd nearly forgot to fear it, four years later, when the family was camping in Y National Park.

At our camp along the banks of the Y River, for reasons unknown to any but her, as ever, my mother had entered again the pit of her disease, sulking about, hissing and hollering insults and threats, shrieking at the heartless mountains, until in the face of her abuse, for the first time ever, I told my mother she was *a fucking bitch*, and she rushed away on her valgus knees screeching my father's name.

I don't remember more than that after I'd sat on a log for a time, wallowing in anger and self-pity, my father appeared lurching from the river. I knew I couldn't expect more than pain. Dimly I foresaw my fate in that dimly I saw the semblance between this moment and the moment four years prior, when I stood in the doorway as my father strode up planning to punch me out. Yet, beyond this vague prospect, I thought nothing else, but remained silent on my log, waiting for my father to reach me and, I'd assumed, with his Fatherly Voice announce my punishment and shame, in concert with his barrage of Fatherly Pokes to my chest or Tweaks to my ear.

But my father did no such thing.

One minute I was brooding on my log by the river.

The next I was reeling in the sand with a head full of pain.

My father, it turned out, had never had a better chance to punch anyone in the face to his satisfaction than the chance I'd given him there on my log by the river, not even the chance he'd had that day years back in the cabin outside our podunk hamlet of cretins and goons.

There on my log by the river, my face hovered before my father three or so feet above the ground, perfect for a knockout blow. Very probably, my father in his rage couldn't help himself. Very probably, my father in his rage, incited not by me but as always by my mother, hadn't wanted to punch me in the face with his giant fist, me, a boy of fourteen, but to punch my mother, his wife, in the face with his giant fist, in return for the catalog of hell he'd let himself suffer across the years, for the resentment and anger that across the years had gathered in him consequent to that hell, which resentment and anger, in his weakness, my father had poured onto me instead, his eldest son, the source of my mother's hatred and fury and hence, ultimately, the source of my father's hatred and fury, too.

But whatever the case, once again my father strode toward me in his rage, my mother as always harping at his back, and once again—the weight of his body behind him, the force of his body in motion behind him—my father punched me in the face—*boom!*—square on the jaw—*boom!*—just like that.

My head snapped back, I felt my feet leave the ground, that was all.

A minute or seconds later, as through heavy rain, my father's face appeared above me in flames. I was still sitting, inverted ninety degrees—my ass pressed into the log, my legs above, bent at the knees, pressed into the log, my calves on the log, my arms spread wide in the sand.

And then my mother and father were gone, and I was alone ...

"Thanks for the camera," I said to my father through the door. "The man at the pawn shop will be glad to see it when I trade it for my guitar."

"Goddamn it, Pat," my father howled, "you open this goddamned door! So help me, you'd better open this door right goddamned now!"

I stayed put till my father tired and returned to the family, then waited for my mother to take my father's place, though she never did.

Soon my brothers' voices joined my mother and father's.

Questions were asked, conjectures made.

The holiday had resumed its face of normalcy.

FOR MY MOTHER ESPECIALLY, THE MYRIAD CONFIGURATIONS of matter that arise in life's natural flow—the fluid entities, in other words, that we called "Mother," "Father," "Pat," "X," and "Z" sitting on a "couch" or standing by a "hedge of roses" or lounging on a "beach"—never sufficed.

Knowing that such configurations of matter *organically* risen never embodied anything remotely approaching harmony, my mother, and, as my mother's accomplice, my father, too, became obsessed with creating the *fictionalized* images of configurations of matter—*photographs,* in other words—by which they could say otherwise. Once the image of such a configuration existed, my mother and father could rest in the fantasy that it reflected a wholesome truth.

We have always been happy. Look, here's the picture to prove it.

And this, I came to see, was the critical part to the subterranean logic by which my mother and father gave me a brand new camera. Rather than destroy me by refusing to give me a guitar and thus destroy my dream to rock, consciously or no, my mother and father believed that by giving me a camera they could win me over, first, to the same twisted ways by which they transformed lies into truth and, second, to the same historical *interpretations.*

With "my" camera in hand, under the same false logic by which my mother and father over the years had striven to rid our family's history of its stink, my dream would've been crushed not by some gargantuan blow but by a quiet slipping into the mists, there to don the same costume my mother and father had been trying to make me believe my version of my life had only ever worn. Preoccupied with my own new camera, I'd function as a conscript in the services of my mother and father, forging with the same mindless earnestness the halcyon days we could all look back on so fondly in the years to come.

Over the years, made as I was time and again by my mother and father to assume this or that configuration of poses and expressions in this or that place, each of which contradicted in every way the true nature of our filthy tale, I grew not increasingly malleable, but hostile, first to being photographed and, second, naturally, to cameras themselves.

I couldn't see a camera as good for anything but service to fantasy, nostalgia, time and stasis and death.

Pictures of lies, pictures of death? I wanted *life*, ferocious and howling.

You dare give me shit? I'll turn it to a storm!

You give me death? I'll make death dance!

My business was glory and wrack.

I would have alchemy, I'd have magic, I'd have mutiny, eternal as untiring.

There—ha! ha!—ran the maverick's way, where angels feared to tread, down onion honey roads, through hymnals of mud, to the place where things made to break and built to spill break and spill that sorrow become joy and tears glee.

I, goddamn it, was going to trade this camera for that Fender Mustang!

And that was what I told my father while he hammered at my door.

For years already I'd been sneaking out my window to join my fellow cretins in nightly sin, smoking weed and guzzling booze, committing petty crimes, vandalizing all things grand and rich, what we didn't have, what we'd been kept from—nice cars, nice houses, the golf course that with gasoline we covered in flames the shape of words—"EAT ME!" "SUCK IT!" "FOOLS!"

Now I put my camera in a bag and stole up the street to the Hashemzadeh's place with their juniper hedge, in whose hollow I stashed the camera, knowing I'd gather it later that day when Tommy Dallen scooped me up in his family's car.

My mother and father and brothers were still in the living room when I returned, jabbering about their presents. I crept down the hall to the phone in my mother and father's room and called Tommy Dallen, then sat back to wait. A few hours later, after my mother and father had taken their turns hollering through my door, I headed out.

My father must've heard me turn into the stairwell, else he wouldn't have leapt from the couch with his shouting. But Tommy Dallen was waiting in his shiny Buick. Before I'd even slammed the door, Tommy Dallen hit it, and we were gone.

THE YEAR 1981 HAD BEEN ANYTHING BUT KIND.

In January, I came down with another of the flus that took me out for months, developing as they always did into bronchitis or pneumonia. This flu, however, was different. Neglecting my lungs, it attacked my ear, and from my ear my face.

The good doctor informed me that the nerve running through a narrow bone canal just beneath my ear had been cut off by an infection that was now become an actual disease.

True to its medical definition—*an idiopathic unilateral facial nerve paralysis . . . whose trademark is rapid onset of partial or complete palsy, usually in a single day*—I went to sleep with my powers intact and woke up helpless to move so much as a cell on the right side of my face—not my eye, not my nose, not my cheek or mouth or anything else. And not only was my right eye unable to blink. My right eye couldn't produce a tear. Nor could I salivate on the right side of my mouth, nor move that side of my tongue, nor even taste with that side of my tongue.

A line had been drawn between my eyes. Everything to the left worked as a matter of course. To the right, I was less than clay.

As for the name of this affliction, it was perfect, both slippery and cruel, as sing-songy and grotesque as the affliction itself: *Bell's palsy.*

So long as I remained passive, my affliction went unseen. But the instant I moved or spoke, the left side of my face leapt into motion while the right lay dead, and this was especially true when I laughed.

I looked so comically hideous when I laughed that none of my friends could help trying to make me laugh. And the second I began to laugh, so did everyone else.

Laughter, one among the few things I loved so well, in which outside of music and books and drugs and booze I'd always been able to shelter, had betrayed me as surely as the rest.

I'd have done anything to be able to laugh.

I'd have done anything to keep from laughing.

But laughter was a thing I could never not do, and I'd been stricken. The people who didn't laugh at me recoiled. And they recoiled because I was repulsive. I knew they were repulsed because I myself was repulsed. I could see the repulsion in their faces—in the tic of an eye, the pinch of a lip, a faint clouding of the gaze.

When finally some guys called me Quasimodo, I wondered why they hadn't done so sooner. I'd seen *The Hunchback of Notre Dame*, I knew it to be true, I looked like Quasimodo. I looked so much like Quasimodo I'd begun to call myself Quasimodo two full weeks before the fucks who called me Quasimodo. I looked in the mirror and laughed. *You hideous motherfucker*, I thought. *You look just like Quasimodo.* (This affliction was itself far from incidental. It wasn't till recently, for example, that I was relieved, at last, of my life-long inclination toward disgust with a person the moment I detected in him or her the suggestion, real or imagined, of some physical aberration or, still more irrationally, of even a mere aesthetic offense that, once noticed, became an obsession virtually impossible to shake. And once the obsession had me, rarely would I fail to see some additional peculiarity in the person of my disgust, such as a lapse of manner or comport—how he or she trimmed their nails in public, for instance, or after a meal sucked their teeth, or sung aloud in grocery stores or malls. Short of something along these lines (or in addition to it), I'd key in on yet another of that person's flaws, often something typically insignificant, an unseemly cowlick or mole, say, but frequently something very much worse—a ring of pimples round the lips, a wart on an eyelid, a neglected broken tooth—at which point the original defect would assume a significance larger than itself and thus grow in me beyond all sense. And the thing is, I always knew my repulsion wasn't right, I always knew my repulsion was absurd. Even so, as soon as my eye had been bruised by this tic or that, I'd see the person's very existence as some ineffable affront. You could argue with me till you were hoarse, detailing Joe Blow's virtues to the last, but nothing could relieve my disgust for him. Dylan Thomas, for instance: I loved his poetry, and still do, yet not as much as before I saw his face. Dylan Thomas's face was the face of a clown without its makeup. Dylan Thomas's face was the face of the haploid in a storm, of the three-armed albino, bitter and defiant, chained to the stage before his roaring master. The slippery jowls, the ropey lips, the bulbous head overrun with knotty unkempt hair, the penetrating eyes of a man who, drunken or no, could be a moron or a genius—all of these features made a face that conveyed the sense of arrogant sadness and vile ennui, the face of a man who's been ugly his whole life and knows it, a man who, because he's ugly, and because he knows he's ugly, and, moreover, because he knows you know he's ugly, too, longs to punish you for having seen his ugliness, first, and, second, for his having been simply born—as if somehow you share responsibility for that grave cosmic oversight. For years, despite his beautiful words, every time I looked at the face of Dylan Thomas, I cringed, for myself and for him. And every time I fell prey to such repulsion, whether for Dylan Thomas or anyone else, even as I thought the things I thought, I knew I shouldn't have thought them, I knew I myself should be abhorred as pitiless, brutal, repulsive, if but for thinking such thoughts, and yet I thought them still, loathing myself all the while for being so sick as to have thought them and too weak to stop. The face of Dylan Thomas, I now know, filled me with such disgust less because it was ugly than because, simply, in his face I saw my own. Likewise, the hideous feet of an old friend's wife repulsed me because in them I saw my feet, or traces of my feet, or chimeras of my feet, mangled in some potential future. And the repellence I experienced kissing the shapeless breasts of a girl I'd known (who in every other way was a creature of beauty) had nothing to do with some imagined tainted nature, but with the memory invoked by her breasts of the breasts of the girl that suckled the baby I was, by whose milk my heart and mind were poisoned to match my deformed body, fashioned by the union of my mother and the monster that was her father and brought to fruition in her corrupted womb. Because at my very worst, when the nightmares of my

233

despair were most pitiless, that was how I saw myself. I was a child of the unspeakable, I'd often believed, an incest baby, born of psychosis and pain, grown to manhood a fraud in a play of frauds, in the shadow of a silent lie. In such moments of despair, wondering whether it was true that I'm not the son of my father but of my mother's father, I wasn't merely the boy for whose unpleasant looks you feel a twinge of charitable pity. Like Quasimodo, the thing I was surpassed description. The thing I was had no name, unspeakable if it did. *Behold this monstrosity, if you dare* (I thought)—*whose nose, cratered with pimples and scars from pimples, forbids countenance—whose eyes are the eyes of a pig—whose brow is the brow of an ape—whose lips are a turtle's lips—whose hair, greasy and shapeless, is the hair of a troll.* My child's body was gangly and weak, awkward at best, accident-prone at worst. My grown-man's body was corpulent past excuse, Orson Welles gone from worse to worst. And even if you could stand to see me, you'd turn away the moment you heard me speak, for while I was dense and dull long before I'd begun to swamp my body with drink and drugs, now that I'd devoted most of my life to the success of that venture, my body and brain were altogether mocus, right down to my least DNA.) And as for treating this new disease of mine—well, it was a horrorshow.

The good doctor pierced my eardrum—a thing so painful as to exceed any worthwhile account and which in the coming months I was to endure not once or twice but three grueling times—then placed a stent in the hole to drain the infection on the other side. Of course this good doctor needed to learn as well the damage to my nerve, so once a week he shocked my face all over, with various degrees of strength. Every week

I lay in the doctor's chair like a monkey for a quack, staring up as the man bent down with his hot wire to zap me here and there, his face knotty with concern. And every week I left the doctor knowing no more than that I'd see him soon to repeat the same.

I began to stay as fucked up as I could short of dying.

I drank as much booze as I possibly could, day and night, and to ingest as many drugs as I possibly could, whenever I could, as often as I possibly could.

I didn't care about the nature of my high, but its class alone. My one standard was whether I fell down. And knowing my chances for falling down ran high, like it was a boast, that was what I'd say.

I'm going to get so fucked up, I'd say, *I'm going to fall down.*

And then, somehow, the palsy passed, and the sunny months, too, and September came, and the first week of my last year of school found me at a party in the hills of Y above the bay, where I faced that moment we all at some point must face, if only once, if only briefly, when laying eyes for the first time on a new human being, everything falls away, life itself falls away, and we feel as though we've been reborn.

It was the turn at the end of summer. Once again the world lay dying. Nostalgia suffused the smallest things, down to pebbles and dust. Nothing was free of what might have been. I stood drinking in a vale, surrounded by trees and fuzzy shafts of sun. In the golden light, full of motes and gnats by the cloud, the world trembled with grace. A bottle cap, a robin, a stone—some girl's hempen bangle, some kid's dirty boot—everything reveled in this final glory, the dignity of the end under God.

And then like a vixen of gold she stepped from the crowd, Valerie Glynn, her flaxen hair and creamy skin, her eyes of sleepy blue, staring into mine, I, for her, the rock of life.

I died, then, beneath her gaze, and then I was reborn, sent back to life as empty of knowledge as a fetus, and as full of meaning.

I had loved before, once, a few years back, Narissa Rentoria, whose island eyes and mane of hair wild with the scent of coconuts and Yardley had never failed to leave me come dawn with my bottomless ache, and yet I'd experienced nothing like it since, and had thought I never would.

Now, here it was another time, as if for the first time, since that is how love works: once again, I was in love.

I still smoked weed, and guzzled booze, and popped pills, and snorted blow, but during my moments with Valerie, somehow my need diminished to vague desire, and, for a time, if just in the back of my mind, I thought, *Life might be worth living, living might be okay.*

I got up earlier and fell asleep later and rushed each day to our meeting place to watch her glide across the yard in whatever light the morning had made.

With Valerie I became a willing cliché. When I saw her, every time I saw her, my hands sweat, my mouth went dry, and by words and thoughts I was betrayed.

Before the time of Valerie, I'd always wanted to give, but never trusted, and so I only slunk and schemed and took. Yet giving to Valerie called for nothing, threatened nothing, no thought, no fear, no shame, no concern for some dreamed exchange. Giving simply happened when it happened, as it happened, the way, I felt, the sky gives rain. I gave that girl my goofy smile. I gave that girl my strange guffaw. I gave that girl my cracked adulation, my stumbling praise, my shaking hands and sloppy mouth, my sighs, my heat, my need, and she, in her quiet distance, took it all like flowers from a field.

And the thing was, in her taking, without knowing or trying, Valerie gave what I'd never been given nor so much as known. Valerie's taking was itself a gift, the gift, holy, of acceptance.

I'd grown half a foot since 1980, from five-feet-seven to six-feet-one, but gained but a couple of pounds, leaving me to navigate the world, literally and figuratively, from a newfound high, like some bony awkward clown. Still, who I was, what I was, how I was and why, for Valerie, nothing else mattered. And from all I could see, these were what she wanted. Valerie wanted me, or so she made me feel, as much as I wanted her, and I'd never wanted anything so much as I had wanted her.

Nothing in my life had come so close to the pain of my wanting Valerie, not even my dream to rock, which wasn't to suggest she rubbed that dream away. If anything, Valerie's arrival in my life fueled my dream the more. She drove me to impress her, since the more I could impress her, I believed, the more of herself she'd give. With Valerie, I didn't want merely to rock anymore but to positively *shred*.

My affair with Valerie lasted from the moment I met her in that vale of trees and fuzzy sun to the moment my mother and father gave me my new camera.

Or rather the moment my mother and father gave me my new camera marked the beginning of the end of my days with Valerie.

But more than everything else, the moment my mother and father gave me my new camera marked the end of my life as a boy, and of my enslavement to them, my mother and my father.

I RETURNED TO MY MOTHER AND FATHER'S HOUSE ON NEW Year's Day without having spoken to them but to say when they called Tommy Dallen's that I was there and wouldn't budge till I felt good and ready.

In the guest room at the bottom of Tommy Dallen's house in the hills of Y, by the great Y temple, I smoked my weed and guzzled my booze and watched MTV while struggling on my guitar to make my blistered fingers mold another chord.

I hadn't changed clothes for a week, not even my skivvies or socks. And whatever Tommy Dallen's grandparents kept— pieces of steak from their nightly meals out, Banquet TV dinners, bologna and crackers and cheese, Otter Pops, Oreos, Cheerios, and Fritos, Pop Tarts and assorted candy from Brach's—that was what I ate.

I didn't give a fat rat's ass. I gave heart.

I'd left my mother and father's with the clothes on my back, and, like I'd said, returned with my boss guitar.

My father had warned there'd be hell to pay if I traded the camera for my guitar, and, no doubt, there was hell to pay. My father hollered in my face, demanding to know what I'd done with "their" camera, to which with great relish I replied as a hundred times I'd dreamed I would:

"I did what I said I'd do."

My mother and father's faces were black with envy and hatred, and that for me was grand, but past all else their faces were stupid with loss.

I had the power, now, and my mother and father knew it.

I'd taken the sword they'd put to my throat and turned it to their own, and I hadn't stalled a beat.

Before they could so much as mutter, I sneered at my mother and father with my whole soul, and stepped into my room as I had on Christmas day.

That afternoon, when I emerged, my father was waiting.

"You," he said, his face in my mine, "are going straight down to wherever it is you pawned our camera and get it back. I don't care if you have to buy it back with your own money, you're going to get that camera. But before you do," he said, "you're going to act like the rest of the members of this family. When we speak to you, you goddamned well better answer. Is that clear, *Son*?"

I looked into my father's face, saying nothing, wanting nothing but to smash my father's face as I'd smashed so many others, as my father had twice smashed my own face, and yet I feared this, knowing that to do it would be to commit the taboo of all taboos.

You do not hit your father—no matter what, you must never strike your father.

The world at the periphery of my vision had collapsed into stasis while at the end of the pinhole through which I now saw, worse than in the worst caricature of a nightmare, my father's jaundiced eye pulsed in ultra slow-mo, grown so huge I couldn't see its ends.

I knew I couldn't look away. The instant I looked away, I knew my father would win.

I stared into my father's eye, mustering for him the totality of my hatred. I wanted my father to know that while I might fear him then, soon enough my fear would cave before my hatred and my wrath, and my father would rue his days of abuse through cowardice and neglect, the whole disgusting lot of it hatched of the terror from which he'd never had the balls to pull himself free.

My father's power was on the wane.

This I also knew. And as I knew this, I knew that despite his show of Fatherly Authority, my father now feared me as much or more than I feared him.

My father knew I'd seen him years before, at the dump, or the parking lot before the lumberyard or hardware store, shaking in the clutches of the angry man.

My father knew I knew that outside the blow he'd delivered to his younger brother, long ago in boyhood—for which my father paid with the loss of his pride when his brother pinned him to the ground and spattered my father's face with blood—my father had never struck a soul but me.

And just as my father knew I knew this, my father also knew I knew he knew that I'd fought, and many times and in many states, against boys much larger than I, and that I had fought and won.

My father's well had near run dry. This, too, my father knew I knew, and well.

Nothing else could account for the desperation of his effort to preserve his power. At all costs, my father knew, he had to hold his sway.

I stared into my father's eye, hideous, wavering how to answer. Then, before I could steel myself further, that old sharp pain blossomed in my chest. My father, clinging to the last of his dirty tricks, had made that dowel of his two locked fingers and begun to jab my chest.

"Is that clear?" my father said.

"Yes," I said, cursing myself for a coward as the word slipped out.

"Now apologize."

"For what?"

"For your inconsideration. For your ingratitude. For your selfishness and rudeness."

"You're crazy," I said.

"If you want to stay in this house, you're going to apologize."

"You're *crazy*," I said.

"Take some time to think it over—in your room. Meanwhile, the rest of the house is off limits. And no food, either. Comprendo?"

A couple hours later, when I came out for a snack, my mother was washing dishes.

"You heard your father," she said.

I ignored my mother and reached into the fridge for some jam and a loaf of bread, but my mother slammed the door on my arm.

"You hateful little brat," she said. "Get back in your room."

My arm bright with pain and my mother's breath in my head rotten with hatred and pain, I was jolted into the sort of super clarity I'd known maybe twice before, in which I saw with simultaneous relief and shame that I was acting so the fool, censoring myself as though there'd been something left to save, as though somehow what I said or did to my mother and father mattered, despite the falsity of that claim, since really not a stitch of it was true, not a stitch was left to save. Nothing I did to my mother and father or even to anyone else any longer mattered, whatever happened to me no longer mattered, either, it was so easy, and so clear, *I was done*, that was all, *I had had my last*—that—was—all.

"Fuck you, you fucking bitch," I said.

I'd called my mother a bitch that day in the mountains a few years back, for which my father punched my face with his giant fist, but I'd never said something like this.

It felt good.

It felt so good, I said it again.

"*Fuck. You.*"

Already my mother's face had impossibly contracted, a marvel I'd witnessed more than should've been legal to say, already my mother's face had wound into the face of a goblin, and yet to my disbelief it began to contract still more, a process that might never end, my mother's face might shrink into itself until at last, with nothing left to twist, it would implode with hatred and pain. All that my mother was—all her misery, all her woe, all her years of abuse and neglect and sadness and rage—had shriveled into the ugliest brightest crimson knot with the tiniest stone-dead eyes.

"You horrible, horrible monster!" she said, and struck at my face.

I'd suffered this act, too, more times than should've been legal to admit. With my forearm I absorbed the blow and swept it away.

"Don't you put your hands up!" my mother shrieked, as if this were reasonable, though when she struck at me again, I did the same.

"Go fuck yourself," I said, relishing the words, and the feel of the words in my mouth, and the sound of the words in the room.

My mother gasped. A genie may as well have roared from a lamp to blight her. My mother was a cartoon creature,

I realized. I was a cartoon creature, and this was a cartoon we were tripping through, frame by absurd frame.

I laughed, then, the worst sort of laugh, something like a snicker, but revoltingly worse.

This, too, was new to my mother.

She'd been dropped into a strange new reality with strange new laws.

The world had changed. No one had told her. She knew only to do the thing she did when I defied her.

On the counter stood the jar my mother kept full of wooden spoons, more for beating me, I'd always believed, than for cooking.

She whirled round to snatch one up, but when she turned back with her spoon raised high, I took her wrist and leaned into her face the way my father had leaned into mine not two hours back.

"How dare you!" my mother said. "How *dare* you! You let me go, right now!"

"I'll let you go. But I'm telling you. If you ever touch me again, I'll *kill* you."

"Ahhhh!"

"And you know I will," I said, and released my mother. "*I will fucking kill you dead.*"

My mother trembled heel to skull, her mouth, from which had slipped a throttled gasp, hung open, the menace in her eyes fell black.

I watched her thinking, pondering her guilt across the years, the crimes repeatedly remorselessly done, weighing them against my threat, seeing at every turn that outside a court of law I'd be right to cut her down any way I pleased. Then the genie took her once more, and she ran off shrieking for my father.

At any moment, I knew, my father would come down.

I didn't care, not anymore. I'd never again let him touch me absent pay. What happened to me no longer mattered, I knew, I had no stitches left to save, I knew, my thoughts, my words, my acts changed nothing, I knew, nor did anything else, it was easy, yes, and so clear, I'd had my last—that was all—I was done—that was all—yes, I was done—that was all, and all.

And then, as from hidden strings, my father appeared, and, like I'd known, it was on.

"Who the *fuck* do you think you are?" he said.

My father had balled his fists to punch me in the face the way he'd punched me years before, since after all, it had been so easy years before, I'd made no shield years before, not when fourteen, not when ten, I'd stood blindly the first time and sat that way the second while my father struck me down, so what the hey, he must've thought, why not have a go again?

A time passed in which I knew these thoughts were at his brain, but just for a moment, because, as I also knew, my father had seen me see him.

My father knew I knew his thoughts, my father knew I knew the thing he'd wanted. And, if but intuitively, my father realized it wouldn't go down now as it had those years before.

So instead of striking me, my father tried to jab me on the soft spot of my chest, the way he'd jabbed me all those years till then, as he'd jabbed me on the chest a while before.

But no sooner had his fingers pierced my field than I took his wrist with one hand and his collar with the other and slammed him to the wall.

And in that single flash, everything changed, the world changed, the universe, too, nothing would ever be the same.

My father hit the wall so much harder than I'd foreseen, so hard full-body the prints on the wall clattered to the floor.

With my hands at his throat, pressing my face into my father's face as he'd pressed his face into mine, a spasm of knowledge shot through me whole: *my father was terrified cold.*

Nor was the knowledge alone. Like the man who'd appeared that long-ago day at the hardware store or lumber yard or dump, from harmless nothing to furious something, conjured by a hocus pocus chant or word to snatch my father by his shirt tight against his neck and press his face close against my father's face and speak to my father with his poison words, so now had I taken my father by his throat to speak to him with poison words.

I had changed.

My father had not.

I was the angry man, now.

And my father—*O my father!*—he was still the coward.

Vilest pleasure had eaten me up. So intense this pleasure was, so horrifically horrific, I was bloody and keyed, despicably oiled, high like a high the world didn't know.

The whole of my life's rage had been distilled to this time.

Everything I had, and everything I was had shrunk to a spot of rage.

My mind was sharp.

My sight was clear.

The unknown laid before me in a limpid gulf, and all the answers to the questions.

Never had I experienced such a reality shy of drugs or booze.

It was as if I'd taken a brew of drugs rendered from the best of every drug—the hypervaluative verve of blow—the hyperepistemic sight of shrooms—the hypercalm assurance of smack—the intuition, hyperabsurd, of hash and weed—the hypercharged courage of booze.

I saw the world and all it held, and all I saw I knew.

And I knew what had been and would be before it had been and was.

Nothing could stop me.

Power was mine, now, yes—*power*—*was*—*mine*.

My true self had emerged, the monster had emerged like the monster from Kane in *Alien*, I was that monster, now, and I was damned.

And yet, somehow, while surely I was damned, I'd also been redeemed. To kill or be killed, I had entered the ring.

But this wasn't just the moment of my damnation and redemption. This was my father's moment, as well, the moment in which my father himself could be damned or redeemed.

My presence in the ring, this alone was dear, my salvation and my sin.

But that my father fled the ring or entered counted very much.

Entering, my father lived.

Fleeing, he passed away.

But his death was least on my list.

I needed my father.

I needed my father to be The Father.

I needed my father more than anything, then, certainly more than some guitar or girl, and definitely more than money or my mother.

I needed my father so badly I'd have died instead, in the grip of his fatherly hands.

That was why we *had* to fight, why my father had to fight *me*. My father *had* to live.

My father could simply have engaged me.

My father could simply have reacted to my parry, answered with his choice of blow, moot behind its strength.

He could've broken my grip with the snap of his arms, my father, he could've thrown me to the ground, he could've hammered my face, stomped my guts, kicked me in the ribs. He—*O my father!*—could've laughed in my face, roared in my stupid ugly face—*Well, let's see what you've got, boy!*—then taken me to the street to thrash for all to see.

But my father made not the slightest move, neither to escape nor to trounce, my father made not the faintest twitch.

To my horror, in the face of my wrath my father had fled.

And when he fled, he died, and when he died, some great part of me died with him.

This was the truth, an unspeakable shame: my father was a *coward*.

My father had shown himself to be a coward years before, in all the ways of his life, smoking his dope, denying blame for this or that mistake or deed, avoiding this responsibility to that obligation, stumbling through his murky world as through a labyrinth of avoidance and denial—that place in which all that *was* was determined by all that *was not*, that place whose meaning derived by perverse elimination, where what was real was what remained after the rest had been destroyed, where the logic of truth was turned always on its head—the thing present never real, only the idea of the thing in its absence—that place of empty remainders, that endless fog of ganja in which his fragile balance could be kept, where, on one hand, he could stay numb enough to ignore what challenged his invented world, a world peopled by children alone, and, on the other hand, aware enough to keep that world's thin façade, the façade not just of a living breathing man, but of a well-adjusted capable man—kindly, laughing, friendly, resolute, stalwart, cool—of a man of fortitude whose life was founded on principle and faith—and aware enough, as well, quickly to patch up this façade those times reality managed to smash on through, his pretexts distilled to their false essence, there in that endless fog of ganja in which panic at the possibility of his façade's collapse, and of the consequent exposure of his charlatanry, always faded, the gloom of forbidden woods brightened always by imagined suns, because, after all, inside his fog of ganja, nothing ever was but what my father said.

But now even my father's ganja had failed him. Now my father found himself in the gloom of forbidden woods, and he was terrified past all measure—the father in the grip of the son who, furious, demanding satisfaction, had stepped up to cut off The Father's head.

Gripping my father's throat that New Year's Day of 1982, I knew beyond question that my father had fled, that in his flight my father had failed, that my father was no longer my father, that my father had never been my father in any sense of the word but an impostor of the most detestable sort, that, because my father had been tainted long ago, my father had perished long ago, crashed into the slime of being with all its hateful masses, that, in fact, my father had never been a father to anyone, ever, but at most the convincing fraud whom time alone had revealed as a frightened little man in a big bad world, incapable of the least defense, a *coward*.

To my unending disappointment and unending sorrow, my father's face hovered before me then as it had hovered years ago before the angry man, in drooping petrifaction, while beneath it, from the neck down, as it had years ago in the angry man's grip, my father's body hung limp with terror, a bag of goo in my furious hands, my father's arms at his sides, his mouth open, his face gone white, the blinking eyes of a stricken man, of a man crippled to his heart with terror.

The pleasure I felt in that moment of power was matched only by my horror at my father's paralysis beneath me, and by my disappointment and my sorrow.

I was at once jubilant and sickened, arrogant and ashamed, prideful and repulsed, certain and confused, powerful and puny, pleased—acutely, maliciously pleased—and helplessly, hopelessly frantic.

That this truth was so ghastly made it no more or less the truth. This was not a notion, this was not the dream of a fevered mind. This was a fact that was the truth. In that moment—*O my father!*—I could do anything I liked with him, *anything at all.*

THE PROCESS I'D BEEN HURLED INTO ROARED THROUGH ITS cycles—rage to censor, censor to need, need to hope, hope to clarity, and on again to panic, to sadness, to anger, hatred, rage.

Round and round I spun while through the cosmos planets burned, quanta met, stars bore and died.

I waited for my father to act, for my father to rise to crush my revolt and thus to save us both. But my father continued to shrink away, smaller and smaller, shrinking as I breathed—*O my father!*—till soon I held but the puppet of a rabbit, the tiniest shabbiest puppet of a rabbit, made of rags and thread.

"You motherfucker!" I said, an inch from my father's face, though still my father did nothing. "You want to throw down? We can head out to the street right now!"

Everything I saw, and I saw just my father's tiny face, hovered in pulsing red.

An atom of morality stood between my fists and my father's face. I wanted so badly to crush him, I wanted so badly for him to crush me—not, with his balled fist, the face of the child I'd been, that would never happen again, but to stand before me as a man, as my true father, to engage in combat the man I'd become, toe to toe, to crush or to try to crush, face to manly face.

The Kraken, however, had been released, its name was Terror, and my father was devoured.

His eyes had expanded with terror, his yellowy eyes were pulsing in terror, his tiny teeth were pulsing in terror, his whole face drained of color, white as paper, white as dough, my father a man consumed by fear—*O my father!*—hopeless, useless coward that he was—*O, O, O my father!*

I'd wrapped my fists in my father's shirt, jacked my fists to my father's chin, hard against my father's throat, and now I was shaking him, now in disgust I was heaving him away. Quite plainly, my father had no means to make sense of the storm into which he'd been cast. Still his mouth hung open, still his eyes spread wide, the whole of my father was rank with terror.

"You!" my father stuttered, backing away, his hands before him. "You!" my father said as he reached into the nook behind him for the phone on its cradle on the wall. "*You* are going to jail!"

Mindless now, in the fog of my wrath, with three quick steps I closed the space between us and smashed the phone. Then, for good measure, when the phone hit the floor, I ripped its cord from the wall.

"Now what, asshole?" I said, and stepped up on my father.

I could hear my mother behind me, shrieking, she was close behind me, I knew, ready to attack. When I spun round, the way I'd spun round so many times before, her hand hung above me, gripping her wooden spoon.

"Stay the fuck back," I said.

"You can't do that!" my father said.

"Go ahead," I said. "Call your little police."

"You are so far out of line!" my father said, struggling, I could tell, to fill his voice once again with the power of The Father. "You're out of control!"

"You're not my father," I said. "*You* are not my father."

"We'll see about that," my father said, and headed through the door behind him, toward the phone at the rear of the house, I knew, in his and my mother's room.

Through the kitchen and down the hall I stormed and ripped from the wall the cord there, too.

"This what you're looking for?" I said when my father arrived.

"You get out of this house!" my father screamed. More and more, he was sounding like my mother. "You get out of this house right now!"

"Fuck you," I said, reveling in the fullness of my power, knowing at last I'd delivered the blow of death to my satanic mother and feckless father.

They were done.

And they knew they were done, better than all they knew they were done, my satanic mother and feckless father knew they were done for good.

"We'll just see about that," my father said, witless now, and stumbled down the hall, toward the stairwell to the family room he and my mother had recently made of the basement with the same filthy money they'd stolen from the insurance company and got from a family death, the same filthy money with which they'd bought pianos and diamonds and sofas and furs for their selfish thoughtless selves, the same filthy money with which they'd refused to buy me a second-hand guitar, the same filthy money with which they'd bought me instead a brand new Minolta XD5 35mm camera, their puny little instrument of fantasy and nostalgia, their puny little gadget of time and stasis and death.

The family room—ha!

The sick irony, the hilarious pathetic idiocy of it all. The family room, I knew, was for my father his last refuge, the final haven, place of the third and final phone.

I took my time behind him, knowing I'd get him well before he could reach an operator, much less his little police. And sure enough, by the time I made it down the stairs, my father as I'd pictured was shielding the phone with his body in a corner, the handset on his shoulder as he fumbled with the dial.

"You get out of here!" he shrieked.

"Ah oh," I said, fully taunting my father, fully mocking my father, then took the cord between him and the wall and ripped it clear. "No mo wittle po-weece."

"You are no longer welcome in this house!" my father shrieked. "This is your last day here. I expect your bags to be packed and ready in an hour."

"You kick me out, Daaaaad, I'll have *you* thrown in jail."

"We'll see about that!" my father said.

"*We'll see about that!*" I said. "*We'll see about that!*"

My father stood before me in shambles, now, out of his wits, utterly feckless, utterly broken, gone.

He had no recourse but to stare as I shook in rage with my knotted fists, knowing he'd failed himself and failed me, knowing he'd lost, knowing, very likely, or at least beginning to glimpse, the dishonor into which he'd irrevocably plunged.

My father was a wasteland, with what little honor he'd managed to keep through the years shattered all around.

And my prize for victory, despite my blindness to the grossest of its implications, which I wouldn't yet see for years, was none other than my freedom.

I could've walked away from my mother and father then, with remorse, yes, and with sadness, yes, but with never a word of regret. I could've walked away with my dignity, too, and the knowledge, as well, that from that day on my destiny was mine alone. Dignity I had in some small portion, and yet of my true power I knew next to zilch. Regret coursed through me like the worst sort of dope, and remorse, and sadness, and hatred, and rage, and thirst for vengeance, and blame.

I hated my mother and father for having made me revolt, and I hated my father for failing to check my revolt, for shirking his obligation to manhood and fatherhood both.

Every last hint of my woes were my mother and father's fault, I believed, every rancid bone of misery, I'd done not a thing, I swore, I was a victim, I swore, I'd been terrorized day by day, helpless as a piglet or a cripple.

That was what I saw.

That was what I believed.

I was a victim through and through, I believed, and victimized, I believed, I could be nothing but right and cold of pardon, a wreaker of vengeance, bloody or psycho, the world would never care.

I had refused to submit to the lash, I had crushed the crushers, I'd stole free of my mother and father's trap, I was the hunted now turned hunter. I had driven my mother and father into their own trap without their least suspicion, then pitilessly sprung the trap.

The proof stood before me in my bug-eyed mother and stuttering impostor of a father.

I had taken my mother and father's camera and turned it into my guitar.

I had taken the past and shaped it to the present.

I'd taken Nostalgia, weepy-eyed and mewling, and made it Satisfaction dancing for the moon, I'd forced him, Old Man Death, to holler and seethe.

Out of the cage onto a wide open plain I'd stepped, and yet—*and yet*—somehow I couldn't see any but black, somehow I couldn't see any but ropes and chains, nor taste but the harshest sadness, the blackest hate, the hottest rage, I was lost in a welter through which all that was good had become all that's creeping and base, the Fog of the Wounded, the Fog of the Crushed, the Fog of Crushing Victimhood.

When my father announced a few hours later that I was no longer part of the family, that I was no longer welcome in the family home, that I'd be sent to southern Y to live with my father's brother in the city of Y, with its engineered wastelands and perpetual smog, the image of myself as this victim coalesced into a toxic jewel.

Long ago, I'd been left to my own devices. Long ago, I'd been abandoned.

Now, for refusing to lie down before the hypocrisy of this false father, in a final, desperate effort to bolster his constructs and smash the doubt in the hearts and minds of his remaining sons, he'd punished me with *exile*.

I was *exiled* now, I was *banished*.

I'd gained my freedom at the cost of everything only to see my freedom flung back like a gummy net.

In name, my childhood had ended.

In reality, I'd been tossed onto the road of manhood, a child in the body of a man, bewildered, absent the way to make my way, bereft of friends, bereft of love, bereft, too, at long length, of the few rags of delusion beneath which I'd somehow managed to shelter.

And I was.

The next day, with my guitar and bag, I caught a bus to downtown Y, and from the depot there a bus to the house of my father's brother ten hours off in a canyon at the edge of Y with its dreary malls stretching on mile after dreary mile, its taquerias in perpetual decline, its shoe stores and liquor stores in perpetual decline, its concrete factories and scrap yards in perpetual decline, its carnicerias in perpetual decline, its pastelerias in perpetual decline, its truck dealers and muffler shops and gun shops and repair shops and donut shops and bars full of flies in perpetual decline, the sky, monotonous and brown, heavy on the boulevards endlessly trudged by assembly-line serfs and delivery men and mechanics and butchers and dolts, by bagboys and clerks, by sick little children and sick old men, and by the endless plenty of sad-eyed tailors and black-eyed bums, and by polyester salesmen, dishwashers, cooks, single-mother waitresses, and whisky-slurping keeps, security guards, bank tellers, cholos, and cops, and helicopter men, and sheet metal men, and Plexiglas cutters and ironwork men and aluminum men and the sons of cops in gangs, the endless vile dust of the walkless ways, the peeling tenements, the tumbledown shacks, the yards of toys all shattered and dogs on chains and car parts and junkies and trash, and the listless bougainvillea, and the pepper trees drooping, and the dusty palms, and the endless anthology of busted furniture and auto parts, broken shovels and jettisoned boots, beer cans and needles and condoms and wigs, and deflated footballs and soccer balls and basketballs and tubes, and power lines and dumpsters and cul-de-sacs of gloom, all of it haunted by mangy cats, and crows, and aimless stoic gulls, and curs as hopeless as fierce, and pigeons and rats and roaches and drunks, pissed on and shat on and puked on and robbed, stumbling through urchins by the band, all of it endless, the endless blare of traffic, the endless blast of big-rig horns, and the stereos booming, and the boomboxes booming, and the septic stink pounding your brain and burning your eyes and clogging your pores, an endless poison cloud, none of it seen on foot, but from my father's brother's car or a public bus, this land of alien people struggling to make their alien ways, ennui like cancer devouring them whole, not a soul free of ennui, not a soul free of ennui or dread, yes, not one soul free of endless bottomless dread.

IN THE MORNING, IN THE HAZY LIGHT, YOU MAKE BOLOGNA sandwiches on white bread with mustard and cheese, then wait out the time by your record, thumping to rock and roll. Then the time comes, and you step into the street. Every house is an empty house, every window faceless. The driveways are filthy with oil. The ruined grass is bound by rows of ruined plants. Orange trees barren of oranges endure, lime trees barren of limes, and lemons barren of lemons. The hills behind the houses walk toward the sea and wait for a smoggy rain. You walk down the street through the septic air, past chain-link fences and cinderblock walls, scanning for butts and coins. At the place where you enter the bus you light your butts with cardboard matches and smoke until the bus pulls up with a hiss. There are no people, just faceless bodies moving in a construct. After a time, you step onto a street like the street where you started and search out a butt to light before you make your way into the zone. Then you enter the zone, and wait for the bell to ring. After a time, the bell rings. Bodies shuffle beneath fluorescent lights, past lockers and doors of frosted glass. A man or woman stands in the distance, speaking of A.E. Housman, the boiling of water, and photons, which are little packets of energy inside all light. Bells ring, bodies shuffle, distant men and women speak of hexagons, theorems, bills. Among the bodies, you see what you see and hear what you hear, you eat your sandwiches and smoke your butts, voiceless with your long hair and pimples and jeans, and wait for the last bell to ring. Then the last bell rings. At the place where you enter the bus, you search for butts, and if you find a butt smoke, or not if you don't find a butt, till the bus pulls up with a hiss. You drop coins in a meter, a driver nods, the bodies begin to sway. After a time, you step through the doors onto a street like the street where you started, where you light what's left of the butt you found before you entered the bus or search for another butt to light before you head up the street beneath struggling trees and power lines, past cinderblock walls and oil-stained drives and stunted grass in which orange trees barren of oranges endure, lime trees barren of limes, and lemons barren of lemons. The yellow hills walk through the smog, on toward the sea. The sky is ceaseless and brown.

THE DRUNK

If not for the beast within us,
we would be castrated angels.
— Herman Hesse

Her window was open.

He heard them fucking.

He knew all along he'd hear them fucking.

The sound was a comfort.

He was glad.

It was why he'd come, to find his wife being fucked by her new lover, some greasy man from The Fake.

Through the curtains he could see her thighs in his hands, her face in tears, the greasy man ruthlessly pounding his wife. Rice stepped in and coughed, then drew a gun whose barrel wouldn't end, but continued to grow like scarves from a trickster's sleeve.

It didn't matter that the man had leapt up to beg.

The gun rose, he pulled the trigger, the man's organs vanished in a spray of red.

He knew the man wouldn't die, and he didn't. He was very much alive, very much conscious, writhing about in empty search while the woman dissolved in her sheets.

Across the hall, a dachshund whined at a bottle of milk. There was a suitcase and hat and scattered deck of cards.

At the foot of the stairs, Rice thought he heard a voice, but looking back, it was plain not a soul had followed.

He knew they were doomed as any couple in the history of rotten love. He'd known it long before, actually, and yet he'd driven out here anyway, to this land of barbequed ribs and noxious air, and magicians and cretins and drunks.

The same imbecilic logic of old had held for them, as well: if they ran fast enough, they figured, if they put distance enough between them and their filth, they might still have a chance at life.

But though they'd only dragged their filth along, it wasn't till the moment he appeared before her in his tee shirt stained with gravy and cheese, his face painted blue and teeth all black—a 240-pound fiend covered in tattoos—that the extent of their imbecility had obtained in full, the repulsion in her eyes, had he somehow doubted, its awful confirmation.

She was in the bathroom, turning herself into a "sexy gothic Martian."

Her own face was green, her eyes in smoky blacks and grays. She'd donned the same red wig she wore the night they met at The Divey Room, when he fell in love with her. On top of this was a barrette with wires for antennae at whose ends dangled Ping-Pong balls, orange. Past these, she wore just her panties and brassiere, the black ones with lace on the fringes he'd bought her back in Y.

"I've decided," he said, as he watched her face contract, "to come to the party after all."

"But it's Halloween," she said, and began to pick her lip.

She knew he knew the day. The last she'd said what she meant or meant what she'd said, he thought, was never. Perpetual code, really—ceaseless inquiry, boundless confusion, hesitation, scrutiny, dread—this was the game they'd been at, both of them, in fact, for years.

"You don't dig my getup?" he said.

"Slackbelcher's going to be there," she said.

"So?"

"So I thought you said you wouldn't go anyplace you might see him."

Slackbelcher was the jerk that had snubbed him, whose ass he'd told his wife he'd kick round the block if the jerk so much as looked his way. A year had passed since then. Now he merely despised the jerk—with his epigone's prose so chockfull of cool pop trivia, and irony, and satire, and distance—as pathetic.

"You know Halloween's my favorite holiday," his wife said, suggesting, inexplicably, a connection between this fact and his contempt for the jerk. She'd been picking at her lip like down inside she might find a chunk of gold. It was bleeding something rotten. "I really want to have fun tonight," she said. "You know?"

"You just call Mr. Slackbelcher up and say I'll be there. Chickenshit'll stay home for sure."

"But what if I don't want to?"

"Call him?"

"Bring you."

Never had his wife used words so clear. And yet, he thought, given the difference between them, now, the wreck he'd become, who could blame her?

She was just twenty-two when they met in the autumn of '96, rooming with some burnouts in a shithole near the cinema. That was her first time without mom, and while the house had been a pit, the night she brought him to her space, she was like a kid showing off a pony.

He took a photo of her then, in her fake-fur coat, smiling from the bed with her things about her—a beat guitar, the album of pix, the wrought-iron chair and its velvet seat, a Jesus candle, a retro-pic of that girl in the window, cupping her cheeks with white-gloved hands, the snapshot of an ex in blackface—what had made Rice think, *Huh?*—then, yes, one of herself in a wig.

Five years later, spurned by every school but one, she jetted out to Y to scope the scene and get a pad. She raved when she returned about the flat she'd taken, swearing it a gem.

But the flat was not a gem, as he found, but a shithole shittier than the hole she'd left.

None of this, in the end, really mattered—not her choices, not her lies, and certainly not her sweetness or beauty or smarts or charm.

His wife, he knew, could've been the clichéd paragon of excellence, chaste as a bird. He was a man prone to fits of suicidal/homicidal dreams, capable in seconds of a drinking binge that, once started, could as quickly find him rubbing his dode on a stranger's cup as throwing some kid from a wharf for picking his ugly toes.

He'd become a menace, in short, for whom such nightmares were routine. And none of this was pretend. The day they left Y, just three weeks had passed between him and his breakdown, the fourth in as many years.

When he saw his father's truck on the street at their new shithole, he hadn't yet known how bad his wife had lied. He didn't know anything more than that the trip had been hell, and that he was glad to see his father had come down from the mountains as his father had said.

Desperation had crushed the worm of fear inside him. For a time, even, desperation had crushed everything but his boyhood hope that his father would save him, that under his father's wing he'd be given the grace he couldn't go on without.

He had nothing left to fight with anymore.

Their silence was ended.

Their nine-year feud, started when Rice had cut him off in '91, was dead.

His father had changed.

His hair had turned silver, and he'd let it grow nearly to the waist in a braid from the back of a cap got off a vendor of grain. With the gall of an uncle come for a stay he doesn't aim to end, a potbelly had moved in on his father, too, a thing Rice had never seen on the man. But scariest of all was his father's arm, maimed by a blow a few years back. His bicep had snapped and, like a window shade yanked, curled up near his shoulder. His father's cave to this loss, both unacceptable and horrific, was astonishing not for its calm alone, but for its total lack of spite. After telling the pain he'd born, his father said that absent the twelve grand needed to repair it—a procedure, his father noted like some scholar his fact, that his doctor had said was commonly waived by all but pedigreed jocks—there was little he could do. "That's just the way it is," his father said, and shrugged.

It filled Rice with awe, this sunny doom, and then with disgust, and then with pity and shame.

And then it struck him that perhaps this man was neither his father nor even his father's harebrained twin, but an android or clone planted there to test him. The man had his father's ears and heavy brow, his father's hands and—minus the inch stripped by the years—his father's average height. And he had his father's laugh, this man, his father's smell and memory of shared events, and yet for these Rice couldn't shake the feeling, uncanny as Freud's uncanny, that this man was a stranger in the strangest sense, the person who, though you thought to know him better than most, in a second defies your belief in the world's ways, and in that defiance breaks the truth you believed had been.

His father wasn't young anymore, he realized, or even middle-aged, but old.

His face had wrinkled, his eyes had watered, and on his body spots had grown like mushrooms after rain. There was a hunch in his father, now, a lurch to his step, it was all too painfully true: his father was a man before the gateway to his dotage, and maybe even death. And throughout this time, the months and years that had brought his father to this place, and throughout his father's grief and bliss, Rice saw, his father had turned something close to wise. For all he'd lost and gained, his father now spoke with the purity of conviction in the voice of the sea on a cloudy day, the desert beneath blue sky: *I have been restored the years that the locust ate.*

Without his father's kindly eyes and cup of morning joe, it was likely Rice had abandoned the works—the flat, his wife, the world itself. His father saved him those first weeks in that contagion of a town, his father was the smiling cause behind everything he did. Without his father, he knew, he could never have repaired the shithole his wife had taken, much less seen the way to it.

He and his father plastered countless cracks, he and his father painted ceilings and walls and trim, he and his father scoured slime from toilets and crud from sinks, and every stick of hardwood floor. It wasn't long, Rice saw, before he'd come to view this process as a trope for fixing busted souls.

In the weeks his father stayed with him, the two had somehow managed to restore most of what had been destroyed those last nine years, to braid this length of trust and that scrap of care, to scrub away the thousand nameless slurs that had for so long polluted their hearts. And fragile as their hearts still were, by the time his father left, they'd furnished them out with their humble best.

But clearly his father hadn't saved him. No sooner had he left than Rice became a Morlock out of H.G. Wells, shuffling between his old-town craphole and the cubicle he spent his days in describing things from Microsoft.

His wife, meantime, after carousing away her nights with the pack of jerks she claimed "colleagues" and "friends," rose each noon to write stories with such lines as, "I'm being hunted by two men—one has a bone, the other a bat named Eugène."

Then he was felled by kidney stones. He underwent the first procedure a month before 9/11 and the second six weeks later, still conscious, no less, during which a tiny claw was crammed up his penis to remove a stent. From the start of his illness to its end, whacked out on so many drugs his doctor refused him more for fear she'd kill him, he ate nothing but root beer floats.

"If I want to go," he said to his wife, "there's nothing you can do."

"It's Vanya's house," she said through the smoke in her mouth. "I'll just tell her to tell you you're not getting in."

Fucking Vanya. This was a woman who'd married a man the month before she came to Y, all because, as she confessed, she was "afraid to do it alone." But once she arrived and found her husband "cramping her style," she started banging a kid from school. Obviously, when her drone of a cuckold, Rick, found out, the man was fit to die. Rice knew. It was through

Rick he'd got his job at the cubicle farm. Working with the kid, or rather sharing the same space—since after his evisceration by Vanya's claws Rick never did work that he could see—was how he'd learned most of what he knew about the couple's grimy saga. More than anything, good old Rick just withered away the months he lingered on. It got especially bad once Vanya shacked up with her new fuckbuddy, a runt of a man named, appropriately, Brian Teany. Poor, poor Rick. The slob did little more than toke on his bong and cry. If ever a woman was vile, he thought, if ever a human was vile, Vanya was, to the deepest marrow.

He told his wife what he thought of Miss Vanya, nothing he'd not said before, and then he told his wife what he thought of her, for having dumped him there in that sub-tropic hell, for so shamelessly lying about the contents of her manic brain, for stringing him along with her fake adoration, blinding him for years to the truth she was.

They swapped obscenities enough to miff a bum till at last he saw that none of this would turn out well and slipped off to buy two quarts of bourbon and a twelver of beer, his hopes for sobriety—three months this round, incredible—flushed away again.

By the time he'd made it through most of the beer and half of that first quart, just under two hours later, his wife was ready to bail.

"Where the hell do you think you're going like that?" he said.

She had on a baby doll dress with the panties and bra, so sheer you could see the panties and bra.

And that was when it hit him, the knowledge, like the memory of an icky dream: if his wife hadn't been doing it with someone else, she was making plans to do so soon. Never in her life had she worn an outfit so plainly scuzzy. Honestly, he thought, it was the outfit of a whore. She looked like an alien that fucks for money, or, more basically, like an alien that wants to fuck.

"I'm not leaving yet," she said.

He laughed. "Just practicing, then, I suppose. Seeing what your purse will look like once you sweat on it."

"You're disgusting. You make me want to slit my throat."

He strode past her, to block the door, and saw she was afraid.

"I just sharpened the knives," he said. "You know where they are."

"I was going to make a call," she said, and reached into the purse for the phone she never answered, the phone she turned off once she'd decided to leave for the night, in spite of her vows to be home soon, by ten, or twelve, or three—whatever time she'd said.

"Your new boyfriend, huh?"

"I hate you so much," she said. "You fat fuck."

Again and again he'd shamed himself, but never with such ease. She'd hinted at his new lard, the way one half does when it's clear the other's lit the fuse, stuff like, "Those floats are really bad for you, honey," and, "How many times a day can a man eat pie?"

But now, like him, she'd abandoned even those respects. It was true. Their kindness had been smashed. Nothing remained but, scarcely pulsing, a spot of the dream they were. From the day they met, despite their moments of tenderness, they'd been busy with destruction. They might have been a type of soul-consuming cannibal, he thought. They'd glutted themselves at the expense of themselves, and now there was nothing left. His wife was an alien whore, and he an old fat fuck.

He didn't know how long he'd stared at that knot in the floor, nothing but that his wife had put a slip beneath her dress and was talking on the phone.

"I don't care what you say," he told her. "I'm coming."

"No," she said, clapping shut the phone, "you're not."

He snatched a pillow and stuffed it beneath his shirt, around the shoulder. "Quasimodo doesn't take no for answers."

"You fat, *fat* fuck," she said, and opened the door.

Goddamn. Perfection of evil that she was, Vanya had appeared from a crack in the sky.

"What do *you* want?" he said.

"Dude, you need to leave her be."

"Eat yourself, why don't you?"

"Watch me," Vanya said, and led his wife away.

He followed them into that sweltering mess, but felt at once he'd been cast to the bottom of a poison sea. His chest was filled with poison, his eyes stripped of light. A swoon engulfed him, then, and he moaned.

"Wait, please, wait . . ."

"Look at you," Vanya said. "You're shitfaced. You're filthy. You stink. Get a freaking clue. *No*body wants you."

That would've done, but then Vanya sneered with more hateful pity than he could've conjured at his worst.

"Do yourself a favor," she said. "Go home."

Forty-five minutes later, he stood by the house where the bash would soon begin, spraying white gas on the hedge that lined its yard. He'd expected a fire to appear when he flicked his lighter, for sure. What he'd not expected was the entire hedge to rise in psycho flames. But things could never have been different. He was under a spell—not of the fire, but the fire that longed to be.

Dusk hadn't fallen, yet already packs of kiddies had taken to the streets. As if from hidden pods, a duo emerged across the way, a clutch up the block, a gaggle more on a nearby porch—bunny rabbits, super heroes, angels, and clowns, the whole prancing bit. More amazingly, he thought, not one of these sprites had noticed his work, much less him. The fire was *huge*, a wall of flames ten feet high and fifty long, black smoke pouring out like water from a busted pipe, and no one had so much as turned their costumed head.

The dreamlike nature of the moment was more than he could bear.

The absence of guilt—the absence of fear—the perfection of fulfillment—the sense of inviolate sway. It was simultaneously thrilling and horrific, too much and too little both.

Once again he took stock, and once again saw what he'd seen: mommies and daddies and kiddies in costumes, innocence on the rage . . .

And then he reached the flat, and then the sirens began, two at first, then three and four, rushing toward his columns of smoke . . .

Later—bottle in hand—he made his way back through the dark, this time to the lot across the street, where, ironically, a house had once burned down.

A split-rail fence had been swallowed by the honeysuckle there. He sat on the log behind it to wait for a sign to show him what to do, the party swelling as he glared through the vines, the music going on—U2, Pavement, KC and the Sunshine Band, James Brown, James Brown, James Brown . . .

Those southern nights were entities all their own, changed with the sun, but somehow ever the same. They pressed against you, those nights, they squeezed you and tore you and licked at you, too, even as they swept you away, just out there, into black predictions. The world smelled of memory, then, of the vastness of space and primordial ooze. Jasmine mingled with moss and mud—endless entropy, endless life, the fern on its putrid stump. And birdcall and catcall fused with the buzz of cricket and cicada. And armies of moths ran beams of light, and geckos hiked fences like phantoms of stone, and centipedes wriggled, and spiders crawled, wherever you looked, they were there . . .

Any moment, he knew, she'd step from the dark in the arms of some man, some pompous twerp, rather, and he'd be free to make Iago's work into something out of Dr. Seuss. But that didn't happen, however much he willed it.

His thoughts wandered, his brain hummed, he fell to evil dreams . . .

He was dead in a field with proverbs, and eyeballs loony with flies . . .

He was nasty on the street with multiple wounds, a note round his neck that said, simply, *PLEASE?*

So be it, he thought, and drank. If his wife wouldn't come to him, he'd go to her . . .

Smoke and light became one, as did faces, blurred to a mask of terror.

A feeling had welled up in the thing that was him, of power and despair. He'd reached the plains of madness, now. No one knew him any longer to laugh at or hurt or jeer. And who guessed what could happen, truly, when the laws had fallen and all that remained was terror?

He saw her.

She'd formed a circle with three boys and a girl, their private galaxy of phoniness and booze. She'd ditched the slip, as he'd foretold, and resumed the guise of an alien whore.

And then she saw him, too, and her voice disappeared, the whole of her collapsed when he pressed in—mumbles all about of *arsonist* and *maniac* and *madman* and *dick*—and his hand, as if its own, shot out to slap those balls bouncing round her head.

In one moment she was an alien whore, the next a girl with a crooked wig. Then destitution took her, and she began to weep . . .

He found himself in darkness scored by planks of light filled with bugs. A window appeared, to the room he'd left, his wife still in it, surrounded by a fresh gang of jerks. She'd restored her wig, but her eyes were ugly with mascara, she couldn't change that, and her makeup was grotesque . . .

He made his way round the house, holding his knife, weirdly enough, then crawled down the drive, on the far side of the two cars in it. He could feel the knife, he knew he was holding his knife, but like a man asleep was powerless. He saw a tire. He saw the knife open and stab the tire. He saw another tire and the knife stab it . . .

The image of his bottle appeared overhead, a beacon to lurch toward, beyond the party's arc of light . . .

Peels of laughter danced his way, a burst of giggles, a rumpus of shock, the shit-faced bawling of some forlorn kid . . .

Far overhead a satellite drizzled, somewhere close a child sprang her tantrum . . .

273

He came to on the floor, one leg beneath him, the other on the bed. His wife had been wailing for some time, he sensed. He'd heard it gathering, louder and louder, till at last he opened his eyes.

He didn't know where he was or why his wife was screaming. He couldn't understand her, either, though with dawning apprehension he saw it was day, and knew he'd gone too far the night before—much, much further than he'd remembered going.

From what he could make of his wife's assault, after setting the yard on fire and storming the party and slapping her wig and slashing the tires of Vanya's car, he'd returned home to piss all over her effects, her jewelry and papers and computer and books.

They were finished. Through his confusion, even, that was clear.

Little did he know, however, that in three weeks, stripped of his health and pride and most of his mind, he'd board a bus full of fantasists and cons, bound for the home of his father in the mountains of Y.

His father, after all, in his way, at least, had addressed his plea for help. It hadn't been hard to take his father's hand. He was ruined, and so was his trust, he and his wife were ruined, he'd done his share of destruction, too, more than his share, he was ready for the end, truly he was ready, yes and yes, it had been more than easy to take his father's hand.

And yet he should've known better than to believe the past was past.

He knew his father. He knew that hope in his father was next to hope in a lie. The years had transformed his father's body but left his father's core. His father was the passive-aggressive wizard he'd always been, able as only his father was to craft the hypnotic charm, the hypnotic kindness needed to transfix him. After all those years, once again he'd been blinded by his father's spell, as he'd always feared to be, as surely as was his father himself still blinded by the father that had got him, too. And neither could he know as he laid on the floor beneath his raging wife that this long ride would mark the beginning of a journey that epitomized forever, from Y, to Y, to Y, to Y, to Y, to Y, and on . . .

Once upon a long ago time, the notion of home had held all he thought true and dear. Become a nowhere man, now, come from nowhere, bound for the same, home had slipped into the bitterness of schemes gone bad, and nothing, not the myth that home was where he lay his head, would help him to see that beneath his hopelessness the world was in order and that, someday, perhaps, his mind would be restored, and he would be okay . . .

She was still wailing, cursing the hoax by which they'd been lured to this demonic town.

He rolled to his side and saw the Glock his uncle had given him for "protection" against the goons in the swamps, the weapon's slide retracted to show an empty chamber.

His urine was everywhere. The house smelled like a cage.

As for his wife's machine, both monitor and tower were missing, and this was the source of her distress. Her novel was on the hard drive. So were her stories and the rest.

He had destroyed it all.

His wife knew he'd destroyed it because he'd told her he'd destroyed it, apparently by way of Zigor, yet another in the line of schmucks from the local hipster bar. He never doubted Zigor's motive for befriending "them." Zigor wanted to fuck his wife. Zigor, too, was a "good friend" to his wife. Zigor "understood" his wife, Zigor "helped" his wife when she was "down." It was his jealously, said his wife, that drove him to leave Zigor a message from his blackout, announcing his intent to "annihilate"—the very word she said Zigor had said he'd used—her machine. And now that the machine was gone, his wife had no reason not to believe he'd done precisely that.

And sure enough, among the palmettos and slime of their ragged yard, they found the missing gear. The tower was destroyed, blasted full of holes and chopped up with a hatchet. The monitor, too, had suffered, but across its screen he'd taped a printout of his beaming face. There were holes through his mouth and both of his eyes.

"I always knew you could do such things," his wife said. He saw no mercy in her face, no tenderness, not a crummy speck of love. "I just never thought you would."

She left that evening with the beat up valise she'd used to move into his joint after their elopement in Y, two weeks to the day from their first date. They'd been inseparable then. Nothing, then, was dull—scraping a spatula, waiting in line at the DMV, plucking an ingrown hair—nothing was dull, all of it was a rocket to D'Qar.

While boredom was that other world's drag, his wife used to say, the world for them was "the playground of a mermaid"—that, too, she'd said—he remembered it like the loss of his virginity—as she climbed from bed at noon with her pack of smokes, headed to the kitchen for a wake-up shot of gin.

He'd seen her first when she was another dude's girl, and

he some other girl's guy. But once he lost that girl, the way he lost all his girls, he went stumbling through the wasteland of one-night affairs—*again*—with girls whose names he never asked.

Finally, six months later, lone-wolfing The Divey, as had become his wont, he saw her playing pool without knowing who she was. He'd been stricken by her—that was what he knew—this weird girl in the bright red wig, the cue above the table jaunty in her hands, that and bazillions more, the smiling gleaming mouth, for sure, he could never keep from kissing once he'd been cursed with its taste.

The girl had been a butterfly on a gator's tongue. She'd been sunshine in a storm, silver on tar, the center of a Tootsie Pop fresh off the belt.

And now she was gone, #149 in The Gone Girl Game, and he was alone among the moss and murk of this demonic town, alone as ever, #149 in The Shithead Game, the ducats in his pocket—from the dole he was on after the fall of the cubicle farm—cutting through the howl in his head—as ever, once he'd started drinking again—weeping and bawling for another bottle and case of beer.

His life was a travesty of déjà vu.

He was a caricature of his own cliché.

Nothing was fresh, because everything he did, the bulk of it catastrophic, had been born of loathing and hate, enforced by the hand in his mind, to which he'd been a slave since way back when, a hand he held that had never done more than hold him down.

This bore no resemblance to a joke, either. He'd once believed, like so many teens who flipped their wigs when they heard it, the mad German's dictum that God was dead, but this "truth," too, had grown stale as the old shoes in his closet.

Life, he well knew by now, was not a hoax, or a joke, or some wicked play enacted on the world's stage, its players stupidly playing their stupid parts doomed to end in mute stupidity, as the Bard had said, sans teeth, sans eyes, sans taste, sans all.

Life was life.

There was nothing else, just *life*, and to think otherwise, he knew—through the foggy lens of metaphor, for instance, worn by so many to ease the truth that life had nothing to do with coming and going but with knowing that where you come from is to know where you are and will always be—was no more or less than a piece of the trick that tricked you to think other.

Life was life, and he'd spoiled it from the start. He had, like a jerk, done scarcely more than spit his beer in its face, thinking himself some dare-all rebel—how pathetic, what a jerk.

At the ABC he nabbed his fix from the guy he'd nabbed it from the day before, a skinny old geez with yellow teeth and yellow eyes and hair slicked up with a tin of Murray's pomade, the same Winston dangling from his mouth as the day before. Rice could scarcely comprehend the man, his drawl so thick, and doubted it would matter had the geez used time to retrieve his smoke so he could move his splintered lips.

Then again, who cared? He had his stuff. He was going to pour his stuff into him and head to his tryst with old Queen Oblivion, to dance with her his lousy dance, same old, same old.

He'd be back later, doubtless, and the geez would stare at him like he was staring now, another of the dirty Yanks that came and went each year with the calendar at school.

The geez, Rice was sure, would sell him his booze anyway. Rice and his kind were the geez's train of gravy and gold.

But, yeah, so what, and who the fuck cared about that anymore than they did the guy who'd made the obit page? What the geez did past selling Rice his stuff could as well be the dream of Schrödinger's cat as the sucking of a pickled egg.

The spare room at their flat he and his wife had made into a study. He spent a good deal of time there, writing, doubtless, but reading and researching, too, and sometimes, like now, during the days and nights he was alone after he'd ceased to be for his wife what he'd once been, he sat at the desk, a bottle of whiskey and many of beer before him, smoking his smokes as he muddled through his perverse dreams, of throttling her dead like a boob from a Johnny Cash song or of very simply packing a bag, as he'd packed so many bags in the years till now, and hitting the road for another girl, the smell of whose hair he'd use to wash out the smell of the last.

Once he was there with his smokes and his booze, the rest became unreal.

The door was shut.

He had his machine.

He had his books.

He had himself a goddamned gun.

People weren't people. People didn't exist, even, to be people or anything else.

The world was his head, and his head the world, and so long as that head stayed on his body and his body in this room with its locked-shut door, the world was anything he said, even, if he wanted, a baboon's stage.

Some hours passed.

She didn't call.

Not that he'd expected she would, given she never had.

That, however, hadn't kept him from looking at his phone. He did this now and then, flipped the gizmo open to see if she'd somehow buzzed while he was on the toilet, but she hadn't.

No one had called.

She hadn't called, and wasn't going to.

She was gone.

And now his booze was near gone, as well, now he'd have to trudge back to the geez to suffer his watery stare and listen to his drawl, slow as molasses from a bottle, as he'd heard some locals brag.

Then, searching through the tin of coins he kept on the desk, picking out the quarters and dimes, he bumped the mouse to his computer and triggered its screen.

Outlook, for Christ's sake, what a shitty program, he was still using the thing, there it was up front, the inbox blinking, at the top of whose list—he looked away and back and blinked and looked away again, addled with disbelief—glowed an email from his wife, its subject line, THANKS LUNATIC NOW GO FUCK SOMEONE BIGGER THAN YOU.

He clicked the message.

The message opened.

Her words, in pixels, appeared on the screen.

He double-clicked a word to see it truly colored, to see it was an actual word in an actual note, which, still, to his abiding incredulity, it somehow was.

Shit on a stick, he thought, it was really so, here was an honest-to-God message, from his wife, no less, he'd not been confused, with just a few short lines, albeit, telling him that while it was a good thing before he wrecked her machine he'd thought to send her a message with her stories and book, that didn't change a thing.

He, she said, was still the psychopath he'd been and would always be.

He, she said, was the most diabolical human she had ever known.

He, she said, had mind-fucked her harder than a victim in a Hitchcock flick.

He, she said, made Caligula look like Gandhi.

But at least she had her stories, she said, at least she had her book, and that was something.

"Don't for second," she concluded, "think to get your hopes up, you fucking prick. And whatever you do, don't you dare call me, not until I call you, if ever I get low enough to do something so clearly insane."

He fell back like an asthmatic under siege, unbreathing, yet somehow clear—as in clear like mountain-stream clear—gobsmacked by the implications of the note on the screen.

After a time, he couldn't say what, he scrolled through the thread to see she hadn't lied.

How could she, now, after all, with a thing of such magnitude? It was so.

He'd sent her an email to which, as his wife had declared, he'd attached a folder of her work.

He could burn property and slash tires and terrorize his wife and piss on her things to little result, but never in years, he'd seen through the rage of his black-out, could he escape the sentence he was sure to call down—what he and she both, really, had believed he'd called down—were he to destroy her writings.

Before he smashed her machine, commanded somehow by the weensy speck of goodness he had left, the spot of love for his wife that yet remained, he'd attached her work to an email and sent it.

But the note to his wife didn't contain merely the stories and books he'd attached, but as well a letter to her, of the dreariest sort, really, angry and sulking and remorseful by turns, in which he'd also pasted, by way of picking at the guilt that against all probability she might harbor, the note she'd written five or six days back.

Dear Boo,

I don't know why, but I feel very unfocused, very muddle-headed, and, in a way, lost. I just don't want to get out of bed in the morning. I know it's "typical." I know I should try to investigate some options. I guess I just need to ride this out for a few days. Please know that I love you very much and feel bad that you're in any way affected by this mood of mine. I really think it's best for me not to be around you, as I will only bring you down too. Please be patient with me?

His letter went on, more of the same, but it was what he'd written at the end, in bolded caps, that broke him.

"**SOMETIMES**," he wrote, "**DREAMS CAN REALLY STINK.**"

HE HAD SET OUT ON A PILGRIMAGE OF NOTHINGNESS.

Then time abandoned him, he became a beggar in a void, no longer searching for his wife, as he realized, but for the self he'd been in the days before they met, when he was a child, before he knew his mother and father and the sadness and rage of his mother and father.

Days turned to nights and nights to days, he ate nothing and drank nothing in a sunless moonless world, but wandered like a beggar in a void with no one to beg from and nothing in the end to beg for but the feeling of what it meant to have to beg.

And then, as if woken from a dreamless sleep into a nightmare of sleeplessness, he found himself groping through a dungeon, its walls slimy with rot.

One chamber led to the next, and corridors ran endlessly on, yet however far he wandered he found but the ghosts of those who'd died behind the castle's walls.

On and on he wandered, forgetful again that the object of his quest had become the memory of the boy he might once have been, and so but a ghost, knowing merely that he'd been searching, like a man dying of thirst helpless to name his need for water.

His quest had become a quest for the memory of his quest, and then for memory itself.

But then one day his wife stepped from behind an enormous block of stone, her belly and thighs thick with hair. Above her navel, he saw, she had a terrible wound, sewn up with a hanger and snatch of twine.

She'd been pregnant, he realized. The monstrosity she'd ripped away was his.

And though her belly and thighs were those of a beast, she was more beautiful now than ever. Dark hair fell round breasts from a dream, white skin glowed, her eyes were wet with hate. His wife stood before him, gorgeous in her hatred, he had so much to say, but her metamorphosis had transfixed him.

Then, from behind the same bloody rock a crone emerged, covered with slime and hair.

"Who is this?" he said.

"She's my doppelgänger," his wife said. "And now that we've found each other, we're never going to part."

Hardly had his wife finished speaking than the crone lunged toward him, and he began to run.

The crone wanted to kill him, he knew, that was its purpose, having learned of his entrance to the castle his wife had invoked her doppelgänger to kill him.

When he looked over his shoulder to prove his fear, the crone reached out and from her hand blew a poison cloud. If he should breathe so much as a speck of this deadly cloud, he knew, his life would end, he would die the most painful, hideous death.

But the faster he ran, the more the crone had gained. And no matter how fast or far, the crone stayed with him, blowing her cloud of death.

Soon they entered a plain so vast he couldn't see its end.

Again he turned back, believing the moment to be his last, but the crone had vanished.

The sun was rising from the west. A shadow swept across him, with nothing to have made it, there was only the plain.

He set toward the castle in the distance, his wife at its gate, staring at her wound.

IT TOOK HIM SOME TIME, BUT EVENTUALLY RICE'S BROTHER Z got a woman at County Mental, behind an office up on Y Lane.

Don't let him out of your sight, she'd said. *An agent from the state will be there soon.*

A car appeared in his brother's drive, some patrol-cruiser

type deal, cream-colored, with that metal grille between the front and back seats he'd once heard a cop call a *transport enclosure*.

The driver, at once clinical and earthy, approached the house more like a man from the IRS than an orderly from the loony bin. And instead of the menacing white tunics Rice had seen on guys in flicks like *One Flew Over the Cuckoo's Nest*, this one wore a short-sleeve button-down of muted plaid tucked neatly into khakis, and white athletic socks in geriatric shoes. The man had shaved that morning, too, and his wavy hair still smacked of a recent trim.

In every way, this man was typical, and yet he was perplexing.

Rice knew he was suicidal, sleepless for three days with the vision that haunted him in his gloom, of plunging a knife into his throat.

Likely he was wrong about the man, likely he'd have suspected evil from any stranger now, it didn't matter where, here in the safety of his brother's home, with his brother's pregnant wife and their little girl, or out on the street with some gold-toothed thugs.

But then he understood: the man's arms were bald while his fingers and hands were thick with hair.

The world had never been stranger, then, or more sadly gorgeous, brimming with such fractal logic, full of men like this man, and children like his niece, gazing up with her judgeless eyes, and the dead gopher on the floor, killed by his brother's dog, and his in-law with her rotund belly, waddling about in a melody of coffee and spoons, all of it a mystery, to the least crumb on the floor.

If only he were the turtle in the warmth of its vivarium, he thought.

If only he'd known how to live.

He wondered whether this man with his furry hands would let him ride up front or stuff him into the *transport enclosure*.

Unfortunately, the man said, there were rules. They weren't his rules, he said, but he had to follow them just the same. "It's a short drive up the hill is all," he said, palming Rice's head as he slid into the seat. "You'll be out in no time."

"Hold on," said a voice from the intercom outside the loony bin.

Rice saw movement behind the window in the door, and then frowning before them stood a man in a parka.

"Wait," he said, after they'd stepped in, as if Rice might rush into some hidden maze.

They stopped in a holding area between a series of doors, the first behind them and two of thick glass before, past which was the ward.

He could make out a couple scruffy sofas there, pleather, it looked like, together with a magazine rack, a cabinet full of antiquated games, and, in the corner above it, a TV on the wall, playing a rerun of *Family Feud*, hosted by Richard Dawson.

"Got any weapons?" the man in the parka said.

"Nope."

"No nail files? No scissors or knives?"

"A pocket knife maybe in my bag. I don't remember."

"Any drugs or alcohol?"

"Wouldn't you like to know."

"Place your feet apart, and raise your arms."

In a recent documentary, two guards had unlocked the cuffs on what had seemed a comatose lunatic only to see the lunatic smash the first on the head and with his fingers stab the other's eyes. Rice had never seen anyone move so quickly or dramatically. Both guards, the documentary said, were hospitalized, the first with a fractured skull, his partner a missing eye. If the man in the parka hadn't dealt with lunatics as deadly as the man in the film, certainly he'd dealt with lunatics crazier than Rice. The man with furry hands stood close, smiling with detached concern, while Rice was searched by the man in the parka.

"Sorry," said the man with furry hands.

The man in the parka knocked on the glass behind him. A buzzer sounded.

They walked through the first door and waited till it closed. Then a second buzzer sounded, and they entered the ward.

Two men had materialized on either sofa, both in V-neck smocks, baggy pants, and socks with rubber treads, all of it the blue of surgical scrubs, both men staring up with druggy eyes as Richard Dawson made his way down a line of frenzied women, kissing them all like they'd just got out of bed.

The first man sat with his hands in his lap. What Rice had taken for an animal on the back of his head, the color and size of a possum, turned out to be a dreadlock.

The other man, hardly more than a kid, had a tic in his eye and a face of violent pimples. The television was muted, but every time Richard Dawson spoke, the kid wagged his head and mouthed along with him. When anyone else talked, the kid began to twitch, and one of his hands flew up like a wounded claw.

Down the hall, a woman with a veil of greasy hair shuffled round in circles. Now and then, like she'd been pricked, she'd gasp, then snatch at her arm with a hand that could've been spattered with ink.

The windows at the front of the room were encased with bars. Through them, across the way, the trees were bare and still, and, but for a defunct Jeep and patchy bushes spoiled with bits of trash, the lot, too, was empty.

A tired-looking man behind a counter to the right stood waiting with a sheath of papers.

"How you doing tonight?" he said, pleasantly enough.

Rice stuck his hands out, palms up, and grinned.

"I see," said the tired-looking man. "Mind if we check your bag?"

"Knock yourself out."

"You wearing a belt?"

"Yup."

"We'll need it. Same with your shoelaces, if you got them. While I'm looking through your stuff, I'll need you to sign a few forms, too.

"All right."

"Do you know why you're here?" Rice tilted his head and looked at the tired-looking man. "It's not a trick question, I promise."

"Is this not the nut house?" Now the tired-looking man tilted his head. "I need help," Rice said.

"Section 5150 of the Welfare and Institutions Code allows a qualified officer or clinician—in your case, Eric, here, Mr. Kowper, I mean—to involuntarily confine a person—in your case, you—deemed, or feared, to have a mental disorder that makes him a danger to himself and/or others. You own a firearm?"

"Not anymore."

"Good. After you sign this, you can't go near a firearm for the next five years." The tired-looking man put the paperwork before him. "You seem like a smart enough fellow. Are you a smart fellow?" Rice held up his hands again. "I'm going to give you this pen. Sign the places I've highlighted in yellow, then set the pen down next to the paper. All right?" The pen was a ballpoint featuring a sketch of three nerdy men beside the words *Pep Boys*. "You can wear your street clothes if you want," said the tired-looking man as he nodded toward the lunatics on the sofa. "Or, if you desire, we can give you the same costume in which those gentlemen there are so gleefully attired. Let us know."

Rice signed his name here and there while the tired-looking man searched his bag and Mr. Eric Kowper, the man with furry hands, completed the paperwork that "authorized" Rice's involuntary confinement. A minute later, the tired-looking man walked Rice down the hall, past the woman in her anguished rounds, and opened a door like the one through which Rice had entered the ward.

"You're in luck," said the tired-looking man. The room had just a single bed. "For the next seven days, minimum, you are the king of this vaunted castle."

"What's your name?"

"My name is Fred," said the tired-looking man, "and I'm not dead."

"You're a generous man, Fred, and I thank you."

Fred pursed his lips in the semblance, near as Rice could tell, of a smile.

"Try to get some rest, Mr. Rice. The doc will see you tomorrow some time near midmorning. Maybe later." He gestured toward the lounge. "As you can see, his caseload is hefty."

Fred closed the door, and Rice began to cry.

After a time, he blew his nose and washed his face, then sat beside the kid with the tic in his eye, who didn't so much as turn his head. The kid was alone with his TV—Charles Bronson, now, a guy the kid could really ID with, Rice thought, given Bronson's own clear bout with acne. Instead of mouthing the words as he had when Richard Dawson hogged the screen, the kid merely wriggled and blinked till Bronson played his harmonica and the kid's hands rose to his mouth in pantomime.

Every ten minutes or so, as if to accompany the kid, someone moaned from a nearby room. More than that Rice heard just the sound of the kid's stifled gurgling and the sometimes-drone of traffic. He went to his room to wait for dawn, rereading Bukowski's *Love Is a Dog from Hell*.

His depressive episodes were more frequent and intense than his manic episodes, which had always been seen, at least by others, as high-functioning, however twisted, behavior, but neither, explained the doctor with his clipboard, could be accounted for by some schizoaffective or delusional disorder.

What Rice had, the doctor said, was *severe, clinical depression, possibly bipolar II*, and what he needed was *pills*.

To put him down, the doctor gave him Ativan.

To haul him up, Wellbutrin.

The latter took some time to hit.

The former dropped him cold.

For the next week, when he wasn't out in dreamless sleep, he could be found shuffling along with the rest of the nuts, staring at stuff mainly—ceilings, walls, TVs, floors, clouds through the window, cars through the window as they zoomed up and down the way.

The sensation wasn't so much unpleasant as vaguely

humiliating, especially those moments when through his haze Rice perceived that to anyone from the outside, to anyone "normal," that is, he wasn't much different than the freaks with whom he shared this void.

To someone from the outside, they were all just "5150s," as lost in space as they were the pathetic menaces tired Fred had told Rice he was.

The notion that this was how others saw him, as a menace, and that this was how others might see him for the rest of his life—since who knew if or when he might ever leave this place or, if he did leave this place, that it wouldn't be for another place like it—that possibility scared Rice blind.

If he wanted to live, which he somehow realized he very much did, he'd have to get his shit together soon. And the first thing on his list to accomplish this getting together of his shit was to quit the drink and drugs.

But it wasn't just the drink and drugs that were his problem, he knew, but Life itself, huckster extraordinaire that Life was, tedium monger, blitzkrieg maker, disgruntled architect of silliness and woe that his Life was.

The ennui was endless, the lunacy, too, and the sadness, and the heartache and injuries and illness, the plain old dirty pain.

His life wasn't his at all, by no means at all was his life his own, but someone else's, a madman's surely, or the specter of that, more like it, who long ago had devised the wherefore by which to inhabit and abandon Rice at will.

Nor had any of this just somehow "started." He hadn't been taken by the scruff of his neck and tossed into his life. His life, all of his life, had been this way always—he couldn't remember a time when it was other.

All he could remember, in fact, was grief.

At five, when a girl had refused to leave his patch of beans, Rice struck her with a hoe.

At seven, aping Evel Kneivel, he'd tried to leap a stretch of garbage cans and Big Wheels and trikes, but got a concussion for his trouble instead, smashing his skull on the walk.

At seven, too, he was taking down boys on the yard at school, at eight he was huffing on smokes and running away, at ten he was robbing his father's weed, and, come thirteen, guzzling booze and snorting cocaine and popping mushrooms and acid and pills.

And plus the fall from that rope swing, thirty long feet onto a dry creek bed.

And plus killing Tommy Dallen's ancient dog, Buster, in Tommy Dallen's car while in the seat behind him Tommy Dallen fingerbanged his girl.

And, with Tommy Dallen, too, lighting some kid's hair on fire just to see what a kid looked like with his hair on fire.

And wrecking skateboards and bikes and motorcycles and cars, and fighting in streets and nightclubs and dives, and contracting VDs and likely passing VDs, and lying and cheating and stealing from more women and friends than he'd deserved, and destroying the faith these women and friends had placed in him, and his habitual dream of killing himself and his regular loss of mind.

He played in rock bands, finally, with Tommy Dallen, he lived the life of the rock (without the) star, he married a woman he never loved and left the woman he never loved, he roamed the streets of cities for nearly two long years, homeless, crashing his way through the maze of ennui and despair and sorrow and madness and rage, bouncing at nightclubs and bars, lost in drugs and heavier drinking, losing his stuff to fire and the rest to the streets, losing confidence, losing will, losing what little he'd been given of generosity and compassion, till at last he met a woman as despairing and as mad as he had been, for whom, after ripping a man's ear off in a brawl on the streets of Y Beach in Y, he set aside what remained of his life and moved to Y, and descended in short order to the depths of hell, where, however impossibly, he found the trapdoor in the basement of hell and tumbled down its stairs, into what couldn't be described as more than a limbo of madness, truly, on the razor's edge.

And while his disease raged, during his windows of puny respite, Gluttony took him again, and again, and again.

He roamed the streets of that shithole town in blackout after blackout, emerging nearly every time in the company of strangers almost as mad, engaged in the madness of men as mad as he was mad.

He carried a gun and shot the gun at more than targets at a range, he bombed with graffiti untold numbers of businesses and homes and flags hanging from businesses and homes in the aftermath of 9/11, he committed vandalism, he committed arson, he committed petty crimes.

And all the while he degraded himself in so many ways, and degraded his wife and let his wife degrade him so many times, in so many horrific ways.

And then, a year ago, almost to the day, his little brother Z, thousands of miles from home, appeared with his truck in Y, to take Rice from his hell.

The bags were packed and the truck was running when

the woman in the shack behind the shithole in which he and his wife had been killing one another waved him to her porch.

"Maybe this will help," she said, handing him a book.

But seeing the book—*When Things Fall Apart*, by Pema Chödrön—Rice's head went light, and the world began to spin. His mind told him to punch this woman on her friendly nose. Instead, he kissed her cheek and slunk away.

For eighteen months he'd been dragging his ass through that demonic town believing his misery a secret, but from the start, evidently, it had been evident to all.

The thought that every time he saw his neighbor, the woman, every time he'd waved to her on the street, every time he'd run into her at a market or restaurant or pharmacy and believed his life hidden behind a greasy pair of shades—the thought that all of this had appeared to her as nothing more than a puppet-show of avoidance and denial—her, whom, sweetly unassuming as she was, he'd written off as some idiot stranger, some lonely lumpy fool of her own—the shock of this thought surpassed all horror.

In the moment the woman gave him her book and looked at him with those knowing eyes, he understood without the teensiest doubt that she'd known everything about him, that his pathetic little sham had never been anything more than that, a pathetic thoughtless sham.

Not once had the woman failed to see through him, not once in all those times had the woman failed to see his crippled heart.

And in her knowledge, he realized, the woman had pitied him, in her knowledge she'd said to herself, and likely to her friends, "That *poor* man. And his *poor* wife. You should hear how he talks to her. You should hear how they fight. They smash things, and scream, and tear each other to shreds. The police were there just last week at three in the morning. The man walks around his house with a gun."

It took a few days before he was able to consider what she'd done for him, but when he did, he wondered at the strength she must've had to summon to show what she knew—that he needed help like sinners their salvation—and to show what she knew with such unassuming kindness, through so simple a way—to hand him a book while looking in his eyes with all that softness in her own.

In the town of Y, where his mother was raised and he was conceived, to which Z had moved and his mother returned, he began to read the book the woman gave him, and then he read others, as well, Suzuki's *Zen Mind, Beginner's Mind*, and one by Alan Watts. And then through those books he began to sit. And while he could only vaguely see why he did these things, much less see their effect, he kept on, feeling that to leave them would trigger some doom in the offing, and he'd be forever lost.

And then one afternoon, as he read on his brother's couch, he was slammed:

Everything he'd ever done was false.

And that was all. He'd been free floating in delusion, he knew, this was the truth. Had he seen it another time, this truth, it could as easily have been the face of a stranger drifting in a trance.

"*What?* This is *it*? We swim our lives through murk with no idea it's murk, till one day we're asked if we know we're swimming through murk? This is the *point*? This is all there *is*?"

Some absurd cosmic grace had been laid on him, he couldn't say why, but it had, he'd been let to see this truth, and, as well, though not till later, how lucky he was, and how lucky, really, he'd always been.

He drove to an abbey at the foot of Mt. Y, in the mountains of Y. Life at the abbey, where he'd be asked to sit for hours and often days on end, would force him to another level, he believed.

He didn't know that he had the strength for such an effort. He knew he had to make the effort, he knew the effort he made would have to be his best.

His days in the abbey were the tolling of bells and clacking of blocks of wood.

He sat on a pillow, watching his thoughts as they came and went.

He bowed to the sun, he bowed to the moon, and to butterflies and monks, and to roots and trees and stones.

He bowed before he entered rooms, he bowed on leaving them, he bowed for the dirt on his hands, and for the soap that washed it off.

It wasn't long before he saw meaning in all he did.

His life, he saw, was grass in the wind.

The world was fleeting, nothing lasted, he himself did not "exist," nothing anywhere "existed," or ever had, and yet still everything was and nothing was not.

It was like he'd been adrift in *ex post facto* memory. His least gesture was the gesture of mendicants and multitudes. His least thought was a purity of significance terribly alien and weirdly everyday.

And then sitting with the monks from dawn to dusk, his body fell away, and his mind fell away, and he knew he wasn't "he," and yet, he knew, as well, he was all, and that all which he was smelled with eyes and tasted with ears, felt with mind and heard with tongue.

He was everything, and he was nothing, he knew, come from nowhere, bound for everywhere, beyond the reach of life and death, the heart of the universe in the center of the heart of the universe in his heart. He was utterly empty, he was full past measure, at one with totality, with nothing to know and knowing all.

He'd swum through the murk into the pool beyond, in which everything was transparent.

The murk through which he'd been swimming was the crystalline waters in which he now swam.

There was delusion in delusion, he saw, and understanding in delusion, and there was understanding in understanding, and in understanding there was delusion.

Understanding and delusion, understanding and delusion—each the mother, father, sister, brother to the next—arising from nothing, descending to nothing, and yet always here, always present, *increasing not, decreasing not.*

And it was then, too, that he knew what old Augustine meant when he said truth gives birth to hatred. We love the truth in every case, he saw, but the one that shows us we've been wrong. It's when we need truth most, when the truth has come at the expense of what we've always believed was true, that we're least inclined to accept the truth, and, ironically enough, most disposed to crush it.

And he saw this so clearly because just then a bell began to ring, calling the monks to dinner, calling him back to whom he knew he wasn't.

He hated his understanding for having shown him his

delusion, and for having shown him the way beyond it. And he hated himself for having wallowed in delusion for all those years, for having never known he'd never known, and for believing that what he hadn't known did not exist.

He hated his delusion, the waters of his deception, for having risen all around him—confusion in the guise of truth—and for the day in those waters that, without the strength or will to swim to the waters that were fast and clear, he'd be confused again.

In his hatred and his fear, however, he was grateful still. He knew what he knew was not the end, but the way. And knowing he knew, he couldn't turn back.

Alea iacta est: the die had been cast.

He'd sat on a cushion and risen from a cushion, just as he'd risen and sat so many times before. But this time the world was one way when he sat and another when he rose. He well knew the world was the world it had always been, and yet everything in it seemed different.

He thought of a story he'd read, about two monks by a flag in the wind. The first monk had said the flag was moving, the second not the flag but the wind. When the master approached, the monks begged him to say who was right. "You're both wrong," the master said. "It's not the flag that is moving, nor the wind, but your minds."

And that, Rice understood, was *it*. All that he now perceived was no different than it had ever been.

Nothing had changed but his mind.

This new vantage had the welcome, if unsettling, effect of donning a pair of glasses after a life without them.

What had appeared the apple was a grapefruit with a bruise.

What had appeared the wig was a head of gorgeous hair.

What had appeared the cat on the road was a swirling plastic bag.

His confusion lay largely in his constant delight. It leapt up at every turn. A joy ran through him, and he wanted to haul through the abbey like some crier of wares.

"Look at the shadow on the mountain!"

"Look at that withered branch!

"And that freckle on her face—is it large or small?

"And is this cheese sharp?

"And that tea strong?

"And the drum on the altar, and the smoke on the breeze, and the birds in the swaying pines?

"What are they to you they've never been to me?"

Then his wife called to tell him she was pregnant—yes, after three months alone at his brother Z's, he'd returned to Y for her and her things, he'd driven cross country yet another time to make yet another preposterous effort to thwart a collapse that was no less inevitable than growing old, senseless as they both knew their efforts were, helpless as they knew they were to escape the demon that had laughingly kept them bound—and once again a thing he'd believed turned into something else.

He was packing his car when a monk appeared, silent and bald, with that smile for which so many monks around the world are scorned.

"It may come as a surprise," the monk said, "now that you've been with us for a time. It may not be as you recall it."

"It?" Rice said.

"The world. But no matter what happens, it's important to be kind to yourself, and patient."

"I'll be back," Rice said. "An emergency came up. That's all." The monk kept his smile. "It's just something I have to do," Rice said. "I'll be back."

"We shall see," the monk said, and smiled a different smile, which had irritated Rice so much his first days in the abbey, because he'd arrived stripped of the means to know the difference. "Won't we?"

Not till now, when it was too late, had Rice seen the smile of this man, how this man had built an absolute code in the shades of a smile. Then, with a swish of his robes, he palmed his hands and bowed.

And by God it was real after all, at the clinic in Y by the bay, it was real by God, the picture of his vilest fear: a mongoloid pulsing in the belly of his blasted wife.

In their fog a date was set to scrape her clean, she wrote it down and said no more till the day had come. And when she said it, he thought it a joke, though it wasn't a joke, she said, not by far, but true, she said, all too true, an abortion on Halloween day, the day to the day a year before, when he'd run amok in Y, setting fires, slashing tires, scaring strangers, crushing work, crushing trust, faith, souls.

And then they were there, him by his wife on a table, sobbing in his ear as a man sucked her dry through a plastic tube.

The engine whirred, his wife moaned, the mongoloid was dying, feverish and dizzy, he watched his mongoloid vanish in a slurry of blood.

And then it was done, then it was over, his mongoloid dead, and his wife began to drink again, and he began to drink again, one more time, yet another unspeakable time he stooped into hell and knew as he knew anything else that whatever God he'd been graced to glimpse had forsaken him again, he was gone for good, he knew, nothing could save him, no one could save him, his days in this world were numbered, for he'd truly lost his mind, hence the man with the fur on his hands appearing to take him away.

After all his efforts, after all he'd done and tried to do, he'd failed yet again. He'd not merely failed, either, but gone mad. He'd lost his bird and been thrown into the loony bin.

And what he saw in the loony bin was a long way off from pretty.

The man could walk as well as Rice—he'd watched the man check in the day after he had—but the man demanded a wheelchair, then refused to leave it. And once he'd established himself, he turned into some autistic master of shit, announcing with ghastly regularity both his stool count and the number and kinds of bacteria in each. Three or four "visitors" would be gathered in the lounge, watching the latest vid from Osama bin Laden, when the shit man would roll up and say, "It's consistent with my previous examinations, of course—seven mutually exclusive units of feces this morning, each of which contains Bacteroides, Clostridium, Streptococcus, and Lactococcus at rates varying from 5.4×10^{10} to 7.2×10^{10} cells per unit . . ." Yet no one but Rice ever heard him. It wasn't till the shit man commenced to roll through the ward with his penis dangling out that anyone took notice. In one moment, the shit man would be mumbling in his chair. In the next, he'd be wagging his junk through another lecture about the life and times of his shit.

A woman was obsessed with the numerology of her name, which was Clementine. According to her system, clearly insane and without the least basis, certain letters in random combinations told the dates and times of certain future events, chief among them her death. "Do you see that?" she snapped at Rice, and pointed to her scribble on a napkin. "September 22, 2014, at 1:37 AM—that's when this little chicken eats the final worm!"

The man with the dreadlock spent an afternoon arguing with his absent mother about why he deserved the money he'd taken from her purse. "The seventy bucks," he warbled, "that was nothing, that was for the long johns and sandals, yeah, and all those rubber bands and cotton swabs and shit. It was the $412.62 you didn't know nothing about, Mommy, I mean, even after I told you, what I bought that bike with, and them beads I put all over it, and . . ."

Lunatics came and went, and while not one received a visitor, Z appeared each day with the candy Rice wanted, twelve-ounce bags of Reese's Peanut Butter Cups that Rice devoured while Z was there. But more than anything, his brother brought him hope. At the end of the day, he'd not been abandoned.

The doctor saw him daily, also, to monitor his "progress," the doctor said. When at length the doctor asked Rice if he felt ready to leave, he froze.

Where would he go, and what would he do once there?

The food in the loony bin may have stunk, and the people in the loony bin may have been loony, but here in the loony bin Rice had nothing to do but eat and sleep and wander and stare. Why on earth would he want to leave?

He told the doctor he thought himself too shaky still, but he would let him know.

The next morning, he read about Shunryu Suzuki's revelation on visiting a great waterfall.

The water fell from such height, Suzuki said, it shimmered like a curtain thrown from the top of the mountain. But looking more closely, Suzuki said, he realized the water didn't fall in a steady flow, but in countless streams of unique drops. How long it takes for each drop of water to reach the bottom of the fall! Suzuki thought. How difficult it must be for each drop of water to fall from the top of so high a mountain! In that moment, Suzuki understood that our human lives were like the drops of water falling from the mountaintop. Just as the water wasn't separated into drops before it swept off the mountain, but was one whole river, Suzuki said, so, too, were we human beings not separated into unique human beings, or even into lizards and flowers and gazelles, nor were we just one human being continuously divided into many. What we were, Suzuki said, was one and the same as the universe itself. It's only after we've been separated from this oneness by birth that we experience any trouble, Suzuki said. And the reason for this trouble is that before we were born, when we were one with the universe, when we *were* the universe, Suzuki said, we had no thoughts, and so we had no desire. It's only after we've been separated from this oneness by birth that we have feelings and desires, Suzuki said, and that we attach the selves we mistakenly believe we are to our feelings and desires without any sense of where these feelings and desires come from or how these feelings and desires were made. In the way that water's always water, whether an ocean or river or ten thousand falling drops, Suzuki said, just so are life and death—one and the same as the universe itself, which has no beginning or end. And while the water may leave the river swept off the mountain, the water will return to the river when it reaches the mountain's foot. The water falls, Suzuki said, but it's never anything but water. And there's no difference, either, Suzuki said, between our lives, as we move from birth to death, and the water, as it falls from the top of the mountain to the mountain's foot. It's because we don't realize this, Suzuki said—that our having "left" the universe at birth is only ever our "returning" to the universe, and that as such we're never *not* one with the universe—that we live our lives in fear. We must see that our lives are as much a part of the universe as the drops of water that make the waterfall are part of the river, Suzuki said. Only then will we be free of the fear of death and, in fact, free of trouble altogether.

Gazing out the window, then, as he'd gazed out the window for ongoing days, contemplating the ray of sun broken through some clouds, a voice spoke in Rice's ear as clearly as a bluebird on his shoulder.

"If you let me out of here with my faculties intact," the voice said, "I will stop the drink and drugs, and I will live."

Hardly had he realized that he was alone in the room, and more, that the voice itself was no more his than another's, than a second voice, strange as the first, replied. "Okay," it said, and that was all.

Every promise he'd ever made to quit his drink and drugs, Rice understood, had been the promise of a man under siege by drink and drugs. Such a man, Rice knew, will say anything for a moment of relief, but then, in the moment of relief, forget his promise and return to the drink and drugs. Over and over, Rice had said, *I will never do this again,* over and over, he'd said, *I'm done.*

But not once had he said he was done, and not once had he said he'd never do this thing again, without falsity in his ear, the echo of that twist of doubt. No sooner would that echo have reached him than another voice yet, the voice of doubt, would sometimes whisper and sometimes scream, *But you are not done, you will do this thing again,* and doubt would've won, he knew even then, it was as true as it had always been true, because he would know his doubt was real, he would know he wasn't done, because in fact he'd do this thing again, and again, and again.

Yet in that moment, gazing at the beam of sun broken through the clouds, there in the loony bin, when the voice that spoke to him as clearly as if it had been a bluebird on his shoulder, Rice heard no other voice, Rice heard not a puny squeak of doubt.

What Rice heard was nothing but the silence of truth.

And three days after he told the doctor he wanted to leave, the doctor released him, into the care of his brother.

And the day after that, Rice met a man who wept for his mother because his mother was dead, a man who when he put his mother in the ground had remembered again what the drink and drugs had done to his life, and what it could do yet without his vigilance. He helped Rice, this man, and with his help and the help of his brother, Rice didn't take another drink or drug.

After all his years of struggle, after all his years of doubt, the drink and the drugs were gone, Rice knew—at least for a time.

THE MAN

And they can do nothing to my son, rather they
will commiserate with him on having had such
a father, and offers of help and expressions of
esteem will pour in upon him from every side.
— *Samuel Beckett*

Father —

In all the years, I can recall but a few times in which you have simply said "I am sorry." Rather (and it hadn't dawned on me until now that this has been the pattern), you say "I am sorry you feel that way, Son."

Your way of "apologizing" undermines the act to the point that it no longer reflects the remorse you say you feel, the will, the desire to expiate the act that rendered the harm. When you say, "I'm sorry you feel that way, Son," you are repudiating not just my feelings, but your involvement in the issue at hand, shirking your responsibility for the effects of your behavior. You are saying, "It is you who feels that way, not I. I cannot help you." But at the same time you are also taking something so desperately needed by the person who has been injured—their belief in your sympathy for them, that you truly care for how they feel, that you are sorry for having had a part in how they feel, that you wish to help them from the inside, not from some remote island where you stand barking heady exhortations.

I felt terribly abandoned by you when we last parted. In light of the circumstances that forced me to you—my fragility, my tenuous hold on sanity, reality, on life itself, my total dependency on you when there was no one else—what did you expect of me? Those days were paramount to my recovery, much less to my survival. I believed those days I spent immersed in introspection, exercising, reading, writing, had been a gift. But they were not a gift, I see now, for I have been paying for them always. Maybe you didn't understand the gravity of the situation. Maybe you just couldn't *see the darkness into which I had lapsed. But I thought you did. You led me to believe that you understood, that you were helping and loving me unconditionally, with nothing expected in return.*

You annihilated me, Father, with your impregnable "dignity," your callous "righteousness," your inability to give without expecting in return. Believe me, had I something to offer, it would have been yours. You seemed suddenly so vindictive and malicious in your treatment of me, as if to punish me for not exalting your "kindness" and your "generosity." But instead of bringing us closer, your "I am sorry you feel that way" pushed us further apart. It is a phrase you have used, I realize now, to shield yourself from the guilt that sometimes comes with the realization that you have hurt someone. It is a phrase you have used, essentially, to keep your hands clean. I do not know what else to say other than that I am sorry myself. For all the times I have not said thank you or shown my appreciation, I am so very sorry.

—Pat

NEARLY TWENTY YEARS HAD PASSED, NINE OF SILENCE AND ten since I'd let my father back into my life.

My brothers had forgiven my father by then, as well, and for the same reason, I suppose, more or less. It had taken almost nine years from my letter of grievances back in the spring of '92 (triumph of bad taste and indiscretion that the letter was), and several from my brothers theirs, but at last my father had made an effort, the first in his life, to hold himself accountable in a letter of his own.

But it wasn't so much the content of my father's letter that softened me as the effort it had so plainly taken to write it. My father had written to express contrition. When I saw the thing for which my father had pronounced himself contrite, however, I was appalled first, and then just disappointed.

That, my father had declared after his bloated run through the list of complaints my mother had been reciting since their divorce, *leaves us to deal with what I consider to be the REAL issues that caused the estrangement between us. I also believe that you see these issues through the prism of your pain, caused by my failures. Let me see if I can restate them correctly:*

* P—You called me with a request for money when you were destitute and I disregarded your need.

* X—I told you S and I would visit you on Thanksgiving if S could get time off. I failed to call you until the day we were supposed to arrive to tell you S couldn't get off.

* Z—The Karmen Ghia I told you you could have and you considered yours was disposed of and I didn't tell you for one whole year.

In the face of all that my father had done and not done across the years, and after everything my brothers and I had ever said about all that my father had done and not done, my father had somehow convinced himself that we had written him off for a single offense committed against us each, that the whole of my sadness and rage could be reduced to what in the scope of things was pathetically superficial, a snubbed request for a couple of hundred bucks.

Had I been stronger, or had more confidence or will, or any power whatever, I might have reacted differently, I might've ignored my father's letter on the grounds that he was deluded, that despite its portion of contrition, more than anything, my father's letter revealed both the true extent of his denial and its consequent misunderstandings, and that the feeling behind his delusion was really the very opposite of contrition, closer, really, to arrogance mawkishly disguised, but the years had been too long, and I no longer had the strength or the will to hold my father to the flames. I was just too tired.

It had taken my father almost a decade to write his letter. In it, my father had given my brothers and me everything he was going to give us, everything he'd had to give. And it wasn't merely the case that my father had given us everything he had to give, but that *my father had given us his best.* I could howl my ruin for another ten years, I could disown my father outright, but none of it would change a thing. When my father wrote his letter, he was incapable of saying or giving more.

And the more I thought about it, the clearer it became that given my father's means, limited as they were, his effort was heroic. It had taken him years to write a single letter, and who knew how many days of anguish and nights of sweat. To want from my father more, clearly, than he could give, I realized, would somehow be unjust.

It wasn't that my father wasn't contrite, but that my father didn't know how to express contrition. Till then, my father had never once thought himself guilty or wrong. On those grounds, to insist that my father say more would be to insist that a baby sing and dance. My father's effort to express his contrition was the effort of that baby learning to walk.

And the truth was, for all my father's weakness, for all my father's failure and doubt and fear, I couldn't deny I missed him.

I just wanted back to my old dream.

I just wanted to pretend again that everything was as it had been with my father, whatever it had been, to pretend to continue to pretend.

And when my father called me up those few weeks before my wife and I left for Y, just days after yet another of the breakdowns whose tides I couldn't stem, and I couldn't get out of bed, and didn't want to get out of bed, and my marriage was stretched to the limits, and I felt I had no one else to turn to, having wasted my connections and friends long since, debacle after pathetic debacle having sapped my connections and friends of sympathy and patience and beds—confronted with all that and more, my father's voice on the line offering his help, promising to meet my wife and me the moment we arrived in Y, sounded like The Voice of Second Chances.

My father had written his letter, and now he'd called to offer his hand, a real gesture, obviously, in a time of real need, something else my father had never done. In his letter, he'd made himself accountable, meagerly at best, but his choice of words had revealed his awareness, however subconscious, of my complaint—that my father hadn't disregarded my need a single limited time, but that his relationship with me amounted to a lifetime's worth of need, overlooked, ignored, unseen.

What I found in that letter was the glimmer of hope that my father's gesture was a start, that with my father's patience, and with my own, my father might someday see more, and I might see more, too.

BY THE TIME MY FATHER HAD RECONCILED WITH HIS SONS and reestablished a habit of connecting, my brother Z had got married and had two kids.

But to remain hidden in his mountains, my father knew,

would be to forsake any potential bonds with the children of his son. My father, therefore, with his wife and mother and my brother X, who'd been living with my father for the last six months to help him pack, returned to the town where my mother grew up, and where I was conceived, and my brother Z had settled to raise his family.

Z and his wife were for my father's move in every way but one.

If my father wanted Z to trust him alone with his children, Z said, my father and his wife had to give up smoking weed.

Of course, maintaining he had no problem with weed— or with anything else—and saying quite honestly he really hardly ever smoked weed anymore, maybe every now and then, recreationally so to speak, as in sometimes on the weekends, with great solemnity and gravitas my father promised Z and his wife that once and for all he and his wife would give up smoking weed.

But not only had my father not given up smoking weed, every day, several times a day, but also my father had never intended to give up smoking weed, nor could my father give up smoking weed if he'd wanted to, leastwise not without help, because after smoking weed day in and day out, every day for over forty years, my father was an *addict*.

Instead of giving up smoking weed, my father did what he'd always done. He said the thing he thought the person he wanted something from wanted to hear, then kept on with the thing he'd said he'd stop—the very thing he'd taught my brothers and me always to do.

It wasn't long after my father and his wife and mother and son had moved to Y and settled in a house beside the sea that my brother found himself confronting my father about his addiction and his lies.

Z had smelled the weed on my father's breath and clothes, Z said, and he'd smelled the weed on my father's wife's breath and clothes. But once again my father set into the two-step shimmy that promised Z that he and his wife would give up smoking weed and then, for a time, to clear the lingering doubts, actually gave up smoking weed, only once again—because my father was an addict—to go right back to smoking his weed, several times a day, every day, day in and day out.

And throughout this time, since my brother X lived with my father in my father's house and knew exactly how much weed my father had at any time and exactly how much weed my father smoked at any time, I knew also exactly what was happening in my father's house.

X, in fact, until he, too, quit the drink and drugs, had smoked my father's weed with my father himself, the way X had smoked weed with my father from the day my father had sanctioned X's weed-smoking when X was thirteen, a couple of years after I'd given X weed for the first time, when X was eleven—weed, no surprise, I'd stolen from my father. Still, throughout this time, I never said a word to my father about his addiction or his lies.

Then came the day my niece went into the car of my father's wife looking for the chewing gum my niece was told she'd find but found instead the bag of weed and rolling papers and sneak-a-toke and lighter that my father's wife had been too stoned to remember she'd left in the car where my brother's daughter had been told she'd find her gum. My niece went straight to her father, Z, to ask him what she'd found in the car of her father's father's wife, whereon, no doubt, Z succumbed to rage.

But this time my father didn't display his former contrition, however insincere.

Having been caught *in flagrante delicto,* my father's pride and my father's character and indeed all that my father was as a man in straits, he attempted instead to flip the blame to Z by announcing with *grave indignation* that he, my father, would no longer tolerate Z's attempts to "control" him and his wife, and that, moreover, there was nothing wrong with smoking weed every day, and who was Z to tell my father otherwise. In fact, my father declared, in his opinion, the best possible solution for all concerned, and especially for the children, would be to introduce them to weed and to the culture of weed by way of an "education."

Z and his wife were aghast, not merely at my father's pronouncement, but at the reality that all along my father had been deceiving them, and—from Z's perspective, at least—making fools of them, to boot.

In reality, though, this wasn't the case, but the case that best suited Z and his wife.

In reality, Z and his wife had known from the start that my father had been smoking weed every day, just as my father had always smoked weed every day.

Z and his wife had merely ignored the evidence, the same evidence as ever, that my father was smoking weed, because so long as they didn't acknowledge that evidence, and so long as my father, nor anyone else, brought that evidence to the attention of Z and his wife—the sort of out-of-sight-out-of-mind elephant-in-the-living-room situation that was so common in that family—Z and his wife could continue to tell themselves that the fabric of things was sound, that all was well and fine, and that, as such, life could go smoothly on.

But reality didn't matter.

Aghast as they'd insisted they were, and wounded as they'd insisted they were, and disappointed and angry as they'd insisted they were, Z and his wife made it clear to my father and his wife that if this was what they wanted to do, smoke weed all day every day, who were they, Z and his wife, to stop them. They could, moreover, do what they liked, said Z and his wife to my father and his wife, but as long as my father and his wife were intoxicated, they could rest assured they'd never spend time alone with the kids.

THIS LATEST FEUD BEGAN AT THE END OF SUMMER '09 AND lingered through the fall.

I'd been clear of the drink and drugs for nearly six years by then and had for the most part got my blues under wraps, as well. I felt so good, actually, I thought if I could manage absent medication I might stop it altogether. I had every reason to believe this likely. That spring I'd gone into another capsule of reflection, studying the sages, writing mystic poems, meditating, working out, fasting. I'd delved into myself more deeply than I'd delved, I'd seen truths inside the truths I'd thought extreme. Come summer, I spent a month on an island off the coast of Y, then toured the wilderness of Y with my wife, J, before driving back to Y in the East, camping in parks along the way.

Life, in short, had become a splendor, somehow, and I was the last to care.

But by summer's end, like a growing shadow, that sense of doom had again begun to creep into my days, until one late September morning I rose feeling badly drugged, the way I'd felt for too many years, feeling, actually, that once more my life was meaningless, that once more nothing mattered, that once more existence itself was a maze of baffling sorrow.

And then the weeping began, and the despair, and then the numbness, and the sloth, and then the lack of will to so much as move, much less to leave the bed, and then, in bed for hours on end, the thoughts of death, and of suicide, and my terminal vision, proverbial by then as any book I'd repeatedly read, of plunging that knife into my throat.

The fit waylaid me as it had dozens of times, yet still I was astounded, as if this specter had appeared from behind a bush that hadn't been the day before.

I was staring out my window at the life below—the honking cars and roaring trucks and the bus that ran my street like time, and the kids on scooters, and the couples arm-in-arm, and the bag lady hanging bags on gates, and the serviceman filling the old man's furnace, and the woman with the tattooed face, while all the while the leaves performed their yearly change, that slow drift, before the fall, across the span from green to brown.

No leaf had fallen.

I'd not yet seen one leaf fall.

Then a bird flew into the tree outside my window, and a leaf, not quite brown, but gold, broke free and fluttered to the ground.

Perhaps it was the child I'd just seen laughing with her mother, or the man yelling from his car at another man in his, or the bird itself that had flown into the tree from which the leaf had drifted, a cardinal, the last of the year, I knew, before it made south for the season, or perhaps it wasn't one of these things but them all—I didn't know—but the leaf as it fell through this tableau was so full of desperate collapsing beauty that a dam opened up inside, the dam that had opened up so many times before, and I gave way and began to sob, and didn't stop for hours.

A part of me—however remote and weak, however much that part couldn't bear the other part of me, the worst of me, that clung to the thought that the slip and fade of things was somehow personal, a deprivation in the host of men imposed on me alone for no more reason than to fill me with despair—that part knew as it had always known that nothing was wrong, that not a thing at all was wrong.

Yet once this cast of mind had taken hold, nothing I did could shake it.

Soon my fits began to take me down me at will.

I was helpless in their clutches, the torment was extreme, my life had become one strictly of endurance.

The melody of a song from a passing car would enter me like a shot of elementary sadness.

I'd see a child cry or even laugh, and the laughter or cries would tear through me whole, and I'd begin to sob.

For weeks this went on, for days and days I'd endlessly weep and sob. And as the weeks passed, my fear grew and my desperation grew until once again I was ready to take my life.

In my slips of the past I'd been on drink and drugs and looked to drink and drugs as both the reason for my madness and my refuge from it. But now that I'd quit the drink and drugs, this slip left me with nothing to say but that I was incomplete.

I was lacking, I'd always been lacking, since birth I'd been lacking, my survival had come by dint of luck and lies, and now that these had left me, I was bereft of means to shore me up. The coming winter would see my end, I believed, I had a few lost days remaining, tops.

Space was churning, matter grinding, I was in the spin of entropy, now, without a hope to see me through, and neither my wife nor my friends could save me, and certainly not my family, twisted as it was. And throughout this latest and, I thought, last descent, the story of my father's enduring addiction and lies, and of my father's resentment before such accusations, wouldn't let me be.

At times my disappointment and shame plagued me in secret, so that I couldn't put words to them but despaired in silent panic. Others these fiends chased me outright, so that in my despair a fury would rise up, and I'd want to kill everything I saw.

My father was a failure.

My father had always been a failure, I saw, my father had never not been a failure, and now that my father was lost, no one or nothing could save him.

But most terrible of all, and what was to me a burden past all burdens, was the truth, inescapable, that I was my father's son. I, too, was a failure, I, too, was lost.

Then, in the midst of this trial, as I strode through my trial with open eyes, the last of my defenses collapsed, and for the first time I began to admit that my father was truly the man I'd known him always to be.

With mortified certainty I realized that though I'd worked for years to repair the damage suffered at my mother's hands,

I'd never so much as glimpsed a scratch at my father's, save in the sense my father was a fixed regret.

It was precisely because I'd let myself gape in awe before the picture of my father as the model of saintly goodness, I realized, that my father's collapse had crushed me. And it was precisely because my father had used my mother's insanity and abuse as a foil against his own terrible flaws that I'd been blinded to them, and that, against the terror and horror of my mother, my father had truly been to me a saint, a saint, moreover, I saw, who in his radical cowardice—which my father had guised as helpless, stoic passivity—could do no more for himself or his sons than quietly endure the storm that was my mother.

Nor had I ever had anyone to direct me to the truth that by failing to protect me first from my mother and then from the world my father had betrayed me at least as badly as my mother had betrayed me, and perhaps even more.

My mother had never had a mask to guise her villainy.

My mother had simply and always been a villain.

But it was precisely my mother's villainy that gave my father the greatest mask of all.

My mother had been my father's mask, I saw, and my father had always known it, and worn that mask to his advantage all my life, casting himself meantime as every bit the victim of my mother's madness as his sons.

Wearing this mask, my father could deflect the misery of both his victimhood and mine back onto my mother, who in her turn prolonged that misery, by which, again and again, my father and I claimed ourselves her victims.

This was the moment, too, when I understood with perfect clarity my recidivation into the nameless conflict with which

I'd grown up, but which for years now had lain dormant, deadly nonetheless, like spores waiting for the shift in things that will guarantee their revival.

It was true. My father in his cowardice, I saw, had failed me in the most critical obligation.

My father in his cowardice had failed to protect me, his son, from my mother in the villainy of her disease. I'd always sensed my father was a coward, who'd failed to do the very thing that should have defined him as a father, but I'd refused to admit it, much less to see and acknowledge that critical lapse, though for all my life I'd wanted and needed nothing more than to do just that, to acknowledge and confront my father's failure and doubt and fear, and the disappointment and shame that over the years had been eating me slowly away.

But inasmuch as I'd needed to acknowledge and confront this parasite, that I might at last destroy it, I couldn't. Like my father, I, too, had been rendered powerless by doubt and fear.

I FLEW BACK TO Y FOR THE FUNERAL OF MY MOTHER'S mother—who, crippled with Alzheimer's for nearly twenty years, was mercifully relieved a few days before Thanksgiving, 2009—and with fresh eyes witnessed once again the calamity that was my father and the hurt he was wreaking on his family still.

Seeing my father shrunken more than he'd already shrunk in our decade apart, almost as if the man were shrinking before my eyes, my vague sense for what that meant and why gathered force and set.

My father's steady dwindling, I realized, quite literally embodied my father's ongoing retreat from the world, a steady fatal regression, back to all things past, all things childish and small—the same tiny, steadily shrinking world that was the house my father now rarely left, its walls the incarnation of the psychic walls he'd erected long before and through the years made stronger, the walls of total avoidance, total denial, total unrepentant fantasy.

In my youth, my father had sung the songs of adventures he'd never lived and values he'd never met, and now in my manhood my father was doing the same, singing the songs of a life and merit that scarcely resembled his life and merit.

My father's life, I realized, was a protracted *zugzwang*.

Everything my father ever did had made matters worse, till finally, having lost everything—his wife, his sons, his home, his job, his money, his reputation, his dignity, his pride—he slunk off to where no one knew him, up into the mountains, under the pretense, no less, of "reinventing" himself, and there began his slide into the fantasy of a life he may or may not have known as a boy, into all the things he'd always wished could always be and never change, that old familiar place of suspended youth, in the days before his own father had been yanked into the sky by some great hand from the clouds, never to return.

The further my father got from the day of his father's death, and the more difficult life became for my father, and the deeper my father's fear, and the greater my father's failure, the tighter my father clung to those seemingly halcyon days. By the time my father had pulled out of his nosedive, restored a hint of stability, and married S in the mountains of Y, his justification for all things had become God Himself.

My father had given his soul to God, he said, and was

rewarded in turn with *the* STRENGTH, DISCIPLINE, GRACE AND COURAGE *to begin rebuilding a* REAL LIFE—a life, moreover, as my father claimed, proudly, tellingly, *like he grew up with.*

So blessed, not only could my father claim the *respect of his business, his community, and his church*, but also the capacity once again *to face himself in the mirror.*

My father's retreat into the past, I knew, was far from a rarity in this hyper-implosive culture of ours, but the rule, expressed in cases great and small down the chronicle of disasters the world calls progress.

Boys in fright cry for the breasts of their mothers, and little girls suck their thumbs. Teenagers sleep with their teddy bears, and young men at war curl into balls while crying, again, for their mothers. Mothers bereft of mothers in their dotage abandon themselves to the pictures of their youth, and fathers bereft of fathers tell of frogs and snails and puppy dog tails to forget the hearts they crushed in love and men they killed in war.

And the disquiet of an unguarded moment sends great singers back to the breath of their apprenticeships.

And the specter of failure makes great actors forget their lines and retreat into paralytic fogs.

Julius Caesar, in the moment of his murder, sought for some imagined haven by reverting out of Latin, the tongue of his empire, into the Greek he spoke as a boy.

And Stalin, stripped of Russian by dementia, babbled in Georgian, language of the mountains where he grew up, though he claimed to've forgotten it long before.

And Molloy and Malone were Beckett's Ghosts of Regression, and Garcia-Marquez's José Arcadio Buendía fled his ghosts by founding a country in remote seclusion, where nothing resembled Buendía's former world but, ironically, mundane objects of antiquity brought to him by gypsies.

And both Napoleon, Corsican-born, and Hitler, child of Austria, fled to lands in which, strangers to all, they could "reinvent" themselves in the image of giants.

And so my father: from city and sophistication to countrified rusticity; from *laissez-faire* liberalism, mature freethinking, tolerance, and experimental openness to status-quo conservatism, jejune thoughtlessness, bigotry, and conventional irrevocability; from hands-off agnosticism and humble contentment to hallelujah zealotry and covetous domineering; from wide-eyed ranger to quaking agoraphobic—in every imaginable way, my father had retreated.

Having left the desert of his youth for a great metropolis, my father supported my mother and me, in the days after my birth, working as a gas-station hand and clerk at Sears, then made his way into the nascent tech industry to advance through the ranks until he was a suit-wearing, mid-tier manager in the purchasing department of a company building brand name computers.

From there he was handpicked by the CEO of a startup to complete the team of VPs charged with launching operations in a second-world country the other side of Earth—he'd made it, at long last the man had made it—only to plummet from that height like Icarus from the sun. The company may have failed, or perhaps it was my father who failed—no one but he would know—but in less than six months my father was sent back to The States with his wings clipped and his tail between his legs, a bird-dog humiliated, jouncing job to job, bewildered and despairing, banished to silence by his sons and bereft of means, and slunk into the mountains to lick his wounds in a cloud of weed.

Ensconced in these mountains nearest the country's belly—a virtual womb, as it were—my father turned away.

In the past, his manners and speech had been impeccable. Now he began to eat and speak like the sort of man who from his stool by the cracker barrel took great pleasure hawking at spittoons.

When it rained, he spoke of his *um*-brella. When he watched shows like *America's Most Wanted*, he'd yell at the screen, "The *po*-lice are comin to git you now, boy!" The expression *y'all* began to feature prominently in my father's speech, and most of his sentences were now prefaced with a prolonged *Weeeeelll* that sounded like *whale*.

But somehow what disturbed me most was the way my father said *root*. He hadn't simply begun to refer incessantly to his roots, almost as if in open confirmation of his increasing regression. Much worse, *root* no longer sounded like *boot* but like *foot*. Asked about some new habit or preference, such as his sudden, equally incessant mention of *The Good Lord*, my father would say, "Weeeeelll, those are my roots." The one time I mentioned this latest affectation—"Since when has the word *root* sounded like *foot*?" I said—my father smiled and said, "Since I realized it's my *roots*, that's when."

In my childhood, my mother and father had referred to city districts whose residents were predominantly black as *Chocolate Town*. But over time, as I conveyed my distaste for that expression and others such as those I recalled my mother and father using to distinguish *black people* and *niggers* and *white people* and *white trash*, the offending language slowly disappeared. Years had passed since my father talked like a bigot, but once again now he began to speak of *wetbacks* and *chinamen*, most of which utterances being tied this way or that to complaints of how *the immigrants* were stealing all of the jobs from *real* Americans and, in the process, like moths, chewing hole after hole through the fabric of America itself.

And then the entire white-collar class—to which his own father had risen from a cotton field in the South, and in which my father had struggled to remain for so many years once he himself had climbed up to it—was the enemy, as was just about everyone with more than a high school diploma.

It seemed no coincidence that the Bush regime had just come into power, with its attendant disdain for someone smarter than a boob. My father, unsurprisingly, had voted for that awful Texan man, and boasted his politics every chance he could, especially after 9/11.

He still had his collection of books—the very books he'd taught me to love almost more than anything else—and sometimes my father even read from them, but never more than pages at most. His flat-screen had taken the place of print, Oprah, Dr. Phil, and Ellen the place of literature, the Weather and History Channels the place of knowledge, and FOX that of news.

For all my life growing up, table etiquette had been strictly enforced. If I wasn't cutting food with a knife, my free hand was to remain on the napkin in my lap. Condiments and dishes beyond my reach were always to be requested with a *please*, as was permission to leave the table, whether during or after a meal, specifically with the question, *May I please be excused?* Dinner was served promptly each night, usually at 6 or, the times my father was late from work, at 6:30 or 7, and, but for the occasional Friday or Saturday evening when the family gathered to watch a special movie or show such as *Mutual of Omaha's Wild Kingdom*, TV while dining was forbidden.

Resting my free hand on the table's edge for much past a few seconds roused a scolding.

Rising from my seat without permission roused a scolding.

Chewing with my mouth open roused a scolding.

Talking with food in my mouth roused a scolding.

Lip-smacking roused a scolding.

Interrupting someone else's speech, at table or anywhere else, roused a scolding.

Scarfing food roused a scolding.

Slurping soup roused a scolding.

Glugging milk roused a scolding.

Licking fingers roused a scolding.

And surely belching and farting roused a scolding.

Now, however, up in the mountains of Y, any show of my father's etiquette, even of the most rudimentary etiquette, forget its memory, had vanished.

The TV blaring at stadium volume, my father sat hunkered over his plate with one arm propped on the table, smacking his lips and hawing through a mouthful of food, licking spoons, licking the rims of mayonnaise jars and jam jars, licking his fingers and sucking his teeth, belching outright as he looked smugly round the table, all before a spread of pure Southern cooking laid out like a smorgasbord at holiday—country ham, black-eyed peas, and cornbread one day, fried chicken, mashed potatoes, and fried jam pies the next.

While my father's wife worked a part-time job with a

government service based in the tourist town thirty minutes off, and made the needed balance at whatever she could find, from cleaning and painting houses to grooming dogs and making cheese at a local dairy, my father now claimed himself a "carpenter" and a "handyman" who, when the work went dry— the way the work so often went dry up in them thar hills—had no qualms churning ice cream and butter at the dairy, too, or clerking at a lumber yard, or running errands for the geriatric couple fettered to their shack in a dale among the oaks.

After my father abandoned his vintage Karmen Ghia for an all-wheel drive pickup truck, king cab, with a toolbox and lumber rack mounted to the bed, he announced the purchase of a semiautomatic .44 magnum, a .22 revolver, a 20-gauge shotgun (for the birds he'd announced he'd hunt, but never did), and a 30-0-6 rifle, for "deer and boar." My father, no doubt, was prevented by law from packing his heat when mobile, an injustice he often bemoaned, but that didn't keep him from ensuring his and his wife's safety by stocking the truck with miniature baseball bats, Bowie knives, and mace.

The home of my father and his wife was everything the home of my youth was not. Truly, the grounds around my father's mountain hideout looked nearly as bad as sets in the film *Deliverance*. Random heaps of branches and logs, lengths of timber, sections of pipe, Glad bags full of garbage and weeds and shit and leaves, rolls of carpet and cans of paint, and stacks of tile, and busted faucets and toilets and sinks, and saw horses, and shovels, and ladders, and rakes, and hammers and hoses and hoes, and plus for sure the stereotypically renowned anthology of auto parts, absent, thank God, the goat atop them—what, it occurred to me, was the "grown-up" version of the fort that as a boy I'd run away to and smoked my cigarettes in, what had in truth been but a hollow bush encircled by objects ruined or unwanted—all this and more was strewn round my father's house in the chaos which a chance observer might generously have described as higgledy-piggledy but in which my father insisted lay order, discernible no less, however hidden.

A dilapidated Toyota next to the garages behind the house gathered cobwebs and rust while a barely running Benz, circa 1970, hunkered out front, embalmed in Visqueen beneath the rickety carport next to a rickety shed.

Once the mound of garbage out back had grown past excuse, my father and his wife hauled it to the side of the hill and burned it whole, anything and everything—empty cans of hair spray, bug spray, and deodorant, too, chicken bones, old shoes, and PVC, a process all told that took two days, and sometimes more.

My father's three dogs, one named after me, and the two cats always near at hand, often with the snout of a freshly killed rat, whiskers and all, never failed to color the scene with hillbilly authenticity.

As for hope for better inside the home, it was no less a fantasy than anything else in my father's world.

My father might've had a lifelong thing for curios and collections, but in my youth what a bedroom closet couldn't hold went to the garage. And if by some terrible chance a thing found itself absent a cubby or, worse, stranded by oversight or neglect, the person responsible for it got fire thrown down in spades.

Everything had its place, right down to nooks for rubber bands and Band Aids, and mugs for pencils and pens, and, for the watches and film and buttons and knives and decals and decks of cards, a wooden box that once held cigars.

But more, during the decade that had swallowed up my and my father's hurt, my father had become something near a hoarder, filling his rooms with things in mounting, vaguely organized piles.

Crammed to the ceiling with crockery and cutlery and silverware and gadgets and spatulas and spoons, the kitchen epitomized the rest. One of anything was far from enough, and never could there be too much. Gallon tins of maple syrup with their tops removed and coffee cans decades-old bound fasces of potato mashers and pastry knives. Cupboards were organized according to types of pot and pan, and those for dishware ranged from saucers, plates, and bowls, to glasses of every sort, and mugs.

In one cupboard my father kept a selection of eight or nine wrought iron skillets, meticulously oiled.

In another were piles of cookie sheets, roasters, grill pans, and griddles.

In another yet was an assortment of paella pans and braisers.

The refrigerator stood jammed and so did the walk-in pantry, ceiling to floor. Whatever was needed, it was there, somewhere, from boxes of cake mix and casserole mix, to baker's chocolate and soda, to pastas and rice, to canned vegetables and fruit, to dried fruit and nuts, to cereal and candy and soda pop by the case, and none of this was to mention the pair of giant deep freezers my father and his wife kept downstairs, in what had been built to be a two-car garage, each of the freezers as full of food as the fridge up in the kitchen.

Not one of three garages held a car, either, or could. The

one attached to the house groaned with more of what was in the two out back, crammed to the rafters with boxes full of anything from doorknobs and photo albums to transistor radios, taxidermied animals, and buckets of tar.

What startled me most about my father's mountain home the first time I saw it, however, was the shrine my father had built to his long-dead father, a man whom I'd never met and whose name I heard but rarely in the gravest of murmured tones.

A memorial in every sense, the shrine consisted of a display case filled with a tightly arranged, ever-growing collection of model airplanes, and pictures of airplanes, and all paraphernalia airplane, among them the Cessna 195 in which my father's father had flown on the day of his ostensible death, built in the year of his ostensible death, 1956. My father, moreover, had positioned the case along the wall opposite the front door, beneath the pass-through to the kitchen, along the top and sides of whose arch he'd hung framed 8x10 photographs of his father—what amounted to a Halo of Fatherdom over the array of machines that had given my father's father not merely the power to fly but, far more importantly, the power to vanish once and for all into the heavens through which he'd daily flown.

My father's father was a vice president for Y Airlines who'd worked his way through the ranks from his initial spot as an engineer. Each day from his home in the desert town of Y, my father's father flew his company plane to corporate headquarters south of Santa Y, where he roamed the grounds directing his lieutenants.

As a boy, I had just the vaguest idea of this man, for whom, the rare times his memory was invoked, my father's voice evinced a solemn awe, an effect which made my father's father, whose image I'd got from a single photograph my father kept above his bench in our garage, more the figure of a myth than any man I ever knew, my father himself included.

I never heard my father say as much—my father didn't need to say as much—but the older I grew, the more clearly I saw that my father's father wasn't just a myth, but a giant of terrible power.

By what other alchemy can a man cast his shadow from the crypt?

In these photographs, my father's father is a lean gap-toothed man with a flattop crew cut—straight up vogue in McCarthy-era USA—and piercing, faintly mischievous eyes.

One photo shows my father's father sitting in an open, carefree manner, his leg dangling from a big oak desk around which two or three other men are standing and seated, examining a set of prints. Juxtaposed against my father's father's insouciance, the postures of these men (angular, focused, intent, tight mouths and furrowed brows, a pencil behind the ear of one) leave no doubt my father's father is in charge. That my father's father is attired in casuals (a polka-dot sport shirt whose collar is flipped over that of his dungaree jacket, worsted serge trousers secured with a thin leather belt above well-shined loafers and a pair of argyle socks) while the others wear suits and ties (jackets off and shirtsleeves hitched), confirms this impression.

In another photo, my father's father stands on a tarmac beside a plane from whose wing the pilot in full flight gear peers onto the document my father's father has on display. As in the other pictures, my father's father is the evident cynosure around which a number of men have gathered, intent on grasping the chief's instructions and, just as importantly, letting my father's father (and the picture's viewer) know they mean business sure. Shot in all likelihood for an ad campaign, or, perhaps, given the fully engaged Korean War, a propaganda push, the photo conveys an operation run by a team of jolly pros—a captain of industry guiding the production of his country's higher works.

Still another photo is a formal portrait of my father's father. Though my father's father emits an aura of clout in every shot, in this one there's more. Taken just before his death, my father's father stands at the height of his power, in his full authoritative glory. No special props or lighting are deployed to manufacture this effect. The power emanates from the man himself, despite its queer sort of incongruence with his image, which at first glance argues to dismiss my father's father as a bumpkin in a monkey suit. My father's father's flattop, his oversized, vaguely protuberant ears, the slightly crooked teeth surrounding his missing upper lateral—these are not the traits of a chief. It is my father's father's broad forehead, his light eyes and probing gaze, together with his carefree bearing and easy open smile that radiate wisdom, good will, and wit, all of which could belong to no one but a man who knows where he's going and how. In this portrait, my father's father is a cross between Will Rogers, that cow-poking jester of the '20s and '30s, and George C. Scott in *The Hustler*, or, better yet, *Patton*. He exudes the goofy but endearing charm of the momma's boy that the crafty horse trader of southern legend deploys so well. At the same time, my father's father radiates the urbanity of a wheeling Vegas gambler. You could imagine him sitting before a card table after having taken his partners to the cleaners, whittling a stick as he jokes about

Khrushchev—guile with a silly grin, fine as frog hair on the front end, tough as a rhino on the back.

The year he died, at thirty-eight, my father's father was the man with the plan, the great provider, loved by all, friends and family alike. At home my father's father's word was Law, his wife as queen and children as princess and princes obeisant to his slightest whim. Or in other words, my father's father was an A-type honcho, a gen-u-wine Übermensch: *The Father*. And with The Father, the last thing you want is to step out from his shadow, where, calm and cool, safety is assured.

I asked about my father's father, here and there I asked my father to tell me some story or tale, but seeing his reaction to these questions, knowing I'd get no more from him than ever—the profound solemnity of expression, the profound sadness, the profound silence—I began to say less and less as time passed until the day came when neither I nor anyone else in our family spoke of my father's father, even, by suggestion, much less by name. But still my father's father's presence, which was the ultimate presence, which was the presence of death, with all of death's great brooding silence, was as palpable as dust or glue.

AND FOR MANY YEARS, THAT, REALLY, WAS THE ONE THING I knew for sure about my father's father, that the man had suffered an ostensibly untimely death, killed in a plane crash over the Y Bay in Southern Y, halfway through my father's sixteenth year. My father's father had left home one morning, the way he left home every morning, to go to work, and never returned.

Up in the high country of the Y Desert, my father's father

had driven his shiny Ford to the town's little airport, then flown away with his two colleagues, destination Y Airlines in Y, never to be seen or heard from again. And since nothing so much as a shred of the plane had been recovered from the ostensible wreck, to say anything of the men in the plane itself, the authorities reasonably conjectured that the plane had gone down in the Y Bay, somewhere along its daily line, between Rancho Y and Santa Y.

Had the plane gone down anywhere else—on land, that is—its wreckage would've been discovered, and the bodies. No other explanation for the disappearance of an entire plane, together with its three lauded men, could suffice. Not that any alternative explanations had been presented to me. My father told me his father had been killed in a plane crash, and I, having no reason to doubt my father, at least at the time, believed him.

But there was an alternative explanation for my father's father's disappearance, as I'd learn many years later from my father's brother's wife.

Not once since the day his father disappeared, my father's brother's wife told me, has my father's brother failed to believe that his father didn't crash into the sea but rather, in fact, that he absconded to a foreign land, that rather, in fact, his father had deserted his old life, forsaken his family, his wife and sons and daughter, that rather, in fact, he'd faked his death for another life, a brand new name and brand new life, somewhere down in Mexico maybe, or maybe South America, what with the Spanish he'd learned growing up on the farm in Y with the Mexicans that lived in the shacks in the fields.

I'd seldom given any thought to the death of my father's father past its legacy and fact, and never to the thought of that legacy on myself, through my father. As for the times I did consider these matters, they were at once exhilarating and horrific, losing myself as I would in the fantasy of the crash itself, imagining the fury and terror of plunging toward death from thousands of feet, of quite literally dropping in flames from the sky.

And I could do this, imagine my father's father's death with such precise detail, because I'd flown in such a plane when I was still quite young, three or four at most, when my father took me flying in it, the Cessna owned by my mother's monstrous father, the details of which adventures had never been anything to me but vivid.

I could imagine my father's father's death with ease. I had but to close my eyes to see it, the instrument panel with its gizmos and dials, the airspeed and attitude and altimeter dials, and the directional gyro thingy and the thingy for vertical speed, and the throttle levers, too, and also the yoke, right down to the least detail I could see it all, and plus through the window the wing struts and wings and flaps on the wings, the endless expanse of cloud and sky, and the sea far below, and the land in the distance to the west, the endless sprawl of city north and south, right up to the edge of the sea on the west, all the way out to its end in the east, at the foothills rising from the haze, beyond which lay the desert—

—*And then above the engine's drone you hear what could've been a shot. A tongue of smoke rushes from the cowling and just as quickly thickens and swells, and then, too, a flame peels out, and then another and another, till soon the plane's enveloped in smoke and flames, it's happened so fast, so unexpectedly fast, it's all just so out of the blue. The man beside you gasps while the man behind you clutches your seat with a scream, the plane shuddering and lurching,* now, the yoke astray in your hands and the pedals gone. And that is it—the plane's nose dips for a moment, then drops utterly away, it's as if you've been shoved from the window at the top of the world, for there you are, now, in a dive, nearly vertical, in fact, inexorable, you know, with all the violence of the inexorable, gripped in a welter of smoke and flames tearing meteoric toward the sea before you like a wall of shifting green and gray, and the man beside you pounds at the throttle, the wall that's the sea sucking up space faster than you imagined space could move till presently the sea has swallowed up the whole of your vision, impossible, you think, but there it is, nothing but sea, now, nothing but a wall of shifting green and grey, the man behind you screaming, the man beside you cursing, how or why your life has come to this you can't say, nothing makes sense, nothing figures, the wall of brutal green expanding still more, if that were possible, crazily shifting, crazily swirling, crazy how nothing figures or makes sense, your mind spins on with its questions, till, as though a switch has been thrown, the questions vanish, like that they're gone, and you know you know, that none of it matters, your questions don't matter, how silly they've been, how silly and stale and trite, everything's gibberish, now, all of it gibberish and spew, this is it, this is the truth, this is how you're going to die, not tomorrow or the next day or the next but now, today, just seconds from now, in fact, yes, today is the day you'll die, this is your hour, this your time, it's stepped up to you as surely as the moment you buckled your belt and tied your shoes the hour before, yes, it no longer matters what you want or think, the sea is almost there, the roar of the engine and the roar of the wind astounding in your head, an awesome wrack of wind and steel like no wrack and roar you've ever heard, agents all, you understand, of what's rushed into your own throat, too, the scream pouring from your lungs, if scream you *can call it, soundless at it is, blotted out as it is by the engine's roar and the howl of wind and wrack of steel, all of it a cacophony that devours both sound and the notion of sound, for the roar is sound itself in all its bottomless worldless fury, there's never been any but this one great sound, you now know, this great vast roar, you now know, always it's been there, this roar, and always it will be there still, wherever you are, whoever has been or will be, always it's been there, and always it will be, since before the beginning began out to the reaches of the endless end, ah, how can you never have known this, never have heard a whit till now, you wonder, though that doesn't matter, either, none of that matters anymore, you realize, because now you've heard it, now you know, this is all that matters, and the wall that's the sea through the smoke and flames is almost there, that is true, that alone is true, you can see the whitecaps clearly, now, the spindrift dancing across the wall of swirling green, the great brutal sea opening up to take you in, this is it, you know, the last you'll see, this is it, yes, this is it—and sssssthwwwwwwwp!—*

—I opened my eyes and knew with relief I was just where I'd been when I closed my eyes to follow my thoughts into the cockpit of the plane in which my father told me his own father had crashed into the sea, in which I myself was not, because I was in my room, lying on my back in the dark.

I'd imagined this scene of my father's father's death in a plane crash in the sea enough times to be certain that as my father's father went down he couldn't have been anything but filled with knowledge and terror.

And, really, that was all I'd needed to know. Two or three times—I couldn't remember just how many, though I knew he wouldn't have told me more than once had I not pressed him for the details he'd given—my father had told me his father had been killed in a plane crash in the sea. My father had been so grave and solemn and sad anytime the subject of his father arose that I'd never conceived that my father's story could've been anything but true. There was nothing more to know, and therefore nothing more to ask to know.

But then, all those years later, decades later, my father's brother's wife told me about my father's brother's explanation for the disappearance of my father's father, and a gash was ripped in the vision I'd created, behind which I realized lay a universe of potential.

What could that mean, if it were true, if my father's brother's belief were true?

The possibility of the truth of such extreme committal, I saw, implied a life other than the life my father had always intimated he'd had as a boy, through the values he espoused to his sons as a man, a hidden life, a life within a life, the true behind the false, a life of nuance and silence and shadow, a secret life of questions without answers, and of doubt and fear.

MY FATHER'S ALLEGIANCE TO THE NOTION OF FAMILY suggested a memory of yesteryears golden beneath the high-desert sun, of halcyon days in the distance of thought, the American Dream in the days of Ike—*rah, rah, rah! sis boom bah!*—football games and basketball games, and pennants and pompoms and flags, student body politics, civic duties and Scouts, dates with Suzy Friday nights, picnics on Saturdays, and Sundays at church, and flat tops and loafers and rolled-up jeans, bailing hay through summers, and swimming in the aqueduct, and apple pie and hot dogs and Mom, and cleaning for Mom, and running errands for Mom, and gobbling up Mom's amazing food, and buffing the car with Dad, and building models with Dad, and flying with Dad in the plane Dad would die in—happiness all in all, a good life all in all, and all of it snatched away in a flash, the sudden fury of loss, the good widow left to fill the void, the good widow left to rear her brood by mainstrength alone, strong in grief, no doubt, but stronger in faith, and in will, and in the memory of her man departed, and of her promise to her man departed, and of their promise together, manifest in the children her man had left behind, whom no amount of yearning could restore but which yearning nonetheless obscured my father's ability to live rightly in the days of now.

And after my father's father vanished, in no regard whatever did my father so much as disagree with his mother, and certainly my father did all he could to fabricate the guise of a life to make his mother proud, and if not a life to make his mother proud then a life to satisfy his mother, or at the worst to prevent the chance of hurting her.

My father's mother was the All-American matron who'd lived the All-American life the All-American way.

Straight out of high school she'd married her sweetheart— the brother of her brother's wife—then born him three children and supported his rise through the ranks as an aeronautics engineer until, by the time he was thirty-five or so, he'd taken the VP's desk at a major American airline. And then, after her purportedly beloved husband's death, my father's mother had waited a good sixteen or seventeen years before embracing another man and returning to the cotton fields and oil fields of dusty Y, from which she made yearly trips back to Y to visit her sons and daughter and the sons and daughters of her sons and daughter, and to which my family, when I was nine or ten, once took a road trip for the occasion of an overdue reunion.

By the picture, my father's mother was immaculate. And she adored not just my brothers and me, but my father, too, her first-born son, and her other son, and her daughter, and their sons and daughters, too, and in fact everyone in her family, huge, to the extent that in her eyes not one of her family could do any wrong, however terribly wrong.

None of this was anything that smacked of secret lives spoiled by secret pasts.

The picture pointed to just what it seemed, an image of mnemonic statuettes wrapped in sun-got gold.

And yet if all this were so, I thought, from what terrible infection had the germ that poisoned the mind of my father's brother risen with such force that he could imagine such a crime, much less truly believe it?

Quite obviously my father's brother believed his father had abandoned him and his brother and sister and mother, by way, even, of a total vanishing sealed with a funeral absent a coffin, a total vanishing utterly severed from explanation, satisfaction, closure, end.

He believed this without doubt, my father's brother, for him this was the truth. Yet, if none of this were so, if indeed my father and his family had lived the life my father and his mother had forever portrayed, a down-home life, a life of earnest striving and contentment, why then were my father and his brother and sister so perversely crippled, why then could none of them scarcely function in the world, why then was it nothing the three of them did worked and everything they touched turned to nastiness and failure and ruin?

If truly my father's father had faked his death and abandoned his family, he couldn't have done so because he was happy, but, all too plainly, because he was miserable, so miserable, it appeared, as to do anything to escape it.

But either way it didn't matter. What mattered—to my father and his family, at any rate, to me, at any rate—was the indisputable evidence that whatever the case, *somehow, somewhere, something was wrong.* And something had always to have been wrong with this picture of my father's family, there had always to've been *that difference between what appeared to be and what truly was.*

I knew I'd always known this.

All my life it was as if a wee shrill noise had sustained in the rear of my thoughts with such brutal purpose that over time I couldn't help but to break. The suspicion broke me, I couldn't escape it, I had no choice but to find its source: the shrine, I saw, built by my father, the notion of which by then had consumed my waking thoughts.

During the forty-plus years since my father's father's vanishing, my father had refused almost entirely to speak of his father. One day my father couldn't bear the sound of his own father's name. The next he was prostrate with candles at the foot of the shrine he'd built for his father. The shrine wasn't hidden in some sacred penetralia, either, but featured at the home's front door, undeniable, inescapable, plush with the image of my father's dead father in its pentagon of worship.

Strangely, even as it needled me, I'd never much considered it. The shrine had been just another version of the bureau tops and walls that families worldwide give to pictures of family past and present.

But then my father's brother's wife revealed to me what couldn't have been less than a well-kept secret, and the air cleared before me, and the nexus of links began to click, and I saw.

MY FATHER HAD BUILT THE SHRINE TO HIS FATHER BECAUSE MY father had finally given in to the ghost of his father, surrendered at last to the unbearable yearning to be once again with his father, even if with his father's ghost, and all the rest, I knew, the forsaking of my father's manner and speech and culture and thought, was a function of that surrender, all the rest was that surrender's void.

Nor was my father's regression a collapse into mere infantilism, I realized, but the last ditch phase of a lifetime's struggle to bask again in universal innocence, security, and love, all of which, in my father's mind, had somehow coalesced in the symbol of my father's father.

My father, I saw, like myself, like the whole of humanity, wanted nothing more or less than to rest again in the bosom of love—that was all, that was all.

And it was in my father's sweet wife, I saw—*whose face looked as close to my father's father's as my father could ever want, shy of the face of his father*—that my father had met his ideal.

The face of my father's new wife, I knew with relief and horror, was the one face that every time my father saw it, that every time my father gazed into it as he looked up from his wife's embrace, could make him feel he was once again embraced by his father, protected again, once again in the shadow of his father's wings.

It wasn't simply that my father's wife was mannish in feature. She was a few inches taller than my father, also, with mannish shoulders and feet and hands. And while my father's wife cropped her hair to a pixie-cut and dressed in sneakers and pants and shirts with stains, my father had grown his hair as long as a beauty queen's—worn in a single braid that ran to his waist—and taken to sporting cargo shorts and Hawaiian shirts and clogs.

Together, my father and my father's wife looked liked the classic hillbilly husband and wife, Ma and Pa, only my father looking up at his wife with his hunched shoulder and withered arm was Ma and his wife gazing down with her sweet smile was Pa.

Yes, I thought, taken altogether, my father's life was the pieces of a puzzle in a box in the closet I'd taken one day and solved. The pieces had always been there, in a jumble in their box. They'd needed merely to be taken from the box and arranged on the table before me. And now the puzzle had come together, now the pieces fit, now I saw the picture whole, finally, now, the mystery had been solved.

The logic of my father's regression had been as fatal as hermetic. His regression amounted to a complete and instantaneous transportation into the Sonhood of Yesteryear, a simultaneous giving of himself to his Father and to God, the Father of All, both of whom, in the end, were One, *gathered in the image of his new wife.*

And nothing could have been better. For my father, his new wife was everything he'd wanted, everything, really, he had ever needed. In her, my father had been restored the paradise of his seeming safety, and everything he did reflected his effort to ensure that paradise remained secure, that he'd never again be stripped of the safety of his paradise.

Not long after my father had retreated into the mountains, a few years before we had reunited in 2000, he destroyed his left arm, the biceps brachii having snapped at the elbow and contracted at his shoulder into something like a knot. Yet rather than find the money to repair his arm, my father neglected the wound, and the obvious consequences of neglecting it, brushing the matter off as something beyond him, as a matter in the hands of God, with the flimsy excuse that the operation to restore his arm cost more than he could get.

In a way, that was what the matter became, for in reality my father had effectively placed the matter in the hands of his wife—*which from the start had been his aim.*

My father had abandoned the life of the executive he'd worked so long to achieve in exchange for the semblance of the life of a backwoods carpenter and handyman.

But a one-armed backwoods carpenter has the usefulness of a one-armed backwoods carpenter.

For all intents and purposes, though he refused to admit it, and though he did well know it, without his arm, my father couldn't work as a handyman or carpenter any more than he could as a juggler in the circus.

By and large, not yet sixty, truly ragtag and bobtail, my father began to rely almost entirely on his wife to win the family's bread. And when at last my father's mother left Y for good to live with her son and his wife in the mountains a little east, my father had the ideal pretext to justify this last departure from the world: he was his mother's caregiver now, his mother in her decline needed him now, his mother couldn't be left alone.

And so the transformation into Sonhood was complete.

Up in the mountains of Y, where no one knew him or his past, my father once again found himself alone with his mother and father and God, once again my father was the thing he'd always ever wanted to be, The First Son, The Good Son, The One and Only Son.

By the time my father and family had moved out to the little seaside town of Y in the west, my father's belief in and reliance on the illusion he'd made was impregnable. That, however, didn't prevent him from bolstering the ramparts yet.

My father had returned to "civilization," but still he left his house less and less, and then not at all, save under various pretexts, most of which involved this or that of his mother's needs, to see a doctor, for instance, or to drive his mother to the parlor for her perm.

And in this house that was his paradise and his prison, my father cooked the lion's share of meals and washed the lion's share of dishes and, amazing to me, somehow even balanced the family's books. Nevertheless, beyond these responsibilities, he was helpless for more, no matter how urgent the need or pressing our advice.

My brothers and I harried my father to enroll in a tai chi class in the little studio just a block from the house, but my father refused.

My brothers and I harried my father to take bicycle rides and walks along the scenic paths that lined the bay, but my father refused.

No matter what my brothers and I harried my father to do, he stubbornly refused, whether to join the Kiwanis Club, or to adopt the hobbies in which he'd long shown interest, or even to take a drive on his own for a movie or cup of joe in town.

Past the meals he made, and the dishes he scrubbed, and the tube he watched, and the naps he took at the tube he watched, and nothing else that anyone could say was more than puttering—sorting through junk mail, watering the yard, feeding the family's six outdoor dogs and three or four cats kept for "vermin," "organizing" his collections (among them now a five-gallon water jug to hold the hair he gathered daily from his brush, and a cigar box for his other bodily excrement, such as the nails he'd trimmed, and teeth pulled, and moles cut off, and gallstones passed, for he couldn't stand, clearly, to see any more of himself go than had already gone)—past these "activities," all of which he never failed to insist were somehow "important," my father did little else than slip away to smoke the weed he'd been smoking every day, day in and day out, for decades.

When at last my father refused an invitation from my brother to go flying in the Cessna owned by my brother's friend—a refusal made time and again—each of them spun from a litany of various but no less vague excuses, I knew for sure that my father was finished, that truly my father would never again return to the world.

My father continued to call himself his mother's caretaker, but by then he knew like the rest of us knew that nothing could be further from the truth.

Despite my father's countless ministrations, the bulk of them cosmetic, everyone knew it was his wife who'd become the caretaker, both of my father's mother and of my father himself, the two of whom, past their meager social security checks (my father having lost his mother's life savings to a Ponzi scheme), relied on my father's wife's salary from the government.

My father blustered constantly about his mother's needs, and of the necessity of ensuring that his mother never for an instant be left alone, and while the former may have been true, the latter wasn't. However old and frail my father's mother might've grown, she hadn't lost her mobility, nor, crucially, her razor's tongue-and-wit, as her readiness to deploy them at will made plain.

Not to mention that my brother, in an effort both to motivate my father and strip him of excuses, had repeatedly offered to cover for my father should he want to leave the house.

Not to mention that, really, my brother's help wasn't wholly necessary, since even when my brother couldn't watch my father's mother, she had neighbors to call in the face of trouble and, if all else failed, 911, which action she was eminently able to take.

It wasn't long before I stopped listening to my father's excuses, or to offer help.

To my ear, everything my father said did nothing but add to The One Excuse, an accurate summary of which, without my father having said the words, might have run something to the effect of: *Though I suffer mightily, I am consoled in the knowledge that I've taken the path of filial obligation, sacrificing my needs for those of my dear mother.*

My father had become the most absurd of martyrs, whose words, whatever he said, were silly and shameful, each new explanation or complaint like another piece of scat on the edifice of the crumbling castle of shit that was the reason for his helplessness, for his dependence on the care of his wife, and, finally, *finally*—this, too, most emphatically never said—for his constant state of befuddled intoxication.

And contemplating this great mess, I understood that none of it was anything new.

As a young man, confronted with his need for a final way out, a way that would let him deny his father's death and escape his father's precepts—which he lacked the courage to disobey—my father had surrendered to my mother's father's demand that my father marry my mother, knowing that once married and with child he'd be free from the obligation to chase his dream, free from his fear of failing to attain his dream, and, most importantly, free from his father, all without the pain of betraying or defying his father. And should anyone dare to question him, my father could excuse this figurative suicide beneath the mask of "principle," saying, simply, that *the right thing had been done.*

SURELY MY FATHER HAD SEEN WHAT HE WAS INTO LONG BEFORE he sowed the girl that bore his sons.

My father didn't know it, but when they met, my mother was just thirteen. She lied to my father, she told my father she was a senior at old Y High, then covered her tale by running from her class at middle school to the front of old Y High, where my father scooped her up in the Chevy he'd bought with monies from the trust left three years back, from my father's father's ostensible death.

No doubt the years between my mother and father's meeting and my father's knocking my mother up gave my father plenty of time to learn the truth, not only of my mother's age, but of her character, the product of a diseased mind, itself spawned by a youth inconceivably horrific. And even if my father hadn't seen through my mother's deceit, my father should've headed for the hills the instant he learned the girl he was bedding was just thirteen.

"You'd better hope she's pregnant, you fuck," my father said my mother's father had said when the monster learned my father had gotten my mother pregnant, "because if she's not, your ass is going to jail."

Given my mother's father's inveterate incest with his daughter, I feel sure my mother's father's reason for jerking my father's chain was motivated not by any sense of injustice, but by the fear that he himself, my mother's father, might've knocked his daughter up, the repulsive implications of which possibility have slunk through my thoughts for years. Whatever the case, my father was trapped in that timeless vise—damned if he did, damned if he did not.

But damnation comes by degree. Dante showed us that.

Had he wanted to, my father could've chosen a softer way.

Marrying my pregnant mother, having the child with my mother, committing himself for the next twenty years to raising that child with my mother, and to the litany of that obligation's attendant concerns—that was all one way.

Going to prison for having illegally screwed my mother, suffering the lifelong stigma that accompanies the sex offender—that was very much another.

If nothing else, my father could've bolted in his hotrod, back to his hometown desert, or, if worse came to worst, at least until the matter had settled, to Canada.

There were no tests for DNA then. The lone way my

mother's father could've so much as implicated my father's guilt—merely of statutory rape—was to have had my mother examined post alleged intercourse. At most, such a test could have revealed what my mother's father already knew, that his daughter had been spreading her legs for another man.

As for proving my father's paternity, science in the '60s hadn't passed the limits of serological testing, which eliminated from question just forty per cent of the male population.

And anyway, had my father actually bolted, shy of great lengths, my mother's father could never have tracked my father down. Even if my mother's father had tried to track my father down, by the time he did track my father down—*if* he tracked my father down—my father could simply have denied the old toad's charge.

Abortion, of course, yet illegal, was an option, too, given the scene.

My mother's father, beyond his questionable practice as an insurance man, beyond his incest and pedophilia, was by my mother and mother's mother's word a drunk, an addict, a philanderer, and a con—all in all, a perfect villain eminently skilled in gathering the reserves he needed to scrape his daughter's basket clean. Failing that, my mother could've elected to birth her baby on her own.

From any perspective, then, my father had not had to do what he did.

My father had his whole life before him.

He could've done anything, gone anywhere, roamed down any number of teeming ways.

How was it, then, he found himself in a slaughterhouse?

The answer was simple—too simple, actually, too immediately embarrassingly obvious to believe.

Many times I've looked directly at this answer only to turn away for other reasons, which, taken together, each with its intrigue and latent motivations, would amount to a sort of punishing thriller, a tale of espionage of the soul beneath whose treachery my father had unwittingly succumbed, like a king poisoned in the night.

But my father wasn't a victim of forces beyond his control, before which he fell after the long good fight.

My father wasn't the maverick who'd leapt into a fray of hustlers only to emerge in the end with a hand so raw it was impossible to surmount.

None of these scenarios belonged to my father.

My father was no hero, just a stoner in a cape whose ruin he himself had wrought with a single deadly blow.

My father was twenty-two when he got my mother pregnant—she a mere sixteen—a year from taking his degree in mechanical engineering at Y University in the seaside town of Y in central Y, where I was conceived. From my father's father's death, my father had a reasonable amount of capital, then, together with youth, good looks, intelligence, charm, and, I can imagine, a range of prospects and leads.

On the surface, it may appear my father squandered these by mistake, like a drunkard on the town.

On closer examination, however, it's clear my father's steps were anything but chance.

My father might never have spoken his intentions, my father's intentions may even have been subconscious, but they were in his mind the same.

If my father's father had proclaimed that my father be an engineer, my father, by golly, would be an engineer. That my father's father was no longer present to enforce his decree was trivial—his presence was no longer needed.

My father's father had his ghost to ensure that task, iron fisted as the shade of Hamlet the First.

It only remained that my father obey, dream of his own or no.

But my father couldn't have cared less about a sheepskin on the wall. My father, in truth, would've done anything to sabotage the taking of some degree. His studies had never been his own. Engineering left him cold, and mathematics he loathed. So long as my father remained loyal to the shade of his father, my father himself would be a lie.

As for my father's dream, as dreams go, it was huge.

Like my father's father, my father, too, loved airplanes and flying.

Unlike my father's father, my father didn't want to design or build or test airplanes, but to *fly* them.

Nor did my father want to fly just any old plane. It was fighter jets in which my father longed to soar, jets from the world's oldest aerobatic squadron, the Blue Angels of the U.S. Navy.

But my father couldn't fly with the Blue Angels of the U.S. Navy, to say anything of an aerobatic squadron or even of a fighter jet.

To fly a jet with the U.S. Navy, my father would had to have become an officer, and to become an officer, my father would have had to take a degree in mathematics, physics, engineering, or the like. And even if my father had adored mathematics, or merely suffered mathematics, he still wouldn't have been able to take his degree.

Doing so would've required he have no reason not to chase his dream.

Doing so would've required he be free.

My father, I now know, was still the boy from the day his father died.

Unable to believe his father truly gone, unable to believe himself alone, to believe he'd never again *not* be alone, my father clung to the notion of his father and, worse, to the notion of his father's shadow. My father had to cling to the notion of his father's shadow.

Belief in his father's death, together with belief in his bereavement, would've been too great a terror. And yet it was this disbelief in his bereavement that bereaved my father of his grief, without which my father could never find his way.

And so my father's scheme: from the frying pan into the fire he leapt, the anti-escape extraordinaire. And at the end of it all, to protect this fragile world, my father numbed himself with dope. In an endless fog of ganja, nothing is but what you say.

Now, all these years later, however unconsciously, once again he was resorting to this insane logic.

In sacrificing himself to his mother, my father could excuse himself from any further pursuit of the values he nonetheless continued to espouse (suggesting that were he not bound by honor to his vow he'd be out and about in the world, mercilessly shaking it down), and, by extension, from meeting his husbandly obligations to his wife, or, for that matter, from assuming any new obligations whatsoever, ever.

Best of all, in the way that this latest ruse would enable

my father's continued immersion in the fantasy that he was at once the King of the Castle, the Patriarch of the Line, and his Father's Beloved Son, just so would the ruse enable him to maintain control of the mechanisms by which he kept his illusion secret from the world, down to the smallest detail, and thus to ensure that its structure remain intact.

In the end, my father in his regression had achieved total withdrawal, total reclusion.

But it wasn't just that he had not a single friend past his brother, with whom my father talked many times a day. My father couldn't bear that his wife have a real friend, either, and especially not the one friend she had made, with whom she'd formed deep bonds, and who, once her friend had been diagnosed with cancer, needed the help and love of my father's wife as much as anyone could need another's help and love.

I'd known all along why my father had no friends, but now I saw as well the reason for my father's demand that his wife have no friends, either.

The more time my father's wife spent with anyone but my father, the less time she spent laving him with the attention of which he could never get enough.

Before long, this conflict had escalated such that every time my father's wife went to see her friend, my father sulked about with the face of a homeless dog. When finally his sulking failed, and his wife refused to abandon her friend, my father ordered his wife never to speak her friend's name if he could hear it. In the end, his tantrums became so insuperable that his wife was forced to pretend to submit, though she never did. Telling my father she was doing "other things," she went on loving and helping her friend.

ALL OF THIS WAS IN PROGRESS THAT NOVEMBER I RETURNED to Y for the funeral of my mother's mother, died at last, in the grip of that virtuoso of disgrace, Herr Rittmeister Alzheimer.

My father and I had been out for twenty minutes or so, on the walk I'd convinced him into after another of his tantrums, my father striding always a step ahead, despite his rotten back and knees, his arms swinging down the lane with its Monterrey pines and soporific air, when I asked why he'd banned his wife from seeing her friend. My father's answer was stupendous.

"Because I don't like change," he said, glaring up with wounded eyes, "and I don't like to share!"

Not two months back—when Z had called to say his daughter had found a baggie of weed in the car of my father's wife, and my father had responded with such bloated indignation (the ironic face of his deepest denial, I realized, a hollered claim of innocence before charges whose factuality only a moron or a man as desperate as my father would attempt to refute), and seeing with certainty in my father's denial that after all these years he'd never change, that he'd never own the truth of his crimes against his sons, that while he had quite literally set his sons on their paths of addiction and disease, he wouldn't remain merely unrepentant to the end but harden further into the lie that was his life in a cloud of weed—I'd been plunged to the depths of the lake of feelings that had been mounting across the years, like a subterranean lake, ancient, fed through rock by the drip of water that eats away the rock, a vast yawning body with but a crust of rock between the world and it, whose existence the world had never known. And while at first I was shocked by these feelings—which for so long I'd failed to see, which had appeared more like a flash flood than the slow drip of eons—once I recognized their scope and depth, I was overwhelmed, then bewildered, then conflicted, and then, at bottom, mute with despair.

The reunion with my father after our decade apart had fooled me.

I'd thought myself cured of my resentment toward my father, I'd thought myself reconciled to my father, to who and what my father had been and become.

I'd put aside my grudges—or tried to, at least—in exchange for the promise, vague as it had always been, of returning to my world of make-believe, to pretend everything was with my father as it had always been, to keep on pretending to pretend.

I was no more exempt than my father, I saw, from that longing for those days of a spotless mind.

I was no more free from the lure of the past than anyone else, much less than my father, a past full of what anyone could ever want—the apricots eaten in the tree from which you'd picked the apricots, the touch of your mother as you lay on her lap in a cool spring noon, the voice of your father as you sped off for the first time on your bike, he shouting your triumph with the pride of a father that every son longs to hear, that will keep him for years to come, that he'll yearn to hear again in years to come, for all the years of his life—a past untouched by harm, exempt from disappointment, sorrow, shame.

And in the moment I saw my father look up with the eyes of the wounded boy he'd never not been, his glasses filmed with grease and dust and his cap askew on his gray head, his beard with its air of noble poise oddly teasing his fragility, in that moment my heart went out to him with the pity of a man for the man who'd always lose.

I looked into my father's face as we stood in the lane by the bay beneath a pilgrimage of clouds, and I saw my father's terror and knew as well my father wasn't simply scared but had declined to sheerest panic.

I thought of the time my father showed me the scar on his belly, a thin white line just above his hip, and I asked him what had happened.

"I was attacked by a puma," my father had said.

"A puma!" I said. "What's that?"

"A mountain lion," my father said. "Just like the lions in Africa, but without all the fur."

"Really?" I said. "What happened?"

"Me and Danny Eagle went off for a drink of water while we were throwing bails of hay, and when we came back, a puma took a swipe at me. But I hollered and jabbed him with my pitchfork, and Danny Eagle got him, too, and he ran off with his tail in his legs."

"That's so cool!" I said. "Were you scared?"

"Sure," my father said. "Plenty. But I wasn't just going to let him eat me."

I was no more than seven when my father told this tale, and more likely five or six. It had been summertime. My father and mother and two brothers and I were at the public pool. My father had climbed up golden from the pool, and, as if for the first time, I saw the scar. His face lit by the sun, his hair swept back shiny and wet, grinning as he told his tale, his gray eyes twinkling with their odd blend of sadness and glee and even a glimmer of that terror, too, returned from the past in his telling—everything about my father, then, had transformed, my father was no longer just my father, no longer even just a man, but a hero of sorts, since that after all was what heroes did, fight lions and monsters and other heroes that fought lions and monsters and sometimes other men, that was what men from legends did, they fought things and killed things and saved the people of the world, it was true, I knew as I looked up at my father, my father was a hero, so big and strong I could climb all over him and pull and drag at his arms and legs and never once make him budge, and now by the pool that summer day I knew that my father had a secret he'd never revealed, that in truth my father was a hero who with pitchforks fought lions in the desert, because he had the scar to prove it, that all this time he'd been a hero, my father, but now his cover was blown, now I knew it to be true, *my father was a hero.*

And it was only then, as I stood with my father in the lane beside an ancient pine, watching my father with his eyes of the frightened boy, that I remembered how long my father had clung to his lie about the puma, and how long it had taken my father to confess that lie—long after I'd become a man, when I was married already or maybe a bit before, when I was down in the dirt with sex and drugs and rock and roll—that there'd been no puma, just bails of hay on a truck in a field, and his friend with the pitchfork that had grazed my father's belly.

Yes, it was only then I thought of this once more, of those days once more, of all these things once more, it was only then I knew what I knew once more. This time, however, I couldn't stem my knowledge, this time I had no place to tamp my knowledge down to, there with my father before me in the lane in the cool sea air, his eyes wet with tears—my father, who, to that day, so numb in his cloud of weed, was still singing the songs of a life and merit that scarcely matched his life and merit—that was him, yes, the man from whom I'd come, whose blood was my blood, that was him, that was the man, stubborn in his treachery, the failure and the coward, buried in his dream in his cloud of weed, this liar and cheat and thief, yes, this impostor, yes, that was him, that was him—*O my father!*

I OFTEN WONDER HOW IT IS A MAN BECOMES HIMSELF IN the world, how a man is made by the world, how the forces of life in this world conspire to exalt or defeat a man, and how a man submits to these forces or conquers these forces to be exalted or defeated. And I wonder, too, how it's possible that my father can embody so many apparent contradictions, the traits of a man who could be both exalted and defeated in this world but in the end suffer only defeat. My father is a man of such a limitless contradictions that it doesn't seem possible he walks this earth. And how is it possible I've survived this long, having been raised in this world by such a man as my father? And how and why have I remained tied to such a man as my father, having lived long enough to see my father for who he is, what he is, and how? And how can I live each day in the midst of such terrible ambivalence, how can I hold at once such awesome love and despicable, burning hatred? I can see my father, years and years back, roughhousing with me, tumbling about the floor, laughing with me, tickling me, swinging me about and tossing me on the bed to press his mouth against my belly and blow so hard the air squirting from my belly and his mouth delighted me always to no end, sounding as it did like the world's greatest fart. And my father loved to drive, my father drove so well, and taught me to love to drive and drive so well that in time I could drive any sort of machine, little car or giant truck or forklift or go-kart or cycle or bus. I could hardly have been five when my father set me in his lap behind the wheel and said, *You're the driver now.* I loved nothing more than to sit in my father's lap behind the wheel of his car, pressed tight against my father's chest, beneath his chin, smelling the smell of my father's breath of cigarettes and coffee and mints and weed mixed with the smell of his cologne and sweat, remembering thinking once that my father smelled like the sandwich I'd always wanted but could never have, because that sandwich didn't exist anywhere but in the smell that was my father, and listening to my father's voice as I steered down the road, *That's it, hot shot,* my father would say, *hold it lightly, a little here and there is all it takes,* my father teaching me the links between gas and stick and clutch, teaching me, though my feet couldn't reach the floor, how to double-clutch, yet another sacred Indian trick revealed to me alone, my father telling me I ought never to look at the road before the car but always at the road in the distance, always at the line in the road in the distance, that, my father said, was how you drove faster through turns, by judging the line of the road over distance, *That's it, hot shot,* my father would say, *that's it,* feeling that thrill as I sat in his lap against his chest, tucked away beneath his chin, smelling his smell, better than any smell ever, better even than the smell of dirt, than which there had never been another better. And I remembered also the first time I'd seen men fishing, at the little lake outside the city of Y in the south-east bay, how I'd fallen instantly under the spell of the call to fish, for years from that moment thinking of little else, of begging my mother and father to buy me a pole and take me fishing at the lake, and of how but a few days had passed before I was presented with a pole and taken to the lake, where, with my father at my side— my father having taught me to construct my pole and tie a hook and bait the hook, stinky cheese and salmon eggs that first time fishing at the lake—I caught a bluegill maybe three inches long, my father guiding me as I reeled in the little fish, my pole electric with the life of that fish thrashing on the hook at the end of my line, *That's it, hot shot, a little more now, that's it, hot shot,* and I, like the fish itself, filled with the sense of having been hooked, of wanting all the time to fish, which—from that day to the day I saw I had no right to torment a fish by snaring it with a hook for the pleasure alone of the challenge of snaring it—I did as often as I could, I fished as often as I could, if but to slip into the mountains for a few to shake away the city. And my father had given me his knack for kindness to strangers. In the depths of my drunkenness I'd been empty of the means to show this kindness, even if I felt it always the same, that instinctive fraternity, that instinctive communion with folks that in the days after I'd quit the drink and drugs emerged somehow naturally but apparently, so that people noticed this in me the way I'd noticed it in my father, and I wondered at it, the easy way that I, like my father, somehow had of smiling at the clerk in the hardware store or winking at the lady at the cleaners or shaking the hand of the mechanic at the station or chatting with the butcher at the market, a manner of being so easy and free with folk in the world, as if the world itself were my family, whom I'd simply never met, that was my father, too, that was what my father had given me, I couldn't deny it, this was so, I, like my father, was the good guy on the street, I had it, too, that special way with people, and I was glad to have it and thankful of my father for having passed it on, though just how my father had got it himself and passed it on, I could never say. And my father had given me his attention to detail, and somehow, as well, for lack of a better word, to what I called my *ethic*, my sense of the obligation to do things *right*, and also to what my father had called *hustle*. A man, I remembered my father saying as I held my trowel in the grass by a flower bed, learning from my father to pull the weeds and till the soil, could never sit on his ass when doing any sort of job, no matter how mean or low the job, my father said, and would say many times more in the days to come, no matter how long a man might be on the ground with his work, a man had always to be at least on a knee, *Like this*, my father said as he pointed to his knee in the grass with a foot before him, because that way, my father said, you could rise at will the better to work your tools, the better to save time, and I'd taken this dictum to heart and never allowed myself to sit while doing a thing that could remotely be called a job, having felt, the few times early on I'd sat while working, an overwhelming sense of guilt and shame. But most of all, I thought, my father had given me a love for books and for the knowledge in books and especially for the stories in books, and from my love of stories my love of art, of every art everywhere, from every time and place, of music and painting and literature and film and sculpture and performance and dance, and then plus, as well, somehow, somehow, from there, a real interest in, a real curiosity about, almost anything of the world, it didn't matter what, almost, the science of a rocket or earthquake or cell, how a worm spun its shell to emerge a moth, how lightning was made or water turned to ice or skyscrapers rose or people took sick and died. And how, I thought, could it be that my father possessed such traits, the traits of the best of the best sorts of people, and yet despite them, these traits, fall prey to the world, or really, I thought, fall prey to his perception of the world, of what he'd somehow come to believe the world was, since in fact it's never the world men and women fall prey to but what men and women think the world is, and then, moreover, I wondered, how my father could possess such virtuous traits even as he possessed such despicable traits, the traits of the coward and failure and liar and cheat and thief and fool, the deadliest of traits, any one of them fatal as a fall from a cliff. My father was generous and gentle and considerate and patient and kind, my father was gracious, my father was friendly, my father was modest and self-sacrificing, all these things and more were my father. But my father was small-minded, too, and selfish and scheming and mean, who demanded unreasonably and punished unmercifully, who reeked of self-loathing, self-pity, and self-doubt, who at nearly everything to which he set his hand struggled to maintain complete control. My father's virtue could as easily have won out, he could as easily have succeeded as failed at anything he chose. On one hand, it didn't make sense that instead of succeeding my father had failed, that instead of rising to his human potential my father had descended to his lifelong mire of apathy and addiction and fear. On the other, I understood perfectly well, all too perfectly well, why my father had descended to his lifelong mire of apathy and addiction and fear. I understood because I was my father's son, because I *was* my father. I, too, possessed all of the virtues of my father, and I, too, possessed all of my father's vices, all of my father's despicable flaws. For most of my life I'd given and loved and waited and considered, yet in those cases alone where it served me, where I knew that for my generosity and patience I'd be repaid. And when I saw no reward for my so-called expense, I lost sight of sacrifice or of any kindness or thoughtfulness at all and resorted instead to the lowliness of a common rogue, sometimes passively but mostly openly, in complete aggression, twisting and abusing and attacking, as the case might've been, whatever it took to achieve my ends, the means nearly always in their service. It wasn't till I'd put aside the drink and drugs that I stood a chance of becoming anything more than the lowest of scum, it wasn't till I'd got any clarity outside the drink and drugs that I began to glimpse just how base I'd been, or, in what was far more meaningful, just how much better a man I could be, just how much better a man, really, I already was, for I hadn't been a *bad* man the whole of my life, but a *sick* man, a man so sick that wherever I looked I saw only reflections of myself, only sickness and misery and death. And that, I saw, was why I'd always depicted the world as I had, because I'd been sick, and in my sickness incapable to see ought but sickness, it didn't matter what, for when I'd seen love, I judged it a lie, and when I'd seen happiness, I judged it a lie, and when I'd seen kindness, I judged it a lie, no one and nothing had been loving or happy or kind but only miserable, only sick and dying. That was how the world was, I'd believed. The world itself, I believed, had been a labyrinthine hoax devised in malice by the most malicious of unseen forces, bent unswervingly on luring us creatures deeper into our labyrinthine hell that they, the forces of malice, could inflict the greatest amount possible on their victims of sickness and misery and death. And in that perverted misunderstanding, I saw, I'd passed my unjust judgments and mean depictions, not with quiet surety but with the brashest nastiest conceit that I could muster, depending on the day, with the nastiness of the villain, always, and always the conceit of the fool. And, what was more, I saw with regret and, the first time I'd seen it, galling shame, I could never have behaved so abominably had it not been for the depth of my perverse confusion. The world had been a lie, I knew, because I myself had been a lie, because I myself had been the gravest incarnation of delusion and deceit, as deluded and deceitful, if not more deluded and deceitful, than my father, who there before me in the quiet lane could so solemnly admit that *he didn't like change and didn't like to share.* Yes, I thought, it's true, my mind also had once been the mind that was my father's then, and therefore, like him, horrifically and comically *insane.* But now I've seen the other side, I thought, now I've seen myself for what I've been and am and perhaps could be, how can I know I've seen my father as clearly, too, how can I know my judgments are just and my depictions true? But then again, I thought, it doesn't matter whether my judgments are just or my depictions true in the sense they can be held to a calculus of justice and truth. The calculus of justice and truth is a figment of memory that's itself never more or less than a cleverly disguised "untruth," and therefore as fickle. At any given moment, then, nothing matters but that I've been as just and as true to myself as I could be, based on what I remember, for if that is so, and only if that's so, only if I can say unflinchingly I've been just and true to and by myself, can I also say I've been just and true by my father, whatever I've judged my father to be, whatever depiction of my father I have drawn. No one, I thought, not even those whose pasts are replete, can say that what they remember is "true." And when we get down to the bones, every man and woman, without exception, has to admit that no matter how extensive or clear, not only are our memories false, but so too is our every thought and word. Our very existences, while we cling to our illusions of self, our illusions of truth, our illusions of knowledge and control, are complete *untruths*. And to stoop to inventing the pasts we fob off as truth, rather than admit that, beyond the *concept* of the Past, the *concept* of Recollection, we have no past at all, but merely the endless dependent co-arising of space, matter, form—that the "past" we do "have" "exists" merely so long as we or others can speak or write it, a task itself dependent on the whim of memory, whose voice can never speak more than lies—to go on blithely acting *as if*—to continue to convince ourselves that what we remember is the truth of what's been—that we have "identities," that we have "selves," despite the tsunami of evidence to the contrary: *This*, I thought, is what's absurd, *this*, I thought, is what's sad, far more so than any conflict that might be hastened by our faculties in decline. I knew all of this. And I knew also that my written words would stand as an ineffaceable refutation of my father's denial and avoidance, and of the ongoing lie that was bred of my father's denial and avoidance, even as I knew the futility that confronted me each time I attempted to explain myself. Explaining myself did nothing to change what had been, what I *knew* had been, as far as my memory told me it had been. And yet just the same I went on with my explanations, despite the futility of my explanations, despite my knowing that Time, that fancy-pants construct invented way back to handle the intransigence of matter, has been twisted to manipulate every human being who's ever lived since the dark day on which it, Time, was invented, despite my knowing that memory, for what it's worth, is itself a scanty puppet, dancing clumsy and bizarre from too many or too few strings, lamer than Plato's shadows on the wall, and less convincing. *And yet I went on.* Like the conquistadors of old exploring the unknown world, tracking down people and things through space and "time," relentlessly colonizing and "civilizing" till the unknown had become known, I, too, explored my past, I, too, stalked my past like the conquistadors of old had stalked their lands like predators their prey, I, too, colonized my past, and colonized my past that I might gain power over it, and gained power over my past that I might ultimately control it. And this power, this control I thought these gestures would bear, depended solely on how successfully I dissected and categorized "my" past. In the winning dissection and categorization of my past alone, I'd believed, did I stand the chance of achieving the Cartesian *clarity and distinctness* required to *understand*, to acquire the *knowledge* and achieve the *meaning* without which I could never control, or *think* I controlled, both my "self" and my notions of "self," what I thought of as *I*, the "I" that I knew was no *I* at all, but only ever an idea, and thus, somehow, at the end of what Galileo had called this *dark labyrinth*, "my" actual "life." And to control "my" past, I had thought, to control "my" "self" and "my" "life," would also have been to control my ever-chaotic present, through which flowed my future, which I'd hoped also to control. Human lives, I thought, all of them, are, have ever been, and will ever be, but endless flux. Memory gives humanity the dubious conviction that we somehow control this flux.

Memory is the magic with which humanity makes its dream of stability in the midst of our flux, which in truth is an order-guised-as-chaos that we can scarcely comprehend. It's only through memory, I thought, that we stand the chance of piecing together in some vaguely sensible fashion the endless torrent of moments in whose midst we stand, forever exposed and frail. And the best we can do when memory fails to suffice is to transform that raging profusion into a catalog of arbitrariness and chance, whose subjects are the clowns we make of order each time it rises from the depths of an apparent chaos to toy with our notions of the way things are. *This*, I thought, is not just the truth of the lives of some men and women, but of *all* men and women, and of my life, certainly, as well—this is how we "live" our lives. We give ourselves over to categorizing the things we've done, I thought, which is the matter and space we've moved through, somehow believing our efforts and categories will give us power over the things we've done in the matter and space we've moved through. And when we aren't lost in this activity of categorizing, we fantasize about the things we might yet do, in the matter and space we haven't yet moved through, somehow believing that by virtue of our power over the past we'll gain power over the future, too, and, though we're rarely, if ever, in it, the present. But despite everything, despite my knowing that in the ultimate scope of things the Word is meaningless, I craved escape from that Word's horrible power. My escape from the Word would be an escape from time and its illusory power, as well, and from my memories, to which, in the end, I saw, I'd always been chained. It was as if I'd been performing an endless exorcism of a ghost that never was. I was in a trance of the belief that by gaining control over my past through writing, I could free myself from my past, and from my father, and from the shadow of my father. I was in a trance of the belief that once my past had been committed to the Word, that once my past had been *given* to the Word, it, my past, and my father with it, would no longer be *in me*. Like that nimrod who thought he could drain the well by pouring water in it, I'd been wielding the Word against itself, hoping to destroy it, only to watch with delight and despair as my words mounted one atop the other, in endless dizzying profusion. I was cursed. The Word had nothing to do with me, but somehow still the Word had everything to do with me, everything, I saw, to do with nothing.

THE FABLE

It was precisely the opposite of forgiveness
… that ultimately freed me from my past.
— *Alice Miller*

AND THEN THE SPIDERS OF GOLD CAME DOWN TO KNIT THE son a dream.

So dazzled was he by the vision they wove that when he awakened, he refused his father's poison meals. Every day the father tried to put the son to sleep, but the son had grown wise and could not be deceived. The father locked him up. The son held fast. He would not settle for less than his dream, and besides, he had nearly dug into the cupboard from which, as his father slept each night, he would steal the fare to see him through.

Now seeing his store dwindle faster than he and his wife could spend it, the father resolved to sit by the cupboard until he caught the thief and killed him. And that very night, scarcely had the father spied a hand in the cupboard than he cut the hand off and threw it out the window.

He did not know the thief was his son. He did not know his son had flown, certain when he was found his father would take his head as surely as he had his hand.

But out in the world, the son met only hardship. He tried to steal chickens, but the chickens slipped away. Thieves stole the crumbs he had gathered and the bed of straw he had made, and everywhere he went children laughed and jeered. Even the rag pickers and harlots joined in, and sometimes even the fool.

At last in his sorrow the son lay down at the edge of a wood to rue his loss and hope for the day his father would rue, as well, for the son would have his revenge, and at his end the father would know it was his son who had shaped his ruin and toted the balance in the father's ledger of weal and woe. For seven days and nights, alone by his tree, the son tore his face and wept. But on the morning of the eighth, a dwarf appeared from the wood.

"Take my hand," said the dwarf, "and I will deliver you to yours."

All day long the dwarf led the son over roots and stones, and by the time the two had reached a glade, night had fallen, and the son was weary, and his body and feet were torn.

"How much farther must we go?" said the son. "Night has fallen, and I am weary, and I have no food or drink. And anyway, I am blind to follow you over the roots and stones."

"But we have reached our end," said the dwarf. "Here you will find what you seek."

"I do not know how I can do such a thing," said the son, "when I can see aught but shadows and night."

"Look to your hand," said the dwarf, "for in it you hold the other."

The son dared not trust his eyes, yet the dwarf had spoken truly, for indeed the son now held the hand he had lost to his father.

But then the dwarf vanished, and it was night, and the way was shut. The son fell asleep, unaware that the spiders of gold had come to make him whole again. And when he awakened, he saw his great fortune, and reveled in it, and gave all thanks, and while the spiders could not be found, he knew it was they that had saved him.

"Now that I have been restored what was lost and am made whole again," cried the son, "I vow by my life to do but good to the end."

And with that he returned to the city and trained himself in the sciences and arts and also in the ways of spirit. And in his labors the son succeeded, and despite his troubles the son prevailed. He routed villains and saw what baffled the sage. Where others had failed, the son was triumphant. He patched bonds, and fixed disputes, and defended the meek, and sheltered the poor, and brought to their senses men in the sway of vice and greed. And truly it seemed there was nothing at which the son could not excel. So great was his prosperity that soon it matched the richest men. And then he married the chandler's daughter, and they had many daughters and sons, and their life was blessed.

The son, however, despite these gifts, was vexed by thoughts of his father, who had cut off his hand and thrown it from the window. The son had become a lord of wisdom and power whose generosity was unsurpassed, and yet nothing could quell his thirst for vengeance. And so he went into the wilds, pledging to stay until his desire had been purged.

One day, when the heat was pitiless and not a shadow could be found, the son spied a figure on the sands. The figure drew near, but the son could not gaze on it long, for he was terrified and appalled.

Before him stood a man scorched by the sun and shriveled by time, his hair lost, his teeth lost, and all of his toes and one of his hands, and two fingers on the other. And his tongue was black, and his eyes were heavy with fog.

But looking at last through the old man's eyes, the son's horror melted and his heart was flooded with care.

"Old man," said the son, "I see that your journey has been long and your misery great. But now I ask that you rest assured you have reached your journey's end. I have a house and a good wife and many daughters and sons, and all good things to sate your hunger and quench your thirst, and your senses will be delighted. In my house, you will hear only wisdom and mirth, and of the ghosts that have haunted you, we will see none more."

"I feel that I have been wandering," the old man said, "since the dawn of time itself. Yet in all these years, not one man has thought to pity me. I had a wife once, and a son, but my son died, and when I could not give my wife another, she abandoned me for a huckster. Through lands far and wide my search has taken me in hopes of restoration, but I have met none but failure."

And so the son took him out of the desert and into his home. And as the son had promised, the old man was restored. Indeed, before long, the old man could see the face of the son. He could taste as well the apples and wine from the son's wife and daughters, and smell the flowers in the gardens at dusk.

As for the son, the old man had delivered his salvation, for he had been purged of his thoughts of doom. Nor had the old man done more for the home of the son than to enter into it, and yet the son's home had been blessed once more with peace.

"Old man," said the son beneath his arbor of roses and grapes, "I see your health returned and your spirits grown. But whereas you may be obliged for your fortune, my gratitude for what you have brought to my home is beyond compare. I am beholden to you, and with all of my heart and all that I have, I give you many thanks."

"You cannot know how it humbles me to receive your gifts," the old man said. "For one who has been so unworthy of even the cheapest grace, I am astonished. That I might in truth have made good for my sins seems almost beyond my ability to reckon, and I tremble to ponder my fortune too well lest it vanish like bubbles on a stream.

"As you know, misfortune has been my bedfellow and anguish my familiar. I have thought well on the provenance of my fate, and seen that despite my conception in sorrow, my travails began truly in the days when my son took to bed and refused to eat and drink.

"I stored up my goods for the day my son would need them again, but after a time it came to my attention that they were dwindling faster than my wife and I could spend them, for I was being robbed by a thief. So I waited by my cupboard, and when the thief's hand appeared, I cut it off and threw it out the window.

"Thinking further, however, it seemed wiser to bury the hand, that my business remain my own. But when I went into the street, a dwarf snatched up the hand and fled. And since like fortune trouble runs in threes, it should have come as no surprise to learn in the morning that my son was nowhere to be found. Nor should I have complained when my wife absconded with a huckster from a passing column."

The longer the old man spoke, the hotter burned the hand the son had lost to his father. And he shuddered with rage, and his mind was taken by visions of blood and steel. It could not be that this man from the desert was his father, returned after these long years, yet somehow it was so.

For all his pledges to do good, and for all his struggles to purge his ghosts, the son's desire for revenge took him once again. He could not slay the old man beneath the roses and grapes, however, since though he drowned in his own blood, a vision of grapes and roses in his dying eyes would be more than so terrible a man deserved. When his doom came, the son resolved, the old man must know its germ, and suffer.

But as he tossed in bed that night, sleepless with his fury, the son recalled the clarity of that long ago day, when he had seen his father as he was, riddled with doubt and fear, and once again the son regained his senses.

Nothing he did to this man could match the penitence he had endured, nor could any force lay down greater justice than he had lain upon himself. The road to perdition, the son well knew, was paved with the skulls of priests, but while heaven and earth might hold a candle to the old man's deeds, here and now those deeds were of no import, for even in his cowardice, the old man's love for him was the love of a father for his son, which the son himself knew as father to his own daughters and sons, and which the power of a galaxy of stars could not equal.

The old man, the son knew, must never see the truth, for to conjure up the ghost of the old man's crimes, and of his penitence for them, might well be more than he could bear. And not only was the old man blind to the man before him, who laved his feet and fed him dates, neither did he know that his son had seen him for the man he had been. The old man, the son determined, would live out the days he had left, surrounded by his family.

He cooled the old man's brow, and spooned good broths to his lips, and the son was glad, and the old man was also glad. But of change comes change, and naught but change endures, and the sun rose at length on the old man's day of truth. Then he called out for the son and took in hand the hand he had taken all those long years back.

"My end is come," the old man said, "but I cannot go to the land of my fathers with my crimes at my feet and truths in my heart. You have given me more than any man could ask for, and far more than I am worth, and yet I ask you still for one last thing, that you listen to this old man well.

"For years I wandered the wilds of contrition, praying for the day I might see the truth, if but a fleeting glimpse. I took no thought for shelter. My robes became rags and my rags filth that turned to dust, and I was handed to the wiles of this world.

"My sight I gave to my search for grubs and my smell to the vapors of perdition. My toes I lost to blizzards, my hand to wolves, and my fingers to wild horses. I tore out my hair to eat it, and when my hair was no more, the stones I ate destroyed my teeth.

"No man may escape himself. No man may run from God. Each we come, and each we go, but the truth walks on forever.

"I was afraid in this world. The truth was to me an abyss of sorrow, not my faithful mirror. So I turned away from the truth, dumb that fast or far, I could never do less than to carry my truth along.

"Misfortune was my bedfellow and anguish my familiar, I now see, in name alone. From the beginning, as to every man, anguish and misfortune are but truth disguised.

"I told you that I had a son and that my son was dead. That was not the truth. I did have a son, but I was not certain he had died. I had said as much because my son ran away. I have rued that day every day since, and longed to see my son once more, yet still he did not return, and I never saw him, and so he was dead to me.

"But my son did not flee because he was bad, nor because

I drove him out. My son was in danger, and it was I who had set him in it. Doubtless I had no sooner committed my crime than seen its folly, but I was afraid to put things right. So instead I locked my son away and fed him a potion that made him sleep, untouched by the horrors that dogged me.

"The night I cut off the hand of the thief was the night my son ran away. And in the days that followed, as I have said, when I failed to give my wife another son, a sugar-tongued man stole her, and I was forsaken.

"I did not know then that the day of my abandonment was the beginning of the end of my own long sleep. I did not know that day was the gift of my chance to set things right. This took time, as is the case with blind men and fools, and I was foolish and blind."

For a year, the old man said, he sat in his garret, bemoaning his fate and despairing of his worth. He was less even than a louse, he said, draining the goodness around him, and that as such it would be best to take his life.

Then the old man recalled the blood the thief had left behind, and determined to follow its trail. The old man did not know why he should do this, when the days that had passed since that night would surely have removed all trace of his son. He had only the sense that he should follow the trail. Somehow, he thought, shy of his son, the trail might deliver some clue from which he could take the strength to carry on.

The trail led for a time through the city, past the brothels, the asylum, the scriveners and esquires and hacks, until finally it turned toward the shambles, and thence to the heath, where in the dusk the old man reached a crossroads. And lo and behold, against all hope, what should he have found where he sat but his son's old charm, the keepsake from his birth, a spider made of iron.

In his misery, the old man took his son's charm as a sign of hope, though what hope a charm might offer, he could not say. His son had not fled the handless thief. The thief had taken the old man's son to ransom or sell for such gold as could be mustered. As surely as water cures thirst, the old man saw, his son's charm had been planted at this crossroads, that he should know the thief would soon return.

The old man waited in that place, and waited, but the thief never came, nor did word of the thief, nor any sign or word of the old man's son, until soon he commenced to cry out his pain and curse the thief that had destroyed him.

Then one day a hermit approached, come from the wilderness on his journey to the city for provisions.

"Brother," said the hermit, "why are you wailing, and to whom? I hear your misery, and understand your woe, but the wrongs you cry are incomprehensible.

"Who do you think is to blame for your fate? Do you think your fate so fickle as to let herself be groped by any who would have her, by strangers, even, with their filthy hands, until her charms are blemished?

"Make no mistake. Your fate is your own, and yours because you have made it. Neither can you make the fate of another, nor in this world of aught else.

"This being so, tell me—on what grounds could you raise your voice in conviction of innocence in this scheme? And wherefore, then, the logic for your accusations, and your slander against the anonymous hosts? Just as well accuse this blade of grass. Yes, just as well throw the noose around your neck!

"Brother, do not forget my words. For so long as you howl your slander, for just that long will you poach in a stew of ass's water and spittle of swine, and for just that long will you stew in that pulp of rancid fat, and rot of moles, and, yes, even dung from the corpses of babes.

"For so long as you accuse even the lowliest man in the name of your salvation, for just that long will your salvation flee you, and you will find no rest, or any peace at all.

"Yet there is hope. Take the rags from your ears and stuff them in your mouth, and in stillness look to the source of what you feel. For only after you have seen your feelings are baseless will you have glimpsed asylum. The one who made your ear can hear better than you, O brother. The one who made your eye can see far. I must go now. This is the city. This is not the city. Do you understand?"

And with that, the hermit poked the old man with his stick, and he fell dumb and made a vow of silence to the hundredth man he saw, and did not speak until he met the son, for he was the hundredth man.

"Do you remember," the old man said to the son, "the story that you told as we crossed the sands, how long ago you dreamed your father had brought you to the tarn in the mountains where the snake bit your foot? Your father sucked the venom from your wound, you said, and then you swam and feasted on duck and beans.

"Hearing your dream, I did not mention that once my son too was bit by a snake along the river at the edge of town, and I cleaned his wound. I wondered at the chance you might be him, but I was a pauper, and my son was his father's son, and you are a great and benevolent lord, so I banished the thought at once.

"You took me out of the desert and into your home, and in my joy I did not think further on these things. I had atoned for my crimes with all that I had, and passed to the other side. I thought so then, and believed so still, until yesterday, when I was ready to pass through once again.

"But as you washed my face, a beam of light fell on the wound at your wrist, and all grew clear, my fate grew clear, and I knew whereof my fate, and why, even if I do not know how, for the workings of this world are a mystery to us all.

"Now hear this. For all that I know, still I know little. Yet in that little I have seen the greatest truth. You are my son, and I am your father, returned one to the other at the end. I was ashamed to tell you, and I did not want to shame you, either.

"I am not, however, afraid any longer. Whatever you do will be just, and you may do with me as you please. I am your father, and you are my son. And though I am not sorry for my life, I grieve for the wrongs I have done you, and know your journey has itself been fraught with hardship and anguish to match my own. Nor do I ask forgiveness. Already you have given me that, and many times over besides. You are my son, here by my side at the end, and I am your father. Nothing can hurt me now. My life is complete."

And with that the son took his father in his arms, and he blessed him, and kissed him on his brow, and the two rejoiced. And then, as he held the hand he had taken from his son all those years before, the father looked into the eyes of his son, and he smiled, and died.

In that moment the spiders of gold came down to knit for the father a shroud so splendid that all who saw it marveled. The son did not mourn his father, nor did the son's wife and many daughters and sons, but rejoiced in his coming, and fixed on his leaving with awe.

And the hand he had lost to his father glowed for the rest of his days, like a jewel in the morning sun.

THE LETTER

By now, all's wrong. In everyone there sleeps
A sense of life lived according to love.
To some it means the difference they could make
By loving others, but across most it sweeps
As all they might have done had they been loved.
—*Philip Larkin*

PAT, I SHOULD HAVE CALLED YOU BACK INSTANTLY WHEN S told me, the same day you made what must have been for you a most humiliating call for help, that her mother had written to tell us S's father had just been diagnosed with old age onset diabetes and asked if we could send them $2,000 for medicine and to have him hospitalized for skin ulcers on his feet and legs. We were broke ourselves and had to borrow money from her credit union to send to them. I didn't want to disappoint you, and I procrastinated calling you, hoping SOMETHING would happen, some BIG JOB would come along to allow us to send you some money, until you wrote me off and wouldn't return my calls at all. My heart broke the day you hung up on me, and has everyday since. I am truly sorry, Pat, that my failures and weaknesses have cost us both so dearly.

However, you didn't have knowledge of my circumstances before you ALL passed judgment on me. No one bothered to find out how I was faring or what my life was like during the period in question. Nor did I want to admit to ANYONE what my life had become and how miserable my existence was. None of you ever knew how close to being homeless and jobless I really came. And I wasn't going to tell ANYBODY! EVER!

No one needs to tell me of my weaknesses and failures—I am painfully, painfully aware of them and how they have affected my life and my sons. Until I met S in 1995, the downhill slide my life started in 1989 was accelerating daily and my self-esteem and pride was non-existent.

And then something wonderful happened! I didn't SELL my soul to God, I gave it to him, and in return I received the STRENGTH, DISICIPLINE, GRACE, AND COURAGE to begin rebuilding a REAL LIFE, a life like I grew up with. I am not perfect, I am not fully healed and may never be. But with God's help and S's support, I am respected in my business, my community, and my church, and can again face myself in the mirror and know that little by little, I am getting better every day.

WAKEFULNESS

Do I contradict myself? So I contradict myself.
— *Walt Whitman*

THERE'S NO RIGHT OR WRONG, ONLY HARM OR NO HARM, and not even that.

Did we eat the bird we shot with our dart of needles and tape? Why did we share with our brother—for fear of judgment? When we cut off the head of that snake, was it because it bit us? And how can we leave a footprint when we've never traced the path?

With knowledge, analysis is empty.

Nor can the truth be squeezed. It knows nothing of fingers, hands, arms—the notion *embrace* is to it an unseen star.

Work the question like a field, want nothing from its labor. Place no stock in the question's worth. Until the question's faded, we'll never find its answer.

The snail is as lovely as the sky, the shade, our wife, and while the thorn attends the rose because it loves the rose, it's the rose that shields the thorn.

Wash our hair in a bucket of mud.

Smile before our killer.

Hand our heart to the dullest stone.

Steal our sister's wound.

Do these things—do them now—and we will know nothing need be done.

Is our tongue a whip, or is our tongue a flower in its field of silence? No one knows, no one understands. *It* is only for us to see, as a child the moon at dawn. Ask the child—any child—she'll tell us with no word. And name our dream, and then forget that name.

Our family is the galaxy, the nest in the leafless tree, our family is a toad. Watch for nothing, cry for all, tend to the meanest fly: we are not ourselves. To believe other is to risk our self—there's no thing more fragile among all the fragile things.

We know what's gorgeous, we know rain, we know of filth, and grudges, and shame, and we know barracuda. But we don't know the soul, and we don't know the war, nor the fetus, nor the king, nor the worm nor whore.

And the living behind the dead? What do they know that the dead do not? And where on earth is no between?

Eternity.

It is now, now is eternity, the ceaseless moment, that from which we came to do just *this*.

Do we know who we are? What do we do, and how do we do it?

For what we resist will persist, and what we force will fail.

And it's okay, it will be okay, it has always been okay. What has not been okay is Time, the bearded liar that has no beard, nor creeps, nor slips away, nor heals all, nor flies. Time is nothing to fear, for fear was its mother, a cloud.

Lay down our life for the one thing we have, our life, and we will live the life beyond our death. All of us—our deaths must die for our lives to live.

Only then will the mundane cease, and all will be made new.

Love, it sees through us, that is all that sees, love is all that sees.

We can't hold what we are.

We can't lose what we aren't.

We can't take from what wasn't there.
We can't arrive when we haven't left.
We can't add to what doesn't lack.
And never can we change the unchangeable.
And the sun always shines, and the dew, it always fades.

GRATITUDE

For all your kindnesses—big, small, and in between—I'm so
very thankful:

Jeanine Durning, Matt Bialer, James Reich, Jeff Jackson, Snorri
Sturluson, Dan Sullivan, Major West, Christopher O'Brien, Augustus
Rose, Anderson Berry, Brian Bennett, Michael J. Seidlinger, Samuel
Sattin, David Gutowski, Matthew Specktor, Terese Svoboda, Sean
H. Doyle, Sean Madigan Hoen, Michele Durning, Carole Doughty,
Oona Patrick, Stephen Dunn, The Eastern Frontier Foundation,
Matty Byloos, Carrie Seitzinger, Rebecca Rubenstein, Taylor Pavlik,
Meakin Armstrong, Stephen Shodin, Ben Barnhart, Joshua Mohr,
Cari Luna, Jennifer Dietz, Dale Bridges, Seb Dubinsky, Trent Tesch,
Laura Tesch, Andrew Megginson, Andrea Johnson, Kris Bernard,
Hilary Clark, Ron Tanner, Jim Ruland, Richard Nash, Jason Diamond,
Tobias Carroll, Rachel Cantor, Andrew Blossom, Todd O'Brien, Janis
Finwall, Tim O'Brien, Mary DiMartinis, Susie Deford, Clark Blaise,
Bharati Mukherjee, Diane Cook, Molly Poerstel, Xander Cameron,
Scott Cheshire, Laura van den Berg, Lance Gries, Lauren O'Brien,
Mark Richardson, Julie Mayo, Glen Griffin, Eric Palmerlee, Will Jones,
Melissa Maino, Anneke Hanson, Germán Sierra, David Connerly
Nahm, Sarah Gerard, Boris Hauf, Litó Walkey, Jocelyn Tobias, Julian
Barnett, Victor Giganti, Neil Wiltshire, Barbara Browning, Janelle
Young, Natalie Eilbert, Dolan Morgan, John Domini, Frances Badgett,
Gabino Iglesias, Elizabeth Crane, Michele Filgate, Penina Roth, Kurt
Baumeister, Tyler Malone, J. David Osbourne, J.S. Breukelaar, Rob
Hart, Jonathan Evison, Porochista Khakpour, August Tarrier, Jeffrey

Calzaloia, Rebekah Lynn Potter, Brandon Hobson, Richard Thomas, CarlaJean Valluzzi, Lauren Cerand, Tabrina Hughes, Jordan Ginsberg, Eddy Rathke, Courtney Maum, Annie DeWitt, Matt Pucci, Steve Karpicz, Kimberly Engebrigtsen, Ben Tanzer, Nick Petrulakis, Wendy C. Ortiz, Gregory Howard, Kera Yonker, Sarah Russo, Jenn Stroud Rossman, Bridget Hoida, Anne Marie Wirth Cauchon, Jean Vitrano, Tim Horvath, Emma Clark, Anisse Gross, Julie Hart, Leah Shapiro, Grant Womack, Tian Rotteveel, Zack Barocas, Michael Kazepis, David Leo Rice, Dennis Widmyer, Jim Warner, Amy Bagwell, Stephanie Dempsey, Shya Scanlon, Jamie Grefe, Christian Kiefer, Harry Stahl, Nathan Knapp, Michael Kimball, Josh Milberg, Gregg Holtgrewe, Leslie O'Neill, Alice Peck, Mark Snyder, Kevin Maloney, Joseph Tiefenthaler, Darcey Steinke, Lindsay Hunter, Adam Wilson, Nick Goode, Mark Cugini, Joseph Riippi, Jason Rogers, James Bennett, Heidi Werner, Dave Housely, John Beckman, Elvis Alves, Gabrielle Gantz, Timothy Gager, Keith Reddin, Anthony Swofford, Naomi Huffman, Ian Douglas, Luke Degnan, Tamara Ober, Sandi Sigurdson, Coleen Muir, Taryn Griggs, Jenn Worthington, Lori Hettler, Bree Ogden, Alice Whitwham, Renée Zuckerbrot, Graham Storey, Jonny Diamond, Mark de Silva, Luke B. Goebel, Halimah Marcus, David Wallace, Isaac Fitzgerald, Sheila Heti, Ron Currie, Porochista Khakpour, Brad Listi, Nina Shengold, Patrick Benjamin, John Madera, Stefanie Diaz, J.T. Price, Joseph Salvatore, Nathan Goldman, David Rice, Samantha Anne Carrillo, Amber Sparks, Benjamin Rybeck, Kim Winterheimer, Michael Jauchen, Alex Kalamoroff, Henry Stewart, Derek Harmening, Westin Cutter, Jon Reiss, Keith Rawson, James R. Kapinski, Larry Nolen, Evan Allgood, Jim Warner, Matt Bell, Gabriel Blackwell, Justin McIntosh, Eric Obenauf, Eliza Jane Wood Obenauf, Ian MacAllen, Dennis Cooper, Peter Tieryas, David Ulin, Berl Harp O'Brien.

ABOUT D. FOY

D. Foy's work has appeared in *Guernica, Salon, Hazlitt, Post Road, Electric Literature, BOMB, The Literary Review, Midnight Breakfast, The Scofield,* and *The Georgia Review,* among others, and has been included in the books *Laundromat and Forty Stories: New Writing from Harper Perennial.* He is the author of a previous novel, *Made To Break.*

www.dfoyble.com

CPSIA information can be obtained
at www.ICGtesting.com
Printed in the USA
LVOW12s1151171116
513382LV00001B/106/P

9 780997 062908